samantha christy

Stealing Sawyer

Books Publishing Group

Saint Augustine, FL 32092

Cover designed by Letitia Hasser | RBA Designs

ISBN-13: 978-1726292320
ISBN-10: 1726292320

For Alex.

You stole my son's heart when you were only fifteen.

I'm honored to have you as my daughter-in-law.

Stealing Sawyer

Samantha Christy

Chapter One

Sawyer

Damn Straight!

I look down at my jersey and see it caked with dirt. Then I stare at my pants to see they are no longer white, but reddish-brown with one of the knees ripped clean through. Bonus points for that.

The state of my clothing always tells me what kind of game I had. The dirtier the better. And today has been exceptionally good, especially for a season opener. Hell, I might even frame this uniform. Four stolen bases. *Four!* I'll bet Rickey Henderson is shaking in his boots thinking I might be the one to break his record.

For two years now, I've held the league record for stolen bases. And if this game is any indication, I'm on my way to year three.

"Take me home, Sawyer!" a woman screams, as I make my way into the dugout.

I turn my head and find a beautiful tall blonde giving me a good look at her cleavage. I take a second to memorize where she's sitting so I can have one of the ushers slip a note to her.

I won't take her home. I never take them home. But the hotel down the street from where I live is convenient, within walking distance of my townhouse, and nice enough that the girls don't complain too much when I leave before the crack of dawn. After all, they do get a hotel-catered breakfast fit for a queen, albeit for one. As for me, I usually hit Starbucks on my walk home.

I put my helmet and batting gloves away and scribble a note to Blondie. Then I hear the disappointment of the crowd and look over to see that Benham got thrown out trying to steal third. I shake my head. I need to give that rookie some pointers.

Brady pats me on the back. "Nice job out there," he says, removing his jacket and grabbing his glove to head out onto the field.

I lift my chin at him. "Let's end this now."

I give my note to an usher, along with a description of the woman and her location. Then I grab my own glove before jogging out to my position. I warm up with the other infielders as the crowd gets louder and louder, wanting us to shut out the Nationals for our first win.

It's the top of the ninth and the score is 4 − 0, so as long as they don't pull a rabbit out of a hat, we'll get the victory.

Before the batter comes to the plate, I take a quick look around Hawks Stadium. Man, I love this. I have the best job. Great pay. Good friends. Killer city. I couldn't ask for things to be any better than they are right now.

Growing up, I could only dream of playing in the majors. My childhood was anything but ideal. My mom was taken from me far too soon. My dad was a drunk. I made so many mistakes. Sometimes I wonder how I ended up here, the shortstop for the New York Nighthawks.

I rein in my thoughts. I need to stay sharp. I am, after all, what most people consider the most important position on the team. I'm the captain. The quarterback of baseball. You don't win games without a top-notch shortstop. And you definitely don't win the World Series. But that's exactly where I plan on taking my team.

I hear the distant sound of thunder as Brady strikes out the first batter to the cheers of the stadium.

The second batter pops one up over the infield. I back up, calling off the center fielder so I can make a clean catch to get the second out.

The third batter dribbles a ground ball past Brady. Conner runs up to the ball, scoops it up and throws the batter out at first, solidifying our first win of the season.

We run off the field just as it begins to rain, celebrating our way back into the dugout.

I catch a glimpse of Blondie as I make my way to the clubhouse. I give her a wink and call out to her. "Give me twenty minutes, sweetheart."

She smiles and then turns around and screams with her friends.

I laugh and shake my head. *Every time.*

Walking up to my locker, I see one of the assistant coaches leaning against the wall. "Rick wants to see you," he says.

"Okay, sure. Mind if I shower first?"

"I don't think he cares how you smell, Mills. Just get your ass in there now."

I watch him walk away, wondering what this is all about. I mean, I just had the best game of my life, why would Coach want to see me?

Caden comes up next to me. "Being called to the principal's office so soon?" he jokes.

3

"I'm sure he wants to tell me how awesome I played. Did you see me out there? I fucking killed it."

My words speak a much different story than my mind. My mind is going crazy wondering why I'm being called to the manager's office after playing such a good game.

I'm no stranger to being in Rick's office. A few times a year he likes to give me the talk about keeping my dick in my pants. Last year they changed the rules of the organization to forbid employees from dating not only each other, but also their family members. Yeah – that was because of me. A pregnancy scare with the daughter of one of the assistant coaches did not go over well.

"I'm sure that's what it is," Caden says.

But I know as well as he does that we're both full of shit.

I walk down the hallway and stand at Rick's door. He's on the phone, but he motions to the chair in front of his desk, so I sit down while he finishes up his call.

I look around his office. The walls are lined with pictures of players. Most of them past players, but there are a few current ones. Most notably, my two best friends, Brady Taylor and Caden Kessler. Caden got his picture on the wall two seasons back for setting a Nighthawks record for hitting the most home runs in a season. Brady got his ugly mug on the wall for the perfect game he pitched last year.

My picture is not yet on the wall. Not even after two years of holding the league record for stolen bases.

Rick has it in for me. It's no secret. I know it. He knows it. Hell, even the press knows it.

I wonder what it will take to get my picture on his wall.

He hangs up the phone. Then he looks at me thoughtfully as he relaxes back into his chair. He crosses his arms and studies me.

He eyes my dirty jersey. "Good game today," he says, with about as much enthusiasm as a pet rock.

"Thanks."

He pushes a folder slowly across his desk, nodding to it.

I pick it up and open it. It takes me a minute to realize what it is before my blood pressure shoots through the roof. I close the folder and throw it back onto his desk. "You're trading me?"

"Yes."

"You're *trading* me?" I ask again, still in disbelief. "But I fucking killed it out there today. I'm one of your best players, Rick."

"Could be a good opportunity for you," he says.

I open the folder again. "Kansas City? Are you kidding me? It's a demotion and you know it."

"They're a solid team, Sawyer. You'll do well there. And they are one of the few teams willing to take you on. Hell, you're lucky we're not straight up releasing you."

"Come on, Rick. Lots of guys have issues like I do."

"Issues?" He walks over to his file cabinet and pulls out a thick folder. He drops it on his desk in front of me. "Your issues take up more room in my file cabinet than the other twenty-four players combined."

He opens the tattered folder and pulls out some papers, shuffling through them. "I've never seen so many complaints. Women, men, old, young. Hell, I had to sit here and get my ass chewed out by some hussy's granny last fall. I don't know how many times you have to be told to stop fucking around, Mills."

"Why the hell does the organization even care what I do when I'm off the field as long as I perform like I did today? I'm making the team tens of millions and you know it."

He shakes his head. "There comes a time when the risks outweigh the rewards. And we've pretty much hit our limit. Your reputation has gone from being the quintessential bad boy of baseball to potentially damaging the Nighthawks' brand and we can't have that."

"What about Brady? He had a chick in every city for Christ's sake. Did you ever threaten to trade *him*?"

Rick shakes his head. "He kept a low profile. We didn't have to hire an additional PR person just to cover up his indiscretions."

"So you'd rather get rid of me than give me a second chance?"

He gives me a stern stare and then nods to the folder on his desk. "The racy photos. The constant stream of tabloid fodder. The goddamn pitching coach's daughter. Need I say more? Mills, you've had a hundred chances and everyone knows it."

"Come on, Rick. You know as well as I do you've never threatened to trade me. Yeah, so you've had it out with me a few times, but if I'd known it was coming to this—"

"You'd what? You'd change? We've been asking you to do that for years."

"Yeah, but I didn't think it was that serious."

"This is a business decision, Sawyer. Nothing personal."

I stand up and pace behind the chair. "Nothing personal? You're not serious, are you? This is *very* fucking personal. You haven't ever liked me, Rick. Not from the very beginning. And you've said nothing to me about this being a possibility. This is bullshit and you know it. I could have done things differently. I *would* have done things differently. You can't do this without warning. You have to give me a chance to prove myself now that I know what could happen. Come on, man. I love it here. And you need me. Please. Give me a chance to show you I can change."

"Pick up, Rick," a familiar voice says from the speaker on his phone.

Shit.

It's Jason. The team owner. He's been listening in the entire time.

Rick puts the phone to his ear. "What is it?"

I pace his office, running my hands through my hair as the two men discuss my fate.

I can't imagine leaving New York. My whole life is here. It's where I started my career. They are the only MLB team I've played for. My friends are here. They are more than friends, they're family.

Rick holds out the phone to me, looking annoyed. "Jason would like a word."

My shaking hand reaches out to take the phone. "Jason, look, I'm sorry, I—"

"Sawyer, shut up and listen. I'm giving you one more shot against everyone else's wishes. One last chance to clean up your act and prove yourself worthy of the Nighthawks' brand. But you should know I'm the only one in your corner. And I happen to agree with you that Rick should have made it clearer about our intentions if you kept going down the path you were on. But kid, you've got one last shot here. No more chances. No screw ups. Do what you have to do to make it right. Find a nice girl and settle down. Swear off women if you have to. Because your job depends on it. And there is a lot of pressure on me. I won't be able to save you again."

"I swear to God, Jason, you won't regret this."

"I hope not. Now if I were you, I'd put down the phone and get out of Rick's office. He's bound to throw a few things around the room."

I laugh half-heartedly. "Yes, sir. Thank you."

I hand the phone back to Rick.

"Don't get too comfortable," he says, walking over to open the door for me. He hands me the file folder with the Kansas City contract in it. "You might want to keep this. I have a feeling you'll be needing it."

I take it from him. "I'm not going anywhere, Rick. You'll see."

He raises his brows at me. "I'm not a betting man, but if I were, I think I'd be betting on a sure thing if I put money on your position opening up in, what, two to three weeks?"

"No way. Not this time."

"I guess we'll see, won't we?"

He shuts the door behind me. Or should I say he *slams* the door behind me. And Jason was right. I'm pretty sure I hear what sounds like a baseball hitting a file cabinet as I walk back down the hallway to the clubhouse.

Most of the guys are gone when I get back. I spot Brady, Caden, and a few others sitting around a table. They all look up at me with questions in their eyes. I bypass them and walk over to the clubhouse door. I stick my head through and ask one of the security team to find a certain blonde girl and tell her I won't be coming.

Then I go sit in front of my locker and hang my head. How am I going to do this? How do I change the person I've always been? I'm the guy who never dates the same girl twice. 'One and done' – that's my motto. No way can I go from that, to what, swearing off women? Settling down? I will never settle down. I'll never find a nice girl. I can't. I know I can't, not without someone getting hurt.

I feel the eyes of my teammates burning a hole into the back of my head, so I turn around and hold up the folder. "They want to trade me. Kansas City of all places."

Chairs fall over as my pissed-off friends stand up and run over to me.

"You're getting traded?" Caden asks.

"Apparently so, if I can't get my ass in gear and stop tarnishing the Hawks' reputation, that is."

"Wait, so you're *not* getting traded?" Brady asks.

I shake my head. "Not yet. But I will be. How in the hell am I supposed to do what they want?"

"What do they want?" Caden asks.

"What do you think?" Spencer says. "They want him to keep his dick in his pants."

"How hard can that be?" Conner asks. "I mean, come on, Mills, this is your career we're talking about. At least fake it for a while, until they get off your back."

"Fake it?"

"Yeah, you know, pretend you're done with women. Become the guy who doesn't date. Become besties with your right hand until things die down. After a while, they won't care if you slip up from time to time."

"Nobody will believe Sawyer Mills has sworn off women," Brady says.

They all laugh.

"So, find one woman and date her until they get off your back," Caden says.

"Not an option," I say.

"You'll figure it out," Brady says. "Just let us know how we can help."

I nod. "Thanks."

"Want to go celebrate the win?" Spencer asks.

I shake my head. "You guys go ahead. I still need to shower. I think I'm going to lie low."

"Probably a good call," Caden says. He grabs my shoulder. "It was a good game, man. The first of many you'll have this season."

I nod again, looking down at my ripped pants. "See you guys. Have fun."

They leave the clubhouse and I find myself sitting alone. I look around. It's filthy in here. Dirty clothes, muddy cleats, wet towels. It smells hideous. It smells like home. This *is* my home. And I will do anything to make sure I can stay here.

After I clean up and get dressed, I pick up the folder Rick gave me and toss it into the trash. But before I reach the door, I go back and retrieve it. I think I'll keep it. I'll keep it as a reminder of what will happen if I don't straighten up.

By the time I emerge from the tunnel, the afternoon storm has passed. The streets are flooded. The air is clean. Night is falling. I decide to walk home. It's only a few miles. It will give me time to think. I sling my duffle bag onto my shoulder and grip the folder tightly in my hand – vowing never to sign the papers inside.

Chapter Two

Aspen

Today could not get any worse. I mean, literally, the only thing that could make it worse is if I get run over by a bus.

My dreams for the future – squashed with a single, solitary phone call.

And on the same day that I got my acceptance letter.

I stare down at the piece of mail that should have me celebrating. The piece of mail everyone in my position dreams about.

Then I think about my brother. That alone makes for a shitty day. And the news about my apartment, that was just the icing on the cake from hell.

I can't go home. I don't want to talk to anyone. Not even my best friend. My best friend who is following *his* dream. My best friend who doesn't have an idiot for a brother.

I read the letter once more before putting it back in the envelope. I rack my brain to see if I can find any way to make this happen. But there *is* no way. The money is gone, and he needs my help. I can't turn my back on him. No matter what he's done, he's my brother. My only remaining family member.

I'll have to go back home. Get a job, or three. I can always give piano lessons to rich snotty-nosed kids for some extra money. What a fine way to use my education. I close my eyes and try to forget about the last few hours of my life.

Then I pull myself together and start to cross the street when a horn blares at me, scaring me back onto the curb just as a bus goes by, its massive wheels splashing water from the gutter, soaking me from head to toe.

"Great! Just fucking great!" I scream at the bus.

I turn around to see people staring. "What?" I scream at them.

They stare at me like I'm crazy as they walk around me.

I look down at my sodden clothes and laugh. It's a maniacal laugh and I think maybe those people are right. I am crazy.

I spot a bar and decide it's exactly what I need right now. I walk over and grab the door handle when I hear, "Miss, you dropped this."

I turn around to see a guy handing me the soaking-wet letter I had dropped on the sidewalk. I look at it and laugh. "A lot of good that'll do me."

"It's not yours?" he asks. "I thought I saw you drop it when you almost got pasted by that bus."

"It's mine. But I don't want it. It represents something I can never have."

He holds up the folder he's carrying. "I hear you. The papers in this folder represent something I can't have either. Or more accurately, something I don't want."

"Maybe we should burn them," I say.

He shakes his head. "Nah. I'd like to keep mine. That way I have a reminder of what I'm working for."

I cock my head to the side and study him. Then I take the wet letter from him and decide maybe I should keep it just for posterity.

"Bad day?" he asks, nodding to my clothes.

"You could say that."

"Bet mine was worse," he says.

"I doubt it."

He holds the door open for me. "Want to have a drink and compare our shitty days?"

"I'd rather not relive mine if it's all the same to you."

He laughs. "Fair enough. But the offer for the drink still stands."

I eye him up and down. He's very attractive in a rugged, athletic kind of way. His dark hair is wavy and haphazard. His smile is crooked and devious. He looks dangerous in the best of ways. And maybe dangerous is what I need right now. I've played it safe for so long. I've been conservative. The good girl. The driven girl. The girl who has no time for danger.

I stuff the envelope in my bag. "A drink is exactly what I need right now."

"Good," he says, walking us over to a table in the darkest corner of the bar. "But you should know up front that I'm not sleeping with you."

I slip into the booth and grab some napkins from the dispenser to wipe the dirty street water from my arms. Then I stare him down. "Is that the standard line you use to get girls into bed?"

He laughs and shakes his head. "No. In fact, I'm not sure I've ever said those words before in my life."

The waitress comes over and takes my order as the guy grabs a non-descript baseball cap out of his bag and pulls it down low on his head. "I'll have a wheat beer, whatever's on tap," he says.

"Coming right up," the waitress says as she walks away.

I eye his hat and then I look around the dark pub. "Too bright for you in here?"

"Just protecting myself from getting splashed from stray buses."

I laugh, looking down at my clothes.

He motions to the bag he put down next to him. "I may have a dry shirt in there if you want it. I can't promise it won't smell like *guy* though."

"I'm fine. But thanks for offering." I hold out my hand. "I'm Aspen."

He takes my hand in his and shakes it. His handshake is strong and confident. "Nice to meet you, Aspen. That's an interesting name."

The waitress brings our drinks over as I wait for him to introduce himself. But he never does.

"I'm not telepathic, you know," I say.

He narrows his eyes at me.

"Your name. Am I supposed to guess it?"

"Oh." He chuckles and stares at me like I'm supposed to know him or something. "It's Sawyer."

"As in Tom?"

"Yup. That's the one," he says. "My mom was a big fan." His hand absentmindedly runs back and forth across his ribs. "And that's not usually what comes to mind when people meet me."

"Really? What does then?"

He laughs. "Nothing. It's just refreshing."

"What's refreshing?"

He shrugs. "You."

I wiggle my toes around in my soaked shoes. "I don't feel so refreshing."

"Well, you are."

"Thanks – I guess. So what do you do, Tom Sawyer?"

That crooked smile of his makes another appearance. "A little of this, a little of that."

I can't tell if he doesn't want me to know what he does, or if maybe he's out of a job and doesn't want me thinking less of him.

"Sorry," he says. "It's just that my job is the reason I'm having a shitty day, and since we're not talking about that …"

I nod. "Got it. Same for me. But not my job. I'm a student. But it's the reason for *my* shitty day."

"You go to college?"

"Yeah. Juilliard," I say sadly.

"No shit? Are you some kind of prodigy or something?"

I wiggle all my fingers. "Hardly. I play piano."

"I'd say you must play it pretty damn well to be there."

I shrug. "I graduate in May."

"Wow. Congrats. What are you going to do after?"

I take a long drink of my beer. "Can we talk about something else?"

"Sure. How about sports? Do you like sports?"

I shake my head. "No time. I spend every spare minute practicing."

He raises his eyebrows. "I thought we weren't talking about that."

"Right."

We sit in silence for a minute as I try to think of something to talk about. I look over at the other corner of the bar and see a band setting up. I look up at the silent television. I look down and examine my fingernails.

"Oh, my God," I say, looking up in disgust. "I literally have nothing to talk about. The past four years I've done nothing but eat, sleep and live piano. Everything has been about Juilliard. I think I must be the most boring person alive. Sorry you ended up sitting with such a dud."

He laughs. "Aspen, I have the feeling you are anything but boring. How about your family? Want to talk about that?"

"Ha! Family is exactly the reason I'm sitting here drowning my sorrows with you. So, no."

"I thought school was why you were here."

"It's both," I say. "But if you want to talk about *your* family, go right ahead."

"Nothing there to talk about," he says.

I take another drink of my beer to hide the awkwardness.

My phone rings. It's Bass. I hold it up and apologize. "I'm sorry, I have to take this. I'll be quick." I swipe my finger across the screen.

"What the hell, Penny? They're going to demo the whole building?"

"That's what the notice said."

"Three months? That's not enough time to find a new place in the city."

"You'll be fine. I'm sure you'll meet a ton of people in training who will need roommates. Plus, you never know where you'll be stationed. I actually think the timing is good for you."

"But what about you?"

I shrug. "I'm probably moving out of New York anyway."

"What?"

"Long story."

The waitress comes by asking if we want another round. Sawyer raises his eyebrows at me and I nod.

"Where are you? Who was that?"

"I'm just getting a drink."

"A drink? Are you at a bar?"

"I might be."

He laughs. "Aspen Andrews at a bar. Wait, did something happen? I mean, other than our impending eviction?"

I sigh into the phone.

"Where are you? I'll come keep you company before my shift."

"No, that's okay. I already have company."

I think I've stunned him into silence.

"Bass?"

"Aspen, you're at a bar and you have company? I know some shit had to happen. Tell me."

"I have to go. I'm being rude. I'll talk to you later."

"Aspen—"

I hang up and put my phone away. "Sorry," I tell Sawyer.

"That's okay. I think you're getting more interesting by the minute. Who's Bass?"

"My roommate."

"Another interesting name."

"It's short for Sebastian."

"Is he going into the military?"

I look at him with questioning eyes.

"You said something about him going into training and not knowing where he'll be stationed."

"Oh. No, not the military. He's going to firefighter school. He spent the past year becoming a certified EMT and paramedic and now he's starting his firefighter training. That will take several months."

"And he's just a roommate?"

"Yes."

"Nothing else going on there?"

I laugh. "Well, we did mess around once, but it was awkward. Kind of like being with my brother. Ewww. We're better as friends."

"Does *he* think so?"

I shrug. "I'm sure he does. Why wouldn't he?"

"Aspen, have you looked in a mirror lately?"

I scoff at him. "Oh, please."

"You're gorgeous."

I feel my face heat up. I take a drink. "Thanks, I guess."

"And I'm hot, too, right?"

"And far too modest," I say, laughing.

The band starts playing a familiar tune and I sit up tall in my seat so I can see them.

"You like this song?" Sawyer asks.

"Yeah."

He nods to the small dance floor. "Want to?"

"You should know I'm a terrible dancer." I wiggle my fingers in the air. "These are the only parts of me that have rhythm."

He laughs, standing up and pulling me out of the booth. He tugs his hat down even lower on his forehead as we reach the dance floor.

I discover that although my dancing leaves much to be desired, it's a way to keep us from feeling the awkward silence. And I find that if I simply mimic what the other girls on the dance floor are doing, I might not look so much out of place.

"You're not half bad," Sawyer says, leaning close to speak in my ear.

"You're not so bad yourself. You do this often?"

"Not really."

"Me neither. I can't remember the last time I danced."

Every time he leans in to talk to me, I smell him. Unlike someone who just got splattered with dirty street-water, he smells clean from a shower. His cologne permeates my senses. His hot words crossing my ear have me feeling things I haven't felt in a long time.

Another song plays. A slower one this time. Sawyer looks at me with raised brows and holds out his arms. I walk into them, drawn like a moth to the flame. I'm not sure what it is about this man. I just met him less than an hour ago. He's dark and mysterious. He's handsome and inviting. He might just be everything I need, to forget about the day I had.

But he's not going to sleep with me.

Suddenly, I feel a sense of loss.

His hands feel like hot lava on my sides. They work around to the small of my back. His thumbs caress me through the thin fabric of my shirt. His eyes take me in now that we're closer.

He looks at me like *I'm* the flame.

"Shit," he says, pulling away.

He grabs my hand and leads me back to the table. He calls out to the waitress to bring another round along the way.

I sit down and stare at him. "What was that about?"

"That was about me not sleeping with you."

"Am I missing something?"

"I can't sleep with you, Aspen. It's against the rules."

I look at his left hand. I don't see a ring. I ask him anyway. "Are you married?"

His eyes snap to mine. "Hell, no."

"Do you have a girlfriend?"

"Never."

"What do you mean *never?*"

"I mean I don't do girlfriends."

I study him. He looks truthful but sorrowful.

"Are you a recovering sex addict or something?" I laugh.

He doesn't laugh with me. "Or something," he says.

The waitress brings our drinks. Sawyer stops her before she walks away. "We'd like some shots, please." He turns to me. "Pick your poison."

"Me? Uh, I don't know." I think back to when I had time to party. "Buttery nipple?"

Sawyer laughs and turns back to the waitress. "Bring four."

"I haven't done shots since the summer after my senior year in high school."

"How old are you, Aspen?"

"Almost twenty-three. You?"

"A solid twenty-five. When's the big day?"

"Next month."

Our shots get placed on the table in front of us. He picks one up and toasts me. "Happy early birthday."

I pick mine up and clink it to his. "Thanks."

"You're different," he says.

"Different from whom?"

"The girls I usually take out."

"This is you taking me *out?*" I tease. "I thought we were just two people drowning our shitty-day sorrows."

"You know what I mean."

"Okay, so tell me about the girls you usually take out."

"They don't go to Juilliard, that's for sure. Most of them can't even have an intelligent conversation." His eyes travel to my breasts that are well-covered by my t-shirt. "And they usually have on a lot less clothing."

I follow his eyes to my chest. "And bigger boobs, I imagine."

"Size doesn't matter to me."

"Me either," I say with a wink.

His head falls back and he bellows out a deep, throaty laugh. "I don't think you'd be disappointed," he says with a cocky grin.

"I'm sure I wouldn't be. I can already tell you have a massive ... ego."

His grin turns into an all-out smile that brings out a slight dimple in his cheek.

"Tell me why you're leaving New York," he says. "You told your friend on the phone that you might. You don't like the city?"

"New York is okay. But why I might be leaving goes along with my shitty day, so I'd rather not talk about it."

He raises his second shot. "To new friends and better days."

I raise mine. "And to buttery nipples."

His eyes go to my chest again and I feel my pulse rate go up. He's thinking about my boobs. I'm thinking about his ... ego.

He pulls out his wallet and puts enough money on the table to cover the drinks for half the people in the bar. Then he grabs his bag, tucks his folder under his arm, and stands up, offering me his hand. "Come on, I'll walk you home."

My heart slumps in defeat. It's not that I wanted to go home with this guy. This guy I don't even know. But after the day I had, it just felt right to do something wrong. Something dangerous. Something out of character.

My head feels a bit fuzzy, so I let him help me from the booth, our hands fitting nicely together. I notice he has callouses on his hand and I wonder if he works in construction. Then I look back at the table and the nice chunk of change he left and I think maybe not.

He drops my hand to open the door and after we walk through, he doesn't take it again.

"I'm this way," I say. "About four blocks over."

He again pulls his hat low on his forehead and keeps his head down, like he's afraid he might run into someone he doesn't want to.

The streets are crowded this time of night and we keep bumping into each other. Every time our hands or elbows touch, we look at each other and smile. It's the oddest thing. I feel more comfortable with him than I did my last boyfriend after weeks of dating.

A bicyclist comes barreling down the sidewalk and Sawyer grabs my arm, pulling me into an alley to avoid a collision.

"Jesus, that was close," he says. "Two close calls in one day is more than enough. First the bus and now this. You *are* having a bad day."

I realize how close we're standing. So close that I have to look up to see his eyes. I shrug. "I don't know. I think it ended up pretty well."

His hand comes up to trace the outline of my jaw. "Aspen." He says my name like it's a prayer. "I can't do this."

I nod and smile. "It's okay."

Before I can turn and back away, he pulls me to him and kisses me. He kisses me softly. Then he kisses me hard. Then I open for him and our tongues meet and mingle as I forget about school, delinquent brothers, and apartment demos. I forget everything, including my own name.

He pushes me gently against the alley wall, his hands moving up and down my arms and then down to my ass. Oh, God, it feels good to have a man's hands on me again.

He breaks our kiss only long enough to utter the words, "I really shouldn't do this." Then he resumes his assault of my lips and my neck.

"Then don't," I say, as he's sucking on a spot beneath my ear.

"I'm not sure I can help it."

I can't help but smile. "Then don't."

"Where's your place?" he asks.

"About twenty steps to the right."

He pulls me by my arm, eager to get where we're going. "Roommate?"

I shake my head. "He works the overnight shift tonight. One of his last shifts as a paramedic before he goes to firefighter school."

We practically run up the two flights of stairs to my third-floor walk-up. I fish through my bag for my keys, pulling out the wet envelope in the process.

"I really want to know what's in the envelope," he says.

I nod to what is tucked under his arm. "I really want to know what's in the folder."

We laugh. Then we stare at each other, the heat between us becoming palpable. When I open my door, all thoughts of envelopes and folders fall away as everything, including most of our clothes, gets thrown to the floor on our way to my bedroom.

In my room, we tear each other's undergarments off in a matter of seconds. Then we appraise each other appreciatively.

"You look incredible," he says, his eyes wandering up and down my body.

"You're not half bad yourself, Tom Sawyer."

He pushes me back onto my bed and climbs over me. "I shouldn't do this. I'm breaking the rules and it hasn't even been one day."

"Sometimes rules are meant to be broken," I say. "Unless it hurts someone. Would you be hurting someone?"

"Just me," he says.

I have no idea what he means by that. But in two seconds, I don't care because his lips are on my breasts. Then my stomach. Then ... *oh, my.*

I writhe and buck beneath him as he brings me to a quick orgasm, likely fueled by alcohol and abstinence.

"That was spectacular," he says, crawling up my body.

"I think I'd have to agree," I say before we share a laugh.

Then I reach over into my nightstand and pull out a condom.

His eyebrows shoot up. "Do this often, do you?"

"Not in a very long time," I admit. "But I was a girl scout. I'm always prepared."

He takes the square package from me and studies it. Then he reaches into my nightstand to grab another one. "Mind if I use two?" he asks.

I shrug. "Suit yourself."

Watching him roll on the condoms gets me hot all over again. I reach out and touch him, running my hand up and down his length. He wasn't lying. It *is* impressive.

When he can't stand my hands on him any longer, he climbs on top of me, looking down on me as he positions himself at my entrance. It's as if he's asking permission.

I reach up, grab his head and pull his lips to mine just as he enters me. I groan into his mouth. I groan from the incredible feeling of his taut skin on mine. It's far different from the feeling of the hard rubber I keep in my night stand. I groan because I haven't had a man inside me for so long, I didn't even remember what it felt like until just now. I groan when he slips a hand between us to stroke my clit, building me back up to what I know will be another explosive climax.

I can see him holding back. He bites his lip so hard I can taste blood when he kisses me. And when I orgasm, he shouts out with his own guttural release.

He collapses down onto me, both of us needing a minute to catch our breath.

Finally, he rolls to the side. He brushes a piece of sweaty hair off my forehead. "Damn, you *are* different," he says.

"Different? I know it's been a while, but I'm pretty sure sex hasn't changed since the last time I did it."

His abs bounce up and down with his laughter.

I put my hand on his stomach, feeling the outline of his chiseled physique. Wow, the guy is in pristine shape. I lay my head on his chest and bask in the afterglow, the strong pull of alcohol drawing me under.

In a haze, the last thing I remember is his strong arm coming around my shoulders to pull me even closer to him.

Chapter Three

Sawyer

I stare at her as the sun comes up and brightens the room. I'm breaking all the rules. Not just the obvious one that will have me traded faster than Rick can tell me to pack my bags.

I glance at her nightstand. She's the first woman to provide her own condoms. I never let them provide condoms. It's rule number one of hookups, and something they warned us about as soon as we got called up to the majors. Girls may try to trap you with a baby, never trust them for birth control.

Then again, our meeting was random. She doesn't even know who I am. Not unless she's a very good actress.

It was refreshing to have a night with someone who didn't want to talk about *me* all night.

I squint when the sun coming through her window hits my eyes. I never stay past dawn. But I have no desire to leave. No desire to walk out that door and never see her again. I've never wanted to stay more than I do right now. But I know it's not an option. Even if this turned out to be it. Even if she's the one. I know better. Nobody can be the one. Because she'd get hurt. I'd hurt her. Because that's what I do. I hurt people. I learned from the best.

I quietly roll out of bed, pick up the condoms from the carpet and flush them. Then I go in search of a glass of water. When I spot my folder on the floor of her living room, the Kansas City contract spilling out of it, I pick it up and study it as I sit down and sink into her couch.

I fucked up. I shouldn't have done what I did last night. Maybe Aspen was right. Maybe I'm a sex addict. I couldn't even keep myself from screwing up on day one. How in the hell am I going to make it an entire season without the organization seeing me for what I really am?

I look at the floor and see Aspen's purse where she dropped it last night. I see the envelope lying beside it. Before I can tell myself what an invasion of privacy this is, I'm opening her letter. The paper is now hard and dry and I have to be careful peeling it apart. Some of the ink is smeared, but not so much that I can't read it.

I look over at her bedroom door and stare at it in wonder. Why would an acceptance letter into the master's program at Juilliard be a bad thing?

I assume, like making it to the majors was my dream, this was hers.

Then I glance around at my meager surroundings and take in what looks like second-hand furniture in a small two-bedroom apartment that could probably fit into my living room.

I hear my phone vibrating and quickly retrieve it from my pants that are still in a heap on the living room floor. I see that it's Danny calling. I really want to answer it, but I don't. I don't want to wake Aspen so I send him a text letting him know I'll call him later.

Then I get dressed and stand in her doorway. I study her far longer than I should. I have thoughts that I shouldn't be having. But when Danny's face pops up on my phone again, this time with a text, I know why I can't stay. I walk quietly across the apartment and gather my things. Then I collect her clothes, fold them neatly, and put them on her dresser. I pick up the condom wrappers and shove them in my pocket. Then I give Aspen one last look before I walk out her door.

As I usually do after a night like last, I find a Starbucks. This time, however, I don't go home. I find myself wandering around the streets of the city, drinking coffee and thinking about the girl I left a short while ago.

I never think about the girl. Why is *this* girl getting in my head? Maybe it's because she seemed so genuine. So sad. So damn real.

I think of her letter again, knowing it probably comes down to money. A graduate degree from the most exclusive fine arts school in the country can't come cheaply. I think about how we are so much alike. We both want something we may not be able to have. I want to stay with the Nighthawks. She wants an education she can't afford.

Suddenly, it hits me, and before I can talk sense into myself, I'm walking back up the steps of her building. I don't know the building security code, so I have to wait around until I can sneak in after someone exits.

I try the door to her apartment, hoping that maybe it's unlocked and I can just slip back in, pretending I never left. But it doesn't budge.

I look at the time. Eight o'clock. I wonder if she's a late sleeper. We did stay up well past midnight last night.

I knock on the door lightly. A minute later, I knock again — harder this time. I finally hear something inside her apartment. It sounds like she ran into a table and is cursing about it.

The door opens a crack and she looks confused when she sees me. She also looks seriously hung over. Her hair is matted down on one side and makeup is smeared down her cheeks. She opens the door a little wider, looking me over from head to toe.

"Why are you wearing the same clothes as last night? And, uh … how did you know where I live?" She pulls her robe tightly around her. Then she rolls her eyes. "Oh, right, you walked me home, didn't you? I'm so embarrassed. I don't normally get that drunk." She looks at her hands and fists and unfists her fingers like they hurt. "It must have been the new stuff I took for my hands. Thanks for getting me home safely. I was obviously out of it. So, why are you here?"

She doesn't remember last night?

"Do you normally get shit-faced drunk with strange men and then let them walk you home?" I ask, not feeling in the least like bursting her bubble and telling her she slept with me.

"No, I don't. I had a bad day. One of the worst I've ever had." She holds the door open and backs away. "Sorry, I guess since you were nice enough to make sure I made it home last night, the least I can do is offer you a cup of coffee."

I watch her as she works in the kitchen, stopping to check her appearance in the mirror and then apologizing to me for how bad she looks before she runs off to the bathroom.

I stare down at the letter that still sits on the floor of her living room. I pick it up and turn it over and over in my hands.

When she emerges from her room, I see she's ditched the robe in favor of yoga pants and a tank top. I wonder if she even thought twice about waking up in the nude. *How could she not know?*

Then I think of the condoms that I flushed and the wrappers I shoved in my pocket. Can she really not tell she had sex last night? Don't girls usually have a feeling?

She pours two cups of coffee and then comes over and sits on the couch opposite the chair I'm occupying. She eyes the envelope on the table, probably wondering if I read it.

"I have a proposition for you," I say.

She belts out a laugh. "If I didn't sleep with you when I was drunk, I'm sure as heck not going to do it now, when I feel like I could vomit at any second."

"That's not my proposition." Then I cock my head sideways and study her. "Well, I don't know, maybe it is."

"Huh?" She takes a sip of her coffee. "You're going to have to be more clear. My head is still a bit fuzzy." Then she eyes me up and down and her face pinks up. "Wait, did we ... uh, did we make out in an alley last night?"

"We might have."

Her head drops into her hands. "Oh, my God. I've hit an all-time low. That isn't me, Sawyer. I don't go making out in alleys with guys I just met."

"It's fine," I tell her. "You're a good kisser. So, about that proposition. I'd like to hire you, Aspen."

She sits up straight and defensively pulls a pillow onto her lap. "Come again?"

"I'd like to hire you to be my girlfriend."

Her nose wrinkles in disgust. "You *what?*"

"For appearances' sake, I need to be seen with a girlfriend." I shake my head because I hear what I sound like and I'm going about this all wrong. "I'll pay you for it."

"Like a whore?"

"No, not like a whore. I just need certain people to think I'm in a relationship." I run my hands through my hair "I – I can't have a girlfriend. But I need one."

"Certain people. A woman?"

"No. It's not like that."

"Was last night at the bar an audition?" she asks abhorrently.

"God, no. I didn't even think of asking you this until just now."

"Get out," she says.

"Come on, Aspen. We had fun last night. We get along great. I need a girlfriend and you need the money."

She throws the pillow off her lap and stands up. "What the hell do you mean by that?"

I nod to the envelope on the table. "I saw the letter. I'm sure grad school will be expensive. Would half-a-million cover it?"

Her jaw drops. "I don't know who you think you are, but you're not anyone I want to know."

She eyes me warily as she skirts around the couch like she thinks I'll pounce on her and keep her from getting away. I put up my hands in surrender, letting her know she's safe.

She backs into the kitchen. "I'd like you to leave. Right now."

I pull my folder out of my duffle bag. "Here, you can read mine, too. It's only fair."

She backs away. "I don't give a shit who you are or what's in that folder." She points to the door. "Please, just go."

"Aspen."

She holds her phone up for me to see. "Do I need to call the police?"

"No. I'm going." I put my duffle bag over my shoulder and walk to the door. "I didn't mean to ruin everything. Last night was incredible – one of the best nights I can remember. I think you're a great girl. I'm really sorry, Aspen."

I walk through the door, closing it behind me. I stand in the hallway and think of what a stupid idiot I am. Then I hear a thump and realize she must have hit the door. I wonder if she's leaning against it. Maybe she's sliding her back down the door until her butt hits the floor. Maybe she's looking at me through the peephole. I look directly into it and put on my best apologetic face. "I'm sorry," I say to the door.

Then I walk away.

~ ~ ~

"You okay, Speed Limit?" Brady asks, walking back to the clubhouse after our practice.

I don't even roll my eyes anymore at the nickname my grandfather gave me when I was drafted by the Hawks and assigned #55 because my favorite number was taken. I stopped trying long ago to get them to quit using it. It was useless. Anytime someone gets a nickname around here, it sticks like white on rice.

"Yeah."

"You seem distracted."

"I'm good."

"Game starts in two hours," he says. "You gonna have your focus by then?"

"I said I'm good."

Brady pats me on the shoulder and nods to our manager who has been sneering at me all day. I swear he's waiting for me to mess up just so he can rub it in my face. "Don't let Rick get to you. Everything will blow over soon enough. Just keep your nose down."

"I wish it were that easy."

Brady cocks his head, studying me. "What did you do?"

I shake my head. "Nothing, man. Everything's fine. Let's get some grub."

I walk over to the buffet table set up with sandwiches and fill my plate. Then I take a seat away from the others while the coaches prepare us for tonight's game. We spend the next hour watching tape from yesterday's game. Well, most of the team does. Me – I spend the hour worrying about what an idiot I was to do what I did last night. And this morning.

This could be bad. This could be very bad. What if she figures out who I am? What if she remembers last night? What if she goes to the press and tells them I tried to hire her to sleep with me? That's not what I was doing, but she doesn't know that. She didn't give me a chance to explain.

I have to make this right. I have to make her understand I'm not the guy she thinks I am.

Well – maybe I *am* the guy she thinks I am, but what she doesn't get is that she really wouldn't be my girlfriend. She'd be able to go to grad school. I'd be able to stay with the Hawks. How does that make it a bad thing?

Hell, I'd write her a contract spelling it out if that's what it takes.

I look around the clubhouse. I have to save my career. Failure is not an option.

As soon as we're done viewing the tapes, I send a text to my lawyer – the one who's had to help me out of some sticky situations over the past few years. She's good. She'll know how to handle this.

Chapter Four

Aspen

"What an asshole," Bass says, as he shovels a forkful of spaghetti into his mouth.

I nod in agreement. "Except the thing is, last night he wasn't. He was the perfect gentleman. It was one of the best nights I've had, and after the day I had yesterday, that's saying something."

"Maybe you were right about it being an audition. Maybe he was putting on an act last night and the guy who came to your door this morning was the real Sawyer." He points at me with his fork. "And, really, Penny? You didn't even get the guy's last name? Are you trying to end up getting robbed or left in a ditch somewhere?"

I sigh knowing he's absolutely right. "It was stupid. But I needed a little crazy after what happened with my brother."

"It's a good thing you have me, then. Because it sounds like between Denver and this Sawyer guy, you're surrounded by crazy."

I reach over and give him a hug. "I'm lucky to have you."

He runs a hand down my back and gives my ass a squeeze. "Maybe you should go out with me again so I can see what all the fuss is about, I mean the guy offered you a half-million to be his girlfriend."

I swat his hand away. "Hey, you had your chance four years ago. And it's not like he was serious about the half-million."

He shovels more food into his mouth. "You never know," he says with a mouthful. "There are some rich douchebags in this city. Maybe he's an investment banker or something. Hell, maybe you should have heard the guy out. There are worse things you could do for five hundred K."

I roll my eyes. "Are you trying to pimp me out, Bass?"

He laughs. "No, not trying to pimp you out. Just trying to figure out how to get you to stay in the city. Think about it for a minute. You're going to give up your graduate degree to move back home and work three jobs just so you can pay off Denver's bad debts. But what will *you* get out of it?"

"You mean other than my brother not going to jail?"

"Of course you don't want him going to jail, Aspen. But you have to look out for your future. Do you really want to teach piano to little kids for the rest of your life? Because you know as well as I do that is all you'll be doing with a pile of shit BM."

I cringe knowing he's speaking the truth. Juilliard or not, it's a joke among music students that a BM, or bachelor of music, isn't good for much. The first week there, we learned the age-old joke, *'What's the shittiest degree you can get? – A BM.'*

Everyone knows going into it that you have to continue on to get your MM – master of music, or even your PhD if you want to do anything more than teach kids. Teaching *is* what I want to do, but not the kind of teaching where you go to rich people's homes and try to teach spoiled, un-teachable kids how to play chopsticks.

My dream is to teach at the collegiate level. Teach students who love the piano so much, they play it in their sleep like I do. Students who would rather stroke the black and white keys until 2:00 AM than party with their friends. People who might even settle for teaching snotty-nosed kids, because even doing that is better than sitting at a desk typing on a computer all day long.

"I've already looked into the University of Missouri – they have an MM degree there."

Bass tilts his head and studies me. "That's bullshit, Penny. You know an MM is a full-time program. There is no way you could help Denver pay off his debts *and* afford to pay for grad school. And while I'm sure Missouri is a fine school, nothing compares to Juilliard. They only accept one hundred and fifty people into the master's program. That's one damn exclusive club you could belong to."

"What about 'my brother has to pay four hundred thousand dollars in retribution' do you not understand? I can't go to Juilliard, Bass. It's not going to happen."

"I'm just saying it could if you took the guy up on his offer."

"Ten minutes ago he was an asshole and now he's my savior?" I get up and put my plate in the sink. "What is wrong with you?"

"Why can't he be both?" he asks. "Why can't he be an asshole *and* your savior?"

"I'm not sleeping with anyone for money, Bass. Not even *that* much money."

"Maybe you wouldn't have to. You said he needed a girlfriend for appearances. Maybe he can get his rocks off somewhere else and just use you for the eye candy."

"First off, I was too busy kicking his ass out of our apartment to get all the details. And second, even if I wanted to consider it, I have no idea who he is or where to find him." I clear his plate off the table. "And third ... just ... gross."

Bass walks over and kisses my forehead. "That's my roommate, squeaky clean Snow White."

I slap him playfully and look at the clock. "Aren't you going to be late?"

He backs away and heads for his room. "Last shift," he says. "I'm so fucking stoked to start fire school next week."

"Don't you ever miss it?" I ask, nodding to his collection of guitars in the corner.

"I play every damn day, Penny. You of all people should know that. It'll always be my passion, just not how I pay the bills. Helping people gives me so much more gratification than entertaining them."

He shuts his bedroom door to change his clothes. Then two minutes later, he emerges looking quite attractive in his paramedic uniform. Some girl is going to be lucky to land him someday.

He puts his arm around my shoulder. "Everything's going to work out, Penny. One way or another."

I nod my head, holding in the tears as he walks out our front door.

I stare at his guitars. Sebastian was the first person I met at Juilliard during freshman orientation. We hit it off instantly, almost like Sawyer and I did last night. We tried dating, but realized we were better as friends. We've been joined at the hip ever since, even after he quit school to pursue becoming a firefighter/paramedic. After freshman year, we got an apartment together. He's as close to me as anyone ever has been with the exception of Denver.

I walk over to the window and look down on the streets of the city I've tried so hard to love. Why did Denver have to blow our inheritance? Why did he have to get caught up in all that crooked shit? He was a cop for crying out loud.

My tears finally fall when I think about his trial last month. While I was there, he pleaded with me to believe him. He said he had no idea the investments weren't legitimate. He genuinely thought he was going to make money for us and all those other people. He was used by some higher-ups in the police department who threw him under the bus when things went south. What *they* did was untraceable, but my brother left a money trail that lead right back to him. And now he's not allowed to leave Missouri, and according to his sentencing that was just handed down yesterday, if he doesn't make regular restitution payments he'll be put in jail. And not just jail. Prison.

A cop in prison is a death sentence. Even if I thought he had known he was scamming all those people, I still would never wish jail on him. He's my brother. My other half. The only person in the world I would do anything for.

A knock on the door startles me. I look through the peephole, not sure I'm seeing correctly. Because I think I'm seeing the asshole. I back away and wipe my tears, checking my appearance in the nearby mirror as my brain tries to tell me it's *not* the asshole, it's my savior.

I pull my hair free of the messy bun it was in and give it a fluff. Then I scold my reflection before I open the door.

Sawyer takes a few steps back like he thinks I'll lunge at him and put my fist through his chest. Not that I could. I felt his abs in the alley when we kissed. They're practically made of steel.

I raise my eyebrows at him.

"Give me five minutes to explain. That's all I'm asking. Please, Aspen?"

I look him up and down. He's not particularly tall. I'd be surprised if he's six feet. But he's pure muscle. I contemplate my choices here, thinking if he wanted to chop me up into little pieces and hide me under the floorboards, he already had a chance to do it.

I step back and walk into the living room, leaving the door open for him to follow. I sit down on my couch. "Don't expect me to offer you a drink."

"I wouldn't dream of it," he says, walking around the coffee table to sit in the chair opposite me.

He looks around my place. "Is your roommate here?"

"No, but he could be back any second," I lie.

Sawyer smirks like he knows I'm full of shit. "Let me cut to the chase," he says. "I believe we are both in need of something we don't have. I need to look like I have a steady girlfriend. And you need money. I can help you go to Juilliard and you can help save my career. This arrangement would be mutually beneficial."

I cross my arms over my chest defensively. "How do I know you even have the money to pay me?"

I cringe after the words come out of my mouth, hating myself for a second that I'm even *considering* considering it. But then I think of Denver, and know I at least need to hear this guy out.

He laughs an arrogant laugh. "I have it." He fishes a business card out of his pocket and hands it to me. "This is my lawyer. If you can meet me at her office for lunch tomorrow, we can go over everything."

I examine the card and then look up at him in surprise. "You want to make this a *legal* agreement?"

"Yes. Wouldn't that make you more comfortable?"

I shrug. "I guess so. But I have class until one o'clock. I couldn't meet you until then."

"And I have to be at … somewhere – by two. That gives us an hour to go over everything."

Somewhere?

I wonder why he's being so secretive. And so totally different from the guy he was last night.

40

He gets up from his chair and comes over to offer me his hand. I shake it, my insides melting from his touch. Flashbacks of last night's kiss race through my head as he holds onto my hand far longer than customary. His electrified touch has me thinking of doing a lot more than kissing him, as thoughts of having him in my bed attack my sex-deprived brain. Then I chide myself for even going there. This guy is an arrogant prick who thinks he can buy me.

I want to pull away. I should pull away. But I can't. Even though he's probably not on the level – hell, for all I know, he could be a criminal, my body reacts to him in a way I can't even explain.

"I look forward to it, Aspen."

"I'm not promising anything, you know. I'm only willing to hear you out."

He nods. "That's more than I expected considering how you kicked me out of here this morning." He looks over at Bass's room. "Did you tell your roommate about me?"

"I tell my roommate everything," I say.

"What did he say?"

"What do you think he said? That you're an asshole, of course."

He laughs. "Yeah. That sounds about right. I'd appreciate it if he'd accompany you to the meeting. Do you think he could swing it?"

"He works nights, so yeah."

"Good."

He finally lets go of my hand and walks towards the door.

I stand up. "Sawyer?"

He turns around. "Yeah?"

"What kind of job do you have that allows you to pay someone a half-million dollars to pretend to be your girlfriend?"

"It's a fair enough question, but one I'd like to answer tomorrow if it's all the same to you."

"So you'll tell me then?"

He nods. "I'll tell you whatever you want to know, Aspen."

He walks out the door and I'm left standing here wondering if this really just happened. Then I look in the mirror, wondering just how far this good little Catholic girl will go to save her brother.

Chapter Five

Sawyer

My phone vibrates in my pocket as I step off the elevator onto the tenth floor of my lawyer's office building. I check it and see it's the only person I never let roll to voicemail if I can help it.

I swipe my finger across the screen. "Hey, buddy, what's up?"

"Are you gonna come over today?" Danny asks.

"Not today. I have a game. But soon."

"Can't you come after? I wanna play baseball."

"No, I can't come after. It takes me a long time to get there, remember? But I promise I'll come next week after I get back from Atlanta."

I can tell he's disappointed. He might even be crying. "I have an idea. Why don't you watch the game tonight and I'll give you a special sign?"

"What's it gonna say?" he asks.

"Not that kind of sign. I'll signal you with my hand when I think the cameras are on me. Maybe when I'm in the dugout, okay? How about I give you a thumb's up?"

"Yes! Yes!" he squeals.

"Great. Now I have to go, but can you put your mom on the phone for a second?"

"Mommy!" he screams into the phone.

I hear Lucy's voice in the background, saying something to Danny before she gets on the line. "Sawyer?"

"Yeah. I was wondering if I could drive out Sunday night after I get back from Atlanta."

"I'm sure Daniel would like that."

"Good. And, Lucy, I told him I'd give him a thumb's up during the game. I'll try my best, but maybe you could play along and make it seem like I did it even if the cameras don't show it."

She sighs into the phone. "You shouldn't make him promises like that."

"I know. But he was upset. I feel bad that I haven't seen him in a few weeks."

"I'll see what I can do."

"Thanks. I have to go now. Tell him I'll see him on Sunday."

"Bye, Sawyer. Good luck tonight."

I slip my phone back into my pocket and open the door to Sarah's law firm.

The receptionist greets me. "Nice to see you, Mr. Mills. Ms. Wilson isn't quite ready for you yet. They will be just a few more minutes. If you'd like to have a seat on the couch, she'll buzz me when you can go back."

"So, they're in there? They both showed up?"

"Yes, they did."

I look at my watch. It's ten after one. Sarah wanted me to arrive late so she could have Aspen and her roommate sign a non-disclosure before our meeting. She thought it best to do it since they don't know who I am yet. The NDA they are signing right now prohibits them from discussing anything we talk about in the meeting. The NDA they will be asked to sign *after* the meeting will include my name and will prohibit them from discussing anything about my on-going arrangement with Aspen.

Assuming she agrees to it, that is.

I'm still surprised she even showed up today.

"They're ready for you now, Mr. Mills. You can go on back."

I breathe a sigh of relief. The fact that I'm being called to Sarah's office means they signed the first NDA – one step closer to making this thing happen.

The receptionist buzzes me through and I walk down the hallway to the large corner office where Sarah is waiting for me at the door. She shakes my hand. "Nice to see you, Sawyer."

I lean in and kiss her cheek. Sarah is a long-time friend of mine. We were introduced at a party by one of my veteran teammates when I first came to New York. I slept with her of course. And fortunately, she wasn't one to hold a grudge, because she's a damn fine lawyer and someone I want on my side.

"Everything okay?"

"So far, so good," she says.

I walk into her office to see Aspen and her roommate sitting at the table by the window. They both look at me with very different reactions. Aspen looks hesitant, scared even. But her roommate obviously recognizes me.

His jaw goes slack as he looks from me back to Aspen. "That's ... that's—"

I step over and offer him my hand. "Sawyer Mills, glad to meet you."

"Holy shit," he says, taking my hand and shaking it with his firm grip. "I mean, Sebastian Briggs, nice to meet you."

"Sorry, ma'am," he says to Sarah. "I didn't mean to cuss, but this is ... surreal."

"It's okay," Sarah says. "It's pretty much the reaction I was expecting."

"What's going on here?" Aspen asks, seeing her friend's reaction.

Sebastian shakes his head, laughing. "This is the guy you met at the bar? Damn."

"What am I missing?" Aspen asks.

"He's a baseball player," Sebastian says.

"Baseball?"

"Yeah, for the New York Nighthawks. He's their shortstop. The best player if you ask me. He holds the league record for stolen bases two years running."

"You're *famous?*" Aspen asks me with a furrow of her brow.

I shrug. "I guess some people know who I am."

"Know who you are? Dude, you might just be the most recognizable face in baseball." He turns to Aspen. "You really didn't know who he was?"

She gives her roommate a scolding stare. "When was the last time you saw me watching a sporting event?"

"Still." He shakes his head. Then he turns to me. "And you want Aspen to be your girlfriend?"

"My *pretend* girlfriend," I correct him. Then I formally acknowledge Aspen. "Thanks for coming." I hold my hand out to her. "I'm sorry about all the secrecy, but in my line of work, you have to be careful."

Aspen shakes her head. "I feel so stupid for not recognizing you. I mean, I don't really follow baseball, but I see the news, and sometimes I read the tabloids."

I laugh. "Never read the tabloids, Aspen. Especially if we're going to do this. You don't want to see what they'll print about you."

"Me?"

Sarah steps over to the table with several file folders. "The press will have a field day with you once you go public with your relationship. They may print things about you that show you in a less-than-desirable light. They will print flat-out lies. It's just one of the things you'll have to deal with if you sign."

With that, Sarah hands everyone a folder. We open them up to pull out a five-page document.

"You are free to take this with you and have your own lawyer look over it," she says.

"What about the NDA?" Aspen asks.

"There is something called attorney-client privilege. It prevents us from talking about anything we discuss with you. It's kind of like our own NDA, but without a signed contract."

"Oh. I don't have a lawyer," Aspen says.

"You sure as hell will be able to afford one now," Sebastian says.

She gives him a dirty look. I can tell she's not completely on board with this yet.

"Let me put it in a nutshell for you," Sarah says. "Mr. Mills will deposit said funds into an escrow account held by my firm. We will, at regular intervals laid out in the contract, disburse such funds to you. You will, for all intents and purposes, pose as Mr. Mills' girlfriend in public from the moment the contract is signed until the end of the baseball season."

"And in private?" Aspen asks.

I try not to laugh. Because I know exactly what we can do in private. We've already *done* it.

"In private you don't have to be his girlfriend, but you can't be anyone else's either. You have to keep up appearances."

Aspen and Sebastian whisper to each other and then she leafs through the contract in silence.

She looks up in surprise. "I have to move in with him in a few months?"

"It's the normal progression of a modern relationship," Sarah says. "Mr. Mills has plenty of room at his townhouse to accommodate you."

Aspen looks ready to argue the point. But Sebastian puts a hand on her arm. "Penny, it could be the perfect solution. We'll be without a place in three months anyway. It's actually pretty good timing."

"Penny?" I ask, amused at his nickname for her.

He shrugs. "It's better than calling her 'Ass,' don't you think?"

I laugh. "Yes, that it is. But I'm not a fan of nicknames."

"But you have a great one. They call him *Speed Limit*," he explains to Aspen. "Because he's so fast and his number is fifty-five."

Aspen doesn't seem to care in the least about what her roommate is telling her. She continues perusing the contract. "But what about you?" she asks Sebastian. "Where will *you* live?"

"Remember what you said about my meeting people at training? I'm sure I'll find other options. Don't worry about me."

Aspen looks at the contract thoughtfully. "Would I get my own bedroom?" she asks.

Sarah looks at me and I shrug.

"Yes," Sarah says. "If that's what you want."

"Can we add that to the contract?"

"Of course," Sarah says, making a note on her legal pad.

I'm trying not to smile and pump my fist. This is going to happen. I can see it in Aspen's face.

"Can we add other things to the contract?" Aspen asks.

"Such as?" Sarah says.

Aspen looks at her friend. "Such as Bass can come stay at Sawyer's place, too, if he doesn't have anywhere to go after they demo our building."

"Penny," he says, chiding her.

"I'm not about to let you be homeless," she tells him.

"I'm not sure that would be good for appearances' sake," Sarah says. "It's tabloid fodder for sure. But how about we add a clause stating that Mr. Mills will help Mr. Briggs find suitable accommodations should the need arise? Would that be acceptable to everyone?"

Sarah looks at me and I nod. Then she looks at Aspen, who seems happy with the compromise.

"Is there anything else you might like to add?" Sarah asks her.

Aspen looks at me and blushes. Then she looks back at Sarah. "I'm not having sex with him. I want it clearly stated in the contract that it's not my obligation to do so."

"You're kidding." I narrow my eyebrows. "We're consenting adults."

"I wouldn't really be consenting if you're paying me, now would I?" she says, looking at me sternly. "I'm nobody's whore."

I sit in stunned silence, wondering just who this girl is. Nobody has ever said they don't want to have sex with me. Especially someone I'm handing myself to on a silver fucking platter.

"You said so yourself that you don't do girlfriends, Sawyer. You said it the other night. So why argue the point?"

Sarah looks at me with raised brows.

"Fine," I grumble.

"Is that all?" Sarah asks.

"No. He can't have sex either. I'm not a whore, but I'm also nobody's fool. I won't be made to look like one if it gets out that he's sleeping around on me."

"Now I *know* you must be joking," I say. "Do you even know how long the season is? That's a ridiculous request."

Sebastian holds up the contract. "No more ridiculous than you paying Aspen to be your eye candy, and forcing her to move in with you. And not allowing her, or anyone, to even talk about anything."

"But six fucking months?" I muse aloud.

"Seven if you make the playoffs," Sebastian says.

"Shit."

I look around at the three pairs of eyes staring at me. Then I look down at the contract knowing I don't have a choice.

"Write it in," I tell Sarah reluctantly.

"And if you screw up and this thing blows up in your face, I still get all the money," Aspen says.

I look at Sarah.

"It's only fair," she says. "Because if Aspen or Sebastian violate the NDA, she gets nothing."

I blow out a long breath. "Fine."

"And when it's over," Aspen says, "I want it known that I left you, not the other way around. You can make up whatever story you want as long as it doesn't make me out to be a bitch or a slut."

I look at Aspen. "You drive one hell of a hard bargain."

Sarah interrupts the staring contest I'm having with Aspen. "You are aware that you'll have to participate in public displays of affection with Mr. Mills, aren't you?"

Aspen nods her head. "Yeah, I get that. But nothing under the clothing."

"Kissing will be required," Sarah says.

"I figured," Aspen replies, looking at me with pink cheeks.

I can't help but smile, because I know she's thinking about the kissing we did in the alley. She doesn't remember it, but we did a hell of a lot more kissing than that. She's an excellent kisser.

"So are we in agreement here?" Sarah asks. "Or do you want to have a lawyer look it over, Miss Andrews?"

Aspen leafs through the pages again. "Do I really have to travel to some of his away games? I have school."

"When are you out of school?" Sarah asks.

"Mid-May."

"Are you okay going to some out-of-town games after that? Say twice a month for three days each?" Sarah looks at me to make sure I'm okay with that. I nod. "That is six weeks away, probably about the time you'd start doing those sorts of things as his girlfriend."

"I guess I could do that," Aspen says. "Until grad school starts up in August."

I see her eyes light up for the first time today when she mentions grad school. That's how I know for sure she's not some chick just doing this to be seen with me. She's the genuine deal. She's not looking for an easy ride or a quick fix. She has an agenda. One I can help her achieve.

"Maybe just an occasional weekend away game after that?" Sarah asks. "People will understand you have commitments."

"That would be okay, as long as it doesn't interfere with a school performance."

"Okay, then, it looks like we might have a deal?" Sarah says.

Aspen and Sebastian whisper to each other for a minute and then they both page through the contract again.

"As long as you add everything we discussed, I'll sign it. It seems pretty straight forward."

"Good," Sarah says. "And when you sign the final contract, you and Mr. Briggs will be asked to sign an additional NDA that prohibits you from talking to anyone about the terms of the contract or the details of the arrangement both now and after the arrangement ends. You've already signed the NDA that forbids you to talk about this meeting."

Sebastian looks confused. "I can't tell anyone I know you?"

I shake my head. "No, you can. You're Aspen's friend, so it will make sense that you know me. I'm sure we might even get to hang out. Do you have a girlfriend?"

His eyes momentarily flash to Aspen. "Not at the moment."

"That's probably for the best," Sarah says. "You won't have to keep anything from a significant other."

Aspen looks thoughtfully at her roommate. Then she turns to me. "You know, Bass is being put into a position here. He'll have to lie about everything. He didn't sign up for this."

Sarah sighs and raises her brows. "You feel he should be compensated?" she asks Aspen.

"Penny, no. That's ridiculous," Sebastian says. "You're making enough already."

"How about a season ticket — club seats?" I say. "For each of you."

Sebastian looks at Aspen like his head will explode if she doesn't accept.

She rolls her eyes. "I guess that's a yes."

"Good," Sarah says. "Because I'm sure you saw on page three that you're required to make a lot of appearances at home games."

"Won't you want her sitting with the other players' wives and girlfriends?" Sebastian asks.

"It might be best if she didn't," Sarah explains. "It will avoid unnecessary questions."

"But if I don't sit with them, won't it look like I think I'm too good for them?"

She has a good point. Women can be super catty.

"We'll say you already had other tickets. And my two best friends on the team have wives who will take you under their wings, I'm sure of it. They can keep their mouths shut. They won't let the other women be mean to you."

"Sawyer," Sarah, scolds me. "The fewer people who know about this, the better. If this gets out, it will be worse for you than what you were dealing with before."

I shake my head. "I'm not worried about them saying a thing. I'd bet my life on it."

"You still haven't said why you're even doing this," Aspen says. "Did you have a bad breakup or something? Are you trying to get someone back by making them jealous?"

"Hardly," Sebastian snorts. "I don't think I've ever seen him with the same woman twice. I'll bet I can tell you exactly why he needs you, Penny. The higher-ups in the Hawks organization are getting tired of him being on the front page of every tabloid magazine with a different woman. They are tired of him parading around like the playboy of baseball. They're sick of having to get their PR person to explain all his indiscretions. I'm guessing there have even been a few lawsuits and some pretty pissed off husbands in the mix, too. Am I right?"

Aspen looks confused. "Are you going to get fired if you don't have a girlfriend?"

"Not fired. Traded. To a team not as desirable as the Hawks. And no, they didn't say I had to have a girlfriend. They know nothing about this and I'm going to keep it that way. They just said I needed to, um ... 'keep my dick in my pants,' to quote my manager."

"So why not just keep your dick in your pants, bro?" Sebastian asks. "Why go to such extremes?"

I don't say anything. What is there to say?

"Oh, my God. Are you really a sex addict?" Aspen asks.

"I'm not a sex addict. I just like to have it. It's fun. Don't you think it's fun?"

She pinks up as she tries to ignore my heated stare.

Sarah points to the contract. "I think Aspen's additions are a good thing. They'll keep you honest."

I turn to my lawyer. "You don't think I could do it on my own? Without her added clauses?"

"I'm not sure you want me to answer that," she says.

I check my phone. "I have to get to practice."

Everyone stands up and Sarah walks us to the door. "I'll draw up the new contracts and messenger them over to Aspen and Sebastian."

"How quickly?" I ask.

"I'll make it top priority. I could have them drawn up by Friday. Why don't the two of you plan a meeting sometime next week so you can figure out how to get started?"

"I'm back from Atlanta on Sunday," I tell them.

"I guess I could meet with you then," Aspen says.

I shake my head. "I have plans."

Six eyes stare at me and scold me like I'm a five-year-old.

"I'm not planning on fucking anyone, guys. I just have other plans. How about Monday night? It'll have to be late, probably ten o'clock or so by the time I'm showered and ready. Is that too late?"

Aspen shrugs. "I don't have class until Tuesday afternoon, so staying up late on Monday is okay."

I turn to Sebastian. "Are you available?"

"Me?"

"Yeah. I kind of figured you guys were a package deal."

Sebastian laughs. "Well, I'm not kissing you, if that's what you're asking, but, yeah, I can come along on Monday night."

"Good." I write down my address and hand it to Aspen. "See you Monday at ten. Now wait five minutes before you leave. I don't want anyone seeing us together until we make it official."

Aspen narrows her eyes at me. "Are you always going to be this bossy?"

"Well, technically, you are my employee for the next six months."

"Seven if you make the playoffs." She gives me a smug smile. "And considering how many revisions I've just made to the contract, you might want to re-evaluate who has the upper hand in this arrangement."

I laugh as I walk out of the office, thinking that this girl might just be the death of me. But, oh, what a way to go.

Chapter Six

Aspen

It's hard to concentrate in class today. I keep going over the contract that was messengered over this morning. I ignore my instructor as I read through the part that covers expectations about my behavior. I must allow him to hold my hand, put his arms around me ... *kiss* me.

The thought of kissing him again makes me squirm in my seat. I remember the night I met him. The surreal night that continues to plague my dreams – or my fantasies if I'm being honest. He was gentle. He was funny. He was unlike anyone I've ever met.

And now, I have to kiss him for the next six or seven months. And I have to 'fawn over him' and 'look at him with dreamy eyes.' It actually says those exact words in the contract. They are even dictating the way I have to look at him.

Five hundred thousand dollars. That is what I think about every time I want to burn the contract that makes me no better than a glorified hooker. But that's the reason I said I wouldn't sleep with him. I'm not about to let anyone pay me for sex.

I'm especially glad I had Sarah add it after all the research I've done on Sawyer the past few days. Bass was right. He's never been with the same girl twice. Not to mention I'm not all that eager to get an STD anytime soon. I question his ability to uphold his end of the contract. No way can he go six months or more without sleeping with someone. But that's nothing I need to worry about. I'll get paid in full if he does. And to my surprise, it was written in the contract that if he does 'cheat,' not only will I get paid the remainder of the money immediately, I will also be released from my duties.

I smile thinking that even though Sarah is *his* lawyer, she might just be on my side. He may be the one with all the money, but *I'm* the one in control.

All the money. I shake my head. I know exactly how much money Sawyer Mills makes. It's not hard to find those things out on the internet. I still can't believe he is who he is. I still can't believe I spent a few hours at a bar with the guy without knowing who he was.

And I'm about to be famous in my own way. Famous for being the girlfriend of the most ineligible bachelor of baseball. It concerns me that we might not even be able to pull it off considering his past. Will people even believe he has a girlfriend? Will he know how to act so that he's convincing? Maybe *he's* the one who needs a contract directing the way he has to look and act.

A text pops up on my phone.

Denver: Hey, sis. Can you talk?

Me: In class. I'll call you after. Everything okay?

Denver: Yeah. Talk to you later.

Denver. I sigh, thinking he's the reason I'm even in this situation. I'm doing this to pay off his bad debts, but at the same time, I'm not allowed to tell him anything. That will be the hardest part of the whole arrangement. My brother and I have always been very close. We tell each other everything. I even knew about the investments he was making. Hell, I gave him my part of our inheritance because it seemed like a sure thing.

Although I was devastated to lose the money that was going to secure my future, it may be the one reason I still have a relationship with my brother. He never would have swindled me. He would die for me. And that's how I know he was duped as well. He was duped by several higher-ups at KCPD. Higher-ups that still have *his* money, *my* money, and the money of a dozen other people. My brother's only crime was being the gullible rookie cop. Unfortunately, that's not the way the judge saw it and Denver ended up taking the fall for everyone.

I wish our mom was alive. She'd have done something. She was a judge herself. A highly-respected circuit court judge. But the judge who presided over Denver's case was a young judge who probably never even met my mom. He was trying to set an example with Denver.

I look down at the contract and re-read the part about how I get paid. I'm going to get fifty thousand dollars as soon as I sign the contract. I'll get two hundred and fifty thousand after our 'break up.' And the rest will be divided into monthly payments in between.

I'm still not sure how I'm going to justify paying off Denver's debts. How will I explain it to him? Do I say I won the lottery or something? How do I lie to the person who I'm closest to in the world? He'll see right through me, I'm sure.

Class is dismissed. I sat through the entire day today without learning a thing. I'd better get my act together or I'll fail my finals and they'll rescind my grad school acceptance.

On the way to the practice hall, I call my brother.

"Hey, little sister, how's it going?"

"Hey, big bro. Fine. Just on my way to rehearsal."

"I can't believe you graduate in six weeks."

"You and me both."

I hear him sigh into the phone. "I'm so sorry I can't be there for your graduation. I asked the court for an exception, but they won't let me leave the state." His voice cracks. "I can't believe I'm going to miss it. Everything you've worked so hard for. And I had to go and ruin everything."

"Stop it, Den. We've been over this a thousand times. What happened is not your fault. I don't blame you."

"I was so stupid. Why did I believe them?"

"Because they were supposed to be the good guys. Your mentors. Your teachers. You were new, and they were supposed to be people you could trust. One day, they will get what's coming to them."

"Maybe. But even if they get caught someday, it won't erase the fact that I'll be labeled a criminal for the rest of my life. Do you know how hard it is to get a decent job with a record? I'll never be able to pay the restitution, Pen. I'm going to prison. Maybe not this month or next, but unless … well, let's just say nothing short of a miracle can help me now."

God, I want to tell him. I want to tell him so badly it's killing me. But it's not just the NDA I signed that's keeping me from spilling my guts. Denver would never let me do this for him. He'd never let me compromise myself or put myself in this position just to help him. He'd never let me do it even though I know he'd do exactly the same for me. He'd do more. He'd go to hell and back if I asked him.

But the thing is, I'm just not sure pretending to be Sawyer's girlfriend will be anything like going to hell. In fact, part of me is excited about it. Part of me can't wait for the touching and the kissing and the 'dreamy' looks – even though it will all be fake.

"You are not going to prison," I say. "I promise we'll figure something out."

"I don't want you moving back here and getting three jobs just to pay off my debts."

"Maybe it won't come to that. Listen, we have six weeks to figure something out. And guess what? It turns out I overpaid tuition this semester," I lie. "I guess I got a scholarship from a local business that I forgot I even applied for, so I'll be able to send you some money as soon as the school reimburses me."

I hold my breath and hope he can't see right through me.

"Really? I'm not surprised, Pen. You are the smartest, most talented person I know. But I hate the fact that you have to send me money. And speaking of school, have you heard about grad school yet?"

"No, not yet," I say, telling him only the second lie I've ever told him in my life. The second of what I know are many more to come. "But we can't think about that right now."

"We have to think about it," he says. "You have a real chance of getting in. I don't want you turning down an opportunity like that because of me."

"We'll cross that bridge when and if we come to it, Denver."

"Yeah, but you and I both know that because of my stupidity, you won't be able to afford it even if you do get in."

I can hear the self-abhorrence in his voice. I know he beats himself up every day over what happened.

"Where there's a will, there's a way, big brother."

"How can you still be so optimistic after everything?"

"I guess I just believe that everything will work out in the end."

He sighs into the phone. "I wish I could believe that, too. But right now, let's just say you are the only thing keeping me from slashing my wrists."

I stop walking and sit on a nearby bench, a viscous knot forming in my throat that's keeping me from speaking. I've already lost my parents. I can't imagine a world without my brother.

"Don't worry, Pen. I'm not being serious. Not really."

"You can't say things like that," I tell him, tears rolling down my cheeks.

"Shit. I'm sorry. That was a dick thing to say. I'm not going to off myself. I promise. It's just that things really suck right now."

Denver lost a lot of friends when he lost all their money. And his girlfriend of two years left him just because people started hating her for being with him. He has no friends, no family, no me. He's all by himself with no way to leave. I guess I'm not surprised that the thought of ending his life has crossed his mind.

Even if I do pay off his debts, he'll still be on probation and unable to leave Missouri. So, no matter how much I want to continue my education at Juilliard, I've considered not doing it. I never planned on staying in New York forever anyway. And sometimes family is more important.

"Hang in there, Denver. Things will get better." I stand up and continue to make my way to the rehearsal hall. "I have to go practice now. I'll talk to you later?"

"Yeah, later," he says.

"Promise me you won't do anything stupid."

"I'm not going to slash my wrists, Pen."

"Or go sky diving without a parachute? Or put a plastic bag over your head?"

"You're being ridiculous."

"Promise me, Denver."

"Jeez, fine. I promise."

"Twin promise?"

He laughs. We haven't made a twin promise since we were kids. We always said twin promises were better than any other promises. They were promises that couldn't be broken no matter what.

"Twin promise," he says.

"Okay, good."

"Do me a favor and record something for me today. Just a minute or two of your practice. I need something to cheer me up and hearing you play always does the trick."

I smile. "You got it. Any requests?"

"Elton John?"

"You do remember I'm a classical pianist, don't you?"

He laughs. Hearing him laugh again makes me smile. "Aspen, you can play anything by anyone and we both know it."

"Okay. Elton John it is. Bye."

I open the door to the practice room and put my bag on the floor. I place my phone on the table next to the piano and then I run my fingers lightly across the keys.

I love the piano. I've loved it since the day my parents inherited a baby grand from my great uncle. I was only four years old. I don't remember it as well as my parents did, but they used to tell me that from the moment I sat on the bench and touched the keys, they knew I had something special. I'd never played before, yet I could put together a tune.

I hit record on my phone and then I sit down and get lost in my passion.

Chapter Seven

Sawyer

Why the hell did our first away series have to be in Kansas City? The whole time we were there, I felt like fate was staring me in the face, challenging me.

While a lot of the other guys were busy partying and scoping out women, I was looking at our surroundings, checking out the city I'm doing my damnedest to stay away from. Who the hell wants to live in the dead freaking center of the United States? What's the draw?

I came to the conclusion that there isn't one. And it's all the more reason to toe the line and not screw anything up.

On the plane, I pull up the new contract on my phone and read through it again. Sarah added a few things we hadn't discussed. Like Aspen being let out of the contract with full payment if I sleep with anyone. And, surprisingly, she added a section about Sebastian Briggs. Not only to cover what we'd agreed to about helping find him a place to live, but clauses concerning my relationship with him. As in, he's to be included in social gatherings and we're to behave like old buddies.

I'm not sure why she put that in there, but maybe it's so the tabloids don't accuse Aspen of cheating on me with him since they're bound to discover they are roommates.

My eyes wander over the section that Aspen insisted on adding about no sex. No sex with her or *anyone*.

I shake my head, still wondering how she didn't remember that night. I just don't recall her being that drunk. Should I have told her what happened? If I had, maybe she'd have left that part out of the contract and I wouldn't have to live with blue balls for the next six months. On the other hand, she may have thought I'd taken advantage of her and nixed the whole damn thing.

I've thought about that night more times than I'd like to admit. I'm drawn to her, there's no denying that. But I'm not a fool. I know she'll only be pretending to like me. In reality, she thinks I'm an asshole. And she's right. I am. It's for the best, anyway. Because anything other than a fake relationship is out of the question.

I look at Caden and Brady in the seats flanking mine, and know I need to start the ball rolling. Sarah assured me that both Aspen and Sebastian signed the contracts. So I guess there's no time like the present.

I get their attention and they pull out their earbuds.

"So ... I met a girl," I say.

Brady leans forward, looking around me to Caden. They share a look.

"What do you mean you met a girl?" Caden asks.

"Just what I said. I met a girl. Last week. She goes to Juilliard. Smart. Plays piano."

I try hard not to laugh as I look at their faces. Brady's jaw has gone slack and Caden has narrowed his brows in confusion.

"Did he say ...?" Brady asks Caden.

"Yup. I believe he did."

"What's the catch?" Brady asks, looking at me suspiciously.

Yeah. That's pretty much how I suspect everyone will take the news. It's why Aspen and I will have to try hard to be convincing.

"I'd like you guys to meet her. Tomorrow, after the game. Bring your wives over."

"You want us to *meet* her? And you want us to bring Murphy and Rylee?"

Caden looks at me like I asked him to go to the moon.

Brady puts his hand on my forehead, checking for a fever. I swat it away. "Cut the shit," I say. "Just come over, okay? And don't make a big deal about it. It's not what you think."

The flight attendant tells us to buckle up and prepare for landing. I put my earbuds in, letting the guys know I'm done with the conversation. I'll answer all their questions tomorrow night.

~ ~ ~

I always have mixed feelings driving up I-95 back towards my hometown of New Haven. It's the place where I grew up – which is probably why I love it and hate it at the same time.

As I get closer, I see the signs for Yale University. Yale students make up a fourth of the population of this modest town. My father was a janitor there for thirty years. It's where he met my mother, who worked in food services until they got married. After they married, he wanted to support her, so she quit her job.

I still can't imagine supporting a family on what he must have made, but he did it. We didn't live in a nice house. The heat didn't always work properly. Christmases and birthdays were sparse. But he said he loved my mom too much to have her working. Raising me and taking care of him was a full-time job. And she did it well. My mother was an amazing woman.

I pass the Yale New Haven Hospital where she died, and I try not to look at the large complex. It's been fifteen years since I was there. Fifteen years since I lost her. I didn't even bother to go when they called me about my dad a few years ago. And I didn't feel guilty about it either. She was the one who held our family together, not him.

I pull into the driveway, tired from my flight and ninety-minute drive. I see the curtains moving in the living room window and then Danny's face appears, lighting up with a huge smile when he sees me get out of the car.

Before I'm to the front door, he rips it open and runs out to greet me. He almost tackles me to the ground with his hug. I laugh. "I'm happy to see you too, buddy."

"Daniel!" Lucy yells from the house. "You are not to run outside without telling me, do you hear me?"

"Sorry, Mommy. Look! He's here," he says excitedly.

"I can see that," she says. "Hi, Sawyer, how are you?"

"Fine. Tired."

"You didn't have to make the drive. I know you're busy."

I shake my head. "No. I did. I promised him. I'm not about to let him down."

"Can we go to the beach?" Danny asks.

"Not today," I tell him. "It's too cold. Maybe next time." I notice he's wearing one of the Hawks jerseys I've given him, and it makes me wonder if he only wears it when I visit.

Danny loves going to Walnut Beach. I hate it. It holds bad memories for me from my high school days. But to him, it's a place of peace. He doesn't even know why he loves it. He shouldn't love it. But he does. And he asks me to take him there every time I come. And most times, I do. Because I'd do anything for him.

Growing up in New Haven, the beach was a big hang out for high school students. And when they built the boardwalk that extended from Walnut Beach over to Silver Sands State Park — well, that just became the place we went to go drinking.

The beach is lined with rocks. Big ones, little ones. There is even a place where people build rock stacks, and it has become one of Danny's favorite activities to try and build the tallest one.

"Do you want to stay for dinner?" Lucy asks.

I try to assess the genuineness of her question. Lucy and I have a tentative relationship at best. We're nice to each other for Danny's sake, but all things being equal, she'd probably prefer I not come around. Too many bad memories.

Fat chance of me not coming around, however. I'm going to be here for him as long as he needs me.

"I don't know, Lucy. I don't want to impose."

"Pancakes!" Danny squeals, clapping his hands.

She laughs and ruffles his hair. "He's right. It's pancake night. Believe me, it's not an imposition."

"Well then, I guess I'll stay. Thanks."

She leads us back into the house and Danny goes straight for the closet. He comes back carrying an armload of games. I run over to help him before they all fall out of his hands. He loves to play games. I let him pick the first one, knowing we'll be at this for a while.

"Candy Land!"

He gets the game out and starts setting it up.

"Lucy, are you joining us?" I ask.

She shakes her head. "You two go ahead. Spend your time together. I've got a mountain of laundry to do."

I nod. It's the answer I expected. She always has an excuse for not joining us. I wish it wouldn't make her sad when I'm here. Because it obviously makes Danny very happy.

Two hours and ten games of Candy Land later, Lucy calls us in for dinner.

"Thank God," I say to her. "If I had to play one more game of Candy Land, I think I'd shoot myself."

She laughs. "It's his favorite."

"I should teach him some new games. UNO maybe."

She looks over at Danny. "I'm not sure he'd be able to play it. It's kind of advanced for him, don't you think?"

I shake my head. "Nah, he can learn it. There's no harm in trying, right?"

She shrugs.

"Danny, sometime soon, I'm going to teach you a new game."

He shovels a forkful of pancakes into his mouth and tries to answer me.

"Danny, don't talk with your mouth full, okay, buddy?"

"I wish you'd call him Daniel," Lucy says.

"Why would I do that?"

"Because it's his name. Danny just seems so childish."

"Oh, like Lucy is such an adult name?"

She rolls her eyes at me. "Just shut up and eat."

"Just shut up and eat," Danny mimics her.

"Don't say shut up, Daniel," she says. "I'm sorry, Mommy shouldn't have said it."

We eat in silence for a few minutes. I stare at Danny. He's so sweet and innocent. Syrup dribbles down his chin and I reach over and catch it with my napkin.

"We watched your game yesterday," Lucy says. "Looks like it was a good one."

I nod. I added two more stolen bases to my record. "It was. I wish you'd bring Danny to one of the games in person."

She shakes her head, looking horrified. "Oh, no. I don't think it's a good idea."

"I know you don't like to drive that far. But maybe one day?"

She shrugs. "We'll see. Daniel doesn't like long car rides."

That's a no. But I don't fight it too hard. Introducing Danny to the world is not something I'm excited about doing. It will cause too many questions that I don't want to answer. Questions about a past that I've tried to put behind me. Questions about a past I can't seem to get away from.

After dinner, I watch a show with Danny. It's getting late and he has trouble keeping his eyes open.

"Time for bed, big guy," Lucy says.

"Can you read me the next part?" he asks, looking over at me with hope in his eyes.

"We're reading Harry Potter," Lucy tells me. "I don't think he understands a lot of it, but the parts he does, he gets really excited about."

"Maybe he should watch the movie," I say.

"I don't know. It might scare him."

"Nah. He's tough. Think about it. Maybe I can bring the DVD over sometime. He and I could have a boys' night."

Danny grabs my hand and pulls me back to his room.

"Make sure he brushes his teeth," Lucy calls out after us.

I help him into his pajamas and watch him brush his teeth. Then he hands me the book and scoots over in his twin bed to allow room for me. I laugh, knowing I won't be able to fit next to him. But I try. And I read him the next chapter, half of me spilling off the bed the entire time.

Chapter Eight

Aspen

Bass and I walk down the street and find the address Sawyer scribbled on the piece of paper for me last week. I stare at the steps leading up to his townhouse. It's in a row of townhouses on a very affluent street in a very nice part of town.

Bass elbows me. "You get to live here in a few months. Lucky you."

"Lucky?" I turn to him. "In case you forgot, we think he's an ass. An ass who doesn't know how to keep a woman around for more than one date. If you think that makes me lucky—"

"You're right. Sorry, I just forgot for a minute." He looks around at the other townhouses that are illuminated by the many streetlights. "Do you think any other famous people live around here? Shit, Penny, you could be neighbors with Robert De Niro or Justin Timberlake."

I roll my eyes and ascend the steps. At the top, I see he's still daydreaming. "If you can get your head out of the clouds for two seconds, we have some business to take care of."

He joins me on the top step. "You really are looking at this as a business deal, aren't you? But, come on, Penny, you have to admit what you're about to do is pretty freaking cool. You'll meet all kinds of people. Celebrities. Sports stars. You'll fly first class and stay in the best places. You'll get to eat at those fancy restaurants we've always walked by making fun of all the stuffy people who eat there. Now you'll be one of those people. And just think, you might make some connections that could help you out in your career long after Sawyer Mills is a thing of the past."

I shrug. He's right. I am looking at this as a business deal. If I think of it any other way, I'm bound to be disappointed. Because even though I'm trying to keep my mind from going there, I can't get over the memory of that kiss. I can't stop thinking about how well we got along that night. And for the life of me, I can't stop fantasizing about having him in my bed. Detailed fantasies. Ones in which I can hear him groan and call out my name.

I'd never hear the end of it if Bass knew just how many times I've used my vibrator in the past week while thinking of the man on the other side of this door. The man who is so untouchable he has to have a contract to get a girlfriend. Or, fake girlfriend. A guy who is so socially inept that he can't fathom settling down.

So, yes, this is a business deal. And for all intents and purposes, I'm a hired actor.

"Ready?" he asks.

"Yeah."

He knocks on the door. While we're waiting for Sawyer to answer, I peek through the sidelight. It's opaque, but I can see shadows moving about. He has company.

"Did he say Sarah was going to be here tonight?"

"I don't think so."

The door opens and Sawyer sees me. He completely ignores Bass while his eyes take me in from head to toe. It's hard for me to stand here and not look affected by his heated perusal. And he *should* be perusing – after all, I broke out my best figure-hugging jeans for this. I'm wearing heels for Pete's sake – something I rarely do, but I figured if I'm to be the girlfriend of a baseball star, I'll need to look the part.

"Aspen, you're looking good," he says. "Come in." He finally looks at Bass. "Sebastian, nice to see you again."

Bass holds out his hand in greeting. "Please call me Bass. Sebastian makes me sound like a stuffy old man."

I look around, surprised to see four strangers standing around Sawyer's kitchen. I turn to him. "I thought we were going to talk about this," I whisper. "I'm not sure I'm ready to jump right in."

"Oh, my God, Penny," Bass says into my ear. "That's Caden Kessler and Brady Taylor."

"Who?"

"Come on," Sawyer says, inviting us into the kitchen. "I'd like you to meet my friends. Aspen Andrews, meet Brady Taylor and his wife, Rylee. And this is Caden Kessler and his wife, Murphy. Guys, this is Aspen and her friend, Bass Briggs."

I don't miss how Bass is impressed that Sawyer remembered his last name. I say hello and shake their hands. Bass is standing in stunned silence as his eyes bounce between the three other men in the room. "Bass," I whisper loudly, hoping he'll snap out of it and quit embarrassing us.

"Sorry," he says, finally shaking hands with everyone. "It's just that this is a surreal moment for me to be standing in a room with all three of you."

"So you guys play baseball, too?" I ask Caden and Brady.

"Oh, I like her already," Murphy says.

"Yeah, we play baseball, too," Brady says, amusement washing over his handsome features.

"Caden is a catcher," Bass says. "He's also pretty good at hitting home runs. Brady's a pitcher. He pitched a perfect game last year."

I look at him in confusion.

"Sorry, guys," Bass says. "Aspen doesn't know the first thing about baseball."

"That's not true," I whine. "I've watched some games on TV before. Just not since I was a kid. And they made us play it in middle school gym class."

"I stand corrected," Bass says. "She's obviously an expert."

I swat him. "Don't mind my roommate. He doesn't get out much."

"You two are roommates?" Rylee asks, obviously as confused as I am about what's going on here.

"Since sophomore year," I say.

"You go to school?" Murphy asks.

"Yes. Juilliard. But Bass doesn't go there anymore. He's training to become a firefighter."

"Juilliard. Wow, impressive." She turns to Bass. "And being a firefighter is a very noble calling."

"He had his first day of fire school today," I say proudly. "He's already a paramedic."

"How was day one?" Caden asks. "Back in college, I had a buddy who became a firefighter. He said it was a bitch."

Bass laughs and stretches his arms over his head. "Let's just say I'll be sore into next week. We did physical assessments today."

"Pul-lease," I say. "You're in great shape, Bass."

It's true. I look around at the three professional baseball players in this room and think of how well Bass fits in. He looks just as fit as the rest of them.

Sawyer gives me a look and I realize what I did. Is he mad at me for talking up my roommate? I guess I'm supposed to be 'making dreamy eyes' at him or something. Is this all starting now? What happened to meeting to discuss how this is going to go?

"Before we get started, can I get you guys a drink?" Sawyer asks.

"Get started with what?" Brady asks. "Is this game night or something?"

"No, not game night," Sawyer says. "Go ahead and make yourselves comfortable in the living room."

I look around at the two couples. They seem to have no idea why they're here, and I'm more than a little uncomfortable. Is Sawyer just going to pull me onto his lap and pretend we're a thing? What must they think of Bass being here?

"Just water for me please," I tell him.

"Me, too," Bass says. "No drinking during training."

I take a seat in a single chair by the fireplace so there's no room for Sawyer to sit next to me. Bass sits on the couch, still starstruck and oblivious to the fact that I've never felt more awkward in my life.

I take in my surroundings. It's a bachelor pad on steroids. It's nice. Not Christian Grey nice, but modern-contemporary-bachelor nice. It looks like he's had the entire townhouse renovated. Most New York City townhouses have been around for a while and have the old-style boxy rooms. This one, however, is an open floor plan, the entire first floor being visible from anywhere you stand.

His kitchen is huge and looks to have all the latest conveniences. I wonder if he cooks. I wonder if he would mind me using his kitchen when I'm staying here.

There's a large sitting area off the foyer that I think would be perfect for a piano. I can't help it. Every time I go into a new residence, I pick the place where a piano should be. Everyone should have one. Then again, I may be a little biased.

"So, what do you study at Juilliard?" Rylee asks.

"Piano."

"You must be very talented to have gotten into such a prestigious school."

"She is," Bass says. "She's the most talented person I've ever met."

"Says the guy who plays guitar better than Jimi Hendrix."

Rylee raises her eyebrows. "A guitar-playing firefighter? Watch out, ladies."

"Thank you. See, I told you, Bass."

"Whatever."

Sebastian isn't cocky. He's humble and modest, and just about the nicest person I know. He's as good looking and as fit as the famous athletes in this room, yet he has no idea the draw he has on women. Probably because he's with *me* ninety percent of the time and women may be too intimidated to approach him with another woman by his side.

Sawyer comes over with two bottles of water, handing one to each of us.

"Are you going to tell us why we're really here?" Caden asks. "You've been acting strange ever since the plane ride home yesterday."

"Yeah, I'm a little confused myself," I say.

"Sorry," Sawyer tells everyone. "I just thought it easiest to only go over this one time."

"Go over what?" Caden asks.

Sawyer comes over and stands behind me, putting his hand on my shoulder. "I'd like to introduce you all to my new girlfriend."

Four pairs of eyes look at Sawyer like he's off his rocker.

"Mills, we already met fifteen minutes ago when she walked in," Brady says.

"What the hell is going on here?" Caden asks.

"So, uh … as of today, Aspen is my girlfriend, but she's not really my girlfriend."

Finally, I understand what's happening. These people are to Sawyer what Bass is to me. His best friends. His confidants. People who will be in on our secret. Now that I think about it, he did mention telling a few of his friends who he thought could help us.

"Dude … explain," Brady says.

"I'm, uh" —Sawyer has the decency to at least look embarrassed before he tells them— "I'm paying Aspen to be my girlfriend for the season."

Samantha Christy

Chapter Nine

Sawyer

Murphy and Rylee sit there with their jaws in their laps while Brady and Caden shake their heads and laugh.

"Are you serious?" Caden asks.

"As a heart attack, bro."

"But … why?"

"Because I'm not going to risk getting traded, that's why."

"And you thought hiring someone to be your fake girlfriend was the way to prevent that?" Brady says. "You realize if this gets out you'll have made things ten times worse. Rick will have a goddamn conniption."

I shake my head. "It's not going to get out."

My friends share looks of disbelief, concern, and maybe anger with each other.

"Where the hell did you find her?" Caden asks.

"How do you even go about hiring someone to be your girlfriend?" Rylee says.

"How did you two meet?" Murphy asks. "And who exactly is Bass? Is he here to protect her or something?"

Bass stands up defensively. "I'm not her pimp, if that's what you're asking. And Aspen sure as hell isn't a hooker."

I see the color drain from Aspen's face as I realize what's going on here. My friends think I hired her through some kind of service. Aspen must be mortified thinking everyone is looking at her like she's a call girl.

"It's not like that, guys," I say. "Aspen and I met last week at a bar."

"You met at a bar?" Rylee asks. "As in she picked you up?"

"Do you even know her?" Brady asks. "She could be playing you."

Aspen holds her hand up. "Can everyone please stop talking about me as if I'm not here?"

"She's right," Murphy says. "We should hear her out."

"Thank you," she says. "When I met Sawyer, I was having a really bad day. And to make things worse, a bus drove by, soaking me with dirty road water. Sawyer saw the whole thing and asked if he could help. We started talking about the fact that we both had crappy days and he invited me to have a drink. We spent several hours in a bar and then he walked me home. He showed up the next morning with this proposition and the rest is history."

"But, why would you want to do this?" Rylee asks her.

"I'm *paying* her to do this," I say. "An education from Juilliard doesn't come cheaply. This will allow her to go to grad school and at the same time, will allow me to be seen as the kind of guy the Hawks want me to be."

"But what about after? How long can you keep this up?" Caden asks.

"For the season," I tell him. "After the season is over, Aspen and I will have an amicable break up. But by then, my reputation will have been repaired in the eyes of the organization."

"And then what?" Rylee asks. "You'll go back to your old ways?"

I shrug. "That's the plan. I'll just have to be more discreet about it."

"How do you know this won't get out?" Brady asks. "There are seven people in this room, that's a lot of people who have to keep a secret."

I know he's not talking about the four of them. He's looking at Aspen and Bass.

"Because we have a contract and they've both signed a non-disclosure agreement."

"You have a contract?" Rylee asks. "What exactly does it say?"

"You know, technical stuff about how she gets paid and what she's supposed to do."

"You mean how I'm supposed to look at you," Aspen says.

Murphy gasps. "You're dictating how she has to *look* at you?"

"With 'dreamy eyes'," Aspen says.

"Oh, my God. Really?" Murphy says, looking appalled at Aspen. "Do you get bonuses for sleeping with him?"

Aspen snorts. "Hardly. I had them write into the contract that under no circumstances would I be having sex with him."

"You did?"

Aspen nods. "Yes. And not only that, I stipulated that he not be allowed to have sex with anyone else, either, for the duration of our arrangement. I didn't want to be made to look like a fool."

Murphy's face turns from a cold, hard stare into a soft smile. Then she laughs. Then my other three friends laugh.

"What's so goddamn funny?" I ask.

When Brady and Caden are done doubling over, Caden says, "This season just got *so* much more interesting."

"Listen, guys," Aspen says. "I know what this must look like to you, but rest assured, Bass and I are good people. And I'm just a poor college student who was down on my luck when I ran into Sawyer. I don't give a rat's ass about him being some famous baseball player. I had no idea who he was when I met him, and if I had my way, I wouldn't even be sitting here. But circumstances dictate I do this, so here we are." She stands up and I'm afraid she might storm out of the townhouse. "Now, if you'll excuse us, Bass and I are going to step out back for five minutes. You can talk about me all you want during that time, but, please, when we come back, can we just sit down and figure this out?"

She looks at Bass, imploring him to follow her. We all watch as they walk out my back door and sit on my porch.

I turn to my friends. "I know you think this is stupid, but the contract is iron-clad. If either of them says anything about it, she doesn't get the money. Even afterwards, she has to pay it all back if she ever tells anyone."

"You really think you can trust them?" Caden asks. "I mean, why not just go find an *actual* girlfriend?"

"Come on, you guys know me. I'm not boyfriend material. This is the only way."

"Having a contract that says you can't have sex for six months is the only way?" Brady asks.

"Yes," I say. "This is my career on the line. I can trust Aspen. I think she's exactly what I need. She's got a good head on her shoulders. You should see all the shit she made Sarah add to the contract."

"She really didn't know who you were?" Rylee asks.

"Not a clue, I'm sure of it."

Murphy looks out my back window. "I think I might like her," she says.

"Ditto for me," Rylee says. "Come on, Murphy, let's go get them."

When the girls leave, Brady scratches his head, still not getting it. "But why not just do what Rick asked and keep your dick in your pants? This seems so much more complicated."

I shake my head. "Because I know I couldn't do it. I didn't even make it one fucking day. The day Rick said they were trading me was the day I met Aspen. We hit it off, had some drinks, and ended up back at her place."

"Wait, you slept with her?" Caden asks. "But she said she wrote the whole 'no sex' thing into the contract. It doesn't make sense."

"She doesn't remember," I tell them. "I swear I didn't think she was that drunk. I would never take advantage of a drunk chick. I slipped out like I normally do, but then I started thinking about her grad school acceptance letter that I saw lying on the floor. She'd said the night before that the letter was why she had a bad day, so I figured she needed money. She needed money and I needed a good reputation. So I went back to her place and told her about my plan. She kicked me out, thinking I was a creepy asshole, which I probably was. But then when I went back that night to apologize, she heard me out."

"Dude, you didn't tell her you had sex with her?" Brady asks.

"Why the fuck would I? I got a free pass."

Brady scolds me with his disapproving stare.

"And I wasn't sure she'd agree to any of this if she knew," I admit.

Caden laughs. "Oh, man, you've got balls, I'll give you that."

"Wouldn't you guys do anything to save your career?" I ask them.

The three of us stare at each other as everyone else comes back in the room. They don't have to say anything. I know what the answer is.

"Okay," Caden says. "Tell us how we can help."

"For starters, you two can validate it when I start talking about Aspen around the other guys. They won't believe me if I say I have a girlfriend."

"Then don't tell them," Murphy says. "Because, you're right, they won't believe you. You should let them see you together. Maybe deny that you have feelings for her. Talk about her like you'd talk about any of the others. It will seem more real to them if they watch it happen rather than being told it has happened."

"This is why we need them," I tell Aspen. "Okay, what else?"

"Maybe you should 'meet' her when you're out with the guys," Rylee says. "That way, they think you are meeting her for the first time."

I nod. "Good. When?"

"We leave for San Diego on Thursday," Caden says. "How about Sunday night after we get back?"

"Not soon enough," I say. "I don't want to give Rick another opportunity to find a reason to get rid of me."

"Isn't Spencer's birthday this week?" Rylee asks.

"How the hell are we supposed to know?" I say.

"Because you're his friends," she says, pulling out her phone to tap around on it. "Yes, it is. It's Wednesday and he's currently unattached, so he probably has no plans. Why don't you guys take him out for a drink after the game?"

"We have an early flight on Thursday," Caden reminds us.

"In and out by midnight?" I ask. "Would that work?"

Caden and Brady look at each other and nod. "We could do that."

"Good," Murphy says. "Take him to Taps Bar. Do you know where that is, Aspen?"

Aspen nods.

Murphy walks around the living room as she talks. "Show up around ten thirty, after they've been there for a while. Go sit at the bar and keep looking at Sawyer. Don't wear anything too revealing, something like what you have on now is perfect. It says 'girl next door' in a sexy kind of way. Sawyer will ask you to join them. He'll hit on you in his usual arrogant way and you'll walk out with them when they leave. Boom – mission accomplished. Some of the guys will have met you and then when they see you again later, they will tease Sawyer about taking out a girl twice, but they won't become suspicious."

Murphy turns to me. "Don't do anything that would make Aspen out to be a slut. In fact, maybe you just want to ask for her number when you walk out. Don't take her home. Caden will remind everyone about the early flight and Aspen will say she has a morning class. You'll gawk after her when she walks away."

She stops talking and we all stare at her.

"What?" Murphy asks.

Caden laughs at her. "I think you missed your calling, Murph. You might just be a little too good at this."

"At what?"

"All the deception. Is there something you're not telling me?"

She laughs. "As in, I was a secret agent in another life?"

"Oh, this is going to be fun," Rylee adds, getting into the spirit of things. "Maybe Aspen should sit and talk to Sawyer, but then reject him when he tries to take her to a hotel. Because we all know he would. Instead of going with him, however, she'll give him her number and tell him if he ever wants a 'nice' girl – one who doesn't have sex with random strangers, to call her. She'll say it in front of everyone."

"Yes," Murphy says. "That's good. Are you guys getting all this?" She turns to look at Aspen and me.

Aspen starts laughing. "I think I like your friends," she says. "Please tell me we'll get to go out with them."

Murphy looks at the other two women in the room and then motions to the kitchen. "Come on girls, let's go get a real drink and come up with some good lines Aspen can feed Sawyer on Wednesday."

The four of us guys watch them walk away, and I know I'm not the only one who's thinking that they just became fast friends.

"Are you okay with this?" I ask Bass. "I guess you can come too if you'd like, but it's probably best if you watch from a distance."

"Aspen is a big girl," he says. "I know the place well. It's safe and close to home. And I know where to find all of you if anything happens."

"We won't let anything happen to her," I say. "I give you my word."

"We'll all watch out for her," Caden says.

Bass nods. "I appreciate that. She's the most important person in my life."

Brady cocks his head and studies him. "You sure you're just roommates?"

"I'm sure," he says, laughing. "That ship sailed long ago."

I'm not sure why, but when he says that, my jaw twitches.

Brady looks from Bass to me and back to Bass. He laughs under his breath and says, "Rylee's right. This is going to be a hell of a lot of fun."

Chapter Ten

Aspen

The camera closes in on Sawyer for a close-up of his slide into home. The stadium erupts in cheers when he is called safe. He gets up, brushes the dirt off his shirt and tips his helmet to the fans. They show replay after replay as the announcers talk about him adding to his record of stolen bases. They put statistics on the screen that compare him to the all-time greats of the past.

I stand here stunned, as I take in just how good Sawyer Mills really is. The way they talk about him – it's like he's a god. After only nine games, they are saying he's already on track to capture another season record.

I fall back onto my sofa, realizing the gravity of the situation. I'm going to be with this man several days a week. I'm going to move in with him in a few months. With a baseball hero. *Me.* How did this even happen?

My phone vibrates with a text.

Rylee: Are you ready for tonight?

I smile. Rylee and Murphy have taken me under their wings. They've both texted me a few times since our meeting Monday night. I get the idea they think I need protection. From what I'm not sure. The notoriety? The crazy fans? *Sawyer?*

Me: I think so. Are you at the game?

Rylee: No. My son is running a fever and I didn't want to leave him with the sitter. But I just saw Sawyer score. He's doing great.

Me: He is. I'm sorry to hear about your son. I hope he feels better soon.

Rylee: Thank you. Do you remember what to say?

Me: Yup. I had good coaches.

Rylee: Coaches. Haha. I like it. I'll be by my phone all night if you need me. Just go to the bathroom and call me, or you could send a quick text. We've got your back.

Me: I hope I don't have to take you up on it, but you never know. I'm kind of nervous, especially after hearing the announcers talk about him. He's really really good. I'm way out of my league here.

Rylee: You'll do fine. Just act natural. And, Aspen – Sawyer's the one who's out of his league. You are definitely too good for him and everyone knows it.

Me: Not Sawyer.

Rylee: You're probably right, he doesn't. But don't take it personally. His ego is bigger than his bank account. But underneath it all, he's a good guy.

Me: I hope you're right. I saw a glimpse of that guy when we first met.

Rylee: You'll see him again. I'd bet on it. Good luck tonight. If I don't talk to you, call me tomorrow. I want to know everything.

Me: Won't Brady be in the bar with me?

Rylee: I promise you his version of tonight and your version will be miles apart. I'll need details. Maybe we could do lunch.

Me: I'd like that. I'll call you tomorrow.

Rylee: Sounds good.

I watch the rest of the game, wishing Bass were here to keep me company. He went out with some of the guys from fire school.

I'm glad he's out living life and making friends. *Real friends*, not fake ones like the ones I'm making. Not ones who will be gone in six months when I'm no longer under the employ of Sawyer Mills.

I check my makeup again before leaving. I look down at my clothes, worried that I've worn the wrong thing even though I followed Murphy's recommendation. I'm not sure why I'm so nervous. This isn't a date, it's a business deal. I need to act like a professional. Like my life depends on it, because although it doesn't, Denver's just might.

The bar is only a few blocks over, and I enjoy some people-watching on my way. Despite the late hour, the streets are well lit. And even though we live in a safe neighborhood, I don't take my hand off the mace in my purse.

I stand outside the bar, staring at the marquee over the door, knowing this is just the beginning. Knowing I'll have to play this part and be someone I'm not for the better part of a year.

"You going in?" a guy asks, trying to hold the door open for me.

"Eventually."

"Well, when you do, I'd be happy to buy you a drink," he says. "That is, unless you're meeting someone here."

"I um ... uh, no, I'm not meeting someone. But I'm not sure, um ..."

Oh, God. I'm blowing this already and I'm not even through the door.

He holds his hand out. "I'm Conner."

"Aspen," I say, shaking his hand.

"Great name," he says. He nods to the door. "Come on, I promise I don't bite."

I search my mind for something to say when my hand touches my phone in my purse, giving me an idea. I pull my phone out. "I'm waiting for a call and it's too loud in there."

"Okay, but the offer stands. Nice to meet you, Aspen."

"You too."

He goes inside, followed by a few more patrons, and I lean against the brick wall next to the door. Why did I think I could do this? I can't even act naturally with a total stranger who has nothing to do with this.

My phone vibrates.

Murphy: Good luck! Call me tomorrow. I need details.

I smile at the text. I really like Murphy and Rylee. Despite the fact that I'm a hired actor, they are treating me like a friend.

Me: Thanks. Going in now.

I tuck my phone away, take a deep breath, and open the door.

The place is dark and not as loud as I thought it would be. I guess that's because it's Wednesday night. There are a few big-screen televisions in the corner and several groups of people sitting in booths. The bar is a large square in the center of the room and I immediately spot Sawyer among a group of guys at one end. I walk to the opposite side of the bar and find an open seat.

"What can I get you?" the bartender asks.

"A glass of the house Chard," I say.

"Coming right up," she says.

I laugh inwardly, because I realize out of habit I ordered the house wine. I ordered the cheap stuff despite the fifty-thousand dollars that showed up in my bank account the other day. But old habits die hard. And, besides, the money is not for me. It's for Denver. It's for Juilliard. It's so the two of us can have the future we always planned.

I pull out my wallet when the bartender puts my wine in front of me. She holds up a hand to stop me. "Don't bother, Dark and Dangerous across the bar took care of it."

Here we go.

I look up, prepared to nod and smile at Sawyer to thank him for the drink, but when I do, my stomach flips over. It's not Sawyer who is toasting me with a raise of his glass, it's Conner, the guy I met outside. The guy sitting right next to the man I'm supposed to 'meet' tonight.

I know the smile on my face is awkward. I look from Conner to Sawyer and see Sawyer shaking his head. He's pissed that someone beat him to the punch. We lock eyes for a half-second, both of us trying to figure out how to get out of this.

I see Caden and Brady among his group of friends. Brady gives me a reassuring nod.

I make some idle conversation with a few ladies sitting at the bar next to me. They obviously know who the guys are as they are planning which one each of them will go home with. I roll my eyes, but then I think maybe I can use this to my advantage.

"Do you think you could help a girl out?" I ask them.

One of them shrugs. "What do you mean?"

"The guy across the bar, the one with the red shirt on, he sent me a drink. But I'm not interested. I don't want to hurt his feelings. I'll buy your next round if you'll … distract him for me."

They look at me like I'm crazy. "Don't you know who that is?" one asks.

"Don't know, don't care," I say nonchalantly.

The redhead loosens a button on her blouse, showing more cleavage than she already was. "No problem. We're good at distraction. And the guy's name is Conner. The one sitting next to him is Sawyer," she says in disgust. "Then there's Spencer, Brady, Caden, and – who's that other one, Carly?"

"Benham," Carly says. "He's a rookie."

"Right. Benham."

"You seem to know them pretty well," I say.

"Just the one. Sawyer," she says. "I know him *very* well. Well, his body anyway. We hooked up once. He's an asshole. Left before I woke up. Didn't leave a note or anything – just a catered breakfast. I hear he does that for all his girls."

"He does?" I ask in disgust.

"Yeah. He's the one-hit-wonder," Carly says.

I almost spit out my sip of wine. "That's what you call him?"

The redhead nods. "He never sleeps with anyone more than once."

"What about you?" I ask Carly. "Have you been with him?"

"Not yet," she says, rising off her barstool. "But there's no time like the present."

Oh, crap. I realize a bit too late that by sending them over to Conner, I'm sending them over to Sawyer.

"Why would you want to sleep with him knowing what he will do?"

We all look over at him to see him watching us.

"Who wouldn't want to sleep with that?" she says. "I mean, look at him. And he's got to pick someone sometime, right? Why not me? Maybe he'll knock me up."

"Oh, my God, you can only hope," the redhead says. "Could you imagine?"

The girls squeal giddily.

I want to stick my finger down my throat.

"Have the drinks sent over to us," Carly says. "That way, they'll think other guys are interested."

I watch them wiggle their asses and toss back their hair as they make their way around the bar. I order their drinks and then I sit back and watch what happens.

The redhead goes up next to Conner while Carly tries to get Sawyer's attention. He ignores her, but she's persistent. He calls one of his friends over and whispers something to him and then the friend strikes up a conversation with Carly.

Sawyer looks at me and shakes his head laughing. This is not how either of us planned for this to go.

He holds up a finger, asking me to wait for something. Then he turns to watch Conner and the redhead as they talk, laugh and eye-fuck each other. After a few minutes, Sawyer leans in and asks him something. Conner nods before he pulls the redhead even closer.

Sawyer calls the bartender over and motions to me. He's sending me a drink.

The bartender laughs, putting another glass in front of me. "I don't know what game you're playing here, but it's working."

I smile and raise my glass, locking eyes with Sawyer. He smiles and toasts me back.

He excuses himself and heads to the bathroom. I want to follow him, but I think maybe that would be too obvious, so I stay put. A minute later, I feel warmth behind me and the hair on my arms stands on end.

"Hi," a deep smooth voice says into my ear.

I spin around.

"I'm Sawyer Mills," he says, offering me his hand. "Nice to meet you, uh?"

"Aspen," I say, laughing. "Aspen Andrews."

I take his hand, liking a little too much how it feels in mine. "Great game today."

He takes a step back and stares at me. "You watched it?"

"I may have caught a minute or two," I lie.

He gives me that sexy smug smile of his before he nods to his friends across the bar. "Would you care to join us?"

I narrow my eyes at him. "Wouldn't that be awkward?"

"Having a drink with me and my friends is what we'd planned."

"No, not that," I say. "I mean with that girl over there."

"What about her?"

"You've been with her."

He looks across the bar, studying both girls. "Which one?"

My jaw drops. "Oh, my God. You don't even know?" I reach around and grab my wine, taking a healthy drink. "Just how many girls have you been with?"

He shrugs. "Enough that I need to hire you so I can save my job."

I shake my head in disgust. Then I finish my wine and pick up the other one. "Fine. Let's go save your job." I plant a smile on my face as we walk around the bar. "It was the redhead," I whisper to him on the way over.

"Good to know."

Sawyer has me sit on the bar stool he was using, then he introduces me to the group.

"Nice to meet you again, Aspen," Conner says.

I don't miss the fact that the redhead drapes herself possessively over him. "I thought you weren't into this," she says.

I give her an innocent shrug and then greet the rest of the guys.

97

Brady and Caden greet me as if they've never met me.

None of the other guys seem suspicious about me being here. I breathe a sigh of relief. I can't believe we pulled it off.

I feel Sawyer's arm come around me and I stiffen. My eyes close briefly at the feeling. I have to remind myself he's playing a part. I take another sip of wine.

Sawyer orders another round of drinks for everyone.

I have to pace myself. I took a muscle relaxant earlier because my fingers were cramping up again. Nature of the business. Playing piano for hours on end does not come without a price. And alcohol and my new muscle relaxants do not mix.

I let the third glass of wine sit untouched on the bar as we all joke around and laugh and enjoy the evening. I realize I'm having a lot of fun with him and his friends. Even with Carly and the redhead here, I'm having a good time. Plus, they pretty much have stayed busy shoving their tongues down the throats of their conquests.

Just before midnight, Caden signals Sawyer and Sawyer nods.

"We should call it a night, guys," Caden says. "We're leaving for San Diego tomorrow."

The guys all open their wallets and throw cash on the bar. I'm sure there is more than enough money to cover all the drinks. In fact, I'll bet the bartender just made a killing in tips.

We walk out of the bar as a group. Sawyer puts his arm around me and gives me a squeeze. "Aspen," he says a bit too boisterously. "Care to join me? There's a great hotel just down the street."

The redhead snorts loudly. "I'll bet there is," she says.

I step away and look at Sawyer like he disgusts me. "You buy a girl a drink and you expect her to sleep with you?"

"That's usually how it works, yeah," he says, sounding like an arrogant asshole.

"Not with *this* girl," I say, noticing that everyone is watching us.

"What makes you so special?" Sawyer asks.

"Maybe I should be asking *you* that," I say. "You think because you're a famous ball player you can just have anything you want? Well, it doesn't work like that. You want a quick lay, go find someone else." I fish around in my purse until I find what I'm looking for. I had scribbled out my phone number on a scrap of paper earlier in preparation. "You want to take someone out for a nice dinner and conversation, call me. Otherwise, don't bother."

He takes the scrap of paper from me, looking dumbfounded as I walk away.

I try not to smile as I pass by Caden and Brady who both wink at me and laugh silently.

I turn the corner and walk right into Bass.

"Shit, Penny, that was awesome. I saw it all go down from here."

"Bass! You scared me." I swat his arm.

"I know you don't think I was going to let you walk home alone after midnight," he says.

Of course he wouldn't. But then I look back at the group of guys walking the other way and I think of how *they* were okay with it.

"Plus, Sawyer texted me earlier telling me he was going to put you in a cab if I couldn't be here to walk you home."

"He did?"

Bass nods. "But I got the idea he'd rather have me here, and now I see why. You walking away was far more dramatic than him putting you in a cab."

"I wasn't aware he had your number."

"He got it from me on Monday. Maybe he's not so bad after all," he says.

I turn around and see the redhead getting in a cab with Conner. Then I think about all the other redheads Sawyer must have been with. All the blondes and brunettes. How many of them are there, I wonder?

"Yeah, he is," I say, threading my elbow with my best friend's before we walk home.

Chapter Eleven

Sawyer

I wake up when the flight attendant comes by and tells me to prepare for landing. I love it when we take the red eye. I can sleep anywhere, and it gives us a full day of free time which we rarely get during the season.

As we taxi up to the gate, I pull out my phone to check the time, calculating how long it will take for me to get home, shower and eat breakfast. Then I send a text.

> **Me: I'll pick you up at noon.**

> **Aspen: Noon? I thought we were doing something tonight. It's barely nine AM.**

> **Me: Were you sleeping?**

> **Aspen: No.**

> **Me: Then what's the problem?**

Aspen: What if I have other plans today? You don't own all my time, you know.

Me: You have other plans? You don't want to go shopping with me?

Aspen: No, I don't have plans. I'll go with you, but it would be nice if you would ask me instead of tell me.

I roll my eyes.

Me: Aspen, will you go shopping with me today?

Aspen: Yes, Sawyer, I'd be happy to. See you at noon.

~ ~ ~

"So, what are you shopping for?" Aspen asks as we walk down the sidewalk.

"I'm not shopping. *You* are."

"Me?"

"Didn't you read the contract? It says I'm to buy you clothes so you can play the part."

She looks down at her t-shirt, jeans, and sneakers. "My clothes aren't good enough for you?"

"Uh, they're fine," I say, looking at her jeans that fit her curves like a glove. "I guess I just thought being a girl, you'd like more shit to put in your closet."

She laughs. "I'm just kidding, Sawyer. And you don't have to buy me anything if you don't want to. You're already paying me a lot of money. But my closet *is* pretty bare and I suppose if we're going to be seen together, I should get some stylish stuff."

"Stylish stuff that *I'm* paying for."

She shrugs. "Okay, I'm not going to argue. But I'm telling you right now, I'm not getting shorts or skirts that show my ass cheeks."

"How about a little thigh – is that okay?"

"Nothing above mid-thigh. And I won't get any tops that show too much cleavage or risk a wardrobe malfunction."

"Do you negotiate *everything?*" I ask.

"I just don't want to come off looking like those girls from the other night," she says.

"Right. No slutty clothes. Got it. We should look for a few formal dresses, too. There are some benefits we'll need to attend."

"I have plenty of dresses. We have to dress formally for performances."

I raise my brows at her. "Performances? I'm envisioning a black dress that starts under your chin and hits the floor."

She laughs. "Yeah, I guess I might want to buy a few. The ones I have might be a bit conservative."

"Lead the way," I say, pulling my hat down low on my forehead.

She watches my movement. "Do you always get recognized?"

"Not if I keep my head down and don't make eye contact. But, yeah, it happens a lot."

We turn the corner and cross the street, heading towards a major department store.

"What did your friends think of me?" she asks.

"Nobody said anything."

"Really?"

"They are used to me picking up girls, so Wednesday night was no different."

"They weren't surprised that I turned down your offer?"

"No. It's happened before. Rarely, but it's happened."

She rolls her eyes melodramatically.

"Spencer made a comment about it being for the best considering the fact that I'm walking on eggshells at work."

"What do you think they'll say when they find out you took a girl out twice?"

"I'll take a lot of flak. They'll ask when the wedding is and shit like that. But it will blow over in a few weeks, I'm sure."

We reach our destination and I hold the door open for her, ushering her inside quickly after I see someone snap our picture.

"Where are we going tonight?" she asks, sorting through a rack of blouses. "What should I look for?"

"We're going to dinner at Eleven Madison Park."

Her mouth opens and I reach out to close it. "You'll catch flies," I joke.

"Why are we going there? It's so expensive."

"Because we'll get noticed," I tell her. "Murphy and Caden are going, too."

She puts back the blouse in her hands. "Looks like we'll need something better than this. LBD maybe?"

"LBD?"

"Little black dress," she says.

She finds a rack of dresses and pulls a few out, holding them up for me to see.

"I don't know. You pick. I couldn't care less what you wear."

She scolds me with her harsh stare. "Listen. I know this whole thing is for show, but it would do you good to learn a thing or two about women. I assume someday you'll need it. So, a bit of advice, never tell a woman you couldn't care less about what she wears."

"First, I *won't* need your advice. Ever. And second, I only meant it doesn't matter what you wear, you'd look good in anything."

Her lips curve up into a smile. "See – *that's* what you should say."

She studies a shirt that has a large screen-printed butterfly on it.

"You like that?" I ask.

"No. I just … well, it's silly, but I've been dreaming about butterflies lately. Not colorful ones like this one, different ones. I can't really explain it."

I touch my ribcage and wonder if my tattoo has anything to do with her dreams.

A few hours later, we walk out of the store carrying one bag and a few dresses. I hold up the bag. "Two hours and this is all you could find? Why are women so damn picky?"

"Lesson number two – never call a woman picky. We're discerning. We like what we like, Sawyer."

"Quit trying to groom me."

She laughs. "Somehow I get the feeling it might be too late to teach this old dog new tricks."

"Who are you calling an old dog?" I wink at her. "Besides, I don't need any tricks. I do just fine."

"Fine if you want nothing but one-nighters the rest of your life."

"Yup. See – no problem at all."

She stops walking and puts her hand on my arm. "Are you seriously telling me you don't want to settle down. As in ever? Not even when you're older?"

I shake my head. "Not even then."

"So why bother with this whole charade if you're just going to go back to your old ways? Won't they just fire you next year?"

"Trade, not fire," I correct her. "And I'll just be more careful."

She pins me to the side of the building with her stare. "As in you'll make every one-night-stand sign an NDA?"

I shrug. "I don't know. Maybe."

She laughs disingenuously. "That doesn't sound like much of a life."

"Good thing you're not me then."

"Yeah, good thing."

We reach her building and I hand her the bag I'm carrying. "Be ready at seven."

She chews her bottom lip as she stares me down.

"Can you *please* be ready at seven?" I ask.

A smug little smile creeps up her face as she spins around and walks through the door. "I was wrong!" she yells back at me. "You *can* teach an old dog new tricks."

~ ~ ~

Dressed and ready for our night out, I follow someone into Aspen's building and walk up the two flights of stairs. When she opens her apartment door, I'm speechless. I'm not sure I've ever seen someone wear an 'LBD' as well as she is right now.

I appraise her from head to toe. Her dark hair looks like silk as it cascades down to her chest in soft waves. The dress she's wearing has thin straps across her shoulders, exposing her toned arms. The hem falls right to mid-thigh, as short as she set her limit.

And, Holy God, the hint of cleavage she's showing has me fantasizing about being in her bed. She's gorgeous.

For a second, I'm glad she put the no-sex clause into the contract, because – fuck dinner – I'd take her to bed right now.

Her roommate comes up behind her. "Cat got your tongue?" he asks, laughing.

I shake off the fantasy in my head, hoping I can tamp down the rising problem in my pants considering Bass Briggs is staring at me right now.

"You look very nice, Aspen."

She takes in my dress shirt, tie, and khaki pants. "You clean up pretty well yourself."

"Shit, you guys will look amazing on the front page of the tabloids tomorrow," Bass says.

Aspen's face goes ashen. "Oh, God," she says.

"You'll do great, Penny," he says. "Just don't look around and you won't be bothered by the fans, the photographers, or the dozens of horny women who want to be you."

"You're not making this any better," she tells him.

"It won't be that bad," I say. "Nobody knows where we're going. We won't make a big deal out of it. And when the photographers get wind of us being there and try to take our picture on the way out, we'll dazzle them with our gorgeousness."

"Our gorgeousness?" Aspen says, raising a brow.

"Yeah. You're gorgeous. I'm gorgeous. *Our gorgeousness*. Like Bass said, we're going to make one hot couple."

She shakes her head. "Good thing you're so humble about it."

"Are you saying I'm not gorgeous?"

"I guess you don't lack anything in the looks department. But we might have to work on your self-confidence," she jokes.

"Aw, come on, my confidence is part of the draw, don't you think?"

"I think you're mistaking arrogance for confidence."

"You don't think it's sexy?" I ask.

"It might get you into a woman's bed, but it won't get you into her heart."

I laugh. "Good. I'm doing things right then."

Bass laughs. "You really are an asshole, aren't you?"

I study him. He's not afraid of me or my fame. He's obviously very protective of Aspen. And they dated before. It makes me wonder if he's still carrying a torch for her.

I shrug. "Never claimed I wasn't."

He hands her a black shawl. "You kids have fun. Don't do anything I wouldn't do."

"Or you mean what the contract doesn't dictate," Aspen says.

I hold the door open so she can walk out.

"Don't forget the 'dreamy eyes,' Penny," he shouts after us. "You gotta earn your keep."

Aspen looks irritated. "Sorry. Even though he knows I need to do this, he's not exactly jumping up and down about it."

I grab her elbow and help her navigate the stairs in her high heels. "I'd be worried if he was."

"He's a good man," she says.

"I can see that."

We leave her building and I hail a cab.

"What, no car? Don't you have one?" she asks.

"I do, but I only use it when I leave the city."

"Do you leave the city much? I mean, other than for games."

I shrug. "A couple times a month, I guess."

"Where do you go?"

"Connecticut mostly."

"Do you have family there?"

"Come on," I say, ignoring her question when a cab pulls up to the curb. "Our ride is here."

We make some small talk on the way to the restaurant. I can tell she's nervous. She has no reason to be. So her picture will be in the tabloids and maybe on TMZ. But quite frankly, it should be. She's got the face and the body of a model. She's exactly the kind of girl people would expect me to date. Actually, she's better. She's smart and cultured. I couldn't have picked a better woman to help fix my reputation.

I smile thinking how Rick will have a conniption knowing he won't be able to trade me.

We pull up to the restaurant and a valet opens the door. I get out and offer Aspen my hand. She looks up at me, takes in a deep breath, and then grabs it.

Just like I told her, nobody is expecting us. There are no fans on the sidewalk. No paparazzi taking pictures or asking questions.

Not yet anyway. Not until we leave. Because it happens every time. A waiter or restaurant patron will notice me and before long, it's all over social media. There are even websites dedicated to posting where famous people have been spotted. I predict by the time we're done with dinner two hours from now, we'll have to be escorted by restaurant security to our cab.

I walk her into the restaurant, my hand on the small of her back. Her dress has an opening that reveals her lower back, so I'm touching her skin. It's soft. I rub my thumb in circles and I feel a shiver run through her.

This is going to be fun. The contract says no sex. But damned if I'm not about breaking the rules. If we break them together, it'll offset the penalties, right? Nobody would have to know.

"Table for Murphy Brown," I say to the hostess.

She smiles at me knowingly before she escorts us to the back corner of the restaurant. It's private, but not so much that people can't photograph us. Which is good. I *want* to be photographed tonight.

"Murphy Brown?" Aspen asks. "Is that really her last name? Isn't there an old TV show with that title?"

"It's not her last name. It's Caden's nickname for her. And we use it to make reservations when we go out together."

"Do you have a name *you* use for reservations?"

"Yeah. Sawyer Mills."

She laughs. "Of course you do. But then why pull your hat down low when you're out in public, like the day we met or earlier today when we were shopping?"

A woman squeals at a table we pass. "Oh, my God!" She stands up to the embarrassment of her teenage daughter. "Can I get a picture with you?"

"I'm sorry, Miss," the hostess says.

"No, it's okay," I tell her. "I can pose for a quick picture."

The woman shoves her phone into the hand of her daughter who looks mortified. "Mo-om," she whines.

"Just take the picture, honey. Your father will be sorry he was late." She turns to me. "He's your biggest fan."

The girl takes our picture and then we continue to our table, loud whispers of recognition from restaurant patrons following us as we walk.

"I don't mind being recognized," I tell Aspen. "I just don't want to be mobbed. Don't worry, you'll see the difference when we leave." I nod back to the woman. "That was nothing."

"Great," she mumbles. "I can't wait."

Chapter Twelve

Aspen

I'm relieved to see Murphy and Caden sitting at the table already. Caden stands up and kisses my cheek.

I find it interesting that they are all treating me like I'm actually Sawyer's girlfriend. Well, all but Sawyer, that is. Because I'm not. So he shouldn't.

But still, it's nice that his friends are being so accommodating and supportive.

"Did you get spotted yet?" Murphy asks me.

"There weren't any photographers out front, if that's what you mean."

She nods to the people in the restaurant behind us who are staring at our foursome. "There will be."

"Don't worry about it," Caden says. "You'll do fine. Just like you did the other night."

I shake my head. "I thought it was all over when Conner sent me a drink. I ran into him outside the bar before I went in. And then when I saw he was with you, I about died."

"It's a good thing those girls came over when they did," Sawyer says.

"I sent them."

"You did?"

"I promised them each a drink if they would distract Conner. I'm sure they would have gone over to you guys anyway. I guess they were just waiting for the right moment."

"Good thinking," Murphy says. "You're better at this than you think you are."

The waitress comes over to take our drink order. She fawns over Caden and Sawyer.

Fawns over.

That's what *I'm* supposed to be doing. And he's paying me a lot of money to do it. After the waitress leaves, I glance around to see that people are still watching, so I give Sawyer my most seductive look while biting the edge of my lower lip.

He gives me his sexy half-smile and moves his chair closer to mine, draping his arm across my bare shoulders.

Murphy appraises us thoughtfully. "You two make a very attractive couple."

"That's what Bass said," I tell her.

"He said we make a *hot* couple," Sawyer says.

"He didn't say that, *you* did. But either way, same difference."

"It's not actually," he says. "Two ordinary-looking people can make an attractive couple. Two good-looking people like us, make a hot one."

"I don't recall the contract saying anything about not bitch-slapping you when you say stupid things."

"No. No, it didn't. That's a different kind of contract. But I'm sure if that's what you're into, we could have Sarah write something up."

"Oh, my God. You're incorrigible," I say, laughing.

"Yeah, but you like it. In an *I'm-paying-you-a-shitload-of-money* kind of way."

I roll my eyes at him.

"So, are you excited to go to the games?" Murphy asks.

"I guess so. I'm sure the more I learn about baseball, the more exciting it will be. Bass, on the other hand, is simply beside himself. He can't wait to go." I turn to Sawyer. "When exactly are we supposed to start coming?"

The three of us look at Murphy. She seems to have all the answers when it comes to our arrangement.

"I think you should wait another week or two. Wait until the pictures have come out. If you're seen at the games before your relationship is established, you might be pegged as just another groupie. It will help his reputation the most if you are seen as someone who didn't go after him because he's famous. Believe me, the public will accept you more if they think you're a nice girl who he met outside of his profession."

"Is that how the two of you met?" I ask her.

"Yes and no," she says, laughing. "You really don't follow baseball, do you?"

I shrug. "Sorry."

"Don't be," Murphy says. "I didn't follow it myself until I met Caden. We met because of baseball, but not by choice. His home run ball hit me." She points to a scar under her eye. "I have a metal plate where my cheekbone is. It messed me up pretty badly."

"Oh, no!"

Caden smiles and puts a hand on Murphy's arm. "And I went to the hospital thinking I'd hit some guy named Murphy. Imagine my surprise when a beautiful woman was lying in the hospital bed."

"Ha! Beautiful my ass," Murphy says. "I was hideous. My cheek had swollen to the size of a grapefruit."

"I love this story," I say. "It's like a fairy tale. Did you ask her out right then?"

"No," he says. "It was months before we started dating. But we did immediately become friends."

"Friends?" Sawyer says. "They were practically joined at the hip – in a very non-sexual, non-fun way."

"I guess we both felt something from the beginning," Murphy says, looking at Caden with admiration. "But it took us a while to realize it."

We have drinks and dinner, being interrupted a few times by people at nearby tables wanting a picture or an autograph. Sawyer keeps some kind of contact with my skin the entire time he's not eating. He puts his hand on mine, clasping them together up on the table for everyone to see. Or he has his arm around me. He even leaned in and kissed my cheek once.

Every touch has my breath hitching. And every hitch of my breath gets me angry. Angry, because even if I weren't being paid to be here, even if his touches and his looks and his kisses were genuine, he'd still be an arrogant ball player. He's not anything like the guy I met that first night. I have to keep reminding myself that *this* is the real Sawyer, not that one.

"When will you two go out again?" Murphy asks. "We should start planning it."

Caden laughs. "Sweetheart, I think you're getting into this just a little too much."

"No way," Murphy says. "I'm having a lot of fun. And Rylee will kill us if we don't bring her and Brady along next time. She was bummed they couldn't come tonight."

"I don't know," I say. "I guess it depends on when they go out of town next."

"Tomorrow," Sawyer says.

"Tomorrow? But you just got back this morning."

"Nature of the business," he says. "We play half of our games on the road. Sometimes we don't even get to come home for a week at a time. We were lucky to have a day off today."

"Do you play every day?" I ask.

"Not every day, but most days. We play one hundred and sixty-two games a season."

My jaw drops. "I had no idea you play that much. Don't football games only happen once a week? Why do you play ten times more?"

"It's the great American pastime, baby," Sawyer says. "Baseball, hot dogs and apple pie."

"Football is a different beast," Caden tells me. "It's much harder on the body. They need a week to recover."

"Do people actually *go* to all your games?" I ask. "How do they have the time? Uh … you don't expect me to go to all of them, do you? I mean, the contract says one game a week."

"Nobody goes to all of them," Murphy says. "I'm sure if you go to a game a week, that will be fine."

"But you have season tickets," Sawyer says. "You know, in case you wanted to come to more."

Caden and Murphy laugh and give each other a look.

"I guess we'll see. But if I can't go, is it okay if Bass takes a friend?"

"Of course. The tickets are for both of you, not just you. He can take whoever he likes, as long as he doesn't say anything about how he got them."

"You don't have to worry about him saying a word. He'd do anything for me."

"Is that so?" he says.

"Your bill, sir," the waitress says, handing Sawyer the check. "And just so you know, there is quite a crowd gathering out front. Would you like us to fetch you a cab and have it waiting?"

"Yes. We'll need two cabs please," Sawyer says, as he puts enough cash in the sleeve to pay my utility bill, cable bill and phone bill combined.

"Our pleasure," the waitress says before leaving.

Sawyer turns to me. "Here we go. You ready?"

"Do I look okay?" I ask Murphy.

"You look stunning," she says. "Doesn't she look great, Sawyer?"

"I told her that when I picked her up."

Murphy gives him a disapproving look. "That doesn't mean you can't tell her again, you baboon."

Caden looks sternly at Sawyer. I get the idea Sawyer could learn a thing or two from him.

Sawyer holds up his hands in surrender. "Geez, yeah, she looks great." He turns to me. "You look great. Can we go now?"

Caden shakes his head and closes his eyes. Maybe he thinks Sawyer is a lost cause. Maybe he is. But part of me thinks Sawyer must be the way he is because of something that happened to him. Maybe he had a bad breakup. Maybe he was dumped by his high school sweetheart and now he never lets himself get close to anyone for fear of getting hurt.

I don't know what makes this man tick. But I have six or seven months to find out. And he doesn't know it yet, but whether he wants to or not, we're going to be friends. Because I'm not spending the next half a year with someone I don't like. And if he ends up a better person because of it, I'd say that will be money well spent. *His* money.

I follow him to the front of the restaurant. "How do you want to do this?" I ask.

He holds out his hand for me to take. "Hold my hand. Stay close."

Murphy pulls us aside before we reach the outer door. "Maybe grab onto him like you're scared of the press. Don't smile and pose for the cameras like the other girls do. You're not with him for the fame. You're with him because you love him for who he is underneath all that."

I find it hard to keep a straight face, as do Caden and Murphy, and we all end up cracking up.

Sawyer looks at each of us, one at a time. "You think the idea of someone falling in love with me is funny? Tons of girls love me."

"You're right, sweetie, they do," Murphy says in a motherly tone.

"What? You think people only like me because I'm rich and famous?"

The three of us remain silent.

"You're all full of shit," he says, pouting. "Come on."

Sawyer grabs my hand and we walk out of the restaurant ahead of Caden and Murphy, only to be blinded by hundreds of flashes.

"What's her name?" someone shouts.

"Pick me instead!" another screams, while restaurant security has to hold her back.

"Over here!" multiple people say, trying to get us to look at them.

"Are you tonight's girl?" a photographer asks. "Where did he get you, Sluts R Us?"

Sawyer stops in his tracks and I run into his back, holding onto him for dear life as I feel claustrophobic with all the people around. Murphy told me I should act scared, but there's no need to act – I *am* scared.

He puts his arm around me and pulls me against him. He singles out the photographer who shouted and yells, "Apologize to her, you prick!"

The guy puts up his hands. "Sorry, Miss," he says. "But really, what number is she? Twenty? Thirty? And that's just *this* year."

Sawyer shakes his head. Then he leans in close and fake-whispers in my ear, after which he holds my eyes with his seductive stare as cameras flash all around us. Finally, he belts out loudly enough for some reporters and fans to hear, "Ignore them, babe."

This puts them into a frenzy. More questions are fired from every direction as Sawyer plows our way to the cab while onlookers try to touch us. A woman bursts through the crowd, tripping and falling at my feet. She claws at my leg as she's pulled back by security.

Sawyer puts himself between the woman and me, then he holds the cab door open for me and climbs in afterward. When we're safely inside, he wraps his arm protectively around me and gives me a tender kiss on the forehead before the cab pulls away.

"That was perfect!" he says, looking back at all the people still taking pictures of us as we're driving down the street. "Rick can take that and shove it up his ass."

He has no idea that I'm shaking. That the last sixty seconds were terrifying. That I'm thinking maybe no amount of money is worth doing what he wants me to do.

Chapter Thirteen

Sawyer

I stand up and shake out the top of my pants, piles of dirt falling onto the ground next to second base. I love sliding head-first. The sound of the ball hitting a glove a microsecond after I touch the base with my fingers is the best sound in the world.

"Eighteen," I say to nobody in particular.

Sometimes I like to taunt them by shouting out how many bases I've stolen this season. But I say it mostly for myself.

I take my lead off second, stretching it to the limit as the pitcher keeps me in his sights.

Do it, I think. *Throw the ball back here.*

I love the game between the pitcher and me. It's a battle of wills. *Will* he throw the ball? *Will* I get a big enough lead to make it to the next base?

But he doesn't do it. Maybe because that was my third steal today and I've already broken his will.

Caden's up at bat and I'm the winning run. A deadly combination for the other team.

He doesn't disappoint and hits a line drive to right field allowing me to score and end the game.

Caden runs over and we bump chests. "You sure earned your name today, Speed Limit. Nice job."

"It helps when you have hits like that, Kessler."

I smile as I look down at my dirty uniform on my way back to the clubhouse. There are a few reporters standing outside the door. One holds up a tabloid with a picture of Aspen and me on it from the other night. It looks like someone snapped it just as I was yelling at the photographer after he made that petty remark about Aspen. I was holding her protectively. It's exactly the kind of picture I was hoping for.

"Who's the brunette?" a photographer asks.

"Is she the same one you were shopping with?" another asks, holding out a photo of Aspen and me walking down the street carrying bags.

Even better.

"She's just a friend," I tell them before I duck inside the clubhouse.

"What was that all about?" Conner asks. "And, was that the girl from the bar last week?"

I shrug.

"Oh, shit. It was. You called her?"

I shrug again.

"You fucking called a girl?" he asks. Then he turns to the rest of the team. "Guys, Mills has a goddamn girlfriend."

"I don't have a girlfriend," I say defensively.

"You met her at a bar. She shot you down. You took her shopping and then out to dinner?" Conner says. "I'd say you're a piece-of-shit liar, Speed Limit. You have a girlfriend."

"Shut up, asshole," I say, stripping off my uniform and heading to the showers with a huge smile on my face. "You don't know shit."

Conner has no idea how much I love him right now, because on my way to the shower, I pass Rick. And I'm one hundred percent sure, based on the look on his face, that he heard every damn word Conner said.

After my shower, I hear the guys making plans to go out. Cleveland is not exactly my favorite place to go, it's nothing like L.A. or Miami, but there are a couple of good places we like to hit when we're here.

Several of us end up at a club. It's no secret that this is one of the hangouts of visiting teams. And there are plenty of beautiful women here to greet us.

Other than the night Aspen and I 'met' in the bar for show, this is the first time I've been out with the guys since starting our arrangement. In San Diego, I blamed jet lag for why I didn't go out. I realize this puts me in a unique situation. And I'm fully prepared to take a lot of shit for not taking home a woman.

What I'm not fully prepared for is how easy it is not to want to do just that.

I shake my head as I look around at all the gorgeous women trying to drape themselves over a professional baseball player. Ordinarily, I'm the one who has to have the prettiest one. The sluttiest one. The one who's a sure thing.

But tonight, I find myself shooing them away. There are cameras going off everywhere. Girls taking photos and video of us. Of them *with* us. And I do my damnedest not to get photographed in a compromising position. After everything I've been able to pull off this last week, I'm not about to fuck it up now. Despite how gorgeous they are and how much cleavage they show me.

I had no idea just how dedicated I could be to saving my career. If I could pat myself on the back, I would.

"Shit, Mills," Spencer says, with one of said girls sitting in his lap. "Are you sick or something?"

I laugh and take a drink. *"Or something."*

Caden, Brady and a few of the other married players decide to call it a night and I head back to the hotel with them. The married players don't give me as much shit as the others, but they still look at me as if I'm a stranger.

"Nice job," Brady says, giving me a fist bump.

"Yeah. I wasn't sure you could pull it off," Caden adds. "But this is just the first of many. You sure you're up for it? There's a lot of temptation."

"There's a lot at stake," I tell them.

"That there is," he says, heading down the hall to his room. "See you two tomorrow."

"G'night."

Before I'm through the door, my phone rings with a call from Bass.

"What's up, Sebastian?"

"I told you to call me Bass."

"I know, I'm just fucking with you, Briggs. What's up?"

"Good game today," he says.

"Yeah, it was. But I'm pretty sure that's not why you're calling. Did you want to make sure I didn't bring a girl back to my hotel?"

He laughs. "No. If you do that, Aspen still gets all her money and she gets to walk away. So, please, by all means, bring a girl to your hotel."

I snort through my nose knowing they've got me by the balls on that one.

"It's not going to happen. This is my career we're talking about."

"And it's Penny's *life*," he says. "I saw the tabloids and I heard her account of that night. It was scary for her. All those photographers and the things they said about her. You might be used to it, but this is new to Aspen. I'm counting on you to protect her."

"If you saw the picture at the restaurant, you'd know that's exactly what I was doing - protecting her."

"I know. But it really shook her up and I'd be remiss if I didn't tell you I'll kick your ass if you let anything happen to her."

I want to laugh at the threat, but I'm pretty sure he's serious. And he's training to be a firefighter, so I don't doubt he could make good on it.

"I'm not going to let anything happen to her. But as soon as people find out who she is, you might have to help me keep her safe. They will follow her and see where she lives."

"We live in a secure building," he says.

"Doesn't matter. You know people can just push a bunch of buttons and someone will buzz them through."

"What are you suggesting?" he asks.

"I'm not sure yet. We'll just have to see what happens and how far the press is willing to go."

"You'd better be willing to do whatever it takes to keep her safe."

"It's part of the contract," I remind him. "It'll be taken care of. How about you go out with us next time? See for yourself how things are."

"I think that can be arranged."

"Can you find a date who won't go bat-shit crazy around me?"

He laughs. "Not everyone worships you, you know."

"Good. Find one of those for Saturday night. We're going to the Knicks game."

"We are?"

"How do courtside seats sound?" I ask.

"I'll wait until you hang up before *I* go bat-shit crazy," he says.

"Okay, see you then."

I hang up the phone and wonder for the hundredth time, what the dynamic is between Aspen and Bass. They claim they're not a couple. And based on the way Aspen acted the day we met, I'd tend to agree. But they seem to be more than friends. They seem a little like the way Caden and Murphy were before they realized they liked each other and started dating.

Maybe I shouldn't have invited him. Maybe she won't be convincing enough with him around. Then again, maybe Bass can end up being the reason for our breakup. I'll have to ask Murphy about it. She seems to be the expert on this sort of thing.

One thing's for sure, Aspen's roommate is a big guy. And I don't doubt for a second he'd make good on his threat if I let anything happen to her. I crawl into bed, exhausted, and fall asleep thinking about Bass Briggs kicking my ass to protect the woman he loves.

~ ~ ~

"What the fuck happened to you?" my father asks, taking a break from his six-pack to look at me.

I reach up and touch the tender skin around my eye as I make my way to the freezer to see if we have any frozen peas.

"I'd give you a shiner myself for being such a screw-up," he says. "But I see someone else already took care of it. You couldn't even win a schoolyard fight?"

"Who says I didn't win?"

I could swear I see a hint of pride cross his face before he goes back to being his asshole self.

"Is this why the school tried to get in touch with me today?" he asks. "You get suspended again? You know if you get suspended again you're off the team, right?"

"No. It wasn't on school grounds. I'm not stupid. They can't touch me."

"Then why the hell did someone from the school leave me a voicemail?"

I shrug. "Beats me. Didn't you listen to it?"

He shakes his head. "Figured you'd tell me whatever I need to know."

"Well, I don't know."

He picks up his phone and taps around on it. I see a smile curve his lips. Then he chugs the rest of his beer. "Seems a scout is coming to Thursday's game. They want permission to tape you, and since you're not eighteen yet, I have to sign something."

"A scout? But I'm only a sophomore."

"Doesn't matter how old you are, just how well you play. You're on their radar now. You play your cards right and we'll be set for life."

"We?"

Maybe I shouldn't have said it so sarcastically, because the ashtray he just threw at me barely missed my other eye.

"Yes, we!" he shouts. "Why the fuck do you think you are where you are? You think you would have gotten there if I hadn't spent ten years driving your ass around to practices and games? You think all that money I shelled out during your travel ball years was so you could have fun? I made you the player you are today. You'll do good not to forget it."

I hold the frozen bag against my sore face. "I'm going to bed."

"Aren't you going to eat?" he asks.

I nod to the bags of greasy take-out food on the counter. "That crap is bad for me. I'd rather not eat."

As I walk away, I'm hit in the back with one of said bags of food.

"You ungrateful shit," he says. "Sit your ass down and eat the food I provide you."

I pick up the bag and walk it over to the trashcan, dropping it inside.

My father stands up. He's pissed. I can see his jaw twitching. He's a big man, but not as big as he used to be. My mother's dying broke him and now he drinks more than he eats. And in the past few years, I've gotten bigger and stronger than he is.

I walk over to him. "I've already won one fight today," I say, not backing down from his threatening stare.

We participate in a stare down before he walks around me to get another beer. "Go the fuck to bed then. Get out of my sight. You really are worthless."

I walk down the hall and slam my door. "Yeah, well, I learned from the best, you asshole," I say to myself.

Then I sit on my bed and wonder if the reason he didn't fight me was because he knew he wouldn't win, or because he might hurt my chances on Thursday night.

I wake with a start, relieved he can no longer control me. I wake up happy that he got what was coming to him.

I wake up grateful that he's dead.

Chapter Fourteen

Aspen

I sit and stare at the covers of the tabloids sitting on my coffee table. I'm not sure why I don't throw them away. All they are doing is causing me anxiety.

I knew it was going to happen. They warned me. It was part of the deal. But that doesn't keep me from dreading it happening again. And once the press finds out who I am, it will only get worse.

I need to get over it. I'm used to being looked at when I'm up on stage and all eyes are on me. But I know I'm just kidding myself. When I perform, people are awed. They are inspired by my music. They applaud me for my talent. Being on stage with Sawyer is entirely different. People, women mostly, will want to tear me down. Find my flaws. Insult me.

I pick up the magazines and rip them into pieces, refusing to let them eat away at me anymore. I turn on the television to see if I can catch the end of the second game in Sawyer's double-header today. Bass took a buddy of his to the game, the first of many I'm sure he'll see. I'm not supposed to go to any games yet. Not until our relationship is more established.

Sawyer must have done something good, because the announcers are talking about him. Then the cameras pan the stadium and show women holding up signs declaring their love for him. *'Marry me, #55,'* one of them says. Another reads, *'I want to have #55 of your babies.'* My jaw drops when I see the one that proclaims, *'I'll do #69 with #55.'*

I can't believe they showed that one on TV. I can't believe some girls are stupid enough to think he might notice them because of their signs. But then I realize who they're talking about and maybe he does. Maybe that's how he picks out his nightly conquests, from the signs they hold up.

Suddenly, I have a strange feeling in the pit of my stomach. It should be disgust. But, oddly, it feels a bit like … jealousy. I shake my head at myself and turn off the television. I walk back into my room and sit at my keyboard. I need an escape, but I don't have enough time to go to school and practice on a real piano. I only have a few hours before our double date tonight – the one that will have us plastered across every magazine and tabloid because of where we're going.

Bass is beyond excited. First, he went to the Hawks game this afternoon and then tonight we're going to see the Knicks. I'm not sure what is so exciting about basketball, about watching grown men run around and sweat. I mean, at least in baseball, the guys look good in their uniforms.

I sigh, thinking of just how good Sawyer looks in his. But then I remember all the women who want to strip him out of his uniform and how willing he is to let them do it. In fact, he's so willing that his team wants to kick him off and he had to hire someone to make him look respectable. He's the definition of a playboy. I'll bet if I Googled the term, his face would show up.

I let my fingers wander across the keyboard, composing a tune that makes me forget about tabloid magazines, rabid fans, and the number fifty-five.

Before I know it, Bass walks into my bedroom, reminding me we have to get ready for our double date. I hadn't even realized how long I was playing and now my fingers are painfully sore. I take a pill to ease the muscle tension and then hop in the shower.

"Who did you find to bring tonight?" I ask Bass, walking out into the kitchen as I towel-dry my hair.

"Do you remember Brooke?" he asks.

"Brooke from school? Cello-playing Brooke?"

"That's the one. Do you ever see her around?" he asks.

"Sometimes. But we don't really talk."

"You should. She's nice. We've kept in touch since I left school and I've always gotten the idea she wouldn't mind if I asked her out."

"Then why wait until now?" I ask.

He shrugs. "Been too busy I guess."

"Remember, we can't say anything in front of her. This is a real date as far as she knows."

"I'm perfectly aware of it, and I think that will make this all the more fun."

"Fun?" I ask.

"Yeah. The three of us have a secret that she can't know. Everything you guys do will be like an inside joke."

I give him a nasty look "This is no joke, Bass. We can't screw this up."

"I know that. It's one of the reasons I asked Brooke and not some random girl. I think we could trust her if one of us slipped up. Tonight will be like a rehearsal to see how the next six months will go." He studies me thoughtfully. "But honestly Penny, I think of the three of us, you are the most likely to screw up."

"Me?"

He nods. "You have to take this seriously. You have to put on a performance. You know how to do that. You're no stranger to the spotlight. But for some reason, you can't seem to get into character. You never talk about the guy. You don't seem the least bit interested in him. That's going to hurt the public's perception of you."

"What is it you want me to do, pretend he's my boyfriend even when he's not around?"

"I don't know, maybe. If that's what it takes to get you through this. There's a lot at stake here. I just don't want you to do something you'll regret. You're a strong-willed woman, and I'm afraid Sawyer will say or do something that will set you off. But you can't let that happen. You have to keep up appearances. Your future depends on it. And so does Denver's."

I want to disagree with him, but I can't. Everything he said is true. I need to pretend Sawyer is the guy I met when I was standing on the street soaking wet when neither of us knew each other from Adam. I can't look at him as the guy who might take one of the sign-holding girls home for the night. The guy who tells me what to do instead of asks me. The guy who has undoubtedly had more women in his bed than a piano has keys.

~ ~ ~

I've never been to a basketball game before – professional or otherwise. But I'm fairly sure this is not how most spectators watch the game. We are sitting in courtside seats. And alongside us are faces I recognize from movies and television.

I have to hand it to Brooke, she doesn't seem to be star-struck. At least not about the people who surround us. She only has eyes for Bass.

Bass, on the other hand, doesn't seem to have a clue about how Brooke is worshiping him. He's too busy doing other things, like watching the game, celebrity-spotting, and making sure I play the part of Sawyer's dutiful girlfriend.

"Lean into him," he tells me. "You're sitting closer to me than you are to Sawyer."

"Maybe that's because I feel safer with you," I whisper.

He smiles. But then he scolds me. "Whisper in *his* ear, not mine. Come on, Penny. Everyone is watching, and you guys seem more like two people who just happen to be sitting next to each other. Nobody even knows you're here together."

I scoot closer to Sawyer, who is watching the game intently. I lean in. "Bass told me I should whisper in your ear because people are watching."

He looks at me and then around the arena like he just realized we are here for show and *not* the basketball game. "Shit, right."

He grabs my hand and brings it into his lap, resting our clasped hands on his thigh. Then he goes back to watching the game.

I really think the guy doesn't know how to date. He's absolutely clueless.

"I think you should pay more attention to me," I say. "I mean, ignoring your date is not something one in a new relationship would do."

"I'm not ignoring you," he says. "I'm watching the game." He lifts up our entwined hands. "And I'm holding your hand."

I throw my head back and laugh, like he just said the funniest thing ever. When I make eye contact with him again, he's studying me in amusement.

"Kiss me," I say out of nowhere. "Not with tongue. Just a peck."

He leans forward and gives me a chaste kiss on the mouth.

"Now take your fingers and brush my hair behind my right ear as you look at me."

He does what I ask, poking my ear in the process. "How's that?" he asks. "Did I do it right? I don't feel like I did it right."

"Are you telling me that's the first time you've ever done that?"

He shrugs. "I told you before, I don't date. I've never had to try to impress anyone, and I couldn't give a shit who likes me."

I paste a smile on my face, knowing we're being watched. "Well you better give a shit if *I* like you, because I promise the next six months will be a whole lot better if I do."

"Is that so?"

I give him a sultry nod and he laughs.

"Well, then, let me try it again."

He reaches up and gently pushes a lock of hair behind my other ear, then he grabs the nape of my neck and pulls me to him until my lips touch his. He kisses me longer this time. It's only a couple of seconds, and still with no tongue, but those few seconds have every synapse in my brain firing at full throttle.

"Now you're talking," Bass says. "You guys are getting better at this." He leans over me and bumps fists with Sawyer.

My lips burn with the remnants of his light touch. Flashes of having more of him, of having *all* of him, bombard my thoughts. I try to push the visions aside, but then I remember what Bass said.

Maybe these thoughts aren't so bad after all. Maybe they will help me play the part.

I look over at Sawyer, letting my heated gaze permeate his profile. I take in his face, the heavy stubble on his jaw giving him a hint of roguishness. I look at his t-shirt that fits him so well I can see the outline of his toned pecs. I follow his shirt down to where our hands rest on his strong thigh, admiring the way his jeans fit while remembering how his backside looked in them when I was following him in.

When the game is over, Sawyer introduces us to a few people who come over to greet him. "Mason and Piper, I'd like you to meet Aspen, Brooke and Bass."

We all shake hands and I wonder just who this Mason is, because Bass is having a conniption. "Oh, man, it's an honor to meet you," he says.

"Do you guys want to join us for a drink?" Sawyer asks them. "I know a nice club not too far from here."

Mason looks at Piper and she shrugs. "Why not?" she says.

As we are escorted out of Madison Square Garden through a private exit, camera flashes go off in all directions. Mason and Piper walk out ahead of us and pose for a few pictures. Then Sawyer pulls me close to his side.

"You should smile for this one," he says. "You have a great smile."

"Okay."

I smile, but I don't look at the cameras. I look at him. When he realizes what I'm doing, he does the thing with the hair behind my ear again. He's getting good at it. It's almost believable thinking we could be a couple with the way he's looking at me and touching me.

"What's her name?" several photographers shout from the other side of the barrier.

"Not a chance," Sawyer says to them, pulling on my hand so we can walk down the sidewalk and get away from the commotion.

Bass and Brooke follow behind us, a few photographers taking pictures of them as well. Maybe the press assumes they're famous since they came out the same door we did.

A few photographers follow us down the street, but as soon as we get into the club, we're whisked upstairs into a private VIP area.

While the guys order drinks, I stand at the railing, looking down on the people below. Down to where I would be if I weren't on the arm of someone rich and famous. It's all so surreal. I step back and take a deep breath.

Piper comes over and looks at me sympathetically. "It gets easier, you know."

"It does?"

She nods.

"I'm sorry, I'm afraid you have me at a loss," I tell her. "I'm embarrassed to say I don't even know who Mason is. Does he play baseball, too?"

She laughs. "Well, then that's quite refreshing. No, he doesn't play baseball. He plays football for the Giants."

Bass butts into the conversation. "He doesn't just *play* for them. He's their quarterback."

"Wow," I say. "He must be really good."

"Just like Sawyer is really good playing for the Nighthawks," she says.

"I guess. I've only seen him play a little bit on TV."

She cocks her head and studies me. "You don't watch him play?"

I look at Bass and he gives me an encouraging smile. This is where I might have to start lying through my teeth. But we said we'd try to keep things as truthful as possible so we don't mess up.

"No. I've never even been to a game."

"Oh? Well, now I'm intrigued. I hear the rumors, and they say he's got himself a girlfriend. I guess you're it."

I shrug. "We, uh, met at a bar. Well, outside a bar actually. I had just gotten some bad news and then a bus splashed me with road water to make my day even worse. He saw the whole thing and thought I could use a drink."

"Ah, great story. And the rest is history?" she asks, smiling.

"I guess we'll see."

"He looks taken with you," she says.

"He does?" I inwardly roll my eyes at my stupidity. "I mean, that's good to hear."

Sawyer and Mason join us at the balcony and hand us some drinks and then we all sit down on a few couches overlooking the dance floor.

"Seems like you and my lovely bride are getting along," Mason says.

"You're married?" I ask. "I didn't realize that."

Piper shows me her rings. "About three years now. But we've been together a lot longer. It took him quite a while to make an honest woman out of me."

"Ha!" Mason laughs. "Don't believe her for a second. She was the one who was dragging her feet, not me."

"Do you have any kids?" I ask them.

"We have a daughter. Her name is Hailey," Piper says. "Well, she's technically his, but I feel like she's mine."

"She's yours," Mason says, leaning over to give Piper a kiss on the cheek. "In every way that matters."

135

Sawyer calls me over to the balcony railing. He nods to the dance floor. "Want to?"

"Gee, with that invitation, what girl wouldn't?" I say sarcastically. "But actually, I'm not sure I'm ready for that. Everyone down there is looking up at you. I think we'd get mobbed."

"We'd get noticed," he says. "Isn't that what we need?"

I shrug. "I guess, but ... there's so many people."

"We could just make out right here instead. Everyone would see us and probably take pictures."

"Make out?" I ask, biding time as my mind goes wild thinking back to the last time we made out in the alley.

"Which is it going to be, Andrews, dancing or kissing?"

I look down at the crowded dance floor and then back at him. I surmise that either option is dangerous. I don't even realize it when my tongue comes out to wet my lips. But *he* does, and he leans in and takes me into his arms. Then he expertly tucks a stray piece of hair behind my ear before his mouth captures mine.

This isn't like the chaste kiss he gave me at the basketball game. He goes all in, parting my lips with his and exploring my mouth with his tongue. He's gentle and demanding all at once. I forget why we're doing this as I get lost in his kiss. He tastes of beer and mint. He tastes like nothing I've ever had. He tastes so much better than I remember.

For a second, I come to my senses and remember this is just for show. I wonder how I'm going to be able to do this for six more months. I mean, holy cow, he's a good kisser. Then he deepens the kiss, and all thoughts of contracts and arrangements cease as his hands explore my lower back and pull me even closer to him. He pulls me so close, I can feel what the kiss is doing to him.

I'm glad it's loud in here, because I can feel the groans emerging from my throat. I wonder if he can too. My knees go weak and he holds me up, pressing me against the railing and dipping me slightly over to make sure people get a good view.

When he finally pulls away, I'm left without any breath. Without any senses. Without any words.

He smiles at me. "That ought to do the trick," he says.

"Uh … Yup," I say, wiping my lower lip.

I hear a slow whistle and then Bass comes to stand next to me. "Damn, guys, that was almost like watching porn."

Sawyer laughs and then flags down the waitress for a few more drinks. I look at Bass, wondering if he meant for his comment to be funny, because he looks a little green around the gills, which confuses me because he's not drinking.

"Don't drink too much, Penny. You know alcohol doesn't mix well with that shit you take for your fingers."

"What's he talking about?" Sawyer asks me.

I wiggle my fingers in the air. "Sometimes when I practice a lot, my fingers and wrists get really tight so I take a muscle relaxant. I'm not supposed to drink too much because I can get a bit loopy."

"Loopy?" Bass says, laughing. "She practically blacks out. The first time it happened she didn't remember half the night. Nobody could tell she was even drunk, but the next day, when I was talking about the night before, she had no recollection."

Sawyer studies me. "Really?" he says. Then he hands my drink to Bass. "Well then no more drinks for you. And you need to make sure to tell me when you've taken one of those pills so I can keep you safe."

Bass puts the drink on a nearby table. "Thanks, but I'm not drinking during my training."

I nod to his date. "Brooke looks kind of bored, maybe you should dance with her."

While they go dance, I talk with Piper.

"Well, after that kiss, there won't be any question as to who his girlfriend is," she says, fanning herself dramatically.

"I kind of get the idea he wants it that way," I say. "I feel like he doesn't want to hide me from everyone. I thought maybe he would because of how he usually is with women."

"He's different with you, that's for sure," she says. "Maybe he's finally ready to settle down."

"Settle down?" I give her crazy eyes and hope I'm playing a convincing part of the skeptical new love interest. "I don't think either of us is looking for that. We're just having fun."

Piper and I get to know each other as she asks me all about Juilliard and I fawn over pictures of their daughter. By the time we say goodbye, we've exchanged numbers and I again wonder how many friends I'm going to make and then lose when this is over.

Thirty minutes later, Bass and I are home, sitting on our couch with my head on his shoulder as we talk about how surreal the night was.

"Penny, I noticed something earlier. You told Piper the wrong story. You said you met Sawyer when that bus splashed you, but the story is you met at the bar when the team went out for Spencer's birthday."

I sit up and cover my mouth. "Oh, my God. You're right. I can't believe I did that. Do you think anyone will figure it out?"

He shakes his head. "No, it's not a big deal. You could say you were confused or something. But I'd try to stick to the same story from here on out. All in all, I think you guys pulled it off. Piper and Mason didn't have a clue, and they are friends with him."

"Good. I'll have to be more careful." I stretch my arms and yawn. "I'm off to bed."

"Goodnight," he says, going to his room.

I lie in bed trying not to think of the kiss but failing miserably. Then I fall asleep and dream of butterflies.

Chapter Fifteen

Sawyer

As I make the drive to New Haven, I think about the tabloid photos Murphy emailed to me early this morning. They're perfect. Photos of Aspen and me at the Knicks game and at the club are all over the internet as well. Photos of us looking at each other, of us touching. And the ones from when I kissed her in the club – those are the best.

Captions read, *'Has the fastest man in baseball finally been tamed?'* and, *'Most eligible Hawk captured.'*

I wonder if Rick and Jason have seen any of them. Those are the two people making the decisions. My manager and the owner hold my fate in their hands. And in a few weeks, when I know I'll be taking Aspen to a benefit put on by the Hawks, they will see I'm in a committed relationship. I can't wait to see the look on Rick's face.

I pull into Lucy's driveway, hoping she'll let me take Danny to Silver Sands to do some fishing. While I still hate going there, he loves it. He gets excited when we go fishing. And today is a beautiful spring day, perfect for being on the coast.

I only have a few hours since we fly to Tampa tonight, but I might not be able to get back here for at least a few weeks, so I wanted to come out this morning.

Lucy answers the door. "Aren't *you* popular today," she says.

I narrow my eyes at her.

"You must know your picture is all over television and social media. Who is she?"

"Just someone I met a few weeks ago. She's nice. We've been out a few times."

"A few times? Isn't that some kind of record?" she says sarcastically.

"I didn't come here to talk about my social life, Lucy. I was wondering if I could take Danny fishing today."

Her lips pucker and she puts her hands on her hips. "Silver Sands, I suppose?"

"Of course."

She sighs and thinks about it. "I don't know."

"Come on, Lucy. You never take him yourself."

"For good reason. It's a terrible place." She rubs her temples like she's got a headache.

"Yes, but he doesn't know that, and he loves it there."

Danny comes into the room, sees me and smiles big. "Is that for me?" he asks, seeing the football in my hand.

"You bet it is. I had my friend, Mason Lawrence, sign it for you. But no throwing it in the house or your mom will kill me."

I gently toss him the ball and am impressed when he catches it. He's normally pretty awkward.

"Can we go outside and throw it?" he asks.

I look at Lucy, staring her down, hoping she'll give in to my earlier demand.

"Okay, fine," she says. "But no going over to Charles Island."

I laugh. "I'm not taking him to Charles Island." I turn to Danny. "Maybe we can take the football with us and throw it on the beach."

His eyes go wide. "Yes! Yes!" Then he runs into his room and comes out with his fishing pole. He tries to open the front door but Lucy stops him.

"Hold on there, big fella. Let me make you two a couple of sandwiches. And you need to take a jacket. It's breezy on the coast."

Ten minutes later, Danny and I are on our way to Walnut Beach and Silver Sands State Park. I tell him all about Charles Island even though I know he doesn't really understand it, but it's something to talk about along the way.

"When I was a teenager, some of my friends and I used to come to the beach, and when it was low tide, we would walk over to Charles Island."

"What's low tide?" he asks.

"It's when the ocean doesn't come on shore as much," I tell him. "When the tide is low and there isn't enough water to cover all the land by the shore, there is a sandbar you can walk on to get over to Charles Island."

Danny is no longer interested in my story, as he's busy studying his new football, so he doesn't ask me any more questions. But I continue to tell him about it anyway.

"Once, a friend and I got stuck over on the island all night because the tide came back in before we could make the half-mile walk across the sandbar."

I laugh, just thinking about it and realize that place does still hold some good memories. "Brandon Miller was the kid I was with. He was scared to death of all the sounds we heard that night on the island. It's a wildlife sanctuary with a lot of birds, so I could see how some people would get creeped out. I wasn't afraid, but I was cold. It was late April and it got cold as shit … uh, cold as heck at night, and all I had on was a light jacket. But our phones still worked, so we called our parents saying we were going to spend the night at each other's houses so we wouldn't get in trouble."

I pull into the parking lot and look in the distance towards the island, wondering what ever became of Brandon. After what happened here, a lot of my friends never came back. Then after high school, most of us went our separate ways and just lost contact.

"We're here," I say. "What do you want to do first?"

We get out of the car, and he stares over at the rocks. "Stack rocks," he says.

I take him over to the area that is cordoned off from the rest of the beach. We walk carefully through the stacks others have built, admiring how high some of them are. A few stacks have fallen down and we collect some of the rocks from them to build our own stack.

"I want mine that high," Danny says, pointing to the tall one that must be over three feet.

"I'll bet they cheated and used mortar or something between the rocks."

"Cheating isn't fair," he says. "Mommy tells me not to ever cheat."

"That's right, you shouldn't. But there will always be people who do."

He looks over at me with his deep blue, innocent eyes. "Why?"

"Because they think it's the only way they will win."

"Do you cheat?" he asks. "You win a lot at baseball Mommy says."

"I never cheat at baseball," I tell him. "I work very hard to be good at it."

"Can you teach me to be good at it?" he asks.

"You bet, buddy."

"Maybe someday I can be good like you."

I look at him, trying hard to keep the sadness out of my eyes. "Maybe you can. Now, what do you say we get your fishing pole and try to catch a big one?"

"Yes!" he screams, pulling me by my hand and leading me away from our pitiful attempt at a record-breaking rock stack.

~ ~ ~

"I'd like to make a toast to the bride and groom," Spencer says, as he stands up and turns around, raising his miniature airplane bottle of vodka from the seat in front of me. "To Sawyer and … what's her name again?"

I knew it. I knew someone would make stupid wedding jokes.

Part of me wants to be pissed – the part that knows it could never be true because Sawyer Mills wouldn't ever have a girlfriend, let alone a wife. But the other part, the part trying to keep my goddamn job, is wanting to do a fist-pump knowing my manager is witnessing this from a few rows over.

I try and think of how I should react to make it believable.

"Two dates, asshole," I say, throwing a packet of peanuts at him. "Two fucking dates. And her name is Aspen."

"Three if you count the night you met her in the bar," Conner adds.

Four if you count the night we really met.

"That wasn't a date," I say, instead.

"And the shopping excursion?" Benham asks. "Hell, when are the invitations going out?"

"Maybe you could all shut the fuck up and mind your own business," I say.

I look over at Brady and Caden who both have shit-eating grins on their faces. "What're you smiling at?" I say, just for good measure.

Then I stick my earbuds in and pretend to ignore the incessant chatter concerning my love life.

I pull out my phone and type an email that I know won't get delivered until we land.

Aspen,

I'm sitting here on the plane listening to my teammates rib me about us. They are buying all of it, hook, line and sinker. And the best part is that my manager is hearing everything. Remember when I told you they'd probably tease me about getting married. Yup — they are. I couldn't have planned it better.

You were great last night. Maybe it's time to ramp things up and come to a game. Next weekend maybe?

Later,
Sawyer

I turn on my music, lean back into my seat, and close my eyes when I realize that is the first email I've ever sent a woman who doesn't either work for me or who isn't part of the Hawks organization. Then I remember that she *does* work for me, and for a second I think I might feel something a bit unusual. Disappointment.

I break the seal of the small bottle the flight attendant gave me and enjoy the burn as I swallow it down.

Chapter Sixteen

Aspen

I re-read Sawyer's email on a break between classes. At least he was nice about it and didn't just demand I show up for a game. I don't care if he's paying me, he still needs to act like a decent human. I type out a reply.

Sawyer,

I'm glad things are going as planned. I keep worrying that I'm screwing everything up. I'm a much better piano player than actress. I spoke with Bass and Saturday works for us if that's okay. Thanks for asking me instead of telling me, by the way. I'm glad to see you're learning something.

Aspen

The cover of a tabloid gets shoved in front of me. "Is this you?" Helen Jensen asks.

Helen also plays piano, so we have a few classes together. I wouldn't exactly call her a friend, but we have been at a lot of the same social gatherings.

I stare at the picture I've already seen, admiring how good Sawyer and I look together. This one was taken at the basketball game when he was doing the thing with my hair.

I shrug my answer.

"Oh, my God, it *is* you. I knew it. You know Sawyer Mills? I mean, you've gone out with him? Are you still?" She sits down next to me. "Tell me everything. Does he have any friends you could introduce me to?"

"There's nothing to tell, Helen. We've only been out a few times."

She points to the article. "According to this, you're his girlfriend."

"Don't believe everything you read," I say. "Those newspapers will print anything."

"So, you're not his girlfriend?"

"No," I say, trying to keep it believable. "We just had some fun together, that's all. There's no label on anything."

"Fun?" She raises an eyebrow. "What's he like – you know, in bed?"

My jaw drops. "Seriously?"

"Oh, come on. Everyone knows he sleeps with every girl he takes out."

I shake my head and stand up. "I have to get to class."

"Okay, but keep me in mind if he wants to double with one of his teammates. I hear Spencer Truman and Dylan Buckley are available."

I wave at her as I walk away, not bothering to reply. How does she know the names of everyone on the team? Am I the only one who doesn't follow sports?

Three more people pull me aside on my way to class. It seems everyone wants to be my friend today. I guess being a talented pianist and a good person wasn't enough for them before. Hypocrites.

I'm ready to throw my phone against the wall, because by the end of the day it's blowing up with texts and social media posts from so-called friends who recognized me. But then one text catches my eye. It's from Murphy. She and Rylee want to take me out to dinner while the boys are away. I solidify plans with them and then shut my phone off. After all, I still have several more weeks of school to get through before graduation. I don't plan on failing my finals and screwing up everything I'm working toward.

~ ~ ~

After my shower, I turn my phone back on in case Murphy or Rylee need to get ahold of me to change or cancel our plans. I'm not really sure why they want to go out with me. It's not like we're friends. I'm the help. The paid escort of their *real* friend. Why they aren't treating me like that is beyond me.

I have quite a few more messages and texts than usual. I guess that's to be expected. And if this is happening now, I can't imagine what it will be like when the press finds out my name.

My phone immediately rings and my brother's face flashes across the screen.

"Hi, Den."

"Sawyer Mills?" he asks. "Is that really you in the pictures? They aren't Photoshopped, are they?"

"Well hello to you, too."

"Tell me, Aspen. What's going on?"

I know he means business when he calls me by my real name.

"It's me. It's not a big deal."

"Not a big deal? You're going out with a Nighthawk? What ... how ...?"

I laugh. But then I remember I can't tell him anything. I have to tell more lies to my brother. Something I'd never done before meeting Sawyer. I think this is the worst part of the whole arrangement, that I can't talk to Denver about it.

"We went out twice. I'm sure it's nothing. You know how quickly he goes through women."

"Jesus, Pen, you didn't sleep with him, did you?"

"Of course not."

"Good. But maybe that's the only reason you got a second date. Did you ever think of that? Maybe he's just keeping you around until you give him what he's after."

"Why would he want to do that? He can have anyone he wants. But maybe you're right. Maybe he's already done with me."

"Shit, really? That's a shame. It would have been so cool. Not that I could meet him or anything with me being stuck in Missouri."

"Because it's all about you?" I joke.

"You know what I mean. So he hasn't asked for another date?"

"Not technically. But he did ask me to come watch one of his games this weekend."

"Are you going?"

"I think Bass and I will go."

He laughs. "Bass? Sawyer won't mind you taking another guy to a game?"

"Didn't you see the other photos?" I ask. "We already went out together. Bass and Sawyer have met."

"He's met your friends? Aspen, what aren't you telling me?"

My skin crawls with all the lies I know I'll have to tell my favorite person in the world over the coming months.

"Nothing. We met in a bar and I shot him down, but I gave him my number and now we've gone out a few times. Is that so hard to believe?"

"No, it's not. You're gorgeous and talented and one of the nicest people I know. But, Sawyer Mills? It's just so unbelievable."

"I agree. That's why I'm trying not to make a big deal out of it. I'm sure it won't last."

"Don't let him fuck around on you, little sister. If he does one thing wrong, cut him loose, alright? Damn, I wish I could come up there and make sure you're okay."

"I *am* okay," I tell him. "You don't have to worry. Bass is watching out for me."

"*I* should be watching out for you."

I sigh. I miss him so much and I know he feels the same way. I had planned on going home for a few weeks this summer. But I wonder if I'm allowed to do that. Would I be violating the contract in some way?

I look at the time. "Den, I have to go in a minute. I'm going out with some friends tonight."

"Speaking of going out, do you have any big plans for your birthday?"

"Not really. I suppose Bass will take me out. What about you?"

"Like there's anyone left here who wants to hang out with me," he says sadly. "Why isn't the baseball star taking you out?"

"I told you it's just casual."

"Okay, be safe tonight. Now that your face is out there, people might recognize you."

I don't tell him they already do. I know he will be beside himself when my name gets published and I become well known for the simple fact that I'm dating a ball player.

"Oh, and I meant to thank you for the check that came today," he says. "It's a lot more than I thought it would be. You must have gotten a good scholarship. I wish you didn't have to spend it on me."

"Of course I'm going to give it to you. And I'm working some extra jobs up here, teaching kids and such, so I should be able to send more money soon."

"Aspen, no. I made my own bed here."

"I'm not letting you go to prison."

"It might not come to that."

"Well, I'm going to make sure it doesn't. We're paying off your debts, come hell or high water."

"I love you, Pen."

"Love you too. I'll talk to you soon."

I finish getting dressed, sad that Denver and I can't spend our birthday together. For the past few years, he's come to New York and we've had a time of it. And now he has no one.

I grab my purse and then re-check the address where I'm supposed to meet Murphy and Rylee. When I open the door, I'm startled by a guy carrying a bag who looks like he was about to knock.

"Can I help you?" I say, looking up and down the hallway.

"I have a delivery for Aspen Andrews."

"That's me. But I didn't buzz you up."

He shrugs. "Someone was going out when I was coming in."

I shake my head in disgust. I hate it when people get in without being buzzed. I wonder if it's going to become a problem.

He holds out the bag for me.

I look at it skeptically. "Who's it from?"

"I don't look at the stuff," he says. "I just deliver it. But I had to pick it up over at Hawks Stadium."

I feel the smile creep up my face as I accept the bag and then dig inside my purse for a tip.

"It's already been taken care of," he tells me before walking away.

"Thank you!" I shout after him.

I go back inside my apartment, needing to see what's in the bag before I head out. I pull out a couple of Hawks jerseys with Sawyer's name and number on the back. I hold them up, wondering why he sent two. But I quickly realize one is too large for me. He sent one for Bass as well.

Underneath those are two Hawks baseball caps, and under those are several assorted ladies shirts. The last thing in the bag is a sleeper set that is shorts and a cami. I didn't even realize they made things like this. He wants me to wear this stuff when I sleep? That may be going a bit too far.

I put my things in my room, leaving the jersey and a hat for Bass on the kitchen table.

On my way to meet the girls, I belatedly realize there wasn't a card or even a note inside the bag. I find that strange.

That's because he's not your boyfriend, my inner voice reminds me.

I pass a few corner newsstands on my walk only to see my face prominently displayed on them. I hide behind other pedestrians so I won't be recognized. It's one thing to have acquaintances at school recognize me from the photos, it'll be something else entirely to have strangers pick me out of a crowd.

I arrive at the restaurant, giving the fake name Murphy asked me to use.

"I'm meeting Mrs. Brown here," I tell the hostess.

"Your party has already been seated," she says. "Please follow me."

We order our drinks and then I have to ask them what's been nagging at me all day. "Why did you invite me to dinner?"

They look at each other, both at a loss for words.

"Okay, now you have to spill. Why are you being so nice to me knowing I'm being paid to do this? If I were actually his girlfriend, I'd understand, but ... why?"

Rylee looks at Murphy again and Murphy nods. "We like you," Rylee says. "And I guess we're hoping that maybe your relationship won't end when the season does."

I look from one to the other in disbelief. "Relationship? We don't have a relationship. We have an arrangement. And from what I've read and what Sawyer tells me, he's not looking for anything. And even if he were, I'm not sure I'd want to be it. You know him, you know his past. He's probably a walking, talking STD. Let alone he's arrogant and bossy. And, okay, so he's a good kisser and he's not so hard on the eyes, but there's only so much that can make up for."

Murphy's brows practically touch her hairline. "He's a good kisser, is he?"

I shrug nonchalantly. "I guess. I mean, I didn't really notice, but I assume he is."

"Based on the pictures I saw from last weekend, combined with what Piper Lawrence told me, you know *exactly* how good a kisser he is."

"You know Piper Lawrence?" I ask.

"We do," Murphy says. "But don't change the subject."

"There is no subject," I tell them. "I'm not in this for anything other than the money. I know that makes me a terrible person, but that's how it is."

"I don't believe you," Rylee says. "You can't fake looks like the ones I saw in those pictures. There's something there."

"The man is trying to save his career," I remind her. "He'd look at Freddy Krueger like that if he thought they'd let him stay on the team."

"Who says I was talking about *him?*" she asks, with a smug lift of her brow.

The waitress brings our drinks, thankfully ending our conversation. For the rest of dinner, they tell me about Piper and her sisters and a few other friends, encouraging me to get together with all of them for a girls' night.

I'm not so sure it's a good idea, however. I'd feel awful lying to their friends who would think I'm genuinely falling for Sawyer. When this is over and I 'leave' him, he will get to keep his friends and I get to go back to being me. We won't be able to co-exist in the same circles. So, my trying to fit into them now just doesn't make much sense. Being seen with Murphy and Rylee is one thing, their husbands are Sawyer's best friends. But I think it's best to leave it at that. Less baggage to deal with when this is just a memory.

When I excuse myself to hit the bathroom, my phone vibrates with a text.

Sawyer: Did you get it?

Me: Get what? I got a delivery today, but there was no card. Is that what you're talking about?

Sawyer: What was in the package?

Me: Some Nighthawks stuff.

Sawyer: And you didn't think it was from me?

Me: Well, I wasn't sure. Maybe one of your friends wanted to make sure I was dressed appropriately when I come to the game on Saturday. But then again, they probably would have included a note. Most normal people would.

Sawyer: Most normal people would just say thank you.

Me: I would have if there had been a note telling me who sent it.

Sawyer: I sent it.

Me: Oh, well, why didn't you just say so? Thank you.

I laugh to myself as I send the text. I know I'm infuriating him.

Sawyer: You are one complicated woman.

Me: I'll take that as a compliment. Now I have to get back to dinner. Goodbye.

Sawyer: Dinner? With who?

I put my phone away, not bothering to answer. He doesn't own all my time. And as long as I don't date anyone else, I'm not violating the contract.

I re-join Murphy and Rylee a minute later and they both narrow their eyes, studying me as I sit down.

"Why the big smile?" Rylee asks.

"Oh, I didn't know I was. Just happy to be here, I guess."

"I'm calling bullshit," Murphy says.

I about spit out my drink. "What?"

I've not known Murphy very long, but I've never heard her cuss.

"You walk out here with a Cheshire cat smile and I'll bet Caden's right arm it has something to do with the text I just got."

"Text?"

She hands me her phone and I read it.

Sawyer: Do you have any idea what Aspen is doing tonight?

I can't help the smile that all but cracks my face in two.

Chapter Seventeen

Sawyer

I curse as I walk back to the dugout two bases too soon. I'm pissed at myself for falling a few inches short of second base. For being tagged out on the steal. I look up to where I know she's sitting, but I can't pick her out. I wonder if she's having a good time. I wonder if she's wearing the jersey I gave her. I wonder if she's disappointed in me.

Then I wonder why I even care.

Some of my teammates give me a supportive pat on the back before I throw my batting helmet down and find a seat on the bench. Then I watch Caden and Spencer each get a single and I'm pissed all over again, knowing I'd be crossing home plate right about now if I hadn't screwed up. After that, the Yankees turn a double play, ending the inning.

We have a couple more particularly bad innings and I wonder if we're just snake-bit today. When I get up to bat again, I strike out. I glance up in the stands again. Yes – definitely snake-bit.

After the game, Rick chews our asses out. But nobody complains. We deserve it. It was our worst performance of the year. In spite of that, there is still a large crowd gathered outside the clubhouse when I emerge. I look around for Aspen. She's supposed to meet me here.

I see a group of reporters huddled off to one side. One of them shouts, "Aspen! Are you going to be the one to settle him down?"

I can't help but smile when I hear the question. Everything is going exactly as planned.

Question after question gets fired at her. And just as we discussed, she's not answering a single one. And it doesn't go unnoticed that they are calling her by her name. One of the reporters calls her 'Miss Andrews' so the cat is most definitely out of the bag.

A reporter shifts over and I see her. Bass is hovering protectively, but she looks terrified. I walk over to the head of security and nod to Aspen. "Drew, can you take care of that for me? She and the guy can come through."

"No problem," he says, before he signals to someone else on his staff and then they clear a path for Aspen and Bass to come around the barriers that separate us from the press and the fans.

I pull Aspen to my side and put my arm around her. Then I lean down and kiss her hello. I can see in her eyes that she's still scared, but she looks relieved to be on this side of the gate.

"Drew, this is Aspen Andrews and Sebastian Briggs. They are both good to have access until further notice."

Drew shakes their hands and pulls some business cards out of his pocket to give them. "Good to meet you. If you have any issues, call or text me at this number."

"I'm gonna go sign a few autographs," I tell Aspen. "You can wait right here and I'll be back in a minute."

When I head over to the fans, the reporters bombard me with questions.

"Are you dating Aspen Andrews?" they ask.

"Yes," I say, trying not to make it seem like a big deal as I sign a few hats and programs.

"How many times have you been out with her?" one yells.

Normally I wouldn't bother to answer these sorts of questions, but in this case, these are exactly the ones I want to answer. "I don't know. I don't keep count. A few."

"How is she different from the others?" one asks.

I look back at Aspen and smile when she gives me an awkward wave. I'm milking this for all it's worth. Damn, I wish Rick were out here to see this.

"Have you *seen* her?" I ask.

"Are you in love?" a reporter shouts.

I have to keep from laughing. I couldn't have scripted this better.

"Come on, guys," I say, trying to look disgusted that he even asked. I do have to make it believable, after all.

A minute later, I'm back at Aspen's side. "They are putty in our hands," I say.

I lean down to give her one more peck on the lips now that I know all the cameras are on us.

"I'm very happy for you," she says, looking up at me the way we discussed she would. Like she's a woman in love. She pulls me close and whispers in my ear. "What happens now?"

I throw my head back and laugh, like what she said was funny. Then I brush a hair behind her ear and run my thumb down the side of her jaw.

"Now we'll go out. Just you and me. Our first solo date. That will have them salivating."

"What about Bass?" she asks.

"We can't always have a chaperone," I tell her. "People will talk. We need to keep this about us. You and me. Not a threesome."

She nods. "Right. So, where are we going?"

"I hope you didn't eat too much at the game, because I'm taking you for a late dinner."

She looks down at her clothing. At the jersey that looks great on her, and her jeans. "But I'm not dressed for dinner."

"You don't need to be. You like pizza, don't you?"

"Sure, who doesn't? But won't we get bombarded?"

"That's kind of the point, Aspen. Consider this our coming out party."

She looks scared.

"Don't worry. I won't let it get out of hand. I know the owner of the place I'm taking you."

"Okay. Let me tell Bass we're leaving."

While she's talking to Bass, I share a few parting words with some of the other guys who hung around to sign autographs. Then I have Drew get us a cab.

"You do what you have to do to protect her," Bass says, walking with us to our ride.

"That's a given," I tell him. "You don't have to keep reminding me every time you see me, Briggs. It's part of the contract."

"And I'm not about to let you forget it," he says.

I shake my head and laugh. "Duly noted."

I put Aspen into the cab and climb in after her. She looks back at everyone who followed us to the street. "Is it always like this, or is this because of me?"

"There are always fans waiting for us outside the clubhouse, if that's what you mean. They can get pretty boisterous sometimes.

But considering we lost the game, there were more than I expected – and that's because of you."

"How long do you think they will make a big deal out of it?"

I shrug. "Don't know. Weeks maybe. Or months. I'm not really sure."

"What do you think will happen now that they know my name?" she asks.

"Some might find out where you live and hang out in front of your apartment building."

"The lease is in Bass's name," she says.

"That's good, but I'm sure it won't be long before they find out his name, too. And everything else about you."

She puts her head in her hands. "Oh, God. Why did I agree to this again?"

I lean into her so the cabbie doesn't hear. "Because I'm paying you a shitload of money."

She looks up at me and takes a deep breath.

I study her face. "That is why you're doing this, isn't it?"

"Of course it is. Why?"

"I don't know. Sometimes the way you look at me, it's just—"

"Sawyer, I *have* to look at you like that," she whispers. "It's in the contract."

"Good. Because I realize all this pretending might seem real and I don't want you thinking … you know."

"That you like me?" she says, sardonically. "I wouldn't dare."

"Come on, Aspen. I do like you. I think you're a cool chick. It's just that I don't—"

"Do girlfriends. Yeah, I know. You've said that like a thousand times. I think I got it by now."

"Are you mad at me?" I ask.

"No. Sorry." She nods to the street behind us. "I'm just not used to this yet."

"Do you have any questions I can answer to make things easier?"

She looks at me thoughtfully. "Yeah, why do they call it a clubhouse? Isn't it just a locker room?"

I laugh. Of all the questions she could ask, she asks such a benign one. "It was a locker room in high school. Now it's a clubhouse. Makes it seem more professional I guess."

"What did they call it in college?" she asks.

I shrug. "Don't know. I didn't go."

"You didn't go to college? Then how are you playing professional baseball?"

"It's not like football," I explain. "Plenty of players get drafted right out of high school. Unlike football, we don't need the extra years to beef up. We're practically at our prime during the college years, so why waste that?"

"*Waste that?* You think college is a waste?" she asks, looking all judgmental.

"I guess not for some people. But for me it would have been. I was never an academic."

"But what about after?" she asks. "You can't play baseball forever. And what if you get hurt?"

I shake my head. "I'm not going to get hurt. Playing shortstop is not as dangerous as some of the other positions, but it is one of the most demanding positions on the team – and the most important one."

"I'll bet Caden and Brady would argue that point."

I laugh. "They would. But they'd be wrong."

"Still, even if you don't get hurt, how long can you realistically play?"

"The average MLB career lasts five years. But that's only because a lot of guys can't hack it in the majors. Some guys play into their upper thirties. I plan on going even longer. I've got fifteen good years ahead of me. Maybe more."

"You don't have a backup plan?"

"Why would I do that? A backup plan assumes you'll fail. Do *you* have a backup plan?"

She shakes her head.

"So you were going to Juilliard no matter what? That's pretty ballsy considering they don't take just anyone."

"Not as ballsy as thinking you'll grow up to play baseball for the New York Nighthawks."

"So, I guess we're two confident people then. We know what we want."

The cab stops, but we don't break our stare. I'm not sure what passes between us, but it makes me uncomfortable as shit.

"Your stop, sir," the cabbie says.

I snap out of it and we get out of the car just as my phone rings. I look to see who it is. "Sorry, I have to take this. I'll just be a second."

I leave her by the entrance to the pizza place and walk over in front of the next store.

"Hey, bud. How are you?"

"I did something bad," Danny says.

"You did? What did you do?"

"I left the water on and it got all over the floor. Mommy's mad at me."

I look over at Aspen to see her watching me. I turn my back and try to wrap up the conversation.

"I'm sure she's not mad at you, Danny. It sounds like it was an accident. Once she cleans it up, she won't be mad anymore.

Maybe you could help her. Why don't you get a towel or a mop and soak up some of the water?"

"Okay. Are you coming over today?"

"No. I can't come over today. But maybe, next weekend. I have a whole day off. Maybe we could go back to the beach."

"Yay! I have to go. Mommy's calling me."

The line goes dead before I can say goodbye.

I spin around and come face-to-face with Aspen. "Ready?" I ask.

She points to my phone. "Who are you planning a beach outing with?"

"None of your business."

"I'd say it *is* my business if you're violating the contract by taking out another woman."

"I'm not taking out another woman."

"It sure sounded like it to me. You have a day off and you want to take her to the beach? I heard what you said, Sawyer."

"Why are you eavesdropping?"

She points behind me. "Because people are starting to gather. They are noticing you. I walked over to tell you since you seemed oblivious to anything but the person on the other end of the phone call."

I roll my eyes. "It's not what you think."

"Then why don't you explain it to me?"

"I don't have to explain anything. I'm not cheating on you and I won't cheat on you. That's all you have to know."

"But even *meeting* another woman somewhere could give people the wrong idea."

"I told you, I'm not meeting a woman. Now can we please go eat," I say, walking over to hold the door open. "I'm hungry."

Chapter Eighteen

Aspen

The waitress brings our beers and almost spills mine in my lap while she's slobbering over Sawyer.

I study him, wondering what that phone call was all about. Who else would he be taking to the beach? And why is he being so secretive about it if it's not a woman?

I shouldn't care. I shouldn't care one tiny bit, because if he does violate the contract, I still get my money and I get to walk away. That should make me happy. But for some reason it doesn't. And that reason nags at me in the pit of my stomach when I realize that even though this is all for show, I still don't want him with another woman.

And that realization makes me just one more pitiful woman in his long line of pitiful women.

I hear a tapping noise behind me, so I look over my shoulder and out the front window to see a crowd gathering and watching us. "Did you have to request a table in the front?"

"It's the best way to be seen," he says.

"But everyone will be watching me eat."

"So don't eat. Most chicks don't eat on dates anyway."

"This isn't a real date," I remind him. "And I'm hungry."

"So eat."

I roll my eyes at him.

"I'm not *most chicks*, either."

He cocks his head to the side and appraises me. "No, you're not, are you."

"Listen, maybe you're used to this by now, but I'm not. I'm not used to people watching my every move."

"You don't play the piano in front of people?"

"I do, but that's different. They watch me play. They don't watch me everywhere else and take pictures of me when I get into a cab. Or when I drink my beer. What if I get spinach in my teeth?"

He laughs. "You'd look great even with spinach in your teeth. But if it makes you feel any better, I promise to tell you if you get spinach in your teeth. Deal?"

I shrug.

"Let's talk about something else to get your mind off it."

"Okay. Tell me why you kiss your fingers and then touch your rib cage every time you go up to bat?"

A smug smile creeps up his face. "Oh, you noticed that?"

"Don't flatter yourself," I say. "It is kind of my job to get to know you."

"I guess you could call it one of my rituals."

"Rituals?"

"Yeah. Baseball is a superstitious sport. Just wait until we get on a winning streak, none of us will shave."

"Really? How many do you have to win to be on a streak?"

"Usually five or six in a row."

"And nobody will shave until you lose?"

"Nope."

I cringe. "I'd hate to be the one to clean up the clubhouse sinks after a loss."

"Yeah, it can get pretty nasty in there."

"So, why kiss your fingers and touch your ribs?"

"It's not so much my ribs I touch, it's my tattoo."

"You have a tattoo?"

"Yup."

"Can I see it?"

He laughs a throaty laugh. "You want me to show you my tattoo with those people out there waiting to pounce on anything we do that's newsworthy?"

I turn around to see the crowd outside that I forgot about for a minute. "No, I guess not. But why do you do it – touch your tattoo?"

"Just something I started back in high school," he says sadly.

"Do your teammates have any rituals?"

"Every single one of them."

"They do? What are they?"

"Some of them will eat the same things before every game. Some listen to specific music or wear a particular article of clothing. Caden plays every game with his wife's engagement ring in his back pocket."

My jaw drops. "Really?"

"Whatever it takes to make us play our best."

The waitress brings our pizza and then a few restaurant patrons ask for a picture on their way out the door. Sawyer stands up and obliges them. Before he sits back down, he picks up his chair and moves it closer to mine. So close that our outer thighs touch.

He puts a slice of pizza on each of our plates and then he puts his arm around me. He leans in and whispers in my ear. "It's hot as shit. Let it cool or you'll burn your mouth."

I turn my head to ask him why he's whispering to me, but when I do, I see he hasn't pulled away and our lips are inches apart. My breath hitches when I look into his eyes. His eyes are what I'd call icy blue. They are so light-blue, they are almost white. It's a contrast to his dark hair which makes him even more striking.

I take a moment to imagine him with a beard. I wonder how many games they would have to win for him to be able to grow one. Then I imagine what it would feel like to kiss him after he did.

"I'm kissing you now," he announces right before his lips find mine.

He doesn't give me a passionate kiss, but it's not exactly a chaste one either. When he pulls away, I ask, "Why did you do that?"

"How could I not when you were looking at me with those fuck-me eyes?"

"I was not," I pout.

"You were. Did Rylee teach you how to do that? I'll have to tell her you were spot on." He nods to the window. "I hope they're getting all this."

I look at the people outside with their cell phones and cameras and I'm reminded why we're doing this. Then I get upset with myself when I realize I wasn't acting. When I was looking at him, I wasn't thinking that I had to look a certain way because someone told me to or because it was written in a contract. I was looking at him because he's a gorgeous man who, despite his arrogance and crassness, seems to have me under some kind of spell.

I push my chair back and quickly stand up.

"Where are you going?" he asks.

"Bathroom. I need to wash up before I eat," I lie.

And as I'm walking to the back of the restaurant, I think about just how good I am at lying. Maybe practice makes perfect.

I stare at myself and shake my head at my reflection. "You can't feel like this," I tell the girl in the mirror. "He's not yours. He'll never be yours. And you don't want him to be."

I hear a toilet flush and I close my eyes. How could I be so stupid?

A woman comes out of a stall and looks at me in the mirror as she washes her hands. "Honey, you're crazy if you don't want that man," she says. "But I wouldn't object if you sent him over to me if you don't."

"I'm just being ridiculous," I say, walking into a stall and locking the door.

I stay behind the door until the woman leaves, giving myself a pep talk. A silent one this time. Then I walk back out to Sawyer, making a vow not to fall for him.

He's eating when I return. "It's good," he says. "I ordered you another drink."

"You didn't want to wait for me?" I ask, ready to give him another lesson on dating. Then I remember the pep talk. "Forget it. Let's eat."

He nods to my phone, not caring in the least about what I was going to say. "Bass called."

"What did he want?"

"I don't know. I didn't answer it. I just saw his name pop up. He texted you when you didn't answer. He wants you to look at some website."

I stare him down. Does he know no boundaries?

"What?" he says. "You left your phone sitting on the table face up, are you saying I'm not supposed to even look at it?"

I pick up the phone and read the text. I click the link to the website and my heart falls into my stomach when I read the article.

My face must go ashen.

"Are you okay?" Sawyer asks.

I shake my head. I'm not sure what I thought would happen, but I didn't think it would be this.

I give him my phone and let him read the screen.

He looks up at me and laughs. "You have a brother named Denver?"

"My parents were big fans of skiing. And Colorado."

"Were?" he says.

I nod.

"I guess I don't know very much about you," he says.

I point to my phone. "Looks like you're about to find out."

He reads silently, scrolling down the page to get to the full story. "Shit. He's going to prison?"

"Not if I pay off his debts."

Sawyer puts down the phone and narrows his eyes at me. "So this isn't about Juilliard after all, is it? Why is it up to you to pay off his debts? Especially when the article says he stole money from *you.*"

"He didn't steal money, Sawyer. He was duped. He thought he was investing it into a sure thing. He had the papers and the statistics. Everything seemed legit. He had no idea this was a Ponzi scheme. It was some higher-ups in the police department where he worked that got him into it. Now they have all his money, all my money, and all the money of a dozen other people in some off-shore account where it can't be traced or touched. And Denver took the fall for everything because he can't prove the others were involved."

"Damn. That's some tough luck. How much does he have to pay back?"

"Almost as much as you're paying me."

He picks at the tablecloth. "So, nothing will be left for Juilliard?"

I shrug. "There's always student loans."

"Fuck."

"It's fine. I'm not sure I want to go there anyway. I don't even like New York all that much. There is a good grad school back in Missouri that I've been considering."

"Missouri?" A look of disgust crosses his face. "But you have to be *here*. At least through October."

"I guess I'll cross that bridge when I come to it. I've been accepted at both places."

"You've been accepted at the school in Missouri? But you have to turn them down. You can't leave until the season is over."

I sigh. "I know. I'll turn them down. I guess I just miss Denver. We've always been close. I don't want you thinking bad things about him. He's a great guy who was just too naïve to be a cop."

"What do you care what I think of him?"

"Because he's the most important person in my life."

"I thought that was Bass," he says.

"Bass is right up there. But Denver is family."

"How much older is he?"

"About three minutes," I say.

"You're *twins?*"

I nod. "And I love him more than anything. We have a bond nobody seems to understand."

"I don't have any brothers or sisters," he says. "But that's a good thing."

I can't imagine growing up without a sibling. "Why is that a good thing?"

He shakes his head. "It just is. Now why don't you eat your dinner and tell me about your family."

I finish a slice of pizza in silence, contemplating what to tell him. He obviously has secrets of his own. Then again, my only secret was just plastered across the internet. He knows the worst thing about me, or about my brother anyway. What could it hurt to tell him about my family?

"My mom was a district court judge and my dad was a CFO for a mid-sized construction company. They both died in a car accident four years ago."

"I'm sorry. My parents are both dead, too."

"But at least I have Denver. You don't have any siblings. That must have been really hard on you."

"My mom dying was hard on me," he says. "My dad, not so much."

"Didn't get along with him?" I ask.

"That's an understatement."

"Well, my family was very close. It was devastating. I was a freshman at Juilliard and Denver was still trying to figure out what to do after high school. He was working odd jobs to afford his own apartment. My parents were taking their first ever vacation without us. A celebration of their freedom, I guess. They went skiing, of course. But they never made it to the ski lodge. Their rental car skidded off the road in the snow. They weren't found for days. I like to pretend they died instantly, but I heard some of the doctors talking and they said they were trapped in the car and probably died of exposure, not injuries. I don't imagine they died at the same time and it must have been horrible for one of them to watch the other go."

"Maybe they both died in their sleep," he says. "In the movies, everyone falls asleep in the cold and then they just don't wake up. Maybe they fell asleep together, in each other's arms."

My lips curve up in a half-smile. Maybe Sawyer Mills *does* have a romantic bone in his body after all. "I hope that's what happened. But knowing how much my dad loved my mom, I can't imagine he would have let them fall asleep. He would have done anything to keep her alive. Anything."

"Yeah, my dad loved my mom a lot, too. Maybe too much."

"How can you love someone too much?" I ask.

He shrugs and picks at his pizza. "So, your parents must have left you pretty well off if you could keep going to school at such a prestigious place."

"They did. They were good like that. And luckily, I'd paid off all my tuition before I let Denver invest the rest."

"How much did he lose?"

"Of mine? A few hundred thousand. Even more of his own."

"He invested his own money?"

"Yeah, you'd think that would prove he wasn't a criminal, but the prosecution didn't buy it. They said he was willing to risk his own money to make so much more."

"What is he doing now? To get by?"

"He's taking whatever jobs he can get. But few people will hire someone with a felony record. So he usually ends up working jobs under the table, which only last for days or weeks at a time and don't pay that well."

"That sucks. How old is he?" Then his head falls back and he looks at the ceiling. "Oh, shit. You said that night we first met that you were almost twenty-three. That means he was too. And it also means I missed your birthday, doesn't it?"

"It was Thursday."

"Thursday? Why didn't you say anything?"

I lean in so nobody can overhear. "Because I'm not your girlfriend and you have no obligation to take me out for my birthday, that's why."

He shakes his head. "Still, you should have said something." He lifts his glass. "To the birthday girl. Now let's drink to you and then I'm going to give you a birthday kiss. And this one's going to be just like the one at the club last week. Do you remember that?"

Remember it? I relive that kiss over and over in my dreams. I relive that kiss and more. In my dreams he's in my bed. In my dreams, he brings me to orgasm every which way possible. In my dreams he's the man I never knew I wanted but would do anything to have. And they just seem so damn real.

"No," I lie. "But I imagine you'll show me."

I take a long drink, eyeing him from over the rim of my glass, seducing him with my eyes for the many onlookers. My panties become damp with the anticipation of what his lips are about to do to me. My mind knows this is all a game, but my body doesn't seem to care.

He puts down our drinks, places a hand behind my neck, and pulls me to him. His eyes lock with mine until our lips meet. His tongue begs for entrance into my mouth and I taste the strong flavor of his wheat beer. One of his hands works the nape of my neck, the other falls to my lap and caresses my thigh. I'm lost in his kiss. In his touch. If this is acting, I'm afraid to know what his real kisses would feel like.

I immediately pull back when I realize his kisses are just like that first one he gave me the day we met. Or at least I think they are. That whole night is a bit fuzzy.

"What is it?" he asks.

"The night we met, when you kissed me in the alley, was that a *real* kiss, or were you just pretending, like now?"

"I wasn't pretending. I didn't know then that I was going to ask you for this arrangement. Why?"

I try not to smile when I think that maybe he isn't acting after all. No way could a man be this good a kisser if he's kissing someone he doesn't want to be kissing. He wants me. He wants me just like I want him.

The problem is – neither of us wants to admit it. Or maybe the problem is neither of us feels we can.

"Just wondering," I say.

"Well, if you're done wondering, can we get on with the show?"

This time, *I'm* the one who reaches out and pulls him to me. I might as well have some fun as long as I'm stuck in this situation. I'm going to see how far I can take this and how long he can resist before he admits to having real feelings for his fake girlfriend.

"Next time, don't start eating until your date comes back to the table," I whisper into his mouth, right before my lips reach his.

He tries to reply, but my tongue enters his mouth and I devour him like I've never done before. My body screams to be closer to his, but sitting next to him makes it impossible, so I just put my hands on his arms and feel the muscles of his biceps.

A slow growl emerges from his throat, letting me know he's getting into this more than he'd like me to think he is. It's hard to smile and kiss at the same time, but I pull it off. I pull it off until someone clears their throat behind us.

We stop kissing and look up to see the owner standing cross-armed and staring at us like a couple of adolescents who got caught making out in the back seat of a car.

Sawyer laughs. "Sorry, Henry. I just can't help myself around her." He pulls out his wallet and throws a fifty on the table. "We're leaving anyway. Our work here is done." He winks at me and stands up, waiting for me to follow.

I don't fail to notice, however, that his pants have a bulge in the front that wasn't there before. He grabs my hand and leads me outside. He pretends he doesn't want us photographed, but I know he does so I try my best to look presentable as we push through the crowd.

When we get in the cab, he says, "I wonder how long it will take those pictures to show up."

My phone pings with a text from Bass. I look at it and laugh. "Not long," I say, showing Sawyer the picture Bass texted me of us kissing just minutes ago.

"Sweet!" he says.

"How did he get it so quickly?" I muse aloud.

"He subscribes to a website that sends him alerts any time something is posted about me."

My jaw drops. "Why would he do that?"

"Because he wants to protect you," he says. "He threatened to kick my ass if I put you in harm's way."

"Are you putting me in harm's way?" I ask.

"I'll do my best not to. But after today, you'll have to be more careful about everything you do. Reporters will want to know everything about you. Right down to every scar and every tattoo."

"I don't have any tattoos."

"I know you don't," he says, knowingly.

"How could you know? I've never told you."

He looks out his window. "Uh, I just meant you're not the kind of girl who gets a tattoo. I can tell."

I remember what he told me earlier about his ritual. "But *you're* the kind of guy who gets them." I nod to his ribs. "Show me."

He looks at the driver who seems to be ignoring us. Then he untucks his shirt and lifts up the side. I turn on my phone's flashlight to get a good look. At first glance, it's a butterfly, but it's one of those pictures that, depending on how you look at it, can be two different things. It can also be a skull. It's the oddest thing I've ever seen. Yet I feel like I've seen it before.

"Wow," I say, tracing it with my finger. "It's horrible and beautiful at the same time."

He huffs out a breath.

"What?" I ask.

"Nobody has ever said that about it."

"Oh. I'm sorry."

"No. It's fine. It's exactly what I meant when I got it."

"Horrible and beautiful?" I ask, confused.

"Yes."

"Did you copy this from someone or something? I feel like I've seen it before."

He pulls his shirt down, looking uncomfortable. "It's not an original. I picked it off the wall of the tattoo parlor when I was eighteen. Maybe a lot of guys have the same one."

"Considering I haven't been with a lot of guys, that's most definitely not where I've seen it before."

He shrugs. "Maybe you saw it in a movie."

"I suppose. So, why did you get it?"

The cab stops in front of my building. "Here we are," Sawyer says, leaning over me to open the door.

I get out but he doesn't follow.

"Oh, no," I say, sticking my head back in. "You're walking me up, Tom Sawyer."

"I am?"

"You'd better believe it. You're walking me up now and after every date we have."

"But it's not a date," he says. He waves his arms at our surroundings. "And there's no one here to see us so what does it matter?"

I point to myself. "*I'm* here to see. And as long as we're doing this, I'm going to make sure you treat me properly. So get your ass out of the car and be a goddamn gentleman."

He laughs as he exits the cab. "Geesh, you've got quite a mouth for a lady."

"Based on that kiss at the restaurant, you should know."

"That I should," he says with a wink. "And that I do."

We walk up the front steps. "Five four nine seven," I say.

"What?"

"That's the code to get in," I tell him. "Because from now on, I'll be expecting you to come to my door."

He shakes his head and smiles. Then he pulls out his phone and types the code into his notes. "Is this part of my training? I told you before, there's no point."

We climb the two flights of stairs to my apartment and then I stop at my door. "Oh, there'll be a point. Someday in the future, there'll be a point. And when I see you one day with the woman who becomes your *real* girlfriend, I'll be able to take all the credit."

"You're wasting your breath," he says. "But I'll play along because you never can tell who might be watching."

"You'll thank me later," I say, putting my key in the door. "Goodnight, Sawyer."

He leans in and gives me a peck on the cheek. "Goodnight, Aspen."

I close the door behind me wondering why he kissed me just now. Nobody was watching. But that little kiss was all it takes to remind me of the bigger ones earlier. The ones that got me worked up. The ones that got *him* worked up. The ones that produced the bulge in his pants that I can't stop thinking about.

I walk back to my bedroom and open the bottom drawer of my night stand. If I can't have a real boyfriend, I might as well make good use of my battery-operated one.

Chapter Nineteen

Sawyer

The awesome crack of the ball hitting the sweet spot on my bat tells me I'm probably getting to second base on this one. I tear down the first-base line and the coach signals me to keep going. I can see the left fielder running to the far corner to get the ball and I know it'll be close. He picks up the ball and winds up for the throw. It's a race to see if I can beat it. The ball is in the air and the second-baseman shifts left so I know I need to go right. I know he has to tag me, so just as he catches the ball and tries to sweep it over me, I dive for the base, catching the outer edge of it with my fingertips just as the umpire calls me safe.

I stand up and brush off my jersey. "Maybe next time," I say to Devin Kirk, the Rays' second-baseman.

"Don't get cocky, Mills," he quips.

He's only half kidding. Devin was drafted by the Hawks the same year I was, but he ended up being traded to Tampa a year later.

Caden comes up to the plate. He's got two strikes on him when I take a big lead. The pitch is wild and I take off for third.

But the catcher must have stopped it, because it ends up in the third-baseman's glove.

Shit. I'm in a goddamn pickle. I turn around and head back for second, but the ball beats me there. I stop and pivot around and head back the other way. I'm fast, but I'm not faster than a thrown baseball. All I can hope for at this point is a mistake by one of the fielders. Otherwise, I'm toast.

I go back and forth, each time the fielders close in on me a little more until Devin Kirk finally tags me out with a smug smirk on his face.

The stadium erupts in displeasure as I make my way back to the dugout. I can't remember the last time I got caught in a pickle. I'm usually smarter than that. I'm usually faster than that. I look up to where Aspen and Bass are sitting – I can't make them out, but I know they're up there.

I throw my batting helmet into the corner of the dugout, hearing it crack as it hits the hard concrete.

Brady pats me on the back. He knows how much I hate to get caught on the steal. "Good try," he says.

I shake my head and look back into the stands. "She's a jinx," I say.

"Who's a jinx?"

"Aspen."

"You have to be kidding."

I look at him sternly. "I'm not kidding, Taylor. This is the fourth game she's been to and I've done something to fuck up in all four games."

He laughs. "Nobody's perfect, Mills. And you fuck up plenty when she's not here."

"I'm telling you, it's her."

He studies me. "Maybe it's not her. Maybe it's *you.*"

"Me?"

"Yeah. Maybe you're nervous about her being here."

I look at him like he's crazy. "I don't get nervous," I say.

He shrugs. "If you say so."

"I do."

He backs away and holds his hands up in surrender as I sit down on the end of the bench.

"You bringing the new girl tonight?" Spencer asks.

I nod.

"What's her name again? Boulder? Vail?"

"Very funny," I say. "It's Aspen, you jackass."

~ ~ ~

I put in the code to get into her building and walk up to the third floor. When she answers the door, I'm stunned. She has on a floor-length icy-blue dress that hugs her tightly in all the right places. I don't remember her buying this one when we went shopping.

"Nice dress," I say, still appraising her. "Is it new?"

"It is," she says, smiling at my obvious ogling.

"I'm supposed to buy your clothes, you know. I doubt you'll be wearing *this one* for any of your performances."

It has a plunging neckline that is far more revealing than she led me to believe she would wear.

"Murphy and I went shopping last week."

"Murphy? Really?"

"Yeah. We hang out sometimes. We do lunch and stuff. Rylee, too."

I had no idea she was getting along with my friends so well. We've all gone out a few times, and Murphy and Rylee have been a big help in making our relationship seem legit. Still, it could get awkward after Aspen and I part ways.

"I'm not sure all the *lunch and stuff* is a good idea," I say.

She waves me inside. "You're worried I might get attached to your friends?"

I shrug. "It might complicate things later on."

"Don't worry, boss," she says with a hint of irritation. "I know how things are."

She busies herself getting her purse, but I wonder if I've offended her. I'm not trying to dictate who she can have as friends, but surely she must understand what's what. I walk over and grab her elbow. "Don't call me *boss*," I say.

"How about *sir?*" she says with a snarky rise of her brow. "Or maybe *master?*"

"Hey, Sawyer," Bass says, emerging from his bedroom. "Damn. You clean up nicely."

I tug on the ends of my sleeve cuffs. "Glad *someone* noticed."

"I noticed," Aspen says. "You just didn't give me a chance to say anything."

She runs a hand from the breast pocket of my tux over to the lapel, smoothing it out as she goes. I feel the tightening in my shorts as I realize it's been so long since I've had a woman, that even a touch as innocent as this is giving me a semi.

"So. Big night," Bass says.

"Yeah. Everyone will be there right down to the guys who make the decision on whether I get to stay or go." I open up the door for her. "We'd better get going, our ride is double-parked. I'll catch you later, Bass."

I help her into the town car, making sure her long dress doesn't get caught in the door.

She smiles up at me. "You're getting better at this," she says.

"I just don't want my date to look like her dress came from Goodwill."

She rolls her eyes at me. "Of course you don't. So, how do you want me to play this?" she asks. "Do you just want me by your side, or do I need to pull out the dreamy eyes and fawn all over you?"

I laugh, thinking of the other times she's looked at me that way. Her looks make me hard, too.

"I usually don't let girls get all touchy-feely with me in public, so if you do, that will send a strong message to the powers-that-be."

"Dreamy eyes and grabby hands it is," she says.

"And kissing," I say. "I think we'll need some of that. Remember that salacious kiss at the pizza place?"

She tries to hide her smile. *Yeah, she remembers it, alright.*

"Some of those will do," I say.

I think I see her cheeks pink up, but the sun is setting so I can't be sure. One thing I am sure of is that she's nervous. Her hands are fidgety. I put a hand on top of them to calm her. "You don't have to worry, Aspen. It's basically just a big dinner party."

"When are you going to get it through that thick skull of yours that I don't live in your world? To you this may be just a dinner party. To me, it's a bunch of high-priced suits and their plastic wives who will be judging me into next week. We may be pretending, but that doesn't mean I don't care what people think of me."

"Everybody loves you. Haven't you been reading the articles?"

She shakes her head. "No, I don't do that anymore. I just know what Bass and Denver and some friends from school tell me."

"Well, it's all good. You are the proverbial girl next door. You're exactly what I needed you to be. Everything is perfect."

She shifts uncomfortably as she stares at my hand on top of hers. "Yeah, we're the perfect couple, aren't we?"

"Is something wrong?"

"No. I'll just be glad when this is all over."

I get a strange feeling in the pit of my stomach. "When what is all over, tonight or our arrangement?"

"Tonight," she says.

Another strange feeling washes over me. I think it might be relief.

The car comes to a stop. I squeeze her hand when I see all the people pouring into the venue past the photographers on the red carpet.

Aspen's eyes go wide. "You didn't say anything about a red carpet. Oh, my God, is that Jennifer Lawrence over there?"

"Come on. We've been photographed a hundred times by now. And you look terrific. Just think of all the great things they'll say about what a hot couple we are."

She turns to me and gives me a hard stare. "Is that all you care about? How hot we look together?"

"All I care about is saving my job, Aspen. And if us looking hot together makes that happen, then yes." I reach up and run my thumb across her pouty lips. "Now paint a smile on those lips and earn your paycheck."

She looks at me. I can tell she wants to argue, but she doesn't. She inhales deeply and blows out a breath so long and slow I can practically see the tension leave her body. "Fine," she says. "I'm going to be the best damn girlfriend money can buy."

"That's the spirit," I say, just as an attendant opens the car door for us to get out.

We make our way up the red carpet and stop several times to pose for photographers. For one picture, Aspen leans into me and puts her hand inside my tux jacket, right over my heart. I look down at her and smile. Damn, she's good. This will make for one hell of a picture.

Luckily for Aspen, we're seated at a large table with Brady and Rylee. Caden and Murphy are across the room with some other teammates. Rylee helps when people come by and ask questions about Aspen and me. She gushes about how cute a couple we are and how perfect we are for each other.

By the time dinner is over, we've become the talk of the benefit. And when the dance floor opens up, I pull Aspen onto it so everyone can see us dance.

"Isn't this a little over the top?" she asks when I dance as close as I can get to her without being overly indecent.

"They're eating it up," I say. "See that guy over there with the bald head by the bar? He's my manager. He hates me. And I'm sure he hates this. *Us.* I'm sure it's why he hasn't introduced himself to you like everyone else has. He's been watching us closely all night."

"And he makes the decisions?" she asks.

"He and Jason, the team owner who you met before dinner. Jason has the final say, which is good, because if it were only up to Rick, I'd be long gone by now."

I feel a tap on my back and turn around to see Rick standing behind me.

"Mind if I cut in?" he asks. "I haven't had the chance to meet your lovely date."

I don't miss the fact that his words are dripping with resentment and sarcasm.

Aspen shakes her head just enough to let me know she doesn't want to dance with him. But I step aside anyway. She's got this. And maybe this is exactly what I need to get him off my back.

"Okay, but I can't stand being away from her for too long."

He laughs disingenuously. "I don't blame you."

I back away and watch the two of them dance and talk. I even see Rick laugh a few times. She's charming him. It's goddamn perfect.

Then halfway through the song, Conner cuts in and dances with Aspen. Then Spencer. Then Benham. I feel myself getting angrier by the minute watching Aspen laugh with all of them. I can't seem to help myself when I storm forward and push Benham out of the way. I hold up my hand and stop Cole, who looks like he was going to be next in line.

"That's it for dancing with my girl," I growl at them. "She's all mine for the rest of the night."

Aspen giggles as Benham and Cole back away. "Wow, you *are* getting good at this. You're very convincing as the jealous boyfriend."

I narrow my eyes at her, wondering what the hell she's talking about. "The press needs to be taking pictures of *us*, not you with them."

She lunges forward and into my arms. Then she whispers, "Dance with me, Tom Sawyer."

The drinks she had at dinner are definitely kicking in. She presses herself against me and I put an arm around her to pull her even closer. I'm not much of a dancer, but with her I don't even have to try to be. It's like we move together in a way I've never moved with anyone else. Then again, I don't dance much. Not like this anyway.

"Is that a gun in your pocket?" she jokes, looking down between us.

"Well, what do you expect when you're grinding yourself against me?"

Amusement dances in her eyes. Then I look at her lips. Her cherry-red lips that I've been wanting to kiss all night. I don't even look around to see if any cameras are pointed at us when I lean down and capture her mouth with mine.

She tastes good. She looks good. She feels good. My mind goes crazy thinking back to the night I had her. She has no idea that she's the only woman I've ever wanted more than once. And the thought of it makes me even harder. If I don't pull away, I'm bound to throw her against the nearest wall.

"Is everything okay?" she asks when I take a step back.

"Yeah." I put my hands back on her waist, trying to keep some distance between us. "I just need to think of something other than your lips for a minute or I can't promise I won't take you into the back hallway and have my way with you."

She follows my eyes down to the front of my trousers and laughs. When her eyes find mine again, she's blushing. And she bites her bottom lip. *Holy fuck that's sexy.*

I raise my eyebrows at her. "It can be arranged, you know, you and me finding a dark hallway to get it on."

"While that might just be the most romantic proposition I've ever gotten, I think I'll pass," she says sarcastically.

"Come on, Aspen. Do I really have to go five more months? You can't tell me dancing like this with me doesn't do anything to you. I can tell it does. We're both adults here. Why can't we just let it happen? It's clear we're hot for each other."

"Let it happen?" she says bitterly. "Sawyer, you're *paying* me to give you fuck-me eyes. You're *paying* me to kiss you and grind against you on the dance floor. I'm *not* letting you pay me to sleep with you."

"What if I fire you and then re-hire you again tomorrow – then could we have sex?"

Her jaw drops. "No, then we could not have sex. You're crazy."

She tries to pull away, but I pull her back towards me. "Fine. But you'd better talk about something to get my mind off it. I've got a painful boner going on thanks to you."

"Okay, let's talk about my graduation next week."

"Your graduation? What about it?"

"You're planning on coming, aren't you? It's Saturday night."

"Why would I do that?"

Her luscious cherry lips turn into a sour pucker. "You're kidding, right? You need to come to my graduation, Sawyer. It's what any boyfriend would do."

"But it's a night off. I have other plans."

The truth is, I totally forgot about her graduation and I had made plans to go see Danny since we have an early game that day.

"Plans? What plans?"

"I don't have to tell you everything I do, Aspen."

"With the girl at the beach?"

I roll my eyes. "There is no girl at the beach."

She steps back, releasing my hold on her. "Maybe I don't believe you."

"Maybe I don't care what you believe."

"You can be a real asshole, you know that?"

"Hey, you two," Rylee says, coming up next to us. "If I didn't know better, I'd think you were bickering like an old married couple."

"What?" Aspen and I both say to her at the same time.

She laughs. Then she waves her hand at our surroundings. "Do you really want everyone to see you fighting? What are you arguing about anyway?"

"He doesn't want to come to my graduation," Aspen says.

"She doesn't want to sleep with me," I tell her. "Even though she clearly wants to."

Rylee shakes her head and then drags us off the dance floor behind her. "First off, you have to go to her graduation, Sawyer. It'll be good for you to make an appearance at something in her life. And second, are you out of your mind asking her to sleep with you? It's against the terms of your contract and it would ruin everything you have going. Do you really want to do that?"

"I just thought—"

"You just thought you'd get a quick lay like you always do. Well, you can't think like that anymore." She motions to my pants. "Now go splash cold water on your face before you hurt someone with that thing."

She hooks elbows with Aspen and they head off in the other direction, Aspen looking over her shoulder at me with a triumphant stare. The woman is infuriating sometimes. I don't see what the big fucking deal is. We're two consenting adults. Why can't we sleep together and still have a professional relationship? Hell, even my lawyer was able to handle it.

I stumble down the hallway to the bathroom, aware that maybe I should stick to water for the rest of the evening. The wine was flowing freely at dinner. Mostly because the more you drink, the more zeros you're likely to write on the check before the evening is out.

Just before I make it to the bathroom, I get pulled aside into a dim hallway.

A blonde woman, with breasts that are overflowing from her dress, backs me into a corner. "Sawyer Mills, I've been wanting to do this all night," she says, jumping up onto me so I have no choice but to catch her.

Her lips crash down on mine. She tastes of vodka and cigarettes – not nearly as good as Aspen tasted. I try to put her down, but her legs clasp onto me like a vice.

"The women's bathroom locks," she says. "Want to join me for a quickie?"

I look at her for a few seconds too long. Long enough for her to think I'm contemplating it. Long enough for *me* to think I'm contemplating it. I mean, in all fairness, it *has* been a long time for me. Over a month in fact. Can I really be expected to be celibate that long? Can any man?

But then I focus on her face, taking in her smeared lipstick and fake eyelashes, and I want to kick myself for even thinking about it. And the reason I want to kick myself is not because of the contract or my job. The reason I want to kick myself is because she's not Aspen. And in this moment, I realize I don't want to sleep with anyone who isn't her. And the realization guts me. It guts me because having Aspen isn't in the cards. Truly having *any* woman isn't in the cards. Not for me anyway. And I wonder if being with the one woman I want but can never have is a cruel twist of fate.

"Get off me," I say to the woman.

Then someone walks around the corner and almost runs into us. "I'm sorry, I was looking for the—"

Aspen's eyes go wide when she sees me holding a woman in a compromising position. She looks from the woman back to me, just shaking her head.

"It's not what you think," I say, trying again to put the woman down. Once I have her off me, I reach out for Aspen. "She jumped up on me. It's nothing."

She looks at the woman. "Yeah, I can see that," she says. "The *nothingness* is written all over her face."

She turns to walk away, but I grab her arm and pull her back. "She's nobody," I say.

Aspen shakes her head at me and I think I see her eyes get glassy. "And that's exactly why you're an asshole." She rips her arm out of my hand. "We're done. This is done. You can go to hell."

Aspen turns and runs down another hallway. The woman grabs me and holds me back. "Let her go. I'm here and willing."

"Just stop," I say, removing her hand from me.

The woman calls out after me as I race down the hallway and open all the doors to try and find Aspen. But she's gone. One of the doors leads to the outside and I can just make out the bottom of her dress as she pulls it into a cab and shuts the door.

Chapter Twenty

Aspen

I put down the phone, still angry over what Sarah told me. But I know she's right. The contract specifically states 'if he was found to have had sexual relations with another woman.' I was stupid not to amend it to cover all activity including kissing and whatever else Sawyer and the skank were doing last weekend.

I look at the tabloid magazines sitting on my coffee table. This is exactly what I wanted to avoid. It makes me out to be just another one of his throwaways. *Trouble in Paradise,'* one headline reads. *'It was only a matter of time,'* boasts another.

Nobody got a picture of Sawyer and the woman I saw him with, but that doesn't matter. They're posting old pictures of him and random women to make it look like I've been getting played all along. I can't even count how many of my classmates and friends have called to console me over our breakup.

But the thing is, when it comes down to it, I had to admit to myself that I was jealous. That I've fallen for a guy who isn't capable of being with one woman. And even if he were, he wouldn't choose the one he hired to play a part.

My ridiculous fantasy of him becoming that guy I met the first night, of him falling for me the way I've fallen for him, of the two of us living happily-ever-after – it's all a silly dream. One I know I've been fighting since day one.

I don't even know how it happened. He's not that great of a guy if I'm being honest. He's self-centered. He has no idea how to treat a woman. And his arrogance knows no bounds. Why would he think he wouldn't have to go to my graduation? It's ludicrous.

I've read his texts and emails a dozen times. Each one seemed more desperate. He claimed he was cornered by that woman. That she came on to him and it had just happened when I ran into them. He practically begged me to let him come over. He *did* come over, but I had Bass turn him away.

But the memory of that woman and her smeared lipstick. And the reality that he'd just said he wanted to find a dark hallway and have sex with me. It all adds up to the fact that he's an arrogant liar. Maybe he's been sleeping around all along but has just been very discreet about it.

"Come on, beautiful, you can't be late for your own graduation," Bass says, looking all handsome in his dress shirt and tie. "And I told Brooke we'd pick her up on the way."

"She really likes you," I say.

He nods. "Yeah, I know."

I narrow my eyes at him. "You don't like her? She's very pretty. And nice. She's the only one of my classmates who hasn't tried to get something out of this whole deal of my friendship with a famous baseball player."

"She got courtside seats," he reminds me.

"But she didn't ask for them."

"So, there's still a deal?" he asks.

I look at the ground. "Yeah. Technically, he didn't violate the contract."

"I'm still not sure why you're so pissed, Penny. You've been moping around the apartment all week. You should be excited. You're graduating. You're getting a shit-ton of money. You can go to grad school. And Denver will stay out of prison." He sees me staring at the tabloid on the table. He runs a hand through his hair. "Shit. You've fallen for the guy, haven't you? It's the only thing that makes sense."

I shrug and try to swallow the tears that threaten to fall.

"Mother fucker," he says, going over to sit on the couch.

He looks mad. Really mad. But more than that, he looks hurt.

"You know it can't happen, don't you?" he asks. "The guy is a womanizer. If you didn't know that before last weekend, you do now. He begged you to sleep with him and when you said no, he grabbed the next person in line. He's not worth it, Aspen. He's not worth your thoughts, your time, and especially not your tears." He stands up and wipes his thumb under my eye to catch one that's fallen.

I shake my head. "I don't know how it happened, Bass. It just did. I don't *want* to like the guy. And when we're apart, I think of all the reasons I shouldn't. But when we're together, something about us just clicks. The way he looks at me, touches me."

"He's paying you to click with him, surely you must realize that. You are his fake girlfriend. He's pretending to like you so he can stay with the Hawks. That's all this is."

"I know. But sometimes I think maybe there's more. He's a baseball player, not an actor."

"His job is on the line. He will do anything to save it."

I nod. Everything Bass is saying is true. Everything he's saying is what I tell myself each night before I go to bed. It's what I tell myself every time Sawyer touches me.

"I didn't mean to fall for him," I say. "I don't want to feel this way. But my mom used to tell me that you can't help who you fall in love with. That the heart wants what it wants."

"Love?" he says abhorrently. "You're in *love* with the guy?"

"I – I don't know. Maybe not. Maybe I'm just infatuated with him and his celebrity and his money."

He shakes his head in disgust. "Since when have you given a rat's ass about someone's fame and fortune? Fuck, Penny, I can't believe this." He looks at his phone. "Damn it, we're going to be late. We have to go. Let me get my jacket."

He goes back into his bedroom and I'm pretty sure I hear him say a few more choice words, and I can't be sure, but I also think I hear him throw something against the wall.

Thirty minutes later, Bass, Brooke and I arrive for graduation.

"I can't believe we're graduating!" Brooke squeals, holding onto Bass's arm. "Oh, and did I tell you I got a job?"

"Congratulations," I say. "What will you be doing?"

"I'll be working with the children's symphony right here in New York."

"That's fantastic," I tell her. "I'm so glad you get to stay here. I know how much you like the city. Isn't that great, Bass?"

I have to nudge him.

"What? Oh, yeah. Congratulations. Nice job."

He seems completely uninterested in her and oblivious to just how much she likes him.

Brooke and I head back for the pre-ceremony instructions and Bass finds a seat in the auditorium. I can't help being upset as I look around at the people arriving. So many people are missing.

Mom. Dad. Denver. But I want to kick myself when I realize the one I miss the most is the person who cares about me the least.

I'm not sure why I thought he would show up. Maybe it was all the groveling he did over the past week. I thought maybe he would come as a gesture of goodwill. But Bass is right. Sawyer Mills cares about one thing and one thing only – Sawyer Mills.

"Come on," Brooke says, hooking my elbow with hers. "Let's go get our diplomas."

~ ~ ~

After the commencement speeches, my name is the first called as they hand us our diplomas in alphabetical order. I'm not nervous. I'm used to being on stage at Juilliard. But when I shake hands with the deans, my spine stiffens when I hear someone shout, "Way to go, babe!"

I turn in the direction of the voice and see Sawyer, Brady, Caden, Murphy and Rylee standing up next to Bass as they all cheer for me. I realize in this moment how grateful I am to have more than one person in the audience clap for me as I cross the stage.

Suddenly, my nerves hit and I become unsteady on my feet. I also feel bad for the next few graduates behind me, as Sawyer and his teammates have caused quite a stir in the auditorium.

I look over at them as I make my way back to my seat. Sawyer looks good. Like Bass, he's dressed for the occasion wearing a nice shirt and tie. He smiles seductively at me. I can't help but smile back. Tingles work up and down my spine as he looks at me. I've missed looking at him. I've missed talking to him. I've missed touching him.

I break our stare when I sit down. I promise myself I will remember what Bass said. Sawyer is not my boyfriend. He's using me. He's *paying* me. It's not real. But then why does it feel like it's nothing but?

I fidget the entire time I'm waiting for the other graduates to make their walks. But it doesn't take long as there are only a couple hundred – less than my high school graduation even.

When it's over, the president directs everyone to the reception hall. I find Brooke and then we find everyone else. Brooke has even fewer people here than I do. Unlike mine, her parents are alive. But they are off jet-setting around the globe and couldn't be bothered to come home long enough to see their only child graduate from college. She's never seemed that upset about it, however. I guess you get used to it after a while, growing up in boarding schools instead of in your parents' home.

Murphy and Rylee run over to hug me, offering me their congratulations.

"Thank you so much for coming," I say. "I thought Bass was going to be the only one clapping for me."

Rylee nods to Sawyer. "It was his idea that we all come."

"Really?"

"I guess when he thought about it, he knew it was the right thing to do. Sometimes he just needs a little nudge in the right direction, but he's a good guy, Aspen. I hope you know that."

I shrug. "Did he tell you what happened at the benefit?"

"He did. I believe he's telling the truth. And so do the guys. As far as we know, he's never lied to them, so why would he start now? Women want him. They will do almost anything to get him. You should give him the benefit of the doubt."

Sawyer walks over to me and kisses me on the cheek. "Congratulations," he says.

"Thanks for coming."

"I should have planned on it all along."

"Well, you're here. And I appreciate it. But I'm sorry you had to change your plans."

He looks down at me. "I didn't have plans with another woman, Aspen."

"Then why are you so secretive about it?"

"There are just some things I don't share with everyone. Not even Brady and Caden."

"Do you have a brother in prison or something?" I joke. "I can see you not wanting that to get out."

He laughs boisterously. "No, not a brother in prison. Just something I do for myself."

I look around to see many people staring at us. "What now?" I ask. "I'm sure you've seen the tabloids. We're supposedly broken up."

He puts his arm around me and pulls me close. "Those rumors will be put to rest by midnight. And speaking of midnight, I'd like to go home with you tonight."

My heart races. He has no idea just how much I want to bring him home and have him in my bed. I dream about it. I fantasize about his hands on my body and my lips on his tattoo.

I say the only thing I can. The only thing that will leave me with a shred of dignity. "No, Sawyer. I'm not sleeping with you."

"I know. You made that perfectly clear last Saturday. But we need to be seen sleeping over at each other's places. You'll have to get used to it sooner or later seeing as you'll be moving in with me in a few weeks." He reaches over and grabs two glasses of champagne from a tray, handing me one. "Come on, Aspen. I'll sleep on the couch."

I sigh deeply. How on earth am I going to manage living with the man if my heart beats this wildly just *standing* next to him? How am I going to handle being around him every morning and night when he's not traveling? Will I go into his room and lie on his bed when he's gone? Will I sneak a t-shirt of his and put it under my pillow so I can dream of him? *Oh, God*, will I see him in a towel when he gets out of the shower?

"Aspen?"

"Oh, sorry," I say, composing myself. "I suppose you can sleep on the couch. Bass will be there of course."

"To protect you?" he asks.

"I didn't say that."

"Do you think you need protection from me?" he asks, looking guilty.

"No. Not from you." *From myself, maybe.*

"What does that mean?" he asks, looking at me strangely.

I ignore his question as Bass, Brooke, and Brooke's roommate, Jordan join us. They are deep in conversation.

"Maybe you can post a sign for a roommate at the new freshman orientation this summer?" Jordan asks. "Surely there will be people who need a place to stay."

"Living with a freshman?" Brooke says. "I'd rather move."

"You need a roommate?" Sawyer asks.

"Are you applying for the position?" Brooke jokes.

"No, but I know someone who might."

Sawyer nods to Bass. "He's getting kicked out of his building at the end of next month."

"I, uh, was looking to live with someone from fire school," Bass says.

"Have you found anyone yet?" I ask.

"Not exactly."

"Then why not take Brooke's spare room?" I ask. "It's in a good location. You're both in need of a roommate. It's the perfect solution."

Bass shoots me an annoyed look. I don't know what the big deal is. Brooke is nice enough. He doesn't have to date her if he doesn't want to.

"That would be great!" Brooke hollers. "It would be a huge relief. What do you say?"

Bass looks at me and I nod in encouragement. I can practically see the wheels spinning in his head as he tries to think of a reason not to live with her. But he can't.

"Let me get back to you after I talk to a few of the guys that were looking into something," he says.

"Okay," Brooke says, looking hopeful. "I promise I'd be the best roommate. I won't play my cello too late at night."

I laugh. "Bass is the one who plays his guitar at all hours. You might want to soundproof his room."

He nudges me. "I thought you loved my guitar playing."

"I do. And I'll miss it."

"Are you moving out of New York?" Brooke asks. "Is that why Bass needs to find another roommate?"

Sawyer and I look at each other, just now realizing his blunder. We hadn't yet announced to anyone that we were going to live together.

"Uh, well we have to move out of the building because they are going to demo it and –" I try to think of a quick excuse.

"Oh, my God, are you moving in with Sawyer?" Jordan squeals, looking between the two of us.

Sawyer pulls me close and kisses my forehead. "It's fine," he says to me and the others. "We weren't going to tell anyone for a while, but yes."

"But I thought you broke up," Jordan says.

"Don't believe everything you read," Sawyer tells her. Then he raises his glass. "Since the cat is out of the bag, I guess we have a lot to celebrate," he says, loudly. "I'd like to make a toast."

Several groups of people surrounding us stop talking and turn around to listen to Sawyer speak.

"I'd like to toast this incredible woman standing next to me. At twenty-three, she's been through a lot, yet here she is graduating from one of the most prestigious music schools in the world." He takes in a deep breath and winks at me. "It's no wonder I'm in love with her."

What. The. Fuck?

Gasps are heard all around us and I think I hear Bass choke on his drink.

"So lift a glass with me and drink to Aspen Andrews," Sawyer says.

"Here here!" many people say as they all take a drink.

Then it feels like the room goes completely silent. He's stunned them. He's stunned *me*. The difference is, most of them think this is real.

Sawyer leans down and kisses me. Then he whispers, "This is when you say it back. Everyone's listening."

"I – I love you, too, Sawyer," I say with shaky words that may have just been barely loud enough for those standing around us to hear.

People erupt in cheers. Snapshots and videos of us are being taken from dozens of cameras. No doubt his toast – and thereby his declaration of love for me – will be on YouTube, TMZ and probably ESPN by night's end.

Then I realize how pathetic I am. I've just said the truest words I've ever spoken, yet this is all a lie.

"I can't believe you just did that," I say so only he can hear.

"Had to redeem myself after the shitstorm I caused last weekend."

"I thought you said it wasn't your fault."

"It wasn't, but I still needed to do damage control."

He leans down and kisses me again. I let him. Of course I let him. I melt into him. I let him wrap me in his arms and hold me.

And as he holds me like I've dreamed of being held, it dawns on me that just like my brother has, I've been handed a sentence. I'm sentenced to five more months of torture being in the arms of the man I love who will never love me back. And Sawyer's house will be my prison.

Chapter Twenty-one

Sawyer

"*I know you love baseball,*" she says. "*And if that's your dream, I want it for you. But remember to be kind, Sawyer. Be kind to yourself. Be kind to others. If you do that, everything else in your life will fall into place.*"

I nod my head. "*Okay, Mom.*" But I know she's lying. Things don't work out that way. She's the kindest person I know, but even at ten years old, I know her life didn't 'fall into place.' I may be young, but I'm not stupid. I know how things are.

"*Do you remember the story of the caterpillar?*" she asks.

I do. She's told it to me a dozen times. But I want her to tell it again, so I shake my head.

"*Baby caterpillars eat and eat and eat. They stuff themselves with leaves and get as big as they can. Then they find a safe place, usually on a stick, and they make a cocoon. Inside the cocoon, they go through a transformation. The caterpillar dissolves into a soupy substance and then rebuilds itself into a new body. But this transformation is not easy. It has to struggle. And it becomes exhausted, because apparently becoming a butterfly is hard work. But then something wonderous happens, it emerges from its cocoon as a beautiful creature with colorful wings. And it can fly. It can go anywhere and do anything. It becomes free.*"

She squeezes my hand extra hard and she starts to cry. It looks like she can't breathe very well.

"Mommy, are you okay?"

"I'm going to be a butterfly soon, my sweet boy. So I never want you to worry about me. I've had my struggle and now I'm going to get my wings. I'm going to be free."

I want to ask her what she means. I think maybe she's confused. She's said things today that don't make any sense. But before I can ask her, the nurse comes in and tells me I need to leave for a minute.

I go down the hall to the chapel where my dad likes to sit when he's not in the room with my mom. I open the door and see him praying on the bench in the front. He knows how to pray because we go to church sometimes. But I don't get why he's praying. What does God have to do with any of this?

I scoot onto the bench next to him and put my hands together and ask God to make Mommy feel better. Then I ask God to make Daddy sick in the hospital bed instead of her. But I know He won't listen. He never does. I've prayed so many times that I ran out of prayers.

I hear the doors open behind me and turn around to see a nurse nodding to my dad. Then Daddy cries out like someone just hurt him. He grabs my hand and pulls me back to Mommy's room. But when I get there, she's lying flat on the bed and her eyes are closed and she looks ... different.

Daddy walks over and collapses down onto her. I worry that he will hurt her, but when he gathers her into his arms, she still doesn't move. Her arms are like those of a rag doll. He cries into her hair.

The nurse comes up next to me and pulls me to her. "I'm so sorry," she says.

I wonder why she's sorry.

Then a man in a white coat walks into the room. I think he's Mommy's doctor. He makes Daddy put her down and he uses that thing around his neck that goes in his ears. He puts the other end over Mommy's heart. He looks at me sadly before he glances at the clock on the wall and says, "Time of death: ten forty-three."

Death? I look around the room to see everyone looking sad. My dad is still crying. I run over to Mommy to try and wake her up, but she doesn't move and her skin isn't warm like it usually is.

The doctor puts a hand on my shoulder. "I'm so sorry, son."

I remember the TV show I saw last week where someone died. She looks just like that person did.

Mommy died? She's dead?

I look at Daddy and get my answer. He looks awful. I've never seen him look so sad. My tummy starts to feel really bad and I need to get away from this. From him.

I run down the hallway until I find the stairs. Then I run down the stairs and out the front doors of the hospital where I throw-up into the bushes. He doesn't run after me. I'm glad he doesn't. It's all his fault and I don't want to see him. I don't want to go home with him. She was the only good thing about home. But I'm only ten. I know I don't have a choice.

I look around the parking lot. I'm not sure what for, a place to hide maybe. I see some kids like me, walking beside their mothers and it makes me cry even harder. I'll never get to walk next to her again.

And I'm mad at myself. If I had known when I saw her this morning that those were the last words I'd ever say to her, I would have made them better words. But I think she knew they were our last. She wouldn't let go of my hand. She knew she was going to die and she didn't tell me.

Out of the corner of my eye, I see something fluttering around. I turn to see a beautiful orange and yellow butterfly. It flies around the flowers by the sidewalk, then it flies around my head. It flies around my head for a long time. Then I watch it fly away. I squint hard and watch until I can't see it anymore.

Then I smile.

I smile because Mommy is a butterfly.

~ ~ ~

Hands on my body startle me and I lash out. Then I hear a cry and a thump. I sit up quickly and try to orient myself. I look around. I'm at Aspen's. I look down at the floor and see Aspen in the darkness holding her cheek.

"Fuck. What happened?"

She shakes her head. "I'm okay. I shouldn't have snuck up on you while you were sleeping. You got me with your elbow."

A sick feeling washes over me as I help her up onto the couch. I reach over and turn on the light. "Let me see."

"It's fine," she says. "You barely got me."

I jump up and go to her freezer in search of something to put on her cheek. I return with a bag of frozen broccoli. I sit next to her and press it to the red spot under her eye.

She tries to take the bag from me, but I don't let her. "Let me do it," I say.

Her lips curve up into a smile. "Is this you taking care of me?"

I shake my head, disgusted with myself. "This never should have happened."

"It's my fault," she says. "I heard a noise coming from the living room. It sounded like ..."

She's afraid to tell me.

"It sounded like what?" I ask.

"It sounded like you were crying, Sawyer."

"That's ridiculous. I don't cry."

"I guess you were having a dream," she says.

I shrug. I know I dream about my mom a lot. But no way do I cry. Aspen has obviously been hearing things.

I pull the bag away from her face, relieved to see there isn't any swelling.

She reaches up to touch her cheek. "See, I told you it was nothing."

"It's not nothing," I say, putting the ice back on.

"If you want me to be mad at you, it won't be because of this, it will be because of what you said earlier."

I narrow my eyes at her. "What did I say?"

"Oh, let's see – first you said we were moving in together and then you announced to everyone that you were in love with me."

"Why would you be mad at me for that?"

She sighs and rubs one of her eyes. "Sawyer, you need to tell me when you're going to do things like that. I need to know how to react."

I laugh, thinking back on it. She did look surprised. "Okay, I promise to give you a head's up before I propose."

Her eyes go wide and she pulls away from the ice pack I'm holding on her face. "What?" she shrieks.

"I'm only kidding, Aspen. I think living together is enough to mollify the organization."

She blows out a slow breath through pursed lips.

"You look tired," I say. "But you should keep the ice on your face for a while." I put a pillow on my lap and pat it. "Lie down on your right side, I'll hold the ice on you. Another ten minutes should do the trick."

She looks at the pillow on my lap like it might burn her. Then she hesitantly lies down on it. I belatedly notice what she's wearing and it makes me glad I have a pillow on my lap. She's wearing the skimpy Hawks sleeper set I sent over.

She catches me looking at her legs and pulls a blanket over her. "The ice is making me cold," she says.

It's a lie. She just doesn't want me ogling her. But damn, she's easy to ogle. And she has no idea what I've seen. No idea I've seen *all* of her. No idea I know every curve, dimple, and freckle of her body. No idea I dream of her at night.

Her hair is messy from sleep and I can't help myself when I brush a few strands off her face. She looks up at me with doe eyes and I have to shift her in my lap. *Fuck, I want this woman. I want her bad.*

"Am I allowed to go out of town?" she asks.

"You want to leave New York?"

"I want to go to Missouri to see Denver. He couldn't come for graduation and I know he's lonely. I'd really like to go see him for a week."

"Is he far from Kansas City?" I ask.

"About twenty miles."

"Do you think he would want to meet me?"

"Are you kidding?" she says. "It would be his dream come true. Does that mean you want to go with me? But, you don't get any time off, do you?"

"We have a series there in two weeks. We fly in on a Wednesday and stay through Sunday. If you go out a few days before we do, that will give you some extra time with him. Then you can bring him to the games."

Her eyes light up. "That could work."

"Kills two birds with one stone. People will see us traveling together and you'll get to see your brother."

"Together?" she asks. "As in you want me to stay with you in your hotel?"

"I think it would be a good thing. Besides, you'll have just moved into the townhouse, so it makes sense."

"Alright, but I want to stay with Denver for a few days before you arrive."

"Just let me know when you want to fly out and I'll make the arrangements."

"You don't need to pay for my plane ticket, Sawyer. You're paying me so much already."

"I'm paying. Now shut up about it and tell me about Bass and Brooke. What's up with them?"

"You noticed, too?"

"Yeah, but I can't figure them out."

"I think Brooke is way more into him than he's into her."

"What's not to be into?" I ask.

"I know, right? She's nice. She's beautiful. She's going to be gainfully employed. And she's got the perfect apartment for him."

"I saw his hesitation. Why doesn't he want to live with her?"

"Maybe because he doesn't want to date her and he doesn't want it to be weird."

I brush another stray hair from her face and feel her shiver under my touch. "Maybe it's because she's not you."

"Not me? What are you talking about?"

"In case you haven't noticed, your roommate seems to be taken with you."

"Bass? No way. We're just very good friends. You're reading too much into it."

"I'm a guy, Aspen. I know when another guy is into a girl. And he's into you. Think about it. Since I've known you, he's only taken Brooke out one time, and he seemed more interested in *me* than her."

"Well, you *are* a baseball star."

"But he can't score with me. You have to think like a guy here. He's got prime pus–, uh, he's got a sure thing, and he doesn't go for it? The only reason a guy would turn that down is because he wants another woman."

She yawns and her eyes grow heavy. "And you know this from experience, Mr. Certified Bachelor?"

I don't answer her question, mostly because it looks like she's falling asleep. But the truth is, I *do* know. I know because when that woman was all over me last week, I couldn't do it myself. She was ready and willing, and it would have been so easy to lock ourselves in the bathroom like she wanted. But I didn't. For the first time in my life, I took a pass.

With Aspen's eyes closed, I can take my time looking at her. She shifts her body and the blanket slips off one of her legs. I follow the curve of her leg up to her thigh where her shorts are riding up and exposing the fleshiness of her butt cheek. It takes all my willpower not to reach out and touch her there.

I avert my eyes, knowing she can probably feel my boner through the thin pillow under her head. When my eyes fall back onto her face, her tired eyes are open and she's staring up at me. I don't think I've ever seen her look more beautiful. The ice pack falls out of my hand as I cup her face and bring it up to mine. Then I kiss her.

Our lips are slow to savor each other. Our tongues almost touch when a noise behind me has me releasing her.

Bass clears his throat and pins me to the couch with his fiery stare.

"Sorry," I say to him. To her. "I guess I forget sometimes."

Aspen sits up quickly, looking embarrassed. I keep the pillow on my lap so Bass won't see exactly what she's doing to me.

"Well, don't," he says. "This isn't a game. This is her life. Aspen, are you okay?"

"I'm fine," she says, getting up off the couch. "I only came out for a few minutes because I heard a noise. I'm going back to bed."

She looks guilty as she walks past him. I wonder why she feels the need to explain anything to him. We're two grown adults. Maybe she knows he likes her but doesn't want to admit it. Or maybe she likes him and is waiting for this to be over so they can be together. Or maybe she's just upset because she let me kiss her.

She *should* be mad at me. I'm mad at myself. What the hell am I going to do when she moves in and wears that kind of stuff every night? What am I going to do when I know she's practically naked and in the next room? This is a bad idea. This is a very bad idea.

As soon as they both go back to bed, I hit the bathroom and take a cold shower. Then I slip out and go home.

Chapter Twenty-two

Aspen

I walk into the living room and see blankets folded neatly on the couch. Sawyer's gone. I'm confused because I thought the whole point of this was for people to see us leaving the apartment together in the morning.

"He's going to hurt you," Bass says.

I look over to see him sitting in the dark kitchen, drinking coffee.

I turn on the light. "Why are you sitting in the dark?"

He shrugs. "Why did you let him kiss you, Penny? Nobody was around to see. Do you think he wants you? For more than one night anyway? He doesn't. He'll use you like he uses everyone."

I pour myself a cup of coffee and sit down next to him. "I know, Bass. But I can't help the way I feel."

"So you'd sleep with him if he asked? Because that would make you a whore."

My jaw drops and my blood starts to boil. I can't believe he said that. "I'm not going to sleep with him, Bass. And if I did, it really would be nobody's business but mine."

"So you would."

"No," I say, mad that he'd even think it. "He asked last weekend and I turned him down."

"That was then, this is now. Last weekend you weren't kissing in private."

I shake my head, still confused over that myself. "I don't know what happened. We were tired. We weren't thinking clearly."

"Why were you even out there with him?"

"I think he had a nightmare," I say.

"He's a big boy, Penny. He can take care of himself. You're not responsible for him. He's going to drop you like a hot potato as soon as the season is over. He's going to break your heart if you let him."

"What would you have me do? End the arrangement and pay back all the money? Money I don't even have anymore?"

"If it means protecting you, then yes."

"I can't," I say.

"You mean you won't. Because you like him."

I shrug.

"Open your eyes, Aspen. Stop being romanced by the fame and fortune and see what's right in front of you."

"What are you talking about?"

Suddenly, he leans over the table and pulls me to him, his lips crashing down on mine before I even realize what's happening.

I pull away. "Sebastian, stop it!"

"Can't you see that he's not the guy for you? I'm right here and I love you."

"You *love* me?"

He points his finger between us. "You and me, we're perfect for each other. We both love music. We're best friends. We know everything about each other. It makes sense."

"Except I don't see you that way, Bass. We tried this once. I thought we agreed that we were better just as friends."

"You decided that. Not me."

I stare at him thoughtfully. "All this time? Why didn't you say anything?"

"I thought you'd come around eventually."

"Oh, Bass." I put my head in my hands, guilty over the fact that I can't reciprocate his feelings. Because he's right – we *would* make the perfect couple. But I can't force myself to love him. Even if I didn't love Sawyer, I couldn't force myself.

"So that's it?" he says, looking dejected.

"I'm – I'm so sorry."

He gets up and throws his coffee cup in the sink, breaking it in the process. Then he walks to his bedroom. "I'm moving in with Brooke," he says, right before going through and slamming his door.

I wipe the tears from my eyes as I sit in stunned silence. Two men have said they love me in the last twenty-four hours. No man other than those I'm related to has ever said those words to me, and now it's happened twice. But my tears fall because I love both of them. One I love like a brother. The other I love from the pit of my stomach to the end of my soul – a love that I know will crush me. Bass is right. Sawyer is going to break my heart. And I'm going to let him. Because leaving now would hurt even more.

And because I'm a stupid, stupid girl.

~ ~ ~

The ringing of my phone wakes me. I guess I fell asleep when I came back in my room and laid on my bed to think things through.

It's my brother.

"Hello?"

"You're moving in with him? And you're in *love?* When the fuck did this happen? When we talked three days ago you were done with him."

He obviously saw one of the many videos all over TV and social media.

My head falls back against the pillow. Why did I call and pour my heart out to Denver last week? He consoled me over my 'breakup.' He told me I was better off without a man who couldn't stay away from women. He thought the whole thing was real. And I know from how I must have sounded, that I probably did, too.

The lines have become blurred. My head understands this is all an arrangement. My heart, on the other hand, doesn't seem to grasp the idea.

"I changed my mind."

"You changed your mind? Aspen, you tossed the guy to the curb because he fucked another woman."

"He didn't sleep with her, Den. All they did was kiss and only because she cornered him. He had nothing to do with it."

"And you believe him?"

It's a question I've asked myself a thousand times this past week. And I'm not sure I know the answer, given Sawyer's track record.

"Yes. I do. Women throw themselves at him all the time. She jumped up on him. He had no choice but to catch her."

"And what do you think would have happened if you didn't walk in on them?"

Visions of Sawyer and the woman assault my mind. The truth is, I just don't know.

"I trust him," I lie. "And that's all that matters."

"I worry about you, Pen. Something just seems off with you."

"Don't worry. I have everything covered."

He's always been able to tell when I'm not myself. I don't know if it's the twin thing or just the fact that we're so close. But I'd better do something to change the subject – and fast, before he calls bullshit.

"Hey, by the way, I'm coming home for a visit in a few weeks."

"You are?"

I can practically hear the smile splitting his face in two.

"The Nighthawks are playing in Kansas City for four days. I thought I'd come out a few days early and stay with you for a couple of nights."

"Holy shit. Does this mean …?"

I laugh. "Yes, this means you will meet Sawyer and some of the guys. But only if you promise not to be a driveling idiot."

"Cross my heart and hope to die. Oh, my God. That will be incredible. Wait 'till I tell … oh, who am I kidding, I don't have any friends anymore."

I feel terrible that he's stuck in a place that abhors him.

"I can't wait to see you, Denver. I really really miss you."

"I miss you, too," he says sadly. "Are you sure everything is okay?"

"Yeah."

"Promise?" he asks.

"Twin promise," I say, feeling guilty as hell that I've tainted the sacred vow.

Chapter Twenty-three

Sawyer

I open the door for Aspen, Bass and Brooke. They stand next to a pile of boxes. I look out front for a moving truck. There isn't one.

"Is this all you have?" I ask.

"Brooke and I will make one more trip, but this is most of it," Bass says.

"Our apartment came furnished," Aspen tells me. Then she looks embarrassed. "Oh, gosh, was I supposed to bring my own bed?"

I look over her shoulder at Brooke. Then I pull Aspen into my arms. "Why would you need a bed, babe? Besides, I've already got a nice guest room for whoever might need to stay with us. I was just going to move all the furniture to the basement if you wanted to put your old stuff there, but now I don't need to." I lean down and grab one of the boxes. "Come on in."

"*Sorry,*" Aspen mouths to me when she realizes her blunder.

As soon as she walks into the foyer, she sees what I had purchased and the expression on her face is priceless.

"You—" She points to the baby grand piano in the front sitting area. "You bought a piano?"

"Do you like it? The guy from the piano store said it's a good one."

She walks over and runs her hand across the glossy black finish. "Did you get this for *me?*"

"Well, I don't know any other concert pianists, so ... yes."

She looks over at Bass and Brooke, now remembering with Brooke here, she has to keep up appearances. She throws her arms around me. "Oh, thank you. It's perfect."

She pulls my head down and kisses me. *Shit.* I didn't realize how much I missed putting my lips on her. We were gone an entire week, going straight from Minnesota to Wisconsin. It's been six days since I've seen her. Six days since I left her apartment after kissing her in front of no one at all. And I spent the week justifying why I did it. I was tired. I had too much to drink. I was trying to forget my dream. But as I kiss her now, everything comes rushing back.

I want her. I want her bad.

I pull away, wishing Brooke weren't here so we wouldn't have to touch each other. "Anything for you, Aspen," I say.

Brooke grabs Bass's arm and pulls him over to look at the piano. I don't miss that she's draped over him like a cheap suit. But for the life of me, I can't figure out if he's enjoying it or not. The look on his face gives nothing away.

I turn to Bass, "Why don't you and I go get the rest of Aspen's things? The girls can stay here and put stuff away."

Aspen narrows her eyes at me, giving me a scolding look. "Uh, why don't we just pile my boxes in your spare room? That way we won't junk up the master and I can take my time unpacking."

Right. Damn. If she unpacks with Brooke here, she'll have to put all her shit in my bedroom and then move it later. For a minute, I forgot she's not moving in for real.

"I don't mind helping you," Brooke says.

"No, that's okay. I think I'd like to check out the piano and get the lay of the land so I know where to put all my things."

"You haven't been here before?" Brooke asks, curiously.

"Of course I have," Aspen says quickly. "But now that we're making it permanent, everything has changed. Like that monstrosity on the wall. I think it will have to go."

She knows my signed and framed Rickey Henderson jersey is one of my most prized possessions. I look over at her to see the smirk on her face. She's just messing with me.

"Come on, Bass, let's head out." I walk over and give Aspen another kiss. Then I point to the wall with the jersey. "It better be here when I get back."

"Or else?" she says with a cocky smile.

"Or else I may have to give you a spanking."

Her face flushes when I say it. My dick twitches. Oh, Lord, these next months are going to be torture.

~ ~ ~

"So you and Brooke seem pretty chummy," I say to Bass, on our walk back to their place.

He shrugs. "She's okay."

"But she's not Aspen," I say knowingly. *All* too knowingly.

He stops walking and looks at me.

"Oh, come on," I say. "It's obvious you want her."

"I – I …"

"It's okay, man. I get it. She's nice and gorgeous and talented. Who wouldn't want that?"

"You," he says belligerently. "*You* wouldn't want that. You're going to hurt her, Mills. This may be just a game to you, a way to keep your job, but you must know women can't separate their feelings like we can. I see how she reacts when you touch her. That's not just acting. She's into you. And it's not going to get any easier for her. She's doing this for her brother. She doesn't have a choice. She can't just walk away no matter how much this will hurt her in the end."

I take a step back and run a hand through my hair. "She told you this?"

"Not in so many words. But I've known her for four years."

"But she thinks I'm an asshole."

"You *are* an asshole," he says, shaking his head. "Apparently she's attracted to assholes."

I absorb what he's telling me. She wants me? Like I want her. I look to the sky. This is bad. I knew it didn't matter if it was just me who was doing all the wanting. That I can handle. I know it can never go anywhere and I know how to handle it.

Hurting Aspen was not part of the plan. But we're in too deep now. She's moving in. Things are going perfectly.

We walk up to their apartment to pick up two more boxes and her keyboard. Bass hits the bathroom before we head out. While I'm waiting, my phone rings and I see that Danny is calling.

"Hi, buddy," I say, keeping my voice down until I can walk into Aspen's room.

Standing in the doorway, I realize I'm back in Aspen's bedroom for the first time. It looks different. There aren't any sheets on the bed. No clothes strewn over the chair. But the smell – the smell of her is still here. I sit on the mattress and take it in.

"I caught a fish," Danny says.

My eyebrows shoot up in surprise. "What? That's great. Did your mom take you fishing?"

"We went to the zoo. They let you fish there. But you gotta put them back, so they can keep swimming."

"That sounds like a lot of fun. Did your mom tell you I'm coming to see you tomorrow?"

I hear a thump and surmise he dropped the phone in excitement. I can't get over how excited he always gets when I visit. I thought that would have worn off by now.

"Can we throw the football?" he asks.

"Sure. We can do whatever you want to do."

"Can we throw a baseball?"

"Absolutely."

"Okay, see you tomorrow."

"See you tomorrow," I say, just as I look up and see Bass walking past Aspen's doorway.

He stops and puts his hands up on the door jam, looking at me accusingly.

"How much of that did you hear?" I ask.

"Enough to know you're going somewhere with someone tomorrow and that you've promised to do whatever she wants you to do." His face turns red in anger. "What the fuck are you up to, Mills?"

"It's not like that," I say.

"You seem to be saying that a lot lately. How can you expect Aspen to hold up her end of the contract when you aren't upholding yours?"

"I'm upholding the contract. I'm not seeing anyone. That wasn't even a woman on the phone."

"You're lying," he says.

"I'm not, but I don't have to answer to you, Briggs."

"The hell you don't if has to do with hurting my best friend."

"You mean the woman you love."

When he doesn't respond, I tell him, "What I'm doing tomorrow will not hurt her, or anyone. I assure you. Just leave it alone."

"I don't trust you." He shakes his head and turns to walk away. But then he spins around. "You have to tell her you don't want her. You have to tell her every day and make her hear it. It's the only way you'll keep her from getting hurt when this whole thing ends."

I've never been a guy to talk about my feelings with other guys. But Bass loves her. He loves her in every way and he's just looking out for her. I walk back into the living room and sit on his couch.

"What if I said I'd be lying if I told her that?"

He closes his eyes briefly and sighs. *He's* the one I'm hurting now.

He walks over and sits across from me. "Don't mess with me, Sawyer. Tell it to me straight. Do you want her?"

I laugh, because it's really all I can do at the irony of it. "I do," I admit. "But I can't have her."

"What the hell does that mean?"

"I can't have her or anyone. Not ever. I won't ever have a girlfriend – not a real one anyway."

"Why not?"

I shake my head. "I just can't."

"A lot of guys think that. You're what, twenty-five, twenty-six? Of course you're not ready to settle down. No one ever is until they find that one person. Don't get me wrong, I really don't want Aspen to be that one person, because I know based on your past that it can't last. But to say you never want a girlfriend is a bit obtuse, don't you think?"

"I'm not being obtuse. When I say I will never have a girlfriend, I mean it."

He cocks his head to the side. "Aspen mentioned a while back that she thought you might be a sex addict — are you?"

I belt out a thunderous laugh. "I like sex a lot, I'm not gonna lie. But I'm no addict. I've gone over a month, I'd think that would prove it."

"Then what? Did you lose someone? Are you scared?"

I shake my head because I'm so over this conversation. I'm sorry I even brought it up. "I just know it can never happen, not without someone getting hurt."

"So you shouldn't even try?" he asks. Then he slaps his hand on his thigh. "Look at me, now you've got me arguing for you to be with her. Shit. That's not what I'm doing and that's not what I want. But I'm just saying you shouldn't let one bad relationship, or whatever it was, determine your entire future."

I stand up and pick up the keyboard. "You don't know anything about it, Briggs, so just shut the fuck up and get the rest of her boxes."

Before I walk out the door, I glance back at Aspen's old bedroom. The bedroom where we had sex. Where she was just another one-night-stand. Where I had the best sex of my life. Where I had no idea who she was or what we would become.

Then I stare at the couch. The couch where I kissed her last weekend. The couch where I realized just how true that toast at graduation really was.

Then I walk out the door knowing how totally fucked I am.

Chapter Twenty-four

Aspen

My fingers are sore, but I don't care. They continue pounding out piece after piece. I play everything I can from memory, savoring how my fingertips flow over the black and white keys.

It's been weeks since I played on a piano this nice. I didn't know how much I would miss it. My keyboard is no substitute for the real thing. I still can't believe he bought a piano. For me. He bought a piano for me even after all the money he's depositing into my account. Even knowing I don't have to pay my own rent again until this is over.

Why would he do that?

Something moves in my periphery and I turn to see what it is.

"Don't stop playing because of me," Sawyer says, walking by with a bag of what smells like take-out food.

My stomach grumbles. "What time is it?"

"After seven," he says.

"Seven?"

I've been playing for four hours. I look down at my screaming fingers and wrists that are about ready to fall off the ends of my arms. I fist and release my hands.

"Come on, I have enough for two," he says, putting the food on the table before he grabs a few beers from the fridge.

I walk into the kitchen and open the cabinet he had designated as mine. I pull out my prescription bottle with my muscle relaxants.

Sawyer eyes my movements and then he looks at the beers in his hands. "Okay, then, no beer for you."

"What? Why?"

"Because you can't drink when you take that shit," he says, looking guilty.

I reach for a beer. "One isn't going to kill me. And, oh my God, what food did you get? It smells divine."

He pulls out several Styrofoam containers. "It's from Mitchells. You know Mason Lawrence's wife, Piper? Her family owns a few restaurants. Their food is good. But I didn't know what you'd like, so I ordered three of my favorites and I figured I'd let you choose."

I smile, knowing that he was thinking of me. We never discussed how this was going to work. Would we eat together? Prepare meals? I guess I'd assumed we would each do our own thing when people aren't watching.

I open the three containers, choosing the pulled pork entrée.

"Good choice," he says.

"I'm sorry, did you want this one?"

He takes a bite of lasagna and says around his food, "I told you, I like all of them." Then he pushes his container towards me. "Here, you have to try this one."

We spend the next half hour sipping beer and sharing the three meals. It feels so ... normal.

"So, Brooke and Bass seem to be getting along well," he says.

I wrinkle my nose. "Yeah, maybe a little too well."

I don't bother telling him that Bass declared his love for me last weekend. And that right after, when I didn't return the gesture, he said he was moving in with Brooke. And then all the whispering and hand-holding and touching they did yesterday. It just seems too fast.

"Jealous?" he asks.

I snort through my nose. "Hardly. I love Bass like a brother. I've told you that before. I just don't want him jumping into anything he's not ready for."

"He's a grown man, Aspen. And Brooke is a great girl from what I've seen. I think they make a good couple. Don't you?"

I shrug. "I guess so."

"We should have them over for dinner," he says.

I cock my head, wondering why he would bother. "Why?" I ask. "Bass knows about us, and it doesn't do you any good to put on a show in front of Brooke."

Then I wonder if he's scared to be alone with me. Every time we're together, things seem electrified. The tension between us is palpable. Maybe he feels it, too. Maybe he knows I'm into him and doesn't want to be alone with me more than necessary.

"Just trying to be friendly," he says. "But if you don't want to—"

"No. I do. It would be nice. I could cook."

"You cook?" he asks with a raised brow.

"Don't look so surprised, Tom Sawyer. I happen to be a very good cook."

"Is that so?"

I nod. "I'd be happy to cook for you," I say, looking over at his immaculate kitchen. "I haven't cooked in a kitchen this nice since we sold my parents' house." Then I laugh, as my eyes wander over his double-sized refrigerator, his stainless steel six-burner gas stove, his high-end quartz countertops. "Who am I kidding? I've never cooked in a kitchen this nice."

"You'd cook for me?" he asks.

"Sure. Why not? And from the looks of things in your cabinets, you haven't had a home-cooked meal in a very long time."

"You noticed that, did you?"

I laugh. "I think it was the over-sized refrigerator containing only beer and condiments that gave you away."

He looks down at our three half-eaten entrees. "As much as I like the food from Mitchells, it will be damn nice to have a home-cooked meal from time to time."

"It's settled then. Why don't you leave me a list of your favorite things and I'll go shopping in the morning."

He shakes his head. "No list necessary. I'll eat whatever you make." He pulls out his wallet and throws several hundred-dollar bills on the table.

"What's this for?" I ask.

"Groceries."

I push it back to him. "Sawyer, you are paying me half-a-million dollars. I think I can afford to buy provisions."

"Take it," he says. "I would have spent a lot more than that on take-out."

"I'm not taking it."

"Well, I'm not taking it back."

"Fine. It'll just sit there on the table then."

"Fine," he says, standing up and gathering the remains of our dinner. He puts them in his trashcan.

"What are you doing?" I shout.

He looks at me like I'm crazy. "Cleaning up. What does it look like?"

"But there was so much food left. We could have had a whole other meal with what we didn't eat."

He looks at the trashcan and back at me, laughing. "You want to fish it out and keep it?"

"Well, not now," I say. "But next time, save the leftovers."

"You want to feed the starving kids of Africa?"

"I want to feed *me*," I say.

"You don't have to do that as long as you're living here," he says. "I'm happy to provide whatever you need."

I get up and put my empty beer bottle in the trash on top of what must be forty dollars of un-eaten food. "I don't want to get too used to things being this way, Sawyer. You may be set for life, but come October, I go back to being a struggling college student."

"A struggling *master's* student," he says.

I could swear I see a hint of pride behind his eyes.

"Same difference," I say.

Then I walk over to the pantry and pull out a cake I bought earlier today when I was exploring the neighborhood. I place it in front of him. "How big a piece do you want?"

He looks at the mouth-watering red velvet cake with disgust. "I don't like cake." Then he points his thumb to the basement stairs. "I'm going to go work out and then hit the shower before bed."

"It's not even eight o'clock. How long does it take to work out?" I take in his athletic shorts and shirt and look over at the duffle bag he dropped by the back door on his way in. "And it looks like you already had a workout today. What were you doing all day, anyway?"

"A lot of things. I played some football. Tossed around a baseball. Went fishing. Stuff that helps me relax on my days off."

I eye him suspiciously. "But you took your car. You once told me you never drive unless you leave the city."

"Yeah? Well, I did all that stuff out of the city."

"Where? With who?"

He sighs and runs a hand through his hair.

Then I realize I'm not his wife. I'm not his girlfriend. He doesn't need to answer to me. "Forget it," I say. "It's just ... please don't violate the contract and make me look like a fool."

"I'm not," he says. "I won't."

As he makes his way to the basement stairs, something dawns on me. "Sawyer?"

"Yeah?"

"It's not good to work out right after a meal, is it?" I ask.

He shrugs. "I have other things I can do down there for a while until I'm ready. I may not be back up before you go to bed. Goodnight, Aspen."

"Goodnight."

I gravitate back to the piano. My hands still hurt too much to play, but I sit on the bench and look at the door to the basement. It's the one place I didn't explore. I'm not a fan of basements ever since Denver played a prank on me when I was five and I got locked in ours for a few hours.

I spent quite a lot of time checking out the rest of the place. I even peeked in the master bedroom. It's a nice bedroom for a guy. Masculine yes, but not dirty, smelly and riddled with heaps of clothing on the floor as I'd pictured. In fact, the whole house is clean. He must have a service. Of course he does. He's paying me half-a-million dollars. Paying for a cleaning service must be like buying a cup of coffee for someone like him.

In addition to the master and my bedroom, there is a third room on the second floor. It's a study. But it's much more than that. While there is a laptop on the desk, most of the room is dedicated to baseball memorabilia. There are jerseys on the walls, signed baseballs on the bookshelves, trophies and rings in a display case. Many of these items are from his own career, but he has a good collection of other memorabilia as well. I wonder why the Rickey Henderson thing is the only one he keeps downstairs.

One thing I noticed is that each room has a wooden butterfly hanging on the wall. They are all different shapes and sizes and each is uniquely painted. I stare at the one hanging to my left. It makes me think of his tattoo. Not that the ones on the wall and his tattoo are similar. His tattoo is rough. Dangerous. Sad even.

A few minutes later, I hear a strange humming noise coming from the basement. I want to go down there and see what it is. But I don't. This isn't my place and I may not have the right to. Well, that and it's a basement.

I go up to my room and watch a movie. Then I turn off the lights and stare at the wall that separates me from the man I don't want to love. I drift asleep thinking of how the wall is the perfect metaphor for our relationship.

~ ~ ~

I'm startled awake by a noise. I check the clock and it's 2:15 AM. I turn over, fluff my pillow and try to go back to sleep. But then I hear it again. It's the same sound I heard last week at my apartment. It sounds like Sawyer is crying. An agonizing sob is more like it.

I sit up in bed and listen for a while longer. When it doesn't happen again, I lie back down. But the effort is futile. I'm awake now.

I get out of bed and quietly open my door and feel my way down the dark hallway to the stairs. I see a faint glow coming from the kitchen and wonder if he keeps a night light on. But when I get to the bottom of the stairs, I see Sawyer sitting at the kitchen counter.

I turn around to go back up.

"It's okay," he says, hearing my footsteps. "You can come in."

I look down at my skimpy sleeper set, contemplating my move. But it's pretty dark in here. Only the dim light over the stove is turned on. So I walk over to the fridge and get a bottle of water.

"Do you normally drink beer in the middle of the night?" I ask.

"Only sometimes. When I can't sleep."

I want to ask him about the noises I heard. But I remember how he denied ever crying when the same thing happened at my place. I surmise he's either embarrassed about it, or he simply doesn't realize he does it.

I take my water over to the couch and sit down.

"You're not going back to bed?" he asks.

"In a little while. I want to finish my water first."

"Mind if I join you?"

I motion to the empty spot on the couch, but then I regret my decision to do so when he stands up and I realize he's wearing nothing but boxer briefs.

He doesn't seem nearly as bothered by my sleeping attire as I am by his. Or should I say *hot* and bothered.

I glance around the dimly-lit room so I'm not left gawking at him. "Why is the Rickey Henderson jersey the only one you have down here? I saw the room upstairs with all your baseball stuff. I figured you'd want that stuff down here to impress the ladies with *your* accomplishments."

"Because he's the reason I play. He's the greatest base-stealer of all time. And one day, I'm going to break his record. I hung the jersey here to remind me of that. I keep it here so I see it every morning at breakfast and every night on my way up to bed. It's my motivation." He looks from the jersey over to me. He reaches out and touches my hand. "And I don't ever bring women here."

"Never?" I say with a slack jaw.

"No. I never go out with a woman more than once, so it would have been pointless."

"Why, Sawyer? Why don't you ever take a woman out more than once?"

He takes a long swig of his beer and I know he doesn't want to talk about it. He never does. Makes me think it's not because he's an asshole, but because there is a deep-seated reason.

"Okay, tell me more about Mr. Henderson," I say, nodding to the jersey on the wall.

"Well, he had over fourteen hundred career stolen bases. They called him 'The Man of Steal.' As in S.T.E.A.L."

"Called? He doesn't play anymore?"

"He retired in 2003. I met him about ten years ago when he was doing some coaching for the Mets. That's when he signed the jersey. When I got drafted by the Hawks, I wanted his number, number twenty-four, but someone else on the team already had it. Then a few months later, that player was released." He laughs. "Boy was I pissed."

"Why were you mad?" I ask. "They wouldn't let you change your number after he left?"

"Oh, they would, but I would have had to buy out all the inventory they had made with my name and number on it — about thirty thousand dollars' worth. And as a rookie, I wasn't in a position to afford it."

"But you can now," I say.

"Yeah. I can. But now I don't want to."

"Why?"

He shrugs. "Because maybe someday, some kid will want *my* jersey hanging on the wall. And number fifty-five has kind of grown on me."

"Someday? Sawyer, kids already have your jerseys hanging on their walls."

He looks over at the wall again. "I can only hope."

"Well, I know it for a fact, *Speed Limit.*"

He rolls his eyes. "And how is that, *Penny?*"

"I've done some research," I say, laughing at his awkward use of my nickname.

"On *me?*"

I nod. "You don't think I was going to agree to live with a guy who could be a serial killer, do you?"

"So you decided I'm a decent guy?"

"Decent enough to be roommates with," I say, nudging him with my elbow.

He grabs my elbow and holds it. "You're different, Aspen."

"Different from what?"

"The girls I usually hook up with."

I look into his eyes, torn between wanting *this* and wanting to be one of those girls. Because my body is screaming to be touched by him. "But I'm not one of them," I say. "And that's why this is different. It's different because I'm your friend, Sawyer."

"Is that what we are? Friends?"

We stare at each other in the dim light, him running a finger across my arm, sending pulses straight to my core. His touch is electrified. His gaze is on fire.

The line is being blurred. I wonder if there even *is* a line anymore. And if so, is it bending? Breaking?

He leans closer, his eyes taking in my bare legs like he's never seen a woman before. His gaze moves to my chest and I know he can see my nipples hardening under the thin material of my top.

He reaches out and touches the hem of my shirt. "I like this. I think I like this a lot," he says.

My mind goes crazy with wonder. What does he like? *The shirt? Me? This?*

Even in the relative darkness, I can see that he's getting an erection. There's no hiding it and I don't get the idea that he cares to.

He brushes a hair behind my ear as he moves even closer. His lips are mere inches from mine. My body is humming with anticipation. And I realize that I want him more than I want to stand by my morals. I want him even though he'd make a fool of me. Even though I can't have him forever. But maybe just having him now is enough.

His hot breath mingles with mine. I close my eyes and surrender myself to him. *Yes*, I think. *Yes.*

Then I feel his weight shift away on the couch and my eyes fly open.

"I – I'm sorry," he says. "Sometimes I forget."

Forget what? I want to scream. Forget we have a binding contract? Forget I'm not one of his hussies? Forget he says he will never have a girlfriend?

He gets up off the couch and throws his beer in the trash. He looks back at me and runs his hands through his hair. From this angle, I can just make out the tattoo on his rib cage. It's mysterious. It's dangerous. It's sexy. Just like him.

He turns away and climbs the stairs to his room.

I sit on the couch and look at the wall. But not at the jersey. I look at the large wooden butterfly illuminated by the moonlight coming through the window. I study it and know that it has everything to do with why he didn't just kiss me.

Chapter Twenty-five

Sawyer

I stare at the email she sent me. She's on the plane and she's bored. I should email her back. But I don't. Because if I do, I'm likely to fuck up and say something I shouldn't. Something like she hasn't even been gone a day and I miss her. Less than two weeks she's been living with me and I already miss her.

It's different when I'm on the road. I'm busy. I'm practicing, playing, traveling, partying. There's no time to think about anything. But here, when I'm at home before a game just sitting in my townhouse, it's seems so ... empty.

How in the hell is that even possible?

I look over at the piano. I can almost hear her playing. I love to watch her play. She doesn't even know I do it. When she plays, her back is to the living room. She has no idea I sometimes sit and stare at her. She has no idea that when she closes her eyes as she plays, I walk into the room and study her. She has no idea how beautiful she is when she's playing. That she looks at the music, the keys, the strings, with as much passion as I've ever seen.

Then it dawns on me, as I remember the night we talked, that she was looking at me the exact same way.

My head falls back against the couch cushion. Bass was right. She *is* into me. I'm not paying her to look at me that way when nobody else is around. Another thing he's right about is that she'll get hurt. She'll get hurt if I let her stay with me. If I let her into my life beyond the arrangement we have.

I can't let that happen.

I dream of Aspen – her and my mom. They are the only women I've ever dreamed of. And they are the only women I've ever had nightmares about.

The night I woke up and she heard me, I wasn't dreaming of my mom dying like I usually do. I wasn't dreaming of the agony she was in for years. I was dreaming of Aspen. I was dreaming of what it would be like to be with her. What it would be like if I let her stay. And the dream was the best one I'd ever had – right up until it turned into the nightmare that woke me.

I'll end up hurting her. I know I will.

My phone vibrates with a call. It's Lucy. Lucy never calls me.

"Is he okay?" I ask, answering the call.

"Daniel is fine. He's getting a swimming lesson now, so I had some time to call you. I've been meaning to talk to you for a while now."

"A while? I was just there last Sunday. Has something come up since then?"

She sighs into the phone. "Yes and no. I mean, this is something I've been contemplating all year, but it's just been finalized recently."

"What's been finalized?" I ask, warily.

There is a very pregnant pause.

"Lucy, what is it?"

"We're moving," she says so quietly that I almost can't make out the words.

"You're moving? Where?"

"To Arizona."

"Arizona?" I yell, standing up and pacing around the room. "Are you fucking kidding me? That's all the way across the country."

"There's no need to use that kind of language, Sawyer."

"The hell there isn't. You're taking him away from me, Lucy. Did you even think for one second how this would affect me?"

"I *have* thought about it. It's why it took me so long to tell you."

"Why are you moving?"

"You know why," she says. "It's hard being a single mom. He's a handful. I need help. My family is down there. My sisters. My mom. They can all help out when I need them."

"I can help out if you need it. I can hire you a damn nanny if you want, just say the word."

"You are not hiring anyone, Sawyer. You do too much already."

I shake my head. "I don't do nearly enough."

"Quit it. Stop blaming yourself for how things are. I'm a big girl and he's my responsibility."

"He's mine, too."

"He's *not* your responsibility. He never has been, Sawyer. I appreciate all you've done for us. But it's time for us to move on."

"Jesus. What the fuck do you expect me to do now? I love that kid."

"I know you do. But the silver lining is that you play in Arizona a few times a year and you can fly down for a few weekends in the off-season. It'll work out. You'll see. And maybe, once we're gone, you won't feel the need to burden yourself with us anymore."

"Burden myself? Are you kidding, Lucy?"

"I know you feel guilty."

"You have no idea what I feel."

"Fair enough. But I'm sorry. I have to do what I think is best."

"When will you go?"

"I have a lease on the house through the end of the year. We'll go then."

I breathe a sigh of relief knowing I can still see Danny anytime I want for the next six months. I start to make a mental list of all the things I want to do with him before he leaves.

"Will you let me fly him up here sometimes?"

"I don't know about that," she says. "We'll see how he does on the flight to Arizona. He's never been on a plane before. But even if he's okay with it, I'm not sure I'd want to put him on a plane by himself."

"They have escorts for that sort of thing."

"We'll see. That's all I can promise for now."

I look at the time and see I have to get to work. "I have to go, Lucy."

"I'm really sorry," she says again.

I blow out a painful sigh. "Yeah. I know."

On my way to head out the door, I walk past the kitchen table. I stop when I see the stack of hundred-dollar bills that has accumulated. For two weeks, I've given Aspen money for groceries. For the incredible food she cooks to feed me. And for two weeks, she's not taken it.

She *is* different.

I take a detour on my way out and decide to write that email after all.

Chapter Twenty-six

Aspen

Denver nudges me when he sees Sawyer come out of the dugout with his bat. "I still can't believe we're going out clubbing with them tonight."

"Get it all out of your system now, big brother. I told you not to go all fangirl on them."

"I'll be cool," he says. "Do you get nervous when he's up to bat?"

I nod. "More than I'd like to admit," I say.

I didn't at first. But the more I watch him and the more I get to know him, the more nervous I become. The story he told me the other night about the jersey on his wall and finally realizing he didn't want to change his number – he not only wants to *play* in the majors, he wants to go down in history. That means every time he comes up to bat, it's an opportunity to add to his record of stolen bases. Of course I get nervous.

"Why wouldn't you like to admit it?" Denver asks. "I'd say it's pretty normal for that to happen when your boyfriend plays in the majors. I'm still not used to saying that. Are you?" He leans close and whispers loudly, "You're Sawyer Mills' girlfriend, Pen. You live with the guy. You may even *marry* him someday." He takes a step back and looks down at Sawyer as he walks up to the plate. "Holy shit, he could be my brother-in-law."

I watch Sawyer swing and miss and then I swat Denver. "Don't go marrying me off just yet. We're still pretty casual about things."

"Casual?" He laughs. "I saw the video, Aspen. The one where he declared his love for you. That's not casual. You've done the impossible here. Well, I think you have. I'm not sure I trust him yet, and a few weeks ago, you weren't either. I'm withholding final judgment until I meet him face to face."

Oh, how I wish I could tell Denver everything. We've talked so much over the past few days. It's like we were never apart. I almost told him. I almost told him about a dozen times. I was so close that I had to call Bass so he could talk me down. But talking to Bass about Sawyer isn't really something I can do anymore. Not since he admitted his feelings for me. And I really need to talk to someone about Sawyer. But I can't. And it's becoming harder every day.

Sawyer hits the next pitch and the ball goes foul, but the first-baseman runs over and makes a diving catch and the ump calls Sawyer out. He's not having a particularly good game. That happens a lot lately when I come to his games. It worries me that the stress of his situation, of possibly being traded, is getting to him.

"I have to hit the bathroom," I tell Denver, excusing myself around him. "Can I bring you anything?"

"I'm good," he says, not taking his eyes off the game.

I locate the ladies room only to find I have to stand behind a dozen women to wait my turn. Someone brushes me from behind and I turn around to see a tall redhead staring me down.

"Sorry," I say, as if it was my fault that she ran into me.

"You should be," she bites back at me.

I turn around and try to mind my own business, when she bumps into me a second time. I scoot up, closer to the woman in front of me, but the redhead crowds me again.

I turn around. "Would you mind backing up a bit, it's too hot in here to stand so close."

"My, my, isn't *she* bitchy?" she says to those around us.

I look around, wondering if I'm the only one who sees what's wrong here. Nobody else seems to care.

When she bumps into me again, I give her a death stare and then step out of line so I can find another bathroom.

"What?" the redhead yells after me. "Are you going to get your famous *boyfriend* to stick up for you? He won't, you know. He'll toss you to the curb soon enough."

I stop walking and turn around, appraising her. "Do I know you?" I ask, wondering if I went to high school with her and maybe now she's jealous of seeing me in the news.

"No, but your boyfriend does."

I roll my eyes at her and walk away.

"He knows me *very* well!" she shouts for everyone to hear. "What makes you think you're so special, you pretentious bitch?"

I walk quickly over to the next set of bathrooms and wait in line there, looking behind me to make sure I've not been followed.

It's nothing new, being bothered by Sawyer's past conquests. It's happened a few times before in New York. And like the redhead, they pretty much just like to tell me they've slept with him. I guess they try to rile me up or something. Get me to fight with him, perhaps, so they can watch our relationship crumble.

What they don't know is that next season, they will have their beloved Sawyer back. I'm sure he'll be more discreet about it, but they'll have him back nonetheless. And the thought of it – the thought of him with the redhead – with *anyone* – makes me sick to my stomach.

When I finally return to my seat, Denver asks why I've been gone so long.

"Big line," I say. "Did I miss anything?"

"Caden hit a double. Benham scored. They have two outs now."

I have a hard time concentrating on the rest of the game. I look around the stands at all the pretty women and wonder just how many of them have been with Sawyer. How many of them will be waiting for him to come out of the clubhouse so they can have a shot with him? How many of them hate me?

The Nighthawks win, but just barely. I know Sawyer will be upset with himself, but it would be worse if they'd lost.

"Come on," I say to Denver, pulling him by the arm. "Let's go get a drink and do some people-watching. It will be a while before they come out."

His face splits in two with a smile. "I can't believe—"

"Yeah, yeah, you can't believe you're going to meet him. I *know*. Get over it."

Thirty minutes later, we're waiting by the clubhouse for the guys to emerge. As usual, fans scream as the players come out. When Sawyer comes through the door, the crowd becomes uncharacteristically boisterous.

"Is it true, you're off the market?" a reporter shouts over the female shrieks.

Sawyer spots me and waves me over. I pull Denver behind me.

"It's true," he says, pulling me close to him.

He gives Denver a lift of his chin. We all know now is not the time for introductions.

"Sawyer!" a fan yells. "Can I have a picture?"

He kisses me on the top of my head before he walks over to pose for pictures and sign autographs. A while later, Sawyer rejoins Denver and me as the crowd starts to thin. But several people linger to get one last look.

A man and a woman approach the three of us and I stiffen. "That's the lady who called me a bitch earlier."

Denver and Sawyer both look surprised. "Someone called you a bitch?" Sawyer asks defensively.

"Yeah, when I was in line for the bathroom. She's a fan of yours, apparently. And according to her, she's seen you do a lot more than play baseball."

"Shit," he says, looking perturbed.

The man and woman come closer, the guy looking pissed as hell. "Is this him?" he asks her. "Is this the asshole you slept with last season?"

She nods.

The man lunges forward and pushes Sawyer in the chest. "You fucked my wife?"

Sawyer backs up and puts his hands up in surrender. "If you're going to be mad at anyone, man, it should be her. I always ask if they're married. I'm not inclined to have meatheads like you coming after me."

"Well she is," the tall, muscular guy says, grabbing her left hand and showing him her ring. "And maybe you should check the ring finger for telltale signs next time, you mother fucker. Or better yet, keep your dick in your pants."

Sawyer pushes me protectively to the side. "It's really not my problem if they lie to me to get into my bed, now is it? And it sure as shit isn't my fault if you can't keep your own wife satisfied."

What happens next, happens in slow motion. The guy takes a swing at Sawyer, but Sawyer ducks and the punch lands right on Denver's jaw. Denver's head snaps back and blood spatters across the wall behind us.

I look at Sawyer, who looks guilty as hell that Denver took the punch meant for him. The guy cocks his arm back, looking like he's going to take another shot at him.

"Stop it!" I yell, putting myself between the two of them.

Denver pulls on my arms, yanking me out of harm's way. "Get out of the way, Aspen."

The guy laughs. "Does your slut always stand up for you, you pussy?" he says to Sawyer.

Sawyer's hands ball into fists and his face turns red. The vein at his temple is throbbing.

"Hit me!" the guy yells at Sawyer. "Hit me, you pussy. Then we'll see who the real man is."

I can tell Sawyer is about to jump the guy. Hell, he's about to *kill* him. Just before I think he's going to blow, he turns and hits the door he's standing next to. I hear a crack and hope to God it's the door and not his hand.

Then security walks up. "Is there a problem here?" a beefy guy with no neck asks.

"Yes, there's a problem," I say. "This jerk just hit my brother."

The security guard looks at Denver to see his bloody mouth and swollen jaw. "Would you like me to call the police so you can press charges?"

Denver looks at Sawyer and then back at me before answering the man. He shakes his head. "No. I'm fine. It's all good."

"Just get them the hell out of here," Sawyer says, motioning to the couple.

"With pleasure, Mr. Mills," the guard says.

We all watch the guy and his wife being escorted away. Then my brother holds out his hand to Sawyer. "Denver Andrews. Nice to meet you," he says laughing.

"You, too." Sawyer shakes his hand, cringing. "I'm sorry about that."

"Shit, did you hurt your hand?" Denver asks.

"I'll be fine. It's my catching hand, not my throwing one. Plus, the door was wood. It had some give. But it looks like we both might need some ice." He nods to Denver's jaw. "And then maybe some shots. Come on, I know a good place. Some of the other players will be there."

On our way to the club, Denver and Sawyer talk while I study them. Neither of them hit the jerk at the ballpark and I wonder why. It's not like my brother to back down from a fight. And why would Sawyer hit the wall instead of the guy's face after the jerk said such terrible things about him?

Once we find where the other players are sitting, I ask the waitress for a couple baggies of ice.

"I know why *I* didn't hit the guy," Denver says to Sawyer. "I'm on probation. I could end up in jail. But why didn't *you?* You had every right. You would have been defending me after that sucker-punch. Defending Aspen."

Sawyer shakes his head. "I'm a lover, not a fighter," he says, disingenuously.

"No, come on, really," Denver says, prodding him. "I mean, I'd get it if you said you didn't want to risk hurting your hands, but you did anyway by hitting the door. So what gives?"

Sawyer looks like he's trying to come up with a reason when Denver says, "Oh, I get it. You don't want a lawsuit. I'll bet people could get millions out of you if you hit them."

"Yeah, that's it," Sawyer says, throwing back a shot the waitress brought. Then he puts a bag of ice on his hand.

That's *not* it. And it's written all over his face.

"Are you okay?" I ask him, reaching out to touch his arm.

"I'm fine. Nothing a kiss from my *girlfriend* can't cure," he says. Then he nods to all the people watching. "What do you say?"

I lean forward and meet him halfway. Our lips touch and I realize just how much I've missed this. We haven't kissed in a while. Haven't touched in nearly a week. Not since he almost kissed me on his couch that night. The night no one was watching.

After our kiss – the one that leaves me disoriented – I sit back and watch Sawyer and my brother become fast friends. Denver knows a lot about baseball, so they have much to talk about. Denver is deliriously happy, despite the split lip and swollen jaw. Halfway through the night, he declares his acceptance of Sawyer, giving us his official blessing and saying our parents would have loved him.

I don't agree. It's *Denver* who loves him. My parents would have hated Sawyer. I can almost hear them say that he's arrogant and crass and not nearly good enough for their daughter.

We sit and drink, the shots going down far too easily; the touches Sawyer and I share feeling far too customary, almost like an old habit.

By midnight, he's got me melting into him on the dance floor. I've shed my Hawks shirt, and the tank top underneath is wet with perspiration. My hair is piled on top of my head in a messy bun. And it's now that I realize I'll be going home with Sawyer, not Denver. People will expect it. He's my boyfriend, after all.

Sawyer looks at me as he's grinding himself into me. His dark hair is matted with sweat. His eyes burn into mine. I know he's putting on a show for everyone else here. But deep down, I think nobody is that good an actor.

He leans down and kisses my neck, licking the beads of sweat that have settled there. "You taste good. Salty and sweet."

Maybe it's the alcohol, but I swear every time he looks at me, he's telling me he wants me. And every time I look at him, I answer him with my own heated stare. One that tells him I want him, too. That I'm tired of resisting. That I'm done using the contract as my shield.

"Fire me," I say, before my brain can filter the spontaneous command.

"What?"

He stares at me, trying to gauge the sincerity in my words. We stop dancing but keep swaying, our bodies pressed together. I can feel his erection. He can see my pebbled nipples through my thin tank top.

I see my brother over Sawyer's shoulder, sitting at a table, laughing with a few of the Nighthawks players.

Nighthawks players.

And suddenly, I'm reminded of who Sawyer is. Who I am. What we're doing. And what I'd be if I let him have me.

I start to pull away. "Forget it. I don't know what I'm saying."

He pulls me back. "Fuck that, Aspen. You said it. I heard it. It's out there. You can't take it back."

"Yes, I can. And I am. Now if you'll excuse me, I'm going to get some water."

Samantha Christy

I walk across the room, aware that he's following me. I keep going past our table and down the hallway until I find the bathroom, knowing he can't follow me in. I take much longer than I need to, hoping he's gotten bored by the time I emerge.

I peek out and see the coast is clear, then I go up to the bar and get myself a bottle of water.

"Aspen Andrews?" I hear from behind.

I spin around and see Trent Dugan. Trent Dugan, my high school boyfriend. Trent Dugan, the guy with an ear-to-ear smile on his handsome, chiseled face.

"Trent," I say, grabbing my water off the bar and reaching into my pocket to fish out some money.

He throws a five-dollar bill on the bar before he pulls me into a hug. "I thought it was you. I've been watching you all night. You look fantastic."

I look down at my sweaty top and think of how my hair must look and I laugh. "I do not."

He nods. "You do, Aspen. You always did."

"You look great, too," I say.

He does. He hasn't aged much in the four years since I've seen him. Except that maybe his baby face is not so babyish anymore. And as I crane my neck to look at him, I could swear he's gotten even taller.

He pulls me off to the side of the bar, where it's quieter. "I guess I don't have to ask you what you've been doing these days," he says, nodding over to where the guys are sitting. "It's pretty much all over the news."

"Yeah, I guess so."

"You've done well for yourself. I'm happy for you."

I stare at him. I think he's serious. I believe he *is* truly happy for me. I've wondered about him over the years. We dated during sophomore and junior year. Then, senior year, he broke up with me when I told him I was going to Juilliard. He didn't want me to go and was mad that I'd go so far away from him. He's one of the few guys I've slept with. And the only one who's broken my heart.

Until now, my inner voice says.

I look over to where the guys are sitting and try to find Sawyer but he's not there.

"What have you been doing since high school?" I ask Trent. "Did you get your engineering degree?"

He nods proudly. "Three weeks ago. I'm back here to pack up my things. I got a job in Austin, Texas."

"That's wonderful. Did you go to school here in Missouri?"

"I went to Cal Tech," he says.

I raise my eyebrows at him, accusingly. "And you thought *New York* was too far away?"

He laughs. "It was only too far away if you were there and I was here. Once I accepted we weren't meant to be, I broadened my horizons."

"I'm glad to hear that. And I'm happy for you."

"I'm glad you found the guy you were meant to be with," he says.

I try to paste a genuine smile on my face, but I know I'm failing miserably.

"What is it?" Trent asks.

"Nothing."

I feel an arm come around my waist. Then hot breath rolls across my neck before Sawyer kisses my bare shoulder. "I lost you for a minute, babe."

I try not to show my displeasure at his use of the endearment. He only calls me *babe* when he's putting on a show.

"Who's this?" he asks, nodding to Trent.

"Trent Dugan, meet Sawyer Mills," I say.

Trent holds out his hand, but Sawyer doesn't shake it. "Sorry," Sawyer says. "I can't risk injuring the hand."

Put off, Trent wipes his hand on his jeans and puts it back by his side.

I try to take a step away from Sawyer and his asshole remark, but he pulls me even closer. "And how do you two know each other?" he asks.

"Aspen and I dated in high school," Trent says. "For over two years."

Sawyer's grip on me tightens. "Is that so? Well, what happened to the happy couple?"

"She wanted Juilliard," Trent says.

"And he wanted Jenna Kinney," I say, joking.

"That's not true," Trent says. "I only dated her after you made it clear that you wanted Juilliard more than you wanted me."

Sawyer's brows shoot up and he looks back and forth from Trent to me.

I shrug. "Doesn't matter now. Everything worked out for the best, didn't it?"

"It did," Trent says. "Well, it's nice to see you again, Aspen. I won't keep you any longer. My number hasn't changed. Look me up sometime if you ever get to Austin, Texas."

"We don't ever go to Austin, so that would be highly unlikely," Sawyer says arrogantly.

I elbow Sawyer hard and give him a scolding look.

"Houston isn't all that far," Trent says.

"We're usually very busy when we travel," Sawyer says. "We don't have any time for socializing."

Trent shakes his head, knowing Sawyer is full of shit. "Yet here you are, hanging out at a bar."

I give Trent an apologetic smile. "I'll look you up if we can find the time. Nice to see you, Trent."

Trent walks away and Sawyer pulls me into the hallway leading to the club offices. "Did you sleep with him?" he asks.

"We dated for more than two years, Sawyer. What do you think?"

If I didn't know any better, I'd say Sawyer is almost as mad now as he was when that guy confronted him after the game. I reach up and run my finger across his throbbing temple. "You're not jealous, are you? There's really no need to be. After all, you're paying me. Trent wasn't. Two totally different things."

Just as intended, my words do nothing to tamp down his anger. But then his anger turns into something else as he looks into my eyes. It turns into passion. Pure unbridled, no-holds-barred passion.

He cages me to the wall, leaning down so his lips are almost touching mine. "I'm not paying you, Aspen. Not tonight anyway. You're fucking fired."

Chapter Twenty-seven

Sawyer

The Uber ride back to the hotel is torture. We have to drop Denver off at his apartment and Aspen runs up to get her things. And when I say runs, I mean *runs*. She takes two stairs at a time as I watch from the car.

She tries to pretend she's not into me. And she can deny it all she wants, but I see the way she looks at me. The way her eyes burn into mine. The way her breathing accelerates and her nipples pebble when I touch her. She wants me as much as I want her.

When she comes back down the stairs with her small suitcase, I take it from her and put it in the trunk. I notice she changed her shirt. This one is not damp with sweat. It's tiny and sleeveless and has me thinking about how quickly I'll be able to strip her out of it.

I scoot in next to her and kiss her neck, smelling the spritz of perfume she must have put on when she was changing.

"Nobody's watching," she jokes. "Are you sure you want to do that?"

I laugh. "Nobody better be watching when I do to you what I've wanted to do for a long time."

She bites her lip. It's an innocent move, but she looks so hot when she does it. She has no idea what she does to me. I look down at the rising problem in my lap.

I rest my hand on her thigh, running my thumb in tiny circles. I feel her tremble and it makes me smile.

She doesn't fail to notice. "Don't get cocky, Tom Sawyer," she says, nodding to my lap. "You have no right to talk."

"I didn't say anything."

"But you were thinking it," she says.

"I'm thinking a lot of things right now," I say, moving my hand up closer to the apex of her thighs.

She looks at the driver to make sure he's watching the road, and then she puts her hand on my lap and moves her fingers around against the fabric of my jeans. *Shit*. I'm not going to be able to get out of the car if she keeps this up.

"What are you doing to me?" I ask.

She giggles. "I figured with your sordid past, you'd know what, Mr. Mills."

I shake my head and laugh. That's not what I meant, but I'm not about to tell her that. This woman – I can't get her out of my head. Maybe a good fuck will do the trick. I ignore the voice in my head that reminds me I already had one of those and it did nothing to squelch my want of her. If anything, it did the opposite.

And I realize I'm in a position I've never been in. I'm about to sleep with a woman for the second time. Sawyer Mills doesn't sleep with anyone twice. *One and done*. I'm breaking my rules with her.

This is different, I tell myself. We're living together like boyfriend and girlfriend. That makes this okay. It's expected of us. It's no big deal. This doesn't affect the contract. It doesn't affect the outcome. Because there can only be one outcome. And I've known that since I was ten years old.

"We're here," the driver says.

We both look out the car window. We were oblivious to the fact that the car had come to a stop. We look at each other and laugh. Then we get out and retrieve her bag.

We run into a few of my teammates going into the lobby bar at the hotel.

"Want to join us for a nightcap?" Caden asks as we walk past.

"Nope," I say, my steps quickening as I pull Aspen towards the elevator.

I hear laughter behind us and glance back to see the guys staring at us. Brady has an amused look on his face.

"Mind your own business!" I yell at him just before pushing Aspen into the elevator.

The doors close. We're the only ones inside. She looks at me. I look at her. She drops her purse on the floor and jumps into my arms. I catch her as I back up into the corner just as our lips crash together.

As the floors go by, our kisses become deeper. Our tongues mingle together as we taste each other. When I'm out of breath, I break our seal and move my lips to her neck. She tastes salty sweet. A mixture of sweat and perfume. A moan escapes her when I suck on a place by her collarbone. I chronicle the exact location in my memory.

The elevator dings and the doors open. I don't want to put her down. I want to carry her like this until I can throw her on my bed. But we have her suitcase in here and her purse is on the floor. I reluctantly let her go and we gather up her things and make our way to my suite.

I unlock the door and deposit her suitcase inside. Aspen immediately jumps back into my arms. It's almost like she read my mind. She doesn't even bother looking around the room. She doesn't notice that I've booked us the Presidential Suite. She doesn't notice the view overlooking the river. Or the ornate flowers on the table. She doesn't notice the stocked bar and the array of food I had pre-ordered for the evening. She doesn't notice because her eyes never stray from mine.

Nobody has ever not noticed. Nobody until her.

I carry her into the bedroom and put her down on the bed, immediately crawling on top of her. Having her under me is like something out of a dream. It *is* out of a dream. *My* dreams. Since the first day I met her, she's plagued me as I sleep.

I pull up the hem of her shirt, removing it when she arches her back and lifts her head. Her white satin bra has a hook in the front and I waste no time unfastening it. The two cups fall to the side, revealing her gorgeous creamy breasts.

I palm them. Then I run my fingers around the edges, teasing her before I pinch her nipples. "If I didn't tell you before, these are incredible."

She laughs. "Of course you haven't told me before. Did all the alcohol fry your brain?"

Oh, shit. That's right. This is supposed to be the first time I've seen her. "I don't know," I say. "That skimpy shirt you had on at the club gave me a pretty good idea."

Thinking about her alcohol comment has me removing my hands from her momentarily.

"How much have you had to drink?" I ask.

She shrugs. "I had a beer at the game and a few shots at the club. Why?"

"You didn't take one of those pills, did you?"

"My muscle relaxants? No. Of course not."

"Good."

She smiles up at me. "Is this you taking care of me again? You'd better watch out, Sawyer, or you'll turn into a nice guy."

I shut her up when I lean down and kiss her again. She arches her back and reaches around to pull me tightly against her.

With my hand between us, stroking her breasts, we kiss until I can't stand it any longer. The pressure in my pants is driving me insane. I sit up and straddle her, reaching behind me to pull my shirt over my head. Then I undo the button on her pants. Her eyes study my chest. My tattoo. She traces the outline of it with her finger.

Her finger stops its path and she looks up at me, cocking her head to the side.

"What is it?" I ask.

She shakes her head, looking at my tattoo. "Nothing. Just a strange feeling of déjà vu."

I move to the side and peel her pants off. "I promise you won't be thinking of *anything* in about twenty seconds."

The sides of her mouth curve into a smile. "Is that so?"

"Oh, yeah," I say, my lips coming down to meet her right breast.

While my tongue is busy playing with her nipple, my hand works its way under her panties. Her very small, very wet panties. My cock strains even harder against the seam of my jeans. I slip a finger through her wetness and coat her tiny nub with it. Then I rub my thumb in circles, extracting a moan from deep inside her throat. When I slip a finger inside her, she pleads with me. "Yes!" she yells.

Her excitement fuels me further and I slide her panties down her legs, removing my mouth from her chest so I can follow every curve with my tongue until I hit her ankle. Her hips buck under me as I slowly work my way back up her legs, tasting every bit of flesh up to the apex of her thighs. When I put my tongue there, she calls out my name three times and I feel like Tarzan. King Kong. Fucking Superman.

The way my name comes off her lips when I'm feasting on her is the most erotic thing I've ever heard. With my tongue on her clit, I use my fingers to stroke inside her, searching for the spot I know will drive her crazy. I know it's there. I've found it once before.

I crook my fingers and she shouts again. Her thighs tighten around my head. Her fingers weave into my hair, tugging, pulling, clawing. When her back arches and her insides clench my fingers, I have to grit my teeth to keep myself from coming with her, because watching her come is fucking hot. And more satisfying than any of my fantasies.

"Holy shit," I say, hopping up to quickly remove my jeans. "I have to see that again."

She throws an arm over her face in embarrassment as she recovers from her orgasm. "It won't happen," she says. "It never happens twice."

"That's not true," I say. "You—"

Damn it.

"I what?" she asks, turning on her side while reaching out to grab my cock.

Jesus, her hands feel good on me. My cock is hard as steel as she runs her hands up and down my shaft.

"Nothing," I say. "I don't even know my own fucking name right now with you doing that to me."

She laughs and then she leans down. "Well, what if I do *this?*" she says, right before taking me into her mouth.

"Aspen!" I shout as her wet warmth encapsulates me.

The seal she has on my cock breaks when she smiles around me. She looks up at me while she takes me in from tip to root and back. Her fingers work fervently around my balls and over my perineum.

I pull away. "I want inside you. Now."

"Condom?" she asks.

"Got it." I reach over the side of the bed and open my wallet. There are two condoms inside. Because I always double-wrap. I look from my wallet back to Aspen. Then I pull out *one*.

I roll it on and climb on top of her. "You sure?" I ask.

She shakes her head. "I'm not sure about anything anymore. But I want this."

Truer words have never been spoken. I wonder if she has any idea that I feel exactly the same way. I've never wanted anything so badly knowing I could never have it. And as I sink myself deep inside her, I know I'll never want anything as much again.

I'm slow and deliberate, allowing her time to get used to me. I watch her as I pull out. I moan with her as I push back in. I reach between us and stroke her, determined to show her she can have a second orgasm. I have to bite the inside of my cheek and hold back, wanting her to come along with me.

I stroke her clit with my thumb, running it in circles before I give it a little pinch. Then I do it again. I do it as I watch her build back up. "Oh, God," she moans, her face looking surprised at the impending encore.

"That's it," I say. "You feel so good."

My words push her over the edge. Her screams push *me* over. We pulsate in and around each other, our gazes never breaking contact. It's as close to another person as I've ever felt. And it fucking scares me. It scares me because I know what happens after. I know I'll hurt her. But little does she know, she'll hurt me, too.

I collapse on top of her as we chase our recovery. Then I roll to the side. She snuggles into the crook of my neck and places her hand on my chest. We lie in silence as she traces the outline of my tattoo once again. I'm beginning to think it's becoming a habit.

I smile down at her as she does it, but she can't see me. She can't see how much I want this. I can never show her.

Suddenly, she stops what she's doing and bolts up in bed. She studies me. She studies my tattoo. Then she stands and picks my shirt up off the floor to cover herself.

"Oh, my God," she says, looking disgusted. "This isn't the first time we've done this, is it?"

"No," I say, guiltily.

She shakes her head in a huff and pulls on her pants. "What the fuck, Sawyer. When?"

"The first night we met."

Her jaw opens. Then closes. Then opens again. "Of course. The alcohol. The muscle relaxants. I should have known. Why the hell didn't you say anything?"

I shrug. "I didn't even realize you didn't know until I came back to your apartment later that morning."

She sits down on the chair next to the bed. "I knew it," she says. "I mean, I didn't know it, but I kept having vivid dreams." She throws my shirt at me before putting on her own. "Why didn't you tell me back then, when I recognized your tattoo in the car? And for that matter, why didn't you tell me when we signed the contract? I'll bet you thought it was pretty funny that I added the no sex clause to it, didn't you? Did you and your friends make fun of me for that? God, Sawyer, you really are an asshole, aren't you?"

She gets up and storms across the room. I dress quickly and follow her. "Aspen, wait." I catch her before she gets to the front door. "I should have told you. I'm sorry."

She spins around. "So you up and left in the middle of the night, just like all your other conquests. You used me and walked out."

I shake my head. "It was different with you," I tell her. "That's why I came back later that morning."

"No. You came back to see if you could use me some more."

"I came back because I liked you. You're different. And because I had read the letter from Juilliard and knew we could help each other out."

"You lied to me," she says.

"Hold on there, I didn't lie. I've never lied to you, Aspen. It's not my fault that you didn't remember. How do you think I felt knowing someone I had sex with didn't remember doing it?"

Her accusing eyes scold me. "Wow – now that's the pot calling the kettle black, isn't it? How do you think every woman you've ever slept with feels? I've probably met a dozen women in the past few months who had sex with you, yet you didn't remember them. It happened earlier tonight, just a couple of hours ago. How can you be so blasé about it?"

I run my hands through my hair and walk over to pour myself a drink. "I never claimed I wasn't an asshole, you know." I hold up the decanter. "You want one?"

"You're kidding, right? After what I just found out?" She nods to her suitcase. "I'm leaving, Sawyer. I'm going back to Denver's place."

"You can't leave. It's in the contract that you go to some away games with me."

"You really think I care about the contract now? Plus, if I recall, you fired me an hour ago."

"Yeah, well, you're re-hired as of right now."

273

Her eyes close and she blows out a long breath. "It doesn't really matter, because any way you look at it, you're still paying me to be with you. And that makes me a whore."

I slam down the drink I just poured, sloshing liquid onto the table. "That's bullshit and you know it."

She points to the bedroom. "What would *you* call me then. After what we just did? I'm not your girlfriend. I'm not your friend. I'm not even your fuck buddy."

"That's not true. We're friends. Friends who had sex. It's not all that unusual, you know."

"It's unusual for *me*. I've only slept with three men. Don't you get that? You're only the third guy I've slept with. *Ever.* I realize that's a novel idea for you."

I raise my eyebrows. "Three? Really?" Then molten lava creeps up my spine. "And that guy tonight, he was one of the three?"

"Trent. Yes. I told you he was."

I realize she's still standing by the front door. "Aspen, I know you're pissed at me. But that doesn't change anything. Please put your bag down and come have a drink."

"So you can take advantage of me again? I don't think so."

"I didn't take advantage of you that night. You only had a few drinks. I didn't know you were on drugs."

"Muscle relaxants," she says.

"Whatever. You seemed fine. And I sure as shit didn't take advantage of you tonight. You were more than a willing participant. Come on. You have to admit, we're pretty damn compatible, sexually and otherwise."

She points her finger between us. "This is not happening again. Not while you are paying me. If you want to, you know, after—"

I shake my head. "There can't be an after. I've told you that."

"How can you unequivocally say that? You said yourself we're compatible. What are you so scared of, Sawyer?"

I silently finish my drink and pour another.

"You got hurt, didn't you? By a woman. Someone you loved?"

"I've never loved anyone."

"I feel sorry for you then," she says. "Because you're missing out."

"You've loved someone?" I ask. "Trent?"

"I was seventeen. Who can really say they are in love at that age?"

"But you thought you were."

She shrugs.

"Who was the third?" I ask. "There's me and Trent, that leaves one more. Was it Bass? It was Bass, wasn't it?"

"No, it wasn't Bass."

"I'll bet he wishes it was."

Her eyes close briefly and I wonder if she wishes it too. "It was just some guy a few years ago. We dated on and off for about a year."

"So, fuck buddies. See – case in point."

"We weren't fuck buddies," she says with an eyeroll. "We just wanted different things out of life."

"You're telling me you went *years* without sex before you met me?"

She nods.

"Years? And here I am giving you free rein." I sweep my hand from my head to my waist, showcasing my body. "Yet you don't want it."

She furrows her brow. "I've had it. Twice, apparently."

"So then why not just keep doing it?"

Samantha Christy

"Because you're *paying* me, Sawyer. What don't you understand about that?"

"Semantics," I say. "And come on, Aspen. Me firing you so we could sleep together? We both know that was a bunch of bullshit. You wanted it. I wanted it. So why fight it?"

"Let me get this straight," she says, walking over to pour herself a drink. "You want me to sleep with you for the next several months, which is decidedly convenient for *you*. But then you want to cut off contact and send me on my way, my pockets stuffed with money, come the end of October."

"It's kind of a win-win, don't you think?"

She puts a hand on her hip. "Are you planning on leaving me with a catered breakfast every time we have sex?"

My eyes widen. "You know about that?"

She shakes her head, obviously frustrated with me. "You really don't have a clue about women, do you?"

I cock my head to the side.

"Let me enlighten you, *Speed Limit*. Men can separate sex and feelings. Women, not so much. You and I are friends. We live together. Surely you've felt the connection we have. Whether you want to admit it or not, we have one."

"Are you saying you have feelings for me, Andrews?"

"I'm saying I think it goes both ways, but you're better at compartmentalizing it."

She takes a swig of her drink, exposing her neck. The neck I was sucking on earlier. I know it well now and I can pinpoint the spot that makes her moan. Her hair is still messy and matted from our activities and she looks sexy as hell in the halter top she's wearing.

She has no idea just how good at compartmentalizing I am. If I had my way, I'd take her right here on the floor of the suite. Then

276

up against the wall. Then on the table. The window ledge. The shower. She doesn't know that every time I look at her, I think maybe she's the one I'll break my vow for. My vow to never let a woman into my life.

She also has no idea that every time I look at her and have those feelings, all I see is my mother.

"Maybe you've just seen too many chick flicks," I tell her.

"So you're saying you have no feelings for me whatsoever?"

"I have a lot of feelings for you." I nod to the bedroom. "I loved the way I felt on top of you. Underneath you. Behind you."

She gives me a biting stare. Then she turns around and grabs the handle of her suitcase on the way to the door.

She opens the door, but before she can walk through, I race over and put my hand on it, pushing it closed. I cage her to the door between my arms and press my face into her hair. "Don't go."

"Why, Sawyer? Why shouldn't I go? Because I signed your damned contract?"

I smell her. She smells of coconut shampoo and sex. A heady combination.

She turns around, putting our faces inches apart, mine hovering over hers. I want to lean down and kiss her. But at the same time, I don't want to mislead her.

"You can't do it, can you?" she asks. "You can't admit you have feelings for me."

"I ..."

When I don't say anything, she spins around in my arms and tries to force the door open but she's no match for my strength and the door doesn't budge.

"Let me go," she says.

"I don't want to."

She sighs and leans her forehead against the door. "See, I have no idea what that really means. You don't want to let me go because it will look bad and the press might print something unfavorable about your love life? Or you don't want to let me go because you don't want me to go?"

I push away from the door and run a hand through my hair. "Fine. You want me to say I feel something for you? I feel something for you. There, I said it. But that doesn't change anything, Aspen. Nothing will change anything. When the season is over, so is this. I can't give you anything after that. I'm not capable. I'd hurt you."

"But you'll hurt me anyway. Don't you know that by now? You'll hurt me anyway."

I pour myself another drink and toss it back. "Not as badly as if you stayed."

"Maybe that's not for you to decide. Maybe you should let me choose if I'm willing to risk it."

I shake my head. "I can't. We can't. It's not possible. I have nothing to give you. And believe me, you don't want what I'd offer."

She studies me for a minute. Then she pulls up the handle on her suitcase and drags it back into the bedroom. She stops in the doorway and looks back at me with sad eyes. "We wouldn't want to ruin your precious reputation. You can take the couch."

The door shuts, leaving me alone in the living room. I bring the bottle over to the couch, and as I drain it dry, I remind myself of all the reasons I can't have the woman on the other side of the door.

Chapter Twenty-eight

Aspen

It's been almost a month. Four weeks without his touch unless it's to keep up appearances for the press. And even then, it seems forced.

I sometimes go to games. We're seen in public per the conditions of the contract. We occasionally pass each other in the night on the way to the kitchen for a drink of water. But what it comes down to is that we're avoiding each other.

I know why I'm avoiding him. I'm mad at him. He went months without telling me the truth about us. But it's more than that. I know deep down, I'm trying to distance myself so when this is over, it won't hurt so much.

But those nights when we do pass each other in the hallway, I swear he wants to tell me something. I think he deliberately brushes against me just to be able to touch me. But then he pulls away, like touching me has hurt him. It's like he's afraid of me.

And the pile of cash on the kitchen table just keeps growing. Every week, he adds more grocery money to it. And every week, I leave it sitting there.

Sawyer and I not communicating isn't the only thing that's changed. Bass and I aren't hanging out like we used to either. I know it's harder since we've both moved into new places, but I miss him. He's my best friend. I'm surrounded by lots of new people, yet I feel completely alone.

Some of those people, I'm going out with tonight. I'm meeting Murphy and Rylee for dinner while the guys are in Atlanta.

On my way to the restaurant, I avoid looking at any news stands. I'm tired of seeing the tabloid magazines that seem to always be showcasing our strained relationship. The irony is not lost on me. We aren't even *in* a real relationship, yet it's strained nonetheless. Oh, how the press would have a field day if they ever found out the reality of our situation.

Denver calls me at least once a week, asking if I'm okay. And I always lie to him, telling him everything is fine. But he knows better. He can sense it. And I know he'd be on the next plane to New York if he had anything to say about it.

Rylee draws me into a hug when I approach. Then she looks behind me. "I thought Bass was coming."

I shake my head. "No. Something came up with Brooke. But he told me to give each of you his best."

He's avoiding me, too.

"Those two are adorable together, don't you think?" Murphy asks.

I shrug. "I guess."

As we're escorted to our table, I can sense Murphy studying me. As soon as we're seated and handed our menus, she asks, "You aren't jealous, are you?"

"Jealous? No. I just don't think their relationship is as genuine as it seems."

"How so?" Rylee asks.

"I don't know. I just think it's moving too fast. One minute he didn't even want to be her roommate because he wasn't into her. And the next minute, he's moving in. And now they're joined at the hip. It just seems so bogus."

Murphy laughs. "I guess it takes one to know one – bogus relationships, I mean."

I stare down at the table and pick at an invisible spot.

"Oh my gosh, that sounded awful," Murphy says, putting a hand on my arm. "I didn't mean anything by it."

"It's okay. I know what this is. And you don't need to apologize. You're absolutely right."

Rylee shakes her head. "What you have with Sawyer is not bogus," she says. "You might have a contract with him, but everyone can see you have feelings for each other."

I laugh. "Have you been paying attention? Have you *seen* us lately?"

"I have," she says. "And that's exactly why I know what you have is real. There is so much sexual tension between you two that it practically lights up a dark room. I don't know what happened with you guys in Kansas City, but you've been different ever since. I can see you fighting your feelings now. I can see how scared he is. That man is seriously in love with you, Aspen. Surely you know that."

My eyes go wide. "In *love* with me? You're crazy."

Murphy smiles across the table at me. "Take it from someone who knows. Caden and I fought our feelings for each other for a long time. You and Sawyer may have had more of an unconventional start, but I predict the ending will be the same."

"The *ending* will be in October. Believe me, he never fails to remind me of that."

"That's a long time from now," Murphy says. "A lot can happen between now and then."

I shake my head, disagreeing with her. "He made it clear from the start that he won't ever be in a real relationship."

"Things change. People change," Rylee says.

"Not him."

"Don't give up on him," Murphy says. "I can see how you love him, Aspen. Love changes people."

"You think I'm *in love* with him?"

"Well, aren't you?"

The waitress comes by to take our drink order, saving me from answering her question. I'm relieved. I'd rather not lie to her. I'm lying to enough people already.

Rylee orders a margarita and I decide I want the same.

"Just a water for me," Murphy says.

The waitress walks away and Rylee pouts. "This is supposed to be a night out. What's girls' night without drinking?"

Murphy's lips curve up into a smile that almost touches her eyes.

Rylee squeals. "Oh, my God! Really?"

Murphy nods.

Rylee all but jumps over the table to embrace Murphy in a hug when I realize what's happening.

"You're pregnant?" I ask.

"I am, but you guys can't tell anyone. The press will have a field day and we'd like to keep this to ourselves for a while. We just had our first ultrasound yesterday."

"Can I see it?" Rylee asks. "Do you have it with you?"

Murphy smiles deviously before she digs an envelope out of her purse and pulls out a black and white ultrasound photo. I stare at it and smile, like I guess I should even though I don't see anything.

"Murphy! Oh, my gosh!" Rylee leans in close, so that only the two of us can hear. "You're having *twins?*"

Murphy laughs and nods her head.

I take the picture from Rylee. "How do know that from this picture?"

"See those two dark spots?" she says. "I only had one of those when I got knocked up."

I study the photo until I can see them. Then I look up at Murphy. "Congratulations! Twins, wow – you'll be busy. I know Denver and I ran my mom ragged. But I can tell you having a twin is the best thing ever. They will be very close."

"I hope so. I can't wait. Caden is already doting over them and I'm not even showing yet."

"He's going to be a great father," Rylee says.

"I think so, too."

Murphy and Rylee spend most of dinner talking babies. Then Rylee apologizes. "I'm so sorry, Aspen. This must be boring for you."

"It's fine. It's nice to see you guys so passionate about it. You're both very lucky."

"Do you want kids?" Murphy asks me.

"Someday, yes."

"Can you imagine Sawyer as a father?" Rylee asks.

"Yes, I can," Murphy says. "He's so fun. He's a big kid himself. I think he'll make one hell of a dad."

I look between the other two women at the table as if they've lost their minds. "Now I *know* you guys are crazy."

We get interrupted by a woman walking by. "You're Sawyer Mills' girlfriend, right?"

I look up at her, not bothering to answer the question she already knows the answer to.

She shoves her phone at me. "I just thought you'd like to know what he's doing while he's down in Atlanta."

I look at her phone to see a picture of Sawyer in a compromising position with a woman sitting on his lap. They are laughing and looking like they're having a great time. I know it's not an old picture, because he's wearing a shirt I bought him last month. I don't normally buy him clothes, but while I was out shopping, I saw a shirt that was the exact color of his eyes and thought it would look stunning on him. It does. Apparently the girl in his lap thinks so, too.

I try to swallow the lump in my throat. I try to pretend that the only reason I'm affected by this is because it's against the terms of our contract. But I'm only lying to myself. I feel a piece of me dying inside.

Murphy pushes the phone away and asks the woman to leave us. "Don't read too much into that," she says. "You know how the press can blow things out of proportion."

"Blow things out of proportion?" I ask, like a jealous girlfriend. "She was sitting on his lap. And her top was practically coming off her boobs."

"Maybe it's an old picture," Rylee says.

"It's not," I say, wiping an unbidden tear from my eye. "I bought him that shirt."

Rylee looks sympathetic. "You can sit here and be upset, or you can ask him about it."

"Like a jealous girlfriend?"

"Like someone who cares about him," she says.

I push my chair back. "I'm going to the bathroom. Please excuse me."

"It'll be okay, Aspen. You'll see. We've both been there. Things like this happen all the time."

"Not to me they d-don't," I stutter. "I n-never expected this. Why did I have to f-fall for a guy who is so clearly unavailable?"

Rylee grabs my arm before I walk away. "*Was* unavailable," she says. "*Was*, Aspen. You are the one who is changing all that."

I nod to the woman sitting across the room who showed me the picture. "Or maybe he hasn't changed at all."

I head to the bathroom and splash some water on my face. I look at my reflection in the mirror. The reflection of a love-sick girl who is getting her heart broken. No amount of money is worth this. I should leave. I should leave now. He obviously doesn't care about me *or* the contract we signed.

Maybe he'd let me out of it. Maybe he'd let me keep the money he's given me already. Then I could go back home and find a job and help Denver pay off the rest of his debt like I'd originally planned.

The door to the bathroom opens and Murphy walks in behind me. She hands me her phone. "Look," she says.

I take the phone from her to see Caden sitting down with the same slutty-looking girl in his lap. My eyes snap to Murphy's. "What?"

"It was a bachelor party for one of the batting coaches who's getting married next weekend. I just got off the phone with Caden. She was a stripper. She sat on their laps. Some pictures were taken and unfortunately, a few got leaked. It was all quite innocent. Caden assured me that Sawyer didn't do anything wrong."

"Oh."

I back up and sit down on the chair in the corner, my head falling into my hands as I try to swallow my tears.

Murphy comes over and rubs my back. "What's wrong, Aspen? It's okay. He didn't do anything."

"I know," I tell her. "I just didn't think I'd be so relieved to find that out." I look up at her with tears pooling in my eyes as I think back over the last few months. The months that have been more confusing than any other in my life. I even think navigating my parents' death was easier than this, maybe because I had my brother to support me – unlike now. Yet, at the same time, these months have been the most exciting I've ever known.

"You were right, Murphy. I do love him. I don't think I knew how much until just now." I shake my head. "What am I going to do?"

"You're going to walk back to our table and sit with Rylee and me so we can come up with a plan. You're going to make that man see what he'd be missing if he tosses you aside when your arrangement ends. You're going to be yourself, because that is the woman he loves – we just need to help him realize it."

I grab the tissue she's offering me and wipe my eyes. "Do you really think we can?"

"I'm sure of it," she says.

Before we walk out the door, I pull her aside. "Murphy, why did you tell me about the babies? You said yourself that you don't want anyone to know about them. Why would you tell someone who isn't even a real friend?"

She narrows her eyes at me and then puts her hands on my shoulders. "Aspen, we've spent countless hours with each other. We've had good times together. We support each other when our men are away. I've laughed with you and cried with you. If you think that isn't a real friendship, then you're not the woman I thought you were."

"Thank you."

"For what?" she asks.

"For being a real friend to me even when you didn't have to."

She pulls me into a hug. A long, tight, all-encompassing hug. A real hug from a real friend.

"Come on," she says, grabbing my hand and leading me out the door. "Let's go figure out how to get your man."

Chapter Twenty-nine

Sawyer

"Ooof!"

I fall back onto the grass when Danny tackles me.

Lucy comes running out of the kitchen. "Are you okay?" she asks. Then she scolds Danny as she helps him get up. "Daniel, you're too big to be tackling anyone."

"But he had the football and that's what football players do," he says.

I brush the grass from my shorts. "It's fine, Lucy. No harm done."

"Your phone was vibrating," she says, nodding back to where I left it in the kitchen. "I couldn't help notice the text that popped up. It's Aspen. She wants to know if you'll be home for dinner."

"Okay. Thanks."

"How come you never talk about her?" she asks. "The only things I know about her are what I read in magazines."

"It's not like you and I have heart-to-hearts about each other's love lives, Lucy."

"True. I guess I'm just surprised that you never bring her name up when you visit. She must mean a lot to you if you invited her to move into your townhouse."

I shrug.

She laughs. "It's *me*. You know I won't say anything to the press. Is it serious? Are you thinking long-term here?"

"When have you ever known me to do long-term?"

"I've never known you to do *any* term, Sawyer. That's why I'm asking."

I look over at Danny, who seems content tossing up and catching the football. I wish he'd just tackle me again, that way I wouldn't have to answer her questions. I'm not prepared to answer them. My teammates don't ask for details and my best friends don't bother because they know about the arrangement. It's easy enough to avoid the press. 'No comment' is not unexpected when it comes to them. But Lucy asking questions is something I didn't anticipate.

"She's nice. Smart, too."

Lucy stares me down. "That's all you have to say? She's nice and smart?"

"What do you want me to say, Lucy? I can't predict the future."

"But you obviously like her. You love her even, according to the articles I've read."

"I'm not discussing this with you."

"Does she know about Daniel?"

I shake my head. "Danny is nobody's business but mine."

"You're ashamed of him."

"The fuck I am," I say, then I quickly look over to see if Danny heard me, but he's running to the other side of the yard. "I'm not ashamed of him, Lucy. But my past is nothing I want to talk about with anyone."

"I suppose our moving will make things easier for you then."

"That's bullshit and you know it. I'm going to fly down and see him whenever I can."

"It's okay if you don't, Sawyer. You have no obligation here."

"I'm doing it," I say, harshly. "Now if you don't mind, I'm going to throw the football with him for a few more minutes before I have to go home."

~ ~ ~

On my drive back to the city, I think about what Lucy said. I've thought about telling Aspen about Danny. I've thought about it a lot. She's the only person I've ever considered telling. But maybe that's exactly why I shouldn't. Then again, maybe if I told her everything, she'd understand why I can't ever be in a relationship.

Aspen is different now. Ever since I returned from Atlanta last week, it's like she's her old self again. She's not avoiding me anymore. She's cooking for me again. Well, she never stopped cooking for me, but now she waits until I get home and she eats with me instead of just leaving me a plate in the refrigerator like she did after we came back from Kansas City.

I think I liked it better when she was avoiding me. Everything was easier. We were like ships passing in the night. There was no dinner conversation. No late-night talks. No joking around. No touching.

But the thing is, I missed all of that. I missed it so much it was messing with my head. I used to think having Aspen at games was a jinx. But after Kansas City, *not* having her there was what screwed up my game.

When I arrive home, Aspen is nowhere to be found despite the incredible smells coming from whatever is cooking in the oven. I decide to get in a workout before dinner, but when I go downstairs, I find Aspen staring at the walls.

"There you are," I say.

My words startle her and her hand covers her heart. "You scared me." She looks over at the stairs. "I hate basements. It's why I've never come down before."

"This is your first time down here?"

She nods as she continues to peruse the room with her eyes.

It makes sense. She's never asked me about the butterflies and I've always wondered why. My basement is split in half, one side is my weight room and the other side is my workshop. Ever since I was a kid, I've made butterflies. It started out as something I'd do at night in the weeks after my mother's funeral. I would draw pictures of them. Then later on, I'd make them out of clay. In high school, I almost got beat up for making one in wood shop. But that was the one I liked the best. So when I moved out of my dad's house into my own place, one of the first purchases I made was a router and a lathe.

I look around at everything I've created over the years. Hundreds of butterflies in all colors, shapes, and sizes hang on the wall. There are wood shavings on the floor. Paint splatters on the table. A pile of various unused wood planks in the corner. And I realize for someone who's never seen this before, it must raise a lot of questions.

Aspen walks around the room, studying each of my creations. I've never shared this room with anyone. Not even my friends know about it. I knew she'd see it when she moved in. I just didn't realize how fucking sexy she'd look staring at my work. Touching them like I want her to be touching *me*.

"These are beautiful," she says, when I walk up and stand next to her.

Then she turns and puts a hand over my rib cage, right on top of my tattoo. It makes me want to wrap her in my arms.

But I don't.

"Tell me about the butterflies," she says.

I think about my car ride earlier and how I've never told anyone about Danny. I've never told anyone about the butterflies either. Or about my mom. Basically, anything about my life.

"My mom really liked butterflies," I tell her. "She would tell me stories about them."

"How old were you when she died?" she asks.

I narrow my brows. "How do you know she died?"

"You told me once, right after you found out my parents died. And you just referred to her in the past tense. And you collect butterflies. I collect poems. My mom loved poetry and now I have a scrapbook I keep, and anytime I read a poem that reminds me of my mom, I make a copy of it and stick it in my scrapbook. I've almost filled up the entire thing." She glances around at the numerous wood carvings and then she touches my tattoo again. "We're more alike than you think, Tom Sawyer."

"She was the only other person to ever call me that, you know."

Her smile broadens. "Tell me about her," she says, picking up one of the butterflies off a shelf and walking over to the couch to sit down.

I follow her over and take a seat. "I was ten."

Her fingers move carefully across the ridges in the wood. "That must have been very hard for you," she says.

"You have no idea," I tell her. Then I realize my comment makes me sound like an inconsiderate prick. "Sorry, I guess you do."

"No. I don't. Every person's experience is different. And you were only ten. I was much older when I lost my parents. Do you want to talk about it?"

I shake my head. "Not really."

She waves her hands around the room. "She loved butterflies and now you have all of these. It's like she's watching over you."

I study her as she continues to appraise the wooden sculpture in her hands. "You don't think that's stupid?" I ask.

"Stupid? God, no, Sawyer. I think it's beautiful. It's how you remember her."

I nod my head. "I saw one right after she died."

"You saw a butterfly?"

"Yeah. I was a mess because she died before I could say goodbye. I was at the hospital and I had just talked to her and she had told me the story of how a caterpillar becomes a butterfly. She loved to tell me that story. Then I went to find my dad and when we came back, she was gone. I ran outside and got sick. I didn't know what to do. And then I saw the butterfly. It flew around my head like it knew me. It stayed with me far longer than I'd ever seen a butterfly stay in one place."

"It was her," she says.

I look at Aspen and see she has tears in her eyes.

"That's impossible," I say, not wanting to admit I thought the same thing. But I was ten. I didn't know any better then.

"It was her," she says again.

A tear falls from her eye and I reach over to catch it. My hand doesn't leave her face after I wipe her tears. I've never told anyone that story before. I've never felt this connection with anyone. It takes all of my willpower not to kiss her. Because I've never wanted to kiss someone as much as I do right now.

I pull away and look back at the wall.

She sighs, and I'm not sure it's a sigh of relief or a sigh of disappointment.

"Is that why you don't like relationships?" she asks. "You saw what losing your mom did to your dad?"

I shake my head. "No, that's not why."

She gets up off the couch and puts the butterfly back in its place. "But there *is* a why," she says.

I ignore her statement. "Tell me why you don't like basements. Doesn't everyone have a basement in the Midwest?"

"Denver locked me in our basement one time. It was hours before anyone found me. And since the light switch was on the outside of the door, I was in the dark."

I try to cover my laugh. She swats me. "Don't laugh," she says. "It was terrifying. I was only five years old."

"Sorry. So this whole time, for months, you haven't come down here? Why now?"

"It's been driving me crazy hearing the noises that come from the basement. I knew you had a weight room down here, but the whirling and buzzing sounds didn't make sense to me. It didn't sound like a treadmill or a weight machine. I just had to find out what it was."

"You could have just asked me."

She raises her brows. "Oh, right. And the most private man on the planet would have just come out and told me."

"I just told you a hell of a lot more than I've ever told anyone else."

I see a hint of a smile. "Only because you caught me looking," she says.

"Maybe. Maybe not."

"Well, I happen to think it's amazing that you do this to honor your mom. And I love that I know this about you."

"Maybe you should tell me something about *you* that I don't know."

"I'm an open book," she says. "I don't try to hide anything."

"You didn't tell me about Denver until I read about it in the news."

"That's different," she says. "It just never came up. And besides, I was … *am* … in your employ, and it's not exactly the kind of thing you tell your boss."

"So it seems we all have secrets at one time or another."

She shrugs. "I guess we do."

"There is something I want to know about you," I say.

"What?"

"What do you do all day? I mean, I'm not suggesting you sit around eating bon-bons, but now that school is over and grad school hasn't started, how do you spend your time?"

She smiles.

"What is it?" I ask.

"Nothing. It's just that you rarely ask about me, I mean except when it has to do with my past boyfriends."

I snort. "Don't let it go to your head, Andrews."

"Oh, I wouldn't dare."

"So, bon-bons?"

"Hardly," she says. "I spend a lot of time volunteering."

"Really? Where?"

"A few different places. Mostly I teach underprivileged kids how to play piano. It's a program through Juilliard that introduces kids to music."

"And that takes up all your time?"

She shrugs. "That and a few others."

"Such as?"

"I help out at a soup kitchen sometimes."

"Feeding the homeless? That's admirable."

"Have you ever tried it?" she asks. "Volunteer work is very rewarding."

"I think I have enough on my plate."

"You do now, but in the off-season I'm sure you have plenty of time."

"Hmmm. Maybe."

"Maybe meaning no," she says.

"I didn't say that."

"Sawyer, underneath your rough and roguish exterior is a nice guy. I know it. I see glimpses of him all the time. That guy wants to come out. Maybe if you did something to help others, that guy will come through and then everyone else will see what I see. What your friends see."

"You think I'm roguish?" I say with a smirk.

"*Rough* and roguish. Big difference."

I smile at her and she rolls her eyes. Damn, I love it when she does that.

"People would see that you're more than a guy who gets lap dances," she says.

I shake my head. "It wasn't a lap dance. She just sat down for a brief second. She sat on every player's lap. Why doesn't anyone get in a tizzy about *them*?"

"Because they aren't you. People are waiting for you to screw up. They are waiting to prove that an old dog *doesn't* learn new tricks. And the women — none of them want you to change, not unless they can be the one to break you."

"Break me?"

"Settle you down."

"Is that what *you* want to do? Settle me down?"

"Settle down *Sawyer Mills?*" she says with distant eyes. "I'm not sure I would dare to try."

I stare at her and try to gauge the sincerity of her words. But I'm calling bullshit because her eyes don't lie. And her eyes are telling me a much different story than her mouth.

I hear the oven timer go off upstairs. Aspen points at the ceiling. "Come on, let's go eat."

Chapter Thirty

Aspen

Tears of pride fill my eyes when I look at Bass in his dress blues. He's graduating from fire school today. He's fulfilling his life-long dream.

That's not to say he doesn't love guitar. He does. He's very passionate about it and plays almost daily. But ever since he was young, he's dreamed of fighting fires. However, his parents are both academics who are heavily involved in the arts and they convinced him to go to Juilliard.

I'm glad he did or we'd never have met. Despite the fact that we haven't been hanging out as much lately, he's still my very best friend. And despite the fact that he declared his feelings for me, I'm pretty sure I'm still his.

I pull him in for a hug. "I'm so damn proud of you."

"Don't smear your girly black eye crap on my nice shirt or white gloves," he jokes.

I swat his arm. "Shut up."

"I'm really glad you came, Penny."

"I wouldn't miss it for the world. You know that. Sawyer's coming, too, but he had a game so he might not get here before the ceremony."

"He shouldn't go out of his way," he says.

"He likes you, Bass. Of course he's going to come."

Sometimes I wonder if it hurts Sebastian to see Sawyer and I together. Although he's one of the few people who knows about our arrangement, he's also well aware of how I feel about Sawyer.

I've often thought about how much easier life would be if I'd fallen in love with Bass instead. There would be no drama. No conflicting feelings. No inevitable heartbreak. He's such a great guy. A better man than Sawyer by most people's standards. He's handsome, funny, and very passionate. Brooke is lucky to have him. I hope she knows that.

Bass introduces me to a few of his fellow graduates and then Brooke joins us. She snakes her arm around Sebastian's waist, almost as if to mark him. She's always been suspicious of us, as are most people. Nobody believes that a man and a woman can live together and be best friends without having some kind of sexual relationship.

Brooke is very sweet, but when it comes to Bass, she's super territorial.

"Where's your boyfriend?" she asks, never failing to mention my relationship in front of Bass.

"He's at a game, but he's coming over right after. I just hope he makes it."

"Don't worry," Brooke says. "I'm going to get the ceremony on video if he ever wants to see it."

"Thanks. I'll let him know. So, Bass, when do you find out what station you get assigned to?"

"Pretty soon. But not tonight. We submitted our top three choices last week."

"Oh, I hope he gets Brooklyn," Brooke says. "Don't you think that would be apropos? You know, because of my name?"

I laugh. "Well, I hope he gets Brooklyn, too. But for an entirely different reason. I know his other two choices were stations in Manhattan and the thought of him having to fight fires in high-rises scares me to death."

"Brooklyn has high-rise buildings, too, you know," Brooke says.

"I know, but not nearly as many as Manhattan. And none that are as tall. I don't want our boy in too much danger."

"*Our* boy?" Brooke says with an accusing brow.

Bass laughs at her insecure comment. I know I shouldn't goad her like that. I knew what I was saying. And maybe *I'm* a bit territorial when it comes to Bass, but it's only because I love him like a brother. Just like he doesn't want to see me hurt, I don't want to see him hurt, professionally *or* personally. But quite frankly, I'm more worried about Brooke. She and I have a lot more in common than she realizes. We both love men who are incapable of loving us back. Or unwilling.

Someone makes an announcement over the loudspeaker and the graduates head to the front of the auditorium to take their seats.

I watch with pride as my best friend walks across the stage and gets the certificate he's worked so hard for.

Sawyer sneaks in from the side, squeezing next to me as I try to make room for him. He leans in and kisses my cheek like it's a habit. "Good," he whispers. "I'm glad I didn't miss it."

I nod my head, unable to speak because of the happy tears that are falling.

Sawyer chuckles in my ear. "Are you going to cry when they give me my World Series ring, too?"

"That depends. Do they give those out right there at the last game?"

Something changes in his eyes. And the way he looks at me is … different. He shakes his head sadly. "No. It normally takes months to make them."

"Oh. Well, that's too bad. I would have liked to have seen it."

He cocks his head to the side. "You really think we'll make it to the Series?"

"Why wouldn't I? The Nighthawks are a great team. And with you leading them, anything is possible."

"Thanks," he says. "It really means a lot to me that you feel that way."

I turn my head and stare at him. "You had the perfect opportunity to say something cocky just now, yet you said something nice again, Tom Sawyer," I whisper. "You'd better watch out or you'll be labeled a good guy before you know it."

"Shhh," he whispers back, his hot breath flowing over my ear and neck. "Don't tell anyone."

He grabs my hand and entwines it with his. I realize he's only doing it for show, but it feels nice. And even though I know he's just playing a part, his thumb rubbing slow circles around my knuckles sends pulses of want and need throughout my body.

Does he know what his touch does to me? Does he even care?

I take a peek at Brooke, who's on my other side, and notice the smile on her face when she sees our clasped hands. She thinks if I'm off the market, she has a better chance with Bass. But I'm not so sure it's me who has anything to do with it. I can see it in his eyes, he doesn't want her like I want Sawyer. But maybe being with *somebody* is better than being with *nobody*.

I look back at Sawyer and realize just how different these two men really are.

Bass wants a relationship so badly, he's willing to accept someone he doesn't love. Sawyer is so scared of one, he'll throw away love without giving it a chance.

And then there's Denver.

Boy, do I have some screwed-up men in my life.

"Come on," Brooke says, standing up and tugging on my arm after the last graduate crosses the stage. "Let's head outside for the reception."

Champagne is flowing freely and Bass quickly gets drunk, making up for lost time after having sworn off alcohol during his training. He grabs two glasses off a nearby tray and hands one to Sawyer after Brooke and I refuse it. "Come on, someone has to keep up with me," he says.

Sawyer takes the glass, clinking it to Bass's.

"See," Bass says, putting an arm around Sawyer's shoulders. "This is why I like this guy. We think alike."

"Oh, you like me now, do you?" Sawyer asks.

"I always liked you," Bass slurs. "It's just that I'm watching out for our girl."

I see Brooke cringe out of the corner of my eye.

"I'm watching out for her, too," Sawyer says.

Bass snorts. "Yeah, right. For what, three more months? Then what?"

"What happens in three months?" Brooke asks.

I kick Bass in the shin and stare him down.

"Oh, shit," he says. "Right. I mean, in three months the season will be over and what then? Are you going to take our girl on vacation? Someplace nice maybe? She deserves it, you know."

"Maybe I will. Ever been to the Florida Keys?" he asks me with a raised brow.

Thoughts of Sawyer and me on a secluded beach infiltrate my head.

"The *Keys?*" Brooke says like it's a bad word. "Take the girl to someplace exotic like Hawaii. I've always wanted to go to Hawaii. My parents got married there and I grew up hearing stories about how wonderful it was."

"That sounds good too," Sawyer says. "I guess we'll have to think about it."

"Brooke, you wanted to meet Jim's wife," Bass says. "She's over there, come on, I'll introduce you." Bass turns to Sawyer and me. "We'll catch you guys a little later. Hang around and enjoy some more drinks."

"We will," Sawyer says, raising his glass to him as they walk away.

As soon as Bass and Brooke leave our side, several people come over and ask Sawyer for autographs and pictures. He obliges. He's always pretty nice about it as long as the fans aren't too unruly.

"I can't take you anywhere," I joke after the last fan snaps a selfie with him.

"Does that bother you?" he asks, motioning to the people watching us from around the courtyard.

I shake my head. "No. As long as they don't drape themselves all over you."

He raises an amused brow. "Jealous much?"

"About as jealous as you were of Trent Dugan."

His jaw tightens and his lips form a thin line.

"See – I knew it. I *knew* you were jealous of him."

"I'll admit to nothing," he says.

I see a fireman's boot being passed around. It's customary at firehouse events to donate to whatever cause they are supporting. But I realize I don't have any cash on me.

"Do you think you could spot me a twenty?" I ask Sawyer, nodding to the boot being circulated.

"Sure," he says, digging into his pocket. His hand comes out with a wad of cash, but then something shiny drops onto the tile pavers with a *ping*.

"Shit," he says, getting down on a knee to retrieve whatever fell. "I forgot I had this." He shows me the beautiful ring that I recognize from Murphy's finger. "Caden was in a hurry today and he left this sitting on the bench by his locker."

"Oh, my God!" someone shrieks. "He's proposing!"

Suddenly, people gather around us, circling us with bodies five-deep.

I look down in panic at Sawyer, who's still on one knee. How are we going to get out of this? Cameras are already out and recording.

"What do we do?" I ask Sawyer through the loud murmurs of the crowd.

A devious smile curves his lips. "Just go with it," he says, so only I can hear.

"Quiet!" someone yells in the background.

The crowd falls silent. You could hear a pin drop. My heart is pounding through my chest wall.

"What do you say, Aspen Andrews?" he says, holding Murphy's engagement ring out to me. "Want to get hitched?"

My jaw drops. I have to keep myself from rolling my eyes at him. I know we're being filmed. I know this will be all over the internet and television in ten minutes flat.

I see him begging me with his eyes. He's begging me to play along. To save his career.

And I'm sure the photogs will go crazy over the shots people are getting of the tears rolling down my face. Tears they think are from happiness. But all I can think about when I nod my head yes, is how ironic that the only proposal I've ever dreamed of, I'm getting from the man who doesn't mean it.

Cheers erupt around us as he slips the ill-fitting ring onto my finger and then pulls me into his arms.

"You're out of your mind!" I shout into his ear.

"Congratulations!" Brooke screams as she drags a stunned Bass over to my side.

Bass looks from Sawyer to me and I can't tell if he's going to hug him or hit him. But what he does next is more surprising than anything. Bass gets down on one knee and holds out his hand to Brooke. "In the words of this tool standing next to me, what do you say, Brooke Carlisle? Want to get hitched?"

Brooke's eyes go wide. "You're drunk," she says, motioning for him to stand up.

"Yeah, Bass, you're drunk," I reiterate.

"Shhh," he hushes me. "This is *our* moment. You already had yours." Then he turns back to Brooke. "I may be a little drunk, but I still know what I'm doing. Come on. We're perfect for each other, don't you think?"

"Yes, I do," Brooke says. "I just wasn't sure you thought so too."

"We are." He turns to me. "Right, Penny? Isn't she perfect for me?"

Brooke puts her hand on Bass's face, forcing him to look back at her. "Is this for real?" she asks. "Because if you're just messing with me—"

"It's for real," he says. "Marry me, Brooke."

A glorious smile creeps up her face and he stands up right before she jumps into his arms.

"What the hell is happening here?" I ask no one in particular.

Sawyer pulls me aside, letting them have their moment. Phones are still videoing. People are still cheering. A waitress comes out offering fresh glasses of champagne so everyone can toast the happy couples.

When the frenzy dies down and Brooke heads for the bathroom, I excuse myself from Sawyer and drag Bass into a hallway. "Have you gone completely bat-shit crazy tonight?"

"No more than you have, *Mrs. Mills*," he spits out.

"You're delusional, Sebastian. My engagement is fake. Sawyer and I both know that. Brooke thinks yours is real."

"It is."

"So you love her? Because I've never heard you say it. And I'm willing to bet *she's* never heard you say it either. You can't hurt her like that."

"I *do* love her," he says without looking me in the eye.

"Are you sure? Because there's a difference between loving someone and being *in love* with them."

"Why can't you just be happy for me, Aspen? I've supported you through this whole charade. I'd think you could show a little fucking excitement for me. That is unless you have feelings for me."

I stretch my neck around the corner and look at Sawyer talking with some of Bass's friends. Bass's eyes follow mine. He watches me watch Sawyer. Then he slumps against the wall and runs a hand through his hair. "You really love him, don't you?"

"I do. And he loves me. But I don't think he'll ever admit it."

Bass laughs at the irony. "We're two messed up people, aren't we?"

I pull him into my arms. "We are. But we'll always have each other. I promise you that."

"I love you," he says to me like he should be saying to Brooke.

"I love you too," I tell him.

"But you're not *in love* with me like you are him."

I shake my head. "I'm sorry."

"I know," he says. "It's okay." He wipes a tear from under my eye. "Now let's go find our fiancées."

"Good idea. But don't be surprised if Sawyer and I duck out of here. I've got some major ass-whipping to do."

He laughs. "Go easy on the guy, Penny. You are pretty irresistible. And a damn fine catch."

I motion to Sawyer as we make our approach. "Maybe you could tell *him* that."

"I have," he says, giving my arm a squeeze. "Time and time again."

Chapter Thirty-one

Sawyer

"Congratulations!" the cab driver says after we get situated in the back.

Aspen gets a disturbed look on her face when the cabbie displays a picture of us on his phone. A picture with me down on one knee.

I grab her left hand and kiss it. "Thanks," I say.

She gives me a biting stare. I shake it off and play with her. "So, where shall we take our honeymoon? Hawaii, like Brooke mentioned? Or maybe someplace more exotic, like Bali."

Aspen shakes her head at me in frustration. I know she's upset with me. But it's more than that. I saw her face when Bass proposed to Brooke. She wasn't happy about it.

We ride in silence back to my townhouse. But once we're safely inside the door, she turns around and punches me in the chest.

"I told you, you can't do things like that, Sawyer!" she shouts, throwing her purse on the table.

"It's not as if I had a choice," I say. "I was down on a knee with an engagement ring in my hand."

"You *did* have a choice. You could have told the truth. That the ring belongs to Caden's wife."

"They wouldn't have believed me."

"Who cares what they believe? But I think they would have," she says. "Lots of people know he carries the ring in his back pocket when he plays. You should have just said that he left it in the clubhouse and you were going to return it to him but it fell out of your pocket. It's the truth. You didn't have to do what you did."

"Come on, it's no big deal. You're blowing this way out of proportion."

Her eyes narrow and I swear I can see smoke come out of her ears. She digs her phone out of her purse and taps around on it. Then she shoves it in my face. "Look! It's all over the internet. We're supposedly engaged. People will ask us about it. I'll be bombarded with questions. *'When's the big day?' 'Who will design your dress?' 'How soon will you have kids?'* Are you prepared to answer those questions? Because I sure as hell am not."

She looks down at her left hand, removing Murphy's ring. "And what do you think will happen when people notice I'm not wearing a ring? I imagine Murphy will want this one back."

"Okay, you've proven your point. I didn't think this through."

"Do you ever, Sawyer? Do you *ever* think things through? I mean, what are we even doing here? You're saving your reputation for now, but what about next season – are you going to hire another girl? And the season after that? When does the charade end? Your whole life is going to be a lie. How can you live that way?"

She has no idea that I already do.

I walk over and take the ring from her. "We'll think of something. We can put people off, saying we want a long engagement and won't make any plans until after the season. That way we won't have to deal with questions. See? Easy."

She shakes her head. "Nothing about this is easy. Don't you realize how your actions affect others? And I'm not just talking about me. Bass proposed to Brooke tonight. That never would have happened if you hadn't done what you did."

I loosen my tie and then pull it off, hanging it over the back of a chair before I remove my suit jacket. "That's really what this is all about, isn't it? You're mad that Bass got engaged."

"Of course I'm mad. He doesn't love her."

"Maybe that's not for you to say."

She looks at me in disgust. "Well, *somebody* has to. He's making a huge mistake. He was drunk and upset about us. He had no right to ask her. She'll be devastated tomorrow when he takes it back."

"How do you know he'll take it back?"

"What is it about *'he doesn't love her'* that you don't understand?"

I go to the bar and pour myself a drink. "Who says you have to be in love to get married?"

"Oh, my God, you did not just say that." She leans against the arm of the couch and takes her shoes off, letting them fall to the floor with a thud. "How can you be so cavalier?"

"I don't know, years of practice?"

She picks up a shoe and throws it at me.

I catch it and walk it back over to her. "The real question here is, why are you so damn upset about Bass's engagement? He's an adult. He can marry for love or money or companionship. It's not for you to decide. Not unless there is something else going on. Not unless you're still carrying a torch for him."

"Carrying a torch for him? Are you crazy?"

I hold up the ring in my hand. "Apparently, I am."

"I'm not in love with him," she says, unconvincingly.

"The hell you aren't."

"What is it with men? None of you seem to understand that you can love someone without being in love with them."

"So you *do* love him?" I ask, pacing behind the couch.

"Of course I love him. I love him like a brother, Sawyer."

"Did you love him like a brother when you were screwing him?"

She throws her shoe at me again. It's a good thing I know how to catch fast moving objects.

"I've told you many times, we never slept together. I don't know why you can't get it through your thick skull. I guess the steroids are making you stupid."

She makes her way to the stairs and I follow her up.

"I've never done that shit, Aspen. That's a low fucking blow."

She walks into her room and tries to reach the zipper around her back. I stand in the doorway for a minute, watching her get frustrated.

"Damn it!" she yells. "Well, are you going to help me with this or not?"

I walk over to help. I unzip it just enough to see the black lacy bra she's wearing under her dress. I look at the creamy skin of her back, thinking of the two times I've been able to touch it. My hands are screaming at me to let them have a feel. It takes everything I have not to let them.

"I just don't get how a man and a woman can live together for years and not hook up. It's unnatural."

She spins around and holds up her dress so it doesn't fall off her shoulders. "Will you get over yourself? Bass is my best friend. He'll always be my best friend. I don't really give a rat's ass if you are too immature to comprehend it."

"Best friends fuck all the time," I say.

"No they don't."

"Yes they do. There have been a dozen movies made about that very thing."

She laughs. "Because that's what sells movies."

"No. Because that's what women fantasize about."

"You *are* crazy," she says.

"I'm crazy to think that you want him? Or that you love him? Maybe *you're* crazy because you won't admit it."

"Oh, my God, would you quit saying that? I don't love him, Sawyer. How could I when I'm in love with *you*?"

The same time the words leave her mouth, her hand slips from her shoulder and her dress falls to the floor, pooling around her feet leaving her standing practically naked in front of me.

She looks horrified after realizing the dress fell when she was yelling at me. She leans down to pick it up.

I'm not sure my brain even comprehends what she said, because it's too busy taking in her body. The body I dream of every night. The body I try to stay away from every day. The body that fits so perfectly with mine.

Before she can grab the dress, I push her gently onto the bed.

"I didn't—"

I kiss her before she gets any more words out.

She tries to push me way. "I don't—"

My lips come crashing down on hers again.

"I can't—"

Her protests cease when my hands grab her breasts and my mouth finds the spot on her neck that makes her moan. I smile against her skin knowing that I've won. I've won and I didn't even have to fire her this time.

She writhes beneath me as my lips explore her neck. Her hands snake around behind me to wander up and down my back, weaving their way under my dress shirt as she grabs every inch of skin she can reach.

I lower the cups of her bra and lick her breasts. I suck on her nipples as she arches into me. I dip my tongue into the depression between her breasts and laugh when she forces my mouth back to the left.

If there's one thing I've learned about her in the two times we've been together, it's that her left nipple is more sensitive than her right one. I tease it incessantly as she bucks underneath me. I swirl my tongue around it. I flick it, suck it, and play with it until she's begging me for something more. I wonder if I could even get her to come simply by keeping this up. It's one of life's great mysteries that I long to solve.

But I'm too greedy and impatient at this moment. And I'm hard as a fucking rock. My cock is pleading for escape. But she could still say no. She could still end this right now. I need to make sure that doesn't happen.

I reach a hand beneath her wet panties and run my fingers along her slit. I easily insert two fingers into her slick entrance as she pushes herself onto me, sinking me in even deeper. She's close. So close I can almost taste it.

I don't even bother removing her panties. I simply rip them off her and swing one of her legs over my shoulder. I climb down her body, licking and laving her soft stomach as I make my way. When my mouth reaches her silky folds, she cries out. When my tongue lands on her clit, her loud moans beg me to make her come.

Her pleas drive me to work harder than I've ever worked before. I want this to be the best orgasm she's ever had. So I pull back and let my tongue wander around her thighs. I let my hands wander around her ass.

I chuckle when a whine of displeasure erupts from her. I run a finger down the curve of her hip, counting slowly to ten before my tongue continues its assault of her clit. As soon as it does, she bucks her hips and calls out to God. So, of course, I immediately ease up and pull away.

She lifts herself up on her elbows and gives me a heated stare. "Sawyerrrrr," she pleads.

"What do you want, baby?"

"You know what I want," she says, her face red with either embarrassment or passion.

"Say it," I say, giving her clit a teasing flick.

"No."

I stick out my tongue and circle it along the edge of her wet pussy as I watch her. Her eyes roll upwards in pleasure. "Say it," I command.

She opens her eyes again and looks right at me. I can tell she's fighting it. She wants so badly to say it, but she doesn't want to give me all the control.

Then she takes her finger and puts it on her clit. "If you don't make me come, I will."

Holy. Fucking. Shit.

My cock swells even bigger at her words. I'd love nothing more than to watch her get herself off. But not now. This one's all mine. And I tell her that.

"Not today you won't. But the thought of you doing that almost made *me* come."

Her sultry smile recedes, and her mouth falls open as I push her hand aside and double my efforts. I bring her to the brink of orgasm over and over, each time, she begs me for more. Every time I pull away, I remove a piece of my clothing until I'm fully naked on top of her. She's on the brink of insanity. I'm on the verge of explosion.

When neither of us can stand it any longer, I push myself inside of her, both of us moaning in pleasure at the exquisite feeling. I know neither of us will last long, so I take my time and savor her, making long slow strokes. She's clawing at my back, meeting me thrust for thrust. She's building up so high, I doubt I'll even have to use my hand to get her there.

Her thighs tighten. Her back arches. Her eyes close.

"No," I say. "Look at me."

Her eyes open and I watch her come as I feel the sweet sensation of her walls pulsating around me. It pushes me over the edge and I join her, shouting out her name and other words of pleasure as I spill myself inside of her.

My eyes close briefly from the intensity. When I open them, she's still watching me. We stare at each other, her waning pulses still milking the last drops from me. She's gorgeous. I wipe away a piece of wet hair that got caught in her mouth.

"God, Aspen, I lo—"

I freeze, mid-sentence. *What the fuck am I doing?*

I quickly pull out of her, jump off the bed and go to remove the condom. "Shit!"

I stare down at my naked cock. I shake my head from side to side. Never have I forgotten to wear one. *Never.*

Aspen is still lying in bed, staring at me with damp eyes. "What were you going to say to me?" she asks.

"I didn't wear a goddamn rubber," I tell her, still in shock over it.

"It's fine. I'm on the pill. What were you going to say, Sawyer?"

I start pulling on my clothes, but she comes to the edge of the bed and grabs my arm. "You love me. That's what you were going to say. Why can't you just admit it?"

I look at her and shake my head over and over. "No. No. This can't happen."

I finish putting my shirt and pants on and walk out of her room. She grabs a robe and follows me. "Why can't it happen, Sawyer? Quit fighting this. I know you love me. It's okay. I love you, too. Don't you think I'm scared, too? We can be scared together."

I run down the stairs and grab my car keys. She tries to take them from me, but I push her away, careful not to push her into the wall. "I can't. We can't." I walk through the back door and turn around to see her tears. "I'd only hurt you," I say, just before closing the door.

Samantha Christy

Chapter Thirty-two

Aspen

I don't immediately hear the loud engine of his uber-macho car, so I peek out the back window to see him sitting in the front seat, pounding his fists on the steering wheel.

What could possibly be going on in his head that has him so messed up? He was going to say he loves me. He *does* love me. I hear it in his words. Feel it in his touch. See it in his eyes.

I want to go after him, but I'm in a robe that barely covers my ass, so I race upstairs, hoping I can dress before he leaves. I throw on a t-shirt and some yoga pants and fly down the stairs, just in time to hear his car driving away.

I pick up my phone, wanting to call him, but knowing he won't answer. I look at it, realizing I can follow him. I eye the pile of money on the table and then grab it before I run out front and hail a cab. I climb in the back seat. "I need you to follow someone."

"Lady, are you crazy?" the cabbie says. "I'm not going to cause an accident. They'd pull my permit."

I shake my head and hold up my phone. "I don't mean you need to chase another car. I know his location. Just drive where I tell you."

He narrows his eyes. "Just how long do you expect to be on this goose chase, Miss?"

I don't tell him it could last a while. That the only reason Sawyer ever drives his car is if he's going out of the city.

I wave around the wad of cash in my hand. "Don't worry, I can cover it."

He eyes the cash. Then he looks at me like I think my father would have under these circumstances. "In my experience, this never ends well," he tells me.

"It may not. But I at least have to try."

"It's your life, Miss. And your money. Where to?"

I open the 'Find My Friends' app – the one Sawyer demanded I install after we signed the contract. He wanted to make sure I was going to be where I said I was. I told him it went both ways, that if he got to know where I was, I should get to know where he was. But I'm fairly sure neither of us has used it until now.

So here I sit in the back of a cab, a desperate woman chasing after an untouchable man, wondering how I could have sunk so low.

I give the cabbie the directions. We're only a few blocks behind Sawyer, so it's not hard to stay close. But thirty minutes later, when we're on a bridge heading out of the city, the cabbie questions my intent.

"Looks like he's headed to Connecticut. You sure you want to do this?"

I throw a hundred-dollar bill in the passenger seat. "I'm sure."

He looks at the bill and laughs. "I hope he's worth it."

"Me, too."

Every so often, I throw another hundred up front just to keep his mouth shut. We pass by Stamford and Bridgeport and eventually turn off I-95 toward the town of New Haven.

This is where Sawyer grew up. Not that he told me, but it's listed on his Wikipedia page. What's he coming home to? His parents are gone and, as far as I know, he doesn't have any siblings.

My thoughts go haywire and my heart falls. It has to be a woman. One he runs to when things get tough. I run to Denver or Bass. He runs to *her*.

As the cab pulls up in front of a small suburban home, I can see Sawyer still in his car. And he's still pounding the steering wheel. Maybe he feels guilty about running to her. Maybe he's going to turn around and leave. Maybe we should drive down the block and let him.

But his car door opens and he gets out, making a bee-line for the front door.

I quickly settle with the cab driver, leaving him an insanely huge tip, and jump out the back door.

"Is this *her* house?" I yell, as he walks up the sidewalk. "Is this where the beach lady lives? Did you run back to your *real* girlfriend?"

I realize I sound like a jealous bitch, but I'm sick of his lies and his excuses. I'm sick of his walking away from me when he gets secret phone calls. I'm tired of loving a man who is incapable of love.

"What the fuck, Aspen? Who's the crazy one now?" He watches the cab pull away from the curb. "You followed me?"

I hold up my phone. "You're the brilliant one who wanted us to be able to track each other."

He looks at the house and then back at me, guilt washing over his features. "Danny lives here."

"Dani? Is that her name? Great, so how about introducing her to the woman you're fucking in her place."

He cringes. "Don't talk like that."

"Too scared to introduce us? You think it might tarnish your precious reputation?"

He looks to the sky and runs his hands through his hair. "Danny isn't a woman, Aspen."

"She's not?"

"No."

I furrow my brow. "Then I'm confused."

He takes in a big breath and lets it out. He *is* scared of something. But now I just don't know what.

"You want to see why I can't do this?" he asks, pointing his finger between the two of us. "Come on. I'll show you."

He grabs my hand and hastily pulls me to the front door where he rings the bell. A woman answers the door. An older woman, probably in her fifties. And she seems surprised to see Sawyer. She recovers from her surprise, quickly looks me over, and then leans out of the doorway to give Sawyer a kiss on the cheek in greeting.

"Hi, Sawyer. I wasn't expecting you," she says. "Did I forget you were coming?"

"I didn't know myself until just a little while ago. Is it okay?"

"Sure. Daniel just had his bath and is putting on his pajamas. He should be right out."

I look from Sawyer to the woman as her words settle in.

He has a secret. A reason he can't be with someone. Danny is a boy not a girl.

Oh, my God. It all makes sense now.

"Sawyer, do you have a son?"

His eyes grow wide. "Uh, no. Why would you think that?"

I shrug. "You're so secretive. I just, I guess I thought …" I nod to the woman.

The woman laughs. "Oh, Lord, no." She holds out her hand to me. "What your rude companion means to say is that I'm Lucy Edwards. And it's a pleasure to meet you, Aspen. I've read a lot about you despite the fact that our mutual friend doesn't talk much."

"Sorry," Sawyer grunts out in apology. "Aspen doesn't know about Danny. She kind of followed me here after we had a fight."

Lucy nods in understanding. "Ahhh. I think I get it. You followed him to find out about his dirty little secret."

I nod in shame.

"He's not my dirty little secret, Lucy," Sawyer says in disgust.

"Both of you, come on in. Daniel should be right out."

We walk into Lucy's house and I look around, searching for clues. Anything to help me understand what is going on here.

Then, suddenly, a man comes lumbering down the hallway and almost tackles Sawyer onto the couch.

"Sawyer! Did you come to say goodnight?" he asks excitedly.

"You bet I did, buddy. And I brought a friend. Danny, this is Aspen."

I stare at the man who is a man, but also a child. He's almost as big as Sawyer, but his words are simple, and something about the way he looks is … off. He looks so innocent and carefree. Much younger than his years would indicate.

I hold my hand out to him but he pulls me into a tight hug instead. "Aspen is a funny name," he says, squeezing me.

"Daniel, that's not a nice thing to say," Lucy scolds.

"It's okay," I say. "It is a funny name. My parents really liked skiing."

"Aspen is the name of a city," Lucy tells Danny. "Can you guess what state it's in?"

Danny thinks on it and then runs over to get a large atlas from the bookshelf. Lucy opens it to the center pages where there is a huge map of the U.S. She gives him clues, telling him he's hotter or colder when he moves his finger around. When he finally points to Colorado, we all cheer.

"Danny, Aspen has a twin brother who is also named after a city in Colorado," Sawyer says. "Can you guess what his name is?"

Looking at the atlas, it doesn't take him long to guess Denver's name.

It's becoming obvious to me that Danny has some major mental deficits. What's not obvious is how this has anything to do with Sawyer and me.

When Sawyer walks Danny back to tuck him into bed, Lucy pulls me into the kitchen. "You look confused."

"I have no idea what's going on here," I say. "One minute we were … we were … and then he almost … and then he ran off and now we're here."

"There's a lot more to this story than you know. But I'm going to leave it to Sawyer to fill you in." She pulls down two bottles of wine from on top of her refrigerator. "Do you like red or white?"

I cock my head to the side.

"Honey, I've never seen a person more in need of a drink than you are right now," she says laughing. "You two can sit out on the back porch. Let him tell you all about Danny. It might explain some things about the man you love."

I let out a sigh. Right. The man I love. The man who the world thinks loves me back. In fact, they think he loves me so much he wants to marry me. What a farce.

"You do, don't you? Love him, I mean. Even though you're faking it. Even though he hired you to be his girlfriend?"

My eyes go wide. "You know about that?"

"I heard him talking to Danny about it one day when he didn't know I was listening. I guess he needed to tell someone and Danny was a safe bet to keep a secret since he wouldn't understand. Sawyer doesn't know that I know. But I've watched him these past months, both in person and in the news. He's changed. Arrangement or not, you've changed him. I see the way he looks at you. There's nothing fake about it."

"He says he can't have a girlfriend. He says he'll hurt me."

Lucy shakes her head. "That man wouldn't hurt a fly. I've known him for a lot of years, Aspen. He only hurts himself."

Sawyer walks into the kitchen and eyes the bottles of wine Lucy's holding.

"Lucy offered us a drink and her back porch so you can get whatever this is off your chest."

"It's time," Lucy tells him. "It's long overdue and you know it."

He nods his head silently, grabs the bottle of red wine from her and then we head out back.

Lucy hands me the glasses and shuts the door behind us, smiling at Sawyer in encouragement before she walks away. I'm so confused I can't think straight. Is Lucy his mother and Daniel his brother? I know it couldn't be so, unless he's been lying to me all this time. And the butterfly thing – surely he didn't make that up.

We sit down on the porch swing and the wood creaks as if it hasn't been sat on in a while. Sawyer opens the screw-top wine and pours us each a hefty glass. Then he proceeds to drink half of his in silence.

It's killing me knowing he's got something weighing on him like this. I can tell he wants to talk. He probably even *needs* to talk. My guess is that nobody knows his secret outside of the people in this house.

"My dad loved my mom as much as I'd ever seen a man love a woman," he says.

I nod my head, thinking the exact same thing about my parents.

"Then again, I was ten," he says. "I didn't know anything. I didn't know that all men didn't hit their wives."

My heart falls into the pit of my stomach when I realize what he's telling me. "Oh, Sawyer." I look back into the house to see Lucy busying herself in the kitchen. "Is that your mom? Did she have to run away and change her identity?"

I try to grab his hand, but he pulls away.

He laughs sadly. "No. Lucy's not my mother. I told you my mother is dead."

"But then who is she? Who's Danny?"

He takes another long swig of wine. "It got worse over the years, my dad hitting my mom. She always defended him. She told me he loved her so much he couldn't help it. She said everything he did was to keep her safe. She said she loved him, too. I couldn't understand why. When she turned up with fresh bruises and a smile on her face, I was so confused. Did she like what he was doing to her?"

"Sawyer – what does this have to do with Danny?"

"You need to let me finish, Aspen. Please. I've never told this to anyone and it's hard for me. You have to let me do it my way."

I nod my head. "I'm sorry. Go ahead."

I've never seen so much pain on a person's face. This man – this big, strong athlete – is letting everything out. He's finally opening up to me. This could be the turning point for us. The moment he realizes his feelings for me are stronger than his past.

"My father killed my mother," he says.

I look over at him in horror, tears welling in my eyes. I grab his hand. This time he lets me. I have a million questions, but I don't ask any of them. Like he said, he needs to do this his way.

"Her official cause of death was multiple major organ damage from an accidental fall. I never even saw her death certificate until I found it after my dad drank himself to death a few years ago. I always wondered what they listed as her cause of her death. It should have been *'being pushed down the stairs by her son-of-a-bitch husband.'* But there was never a mention of any abuse in her medical records. They hid it well. *She* hid it well."

He puts down his glass and touches his rib cage where his tattoo is. "I should have known she was miserable. How could any person endure what she did and not be? But I guess she was afraid of what would happen to me if she tried to leave him. We were poor. She would have had no way to hire an attorney. I guess she thought that if my dad was hitting her, he wouldn't have to hit me. And she was right, because after she died, I became his punching bag."

My hand goes to cover my mouth. "Oh, Sawyer," I cry.

He shakes his head. "Don't feel too sorry for me. It didn't last long. I was fast and could usually outrun him. I'd hide somewhere in the neighborhood and wait to go home until he left for work. By the time I was thirteen, I was almost as big as he was. He'd try to hit me, but I wouldn't let him. By the time I was fifteen, I got the courage to hit back."

"You were fast even then," I say, with an elbow to his rib in an attempt to lighten the mood.

He laughs a painful laugh. "Hell, he's probably the reason I'm such a good sprinter. But never in a million years would I admit he has anything to do with my success in baseball."

I zip my lips. "Your secret is safe with me."

He appraises me silently. "Are *all* my secrets safe with you?"

"Yes." I nod reassuringly. "They are."

He studies me, gauging the truth to my words.

"I promise," I say, squeezing his hand in encouragement.

He draws in a deep breath. Then he blows it out. Then he takes another drink. Then he looks anywhere but at me. "I'm the reason Danny is the way he is."

I narrow my eyebrows in confusion. "I ... I don't understand."

He still won't look at me as he continues to explain. "Being around my dad, fighting was all I knew. I got suspended three times for fighting in middle school. And in high school, it happened so often, they threatened to kick me off the baseball team. Anyone else would have been. But I was their star player and the coach was always able to convince them to give me another chance.

"Danny wasn't always the way he is now. He was a baseball player, too. A teammate of mine."

He glances at me briefly to see how shocked I am. I'm stunned. Danny doesn't seem like he could have ever played organized sports.

"We were hanging out at a place on the coast called Silver Sands. There was a boardwalk there that ran from the beach to the state park. It was a drinking place for local high school students, but it was new enough that the cops hadn't caught on yet.

"Danny and I, we ..." He looks back into the house, choking on his words. "We had a disagreement about what happened in the game we had played earlier that night. He played second base and I played short. We lost the game because a hit made it past both of us, going right between where we were standing. Each of us claimed it was the other's ball.

"Danny and I weren't such great friends to begin with. We were always butting heads over something. But we hung out with a lot of the same people and always ended up at the same place somehow. And once we started drinking that night, our argument got worse. And in true Sawyer Mills fashion, we got into a fight."

His eyes close. He pulls his hand away from mine. "We got into a fight and that's why he is the way he is."

My heart sinks for him. For Lucy. For Danny. I don't even know what to say.

"And to make matters even worse, he was right all along. It *was* my fucking ball."

I can't imagine what he must be going through carrying that burden all this time. But I still don't understand what that has to do with me and why he can't have a relationship.

"Can I talk now?" I ask.

He nods.

"I know you must feel incredibly guilty over that. And I realize that maybe you think you should have done something to save your mom, too, even though you were only ten and you couldn't have. But, Sawyer, what does that have to do with us? I know it's an incredibly selfish question considering what you just told me, but I need to know."

He gets up off the swing and paces around the porch. "What does it have to do with us? It has *everything* to do with us. I hit people, Aspen. It's what I do. It's how I grew up. It's all I know. I've told you since day one that I'd hurt you. And now you know why." He motions to the house. "If that isn't evidence enough for you, I don't know what is."

"Do you love me?" I ask.

He stops walking and stares at me.

"Do you love me, Sawyer?" I ask again.

"That's irrelevant," he says.

"Irrelevant? It's the most relevant thing there is. You do. I can tell you do. You were even going to say it earlier. It's why you ran away. You love me, Sawyer. You won't hit me."

"Ha!" he belts out, with a painful laugh. "Were you not listening to me? My dad loved my mom, Aspen. He loved her to death."

"But you're not him."

"I'd hurt you," he says. "Not a lot at first. Maybe just a strong hold on your elbow as I drag you behind me, or a swift push to get you to go where I want you to go. But eventually, those holds and pushes would turn into more. They would turn into slaps, and then punches, and then" —his voice breaks— "pushes down a flight of stairs."

"That won't happen," I say. "I won't let it."

"Neither will I," he says, with distant eyes.

My heart starts to break for the umpteenth time.

"I already hurt you once," he says.

"What are you talking about?"

"The elbow to your face that night on the couch."

"That wasn't you hurting me, Sawyer. That was an accident."

"See – that's what they all say. Is that what you'll tell the doctor when I take my fist to your face?"

I shake my head at him in confusion. I've known this man for four months and I've never seen him raise a hand to anyone. I've seen him get mad, infuriated even, but never once has he hit anything but a wooden door. And I've done hours of research on him. Never was there a mention of a violent past. Surely if he still got into fights, it would hit the news.

"So you'd rather throw this all away than take a chance on us?"

He nods. "If it keeps you safe. Yes."

"When is the last time you hit anyone?" I ask.

Sawyer nods to the house. "Danny was the last person I hit."

The sliding glass door opens behind me. "That's a lie," Lucy says.

"Stay out of it, Lucy," Sawyer warns her.

"And what, sit here and watch you throw away a perfectly good relationship because you have a distorted view of what really happened? I won't let you do that. My walls are thin, Sawyer, I could hear everything you said. You have to get over this, son. It's eating you alive."

"You weren't there," he says.

"No, I wasn't. But a dozen other people were. And their stories to the police were all the same. Are you saying they all lied?"

"It's my fault, Lucy."

"It's not," she says. "In fact, from what everyone else said, it was Daniel's. He took a swing at you. He hit you. Even the police records show you with a black eye."

"I took a swing at him, too," Sawyer says, his face filled with excruciating pain.

"Of course you did. You had just been hit," she says. "And the fact that he stepped out of the way and then tripped because he was drunk, was not your fault." Lucy turns to me. "They were on the end of the boardwalk at a place where there are a lot of rocks in the sand. Daniel tripped and fell head-first into a rock. He was too drunk to have good reflexes so he didn't brace himself. The rock ripped through his skull causing a traumatic brain injury. He damaged the frontal cortex of the brain where the higher learning and thought centers are. So now he has a mental handicap, a cognitive deficit, and he will always have the mental capacity of a six-year-old." She walks over to Sawyer and places a hand on his arm. "And it is not your fault. So quit blaming yourself."

Sawyer shakes his head over and over.

Lucy sits down next to me as we watch Sawyer pace around the yard. "At first, I think he came around to punish himself. He visited Daniel in the hospital every single day. And after Daniel's release, Sawyer came to dinner every Sunday. It was hard, seeing my strong and vibrant son revert to such a low level of learning. Even Daniel's father couldn't handle it and we divorced a year later. But Sawyer stuck around, visiting him often. Eventually, they became more like brothers." She nods at Sawyer. "That man has been a Godsend. He's the light of Daniel's life. He could have walked away. Most other seventeen-year-olds would have."

"Do you know about his mom?" I ask.

"I do. In the early days of Sawyer's coming around, he told me. He told me he was just like his father and that's why Daniel got hurt. It wasn't true, of course. He's nothing like his father."

"He thinks he'll hurt me," I say. "I used to think what he meant was that he would leave me. But he literally thinks he will hurt me. He thinks he'll hit me like his dad hit his mom."

"He won't. I'm sure of it. And even if he had the inclination, I think knowing what happened to his mom and to Daniel would keep him from ever doing it." She puts her hand on mine. "If I had a daughter, I'd give her my blessing to be with him. That's how much I trust him."

"But he doesn't trust himself," I say.

"Are you two done talking about me?" Sawyer says, coming up to join us. "Because I need to get back. I have an early flight tomorrow."

Lucy gives me her phone number and tells me to call her any time. Somehow, I have a feeling this won't be the last time we talk.

In Sawyer's car on the way home, I think about everything I found out tonight. Sawyer probably believes it made me think less of him. That couldn't be further from the truth. If it's possible, I love him even more.

I look down at my hand and remember the fake proposal from earlier. "We could always tell people the ring had to be sized."

"What?"

"You know, to explain why I'm not wearing one."

He cracks a smile. "My fiancée is one smart cookie."

"Please don't call me that when it's just the two of us," I say, looking out the window, once again being reminded of what can never be.

"Fair enough," he says.

I stare at the streetlights as they go by, knowing he's wrong. There's nothing fair about it.

Chapter Thirty-three

Sawyer

I hide in my closet. Not because I think he will come for me. He never comes for me. But it's quieter in here, and I bring my Gameboy with me so I don't hear him yelling. So I don't hear her crying.

She never cries in front of me. She just smiles. She smiles even though she has a bruise on her arm or a cut on her face. I don't get it. When I fall off my bike, or rip my pants when I'm sliding in baseball, it hurts. No way would I smile. But she smiles. And she bakes. Usually, after my dad yells and throws things around the house, I get to eat cake. Or cookies. Or brownies.

I hate cake and cookies and brownies.

I hear a crash. Something hits the wall. Probably something my mom loves. Like a vase or a framed photo. He likes to break things she loves. He likes to break her. He loves her. Why does he like to break things he loves?

"I'm sorry," she cries.

I wonder what she's sorry for. She does everything he wants. She even makes steak for dinner. She hates steak. But she makes it because she loves him. She loves him so much. She tells me that all the time. She tells me he loves her too. And me. She says he loves me.

But all he ever does is complain that he has to spend money on baseball. Last week, my coach said my bat was getting too small for me and Daddy got *mad that he had to buy me a new one. I think he spent fifteen dollars at the second-hand store to get me a bat that was all scratched up. I'm not sure why he got mad at Mommy for that, but he did. And the next day, we ate chocolate cake.*

Finally, I hear Daddy's car start and pull out of the driveway. That's when I know it's safe to go out.

"Mommy?" I ask, from outside their bedroom door.

"I'll be right out," she sings from inside.

I go wait on the couch. It takes her a long time to join me. When she does, I can tell she's been crying. And I know what she was doing in her bedroom. She was using that brown stuff on her face. The stuff she usually puts on when we go out somewhere. It makes her look prettier than she already is. She always puts it on after she fights with Daddy.

"Okay," she says, walking into the room. "What shall we do for the rest of the evening?"

I shrug. "Can you toss me some baseballs out back?"

She smiles at me. "Of course."

I run to my room and get my glove. But as soon as we're out back, I feel bad, because I notice she's trying to throw balls to me with her left hand because her right hand is hurt.

I put my glove down. "I don't want to throw balls anymore," I say. "Let's do something else."

"Want to help me bake something?" she asks.

I shake my head. "I don't like it when you bake."

"You don't? Well, that's silly. Who doesn't like cookies and cakes?"

I shrug.

"Well, what would you like me to make you then?"

"Nothing," I say. Because I know whatever she would make would become something I hate, too.

"How about we go inside and play Scrabble?"

I nod. *"Okay, Mommy. But don't let me win. I don't like it when you let me win."*

She studies me, probably reading more in my eyes than she ever has before. I'm almost ten. I'm growing up. I see things. I get things. And maybe she's beginning to understand that.

"We'll be okay, Sawyer," she says. *"Everything will be okay."*

"Nothing will be okay!" I yell at her. *"Nothing will ever be okay!"*

"Sawyer, don't yell at me."

I look at Mommy, but it's not Mommy. It's Aspen. And she's beautiful. Just like a butterfly. I brush a hair from her face and notice my hands are big. Big like a man's. I'm a man.

Then someone else walks into the room. *"Penny is mine,"* Bass says. *"She's always been mine and she'll always be mine."*

I step across the room and punch him. *"She's mine!"* I yell, as he falls to the floor.

"Sawyer, stop it!" Aspen shouts, running over to help Bass.

"You love him, don't you?" I ask. *"You lied. You said you loved me, but you really love him. You're a liar. Just like my mom was when she said she loved my dad."*

Then Aspen hits the floor, falling on top of Bass, blood trickling from her mouth. She looks up at me and smiles. *"I told you you were just like your father."*

I look at her swelling face and then at my hands.

I look at myself in the mirror and then I fall to my knees, knowing she's right. I'm not only just like him — I am him. And I know for sure I can never, ever have her.

"Sawyer!" someone shouts.

I feel a hand on my shoulder.

I wake up and look around my dark bedroom. I let out a sigh. "What is it?"

"I think you were having a nightmare," Aspen says.

I try to shake off the dream. The vision of her on the floor, swollen and bleeding from *my* fist. I close my eyes, willing myself to speak without my voice cracking. "I guess I should start sleeping with my door shut."

"No. It's okay. You didn't bother me. I'm sure all our talking earlier brought a lot of stuff to the surface."

"I'm fine. You can go back to bed."

She climbs into bed with me, sitting up against the headboard. "I'd rather stay in here."

"Suit yourself," I say, turning away from her and lying back on my pillow.

"Is that really how you're going to play this? I'm not her, Sawyer. You're not him."

"I can't risk it."

"Risk what? Hitting me? Or loving me?"

"He *killed* her, Aspen. He killed her and she never admitted it, not even on her death bed."

"I wouldn't let anything happen. And I don't think you would either. You didn't do that to Danny. So you got in fights back in school. A lot of boys did. That doesn't mean they will grow up to abuse their girlfriends."

"Do you know what the statistics say? Have you even bothered to look? Kids who grow up in an abusive home are three times more likely to be abusive in an adult relationship. *Three times.*"

"But you've proven you're not like that. Have you ever hit a girl? Have you even been in a fight since high school?"

"That's not the point. There is no way to know if I'll hurt a woman until I do. I'm not willing to let that happen. Not to anyone, but especially not to you."

"Why especially not to me?"

I jump out of bed and pull on a pair of sweats. "I'm going to the basement."

"To get away from me?" she asks.

"Nobody's keeping you from going down there."

"But you know I won't."

"I guess that's your choice, then, isn't it?"

I walk down the stairs, grab a bottle of water and head down to my workshop. A few minutes later, I hear Aspen playing the piano. I stop what I'm doing and listen. I *always* listen. I love to hear her play. It's the only time my mind is truly at ease.

After a while, I look down at the template I've drawn. And for the first time, it's not a butterfly. I realize what I've been drawing is Aspen's hands on a set of piano keys.

Chapter Thirty-four

Aspen

"What the hell are they thinking?" I shriek into the phone.

I rarely call Sawyer when he's on the road. We text sometimes to make plans. We email. But we never call. And I realize that even though he's laughing at me right now, I like it. I like hearing his voice when he's been away for a while.

"It's been a week," I cry. "*One* week. That's not even enough time to *pick* wedding invitations let alone *mail* them. Did they go home that night and plan the entire thing in ten minutes? And two weeks from now. Are they crazy? Who has a three-week engagement?"

"Maybe she's pregnant," he says.

"She's not. I asked."

"You talked to him already?"

"Of course I talked to him. Why do you think my voice is so hoarse?"

He laughs. I'm sure he's imagining me tearing into Bass. He thinks I'm stubborn. And a meddler. He thinks I'm a stubborn meddler. "Well, did he say why they're doing it so quickly?" he asks.

"He claims it's because of her parents. The ones who didn't even come to Brooke's Juilliard graduation. They will be in town for the next three weeks before they go cruising around the world on some multi-millionaire's yacht for five months. So they insisted it happen before they leave."

"What kind of father insists that his daughter have a short engagement just to fit into his schedule?"

"Exactly!" I yell. "See – even *you* understand that. Why not just push it out and be engaged for six months? Or a year, even? People can stay engaged indefinitely."

"Maybe Brooke wants to make sure he doesn't change his mind."

I think about his words. And everything starts to make sense. Especially about how even Bass was surprised about the abbreviated engagement.

"Aspen?"

"I never thought of that," I say. "But, oh my God, I bet you're right."

"You've always said she's way more into him than he is into her."

"It's true. She is."

"Well, there you have it."

"He wants me to be his best man, or best woman, or whatever you call it when a girl stands up with a guy."

"You didn't turn him down, did you?"

"Of course not. He's still my best friend. And even though I don't agree with his choices, I'll still be there for him. Oh, gosh – please say you're in town on the fourteenth. I don't want to have to go through that by myself."

He laughs. "Yeah, I'll be in town. But I hope it's a night wedding because we play a double-header that day."

I rifle through the ornate wedding envelopes to find the invitation. "It's at six-thirty."

"Good. Then I'll be there. Just don't expect much. Weddings aren't really my thing."

"Do you think he's really going to do it?" I ask, ignoring his comment that was obviously directed at *me*. "I'm still not convinced he loves her. Why would he go through all the trouble?"

"Because the one he really wants is unattainable," he says.

I snort into the phone. Then I let out a huge sigh. "Well then, I guess Bass and I have one more thing in common, don't we?"

"Come on, Aspen. Don't be like that. We've discussed this."

"No. *You've* discussed it. You've unilaterally decided we can't be more than friends based on a notion of something that will never happen."

"Yeah, but what if we're friends, who, you know—"

"Fuck?" I bite at him. "You want to fuck me, but you don't want to love me?" I belt out a maniacal laugh. "Oh, that's precious. And what will the press call us then?"

"Fiancés," he says. "Just like now. It could work. We could just extend the contract."

"Extend the contract?" I huff in anger. "You're asking me to be your long-term fuck buddy? And you'll *pay* me for it? To pretend for the sake of your career that we're in love, which – news flash – *we are*, and despite the fact that we're *supposed* to be, for appearances' sake, you're bound and determined to deny it in front of the only person who really matters. Oh my, I don't think I've ever received a more romantic proposition."

I realize my sarcasm is dripping through the phone, but at this point, I don't really care.

"I'm not capable of more, Aspen."

"Yes, you are. You're just scared of more. You're scared of *me*."

"No. I'm scared of what I might do to you."

"Then buy me a gun," I say. "And if you touch me, I'll shoot you in the leg."

"It's more than just physical hitting, you know. Abuse is emotional as well. Abuse is wearing someone down until they feel they are nothing and no one without the abuser. You deserve so much more than that."

"Yes. I do. And you deserve to not live your life in fear of love, missing out on one of the greatest things in life."

He sighs into the phone. There's a lot of sighing going on in this conversation. I guess he thinks there's really not much more he can say that hasn't already been said.

"I'm sorry," I tell him. "I know we're not going to settle anything when you're a thousand miles away. I just called because I was surprised and upset by the invitation."

"Things have already been settled."

"Sawyer …"

"Aspen …"

I expect him to make an excuse to hang up the phone. But he doesn't. I hear him breathing. I hear him *thinking*. He wants to stay on the phone with me.

Things have most definitely not been settled. Not by a long shot.

"Where is the wedding?" he asks. "I'm sure all the best places have been taken."

"The ceremony will be at her parents' church on Long Island. The reception will be at their house. They already planned the honeymoon and everything. Do you know her parents bought them a two-week trip to Hawaii? Paid for it all in advance. They can't even go for six months since Bass is just starting his new job next week. Can you believe that?"

"Must be nice to have rich parents."

"No thank you," I say. "I'd rather have had only nineteen years with parents who loved me to the ends of the earth than parents who could *buy* it for me."

"You were lucky to have them."

"I know," I say. "I know that now more than ever."

"I have to go. I need to report to pre-game in thirty minutes."

"Good luck today, Speed Limit. Steal a base for me, okay?"

"How about I steal two?"

I stare at my phone long after the call disconnects, knowing the man on the other end of the line has stolen a lot more than just bases for me. He's stolen my heart.

And I'm not sure I'll ever get it back.

Chapter Thirty-five

Sawyer

Entering the dugout before our first game, I think about how today is going to be a long day. Two games and then Bass's wedding. I can't help but dread it a little – the thought of attending a wedding with Aspen. Weddings make girls get all mushy and emotional. As if she hasn't been already.

She's tried for weeks to get me to change my mind about us. It's no use. No way in hell would I ever put her in danger. And being with me is exactly that. Dangerous.

I, on the other hand, have tried to talk her into extending our contract beyond the season. In a little over a month, the season will be done. *We'll* be done. I'm not ready for that. But I'm also not willing to do what she wants – have a real relationship.

The contract makes things safer for everyone. I don't get why she won't agree. She still gets me. She gets me for as long as she wants to extend the contract. She gets me for as long as she's willing to keep things the way they are now.

Why do women always need more?

I look out into the stands, up to where she normally sits, wondering if she's even going to come today. It's Bass's wedding day. Maybe she's hanging out with him doing 'best man' duties or whatever.

Just as the pre-game festivities end, I take a seat on the bench, waiting for the ceremonial first pitch to take place. Caden elbows me. "You might want to watch this one, Mills."

He walks out on the field, presumably to be the catcher of the first pitch. Curious, I stand up and walk to the railing. Then my jaw drops when I see Aspen and Danny walking out onto the field. Aspen is talking into Danny's ear. They walk to about the half-way point between home plate and the pitcher's mound and then she hands him a ball, pointing to Caden as she gives him a few words of encouragement.

I stand here, stunned, wondering how this even came about. I've been trying to get Danny to a game for years, and now, not only does Aspen get him to one within weeks of meeting him, she's arranged for him to throw the first pitch.

He throws the pitch. Caden catches it. The crowd cheers.

Danny jumps up and down, clapping. Aspen finally looks over at me and smiles.

I smile back. I can't help it. She looks so beautiful out on that field wearing my jersey. And she got him to a game.

Caden comes back into the dugout and looks at me. "Are you pissed? Aspen thought you might be pissed."

"Pissed? No. Not even close. But how? And, uh … how much do you know?"

"As far as the how – maybe you should ask Aspen. And all I know is that Danny is someone special to her, and, I guess, you."

I nod my head. "Yeah. Yeah he is."

Caden puts a supportive hand on my shoulder. "Whenever you want to talk, brother. I'm here."

I nod my head again, then I walk away to find a piece of paper.

I write a note for Aspen, asking her to bring Danny to meet me outside the clubhouse in between games. I have to know how she made it happen. I give the note to the security guard standing near the dugout and ask him to deliver it to her.

When I walk out to bat, I can't get the picture of them out of my head. Aspen and Danny, both wearing my #55 jersey, walking out onto the field. They are the two most important people in my life.

Then it hits me like a hundred-mile-an-hour fast ball. I fucking love her.

I almost said it to her weeks ago. I've said it to her in my dreams. I know she already knows it. But now *I* know it. I know it for sure.

I touch my tattoo before I stand at the plate. *He* loved *her*, too.

I stare at the pitcher, wondering what he's going to throw me. *Baseball.* That's what I love. That's what I can control. Nobody gets hurt in baseball. And when I take a swing and hear the crack of wooden bat on ball, I run my ass off. I run around to second, thinking of Danny the entire time. And when the ball gets thrown back to the pitcher, I take off for third. I run for him, for Danny. I run because he will never be able to.

Having caught the pitcher off guard, he's late on the throw, and I just beat it, sliding feet first into third base, touching the bag with the side of my cleat before the glove with the ball in it tags me.

I stand up, brush myself off, and look up to where I presume Danny is sitting. I point to him and say, "Eighty-eight."

God, I love baseball.

~ ~ ~

Still in uniform since we have another game, I exit the clubhouse and look around. When I see Aspen standing with Lucy and Danny over by the wall, I wave them over and tell security to let them through the barrier.

Caden and Brady come out right behind me, just as Aspen and the others walk up.

"Danny, I'd like you to meet some of my teammates, Caden Kessler and Brady Taylor. Caden and Brady, Danny is a very special friend of mine. And this is his mother, Lucy."

In typical Danny fashion, he hugs Caden and Brady and then they sign his program.

I grab Aspen's elbow. "How did you do this?"

"She pretty much knows everyone in the Hawks organization," Lucy says.

I shake my head, confused. I introduced her to Rick and Jason and some of the coaches, but that was just the one time. And it was months ago.

"Remember when I told you I do a lot of volunteering?" Aspen says. "Well, the Nighthawks is one of the places I do it."

"You do?" I ask, surprised. "Why didn't you tell me?"

"Because I didn't want you to think I was doing it for you."

I study her, and then I motion to Lucy. "And how did you get her to agree to this? I've been trying for a while to get Lucy to bring him to a game."

"Your, uh, *girlfriend* is very persuasive," Lucy says.

Something about the way she says it makes me wonder if she knows about Aspen and me.

"Aspen and I have become close in the past few weeks," she says. "Daniel has really taken to her."

I raise my eyebrows at Aspen. "You've been out to see them?"

"A few times, yes."

I pull her to the side. "Why?" I ask. "You don't think this will change things, do you?"

She shakes her head sadly and looks at the ground. "Everything is not about you, Sawyer Mills."

I feel like a douchebag. "Sorry. I guess I just thought—"

"You thought everything was about you," she says.

She's right.

"Shit. I'm ... I'm sorry. I'm glad you and Danny have become friends. He needs more of those."

"I can see why you like him so much," she says. "He's absolutely delightful."

"Did you see me throw the ball?" Danny asks excitedly, coming up beside me. "I'm a baseball player like you, Sawyer."

"You sure are, buddy. You were great."

I look at Aspen, her face glowing when she sees how happy he is. She's responsible for that. She made his dream come true. All Danny ever wanted was to play ball. And she made it happen. She changes people's lives. She changes people's dreams.

But she can't change the past. She can't re-write history. Oh, but how I wish she could. I'd give anything – *do anything* – to make that happen.

I bring Danny into the clubhouse and give him a tour, introducing him to all the guys along the way. They treat him like he's a celebrity. I've never seen him happier. By the time we re-join the ladies out in the tunnel, Danny looks exhausted.

"I'm going to see them off now," Aspen says. "Then I have to go get ready for the wedding. I told Bass I'd get there early."

"I'll be there as soon as I can," I tell her. "But it will be pretty close."

"No extra innings," she says, as they walk away.

I laugh. "As if I can control that, Andrews."

"You're the great Sawyer Mills," she says. "I thought nothing was beyond your control."

I wave at all of them as they leave, wondering if she was even talking about baseball at all.

Chapter Thirty-six

Aspen

I walk into the groom's room in the back of the church only to see Bass's head between his knees.

"He's a bit nervous, dear," his mom tells me. "Maybe you can calm him down. You've always been good with him."

"I'm not sure what I can do," I say. "But I'll try."

He wasn't nervous at all earlier when we were hanging out at his apartment. Brooke wasn't there. She stayed at her parents' house last night so they wouldn't see each other this morning. Bass and I spent the afternoon talking about his new job as a firefighter. And music. He played a new song for me. He's a true virtuoso on the guitar. He seemed fine. Relaxed even.

Bass's mom brings me in for a hug. "If only *you* were the one walking down the aisle," she whispers in my ear before walking out of the room, leaving me alone with him.

I stare at the empty hallway, not quite believing she just said that. I get that it was a short engagement, and it came as a surprise to everyone, but she needs to accept Brooke as her daughter-in-law or they will get off to a very bad start.

I walk over to Bass, wondering why he's so nervous. He doesn't get nervous. Not when he plays guitar in front of a thousand people. Not when he rescues people from burning buildings. Not even when he meets famous baseball players. So — why now?

"Bass," I say, reaching out to rub his shoulders. "Is everything okay?"

He nods his head. Then he reaches over to grab a glass off the table, downing a large swig of light-brown liquid. I raise my eyebrows at it.

"Crown and Coke," he says. "Just a little liquid courage."

"If you need courage to do this, maybe you shouldn't be doing it."

He laughs. "As my best man, I'd think you'd be more supportive than that, Penny."

"Sorry. In that case, where can I get one?"

He holds his drink out for me. "I'll share it with you."

I take a drink, feeling the burn as I swallow. "Ick!"

"You always were more of a beer and wine girl," he says.

I take another sip, careful to control my facial expression this time. "A girl can change," I say.

He eyes me speculatively. "Yeah, I guess she can."

"Sebastian, are you ready for this?"

"Have you seen the decorations in the church?" he asks. "And holy shit, Penny. Her parents' house — we were there yesterday, you wouldn't believe what they've done. There's a huge tent out back with dozens of tables. And there's a stage for a band." He shakes his head. "They hired a fucking band. In less than three weeks. They've probably dropped more than fifty grand on this. There will be two hundred people here. Who the hell are they? I know about twenty people and that includes the guys from the firehouse. I know her parents can afford it. But I guess I never thought it would turn into such a big deal."

"Their only daughter is getting married," I say. "Can you really blame them?"

He shakes his head. "I guess not."

"Think of the pictures," I say. "They'll be wonderful. And everything will be top-notch."

"I don't give a shit about the pictures," he says.

"And you shouldn't. The only thing you should care about today is the person coming down that aisle."

He sighs. He sighs big. Then he takes another drink.

"You do care about the person coming down the aisle, don't you?" I ask.

I can't help but wonder, as I have a thousand times in the past few weeks, if this is really what he wants.

"Of course I do. Brooke is a great girl."

"Yes, she is. And she deserves someone who loves her more than anything."

"Yes. She does."

"Are you that person, Bass? Because if you're not ..."

The door opens and Sawyer walks through. "Can I come in?"

Bass waves him over.

"How's it going in here?" he asks.

"Just the usual case of cold feet," Bass says, jokingly.

And, again, I wonder.

"Is that really a thing?" Sawyer asks. "Like, do all grooms want to bolt right before they get hitched?"

"I think you've both seen too many movies," I say.

"Where is everyone else?" Sawyer asks.

"Who do you mean?"

"You know, the groomsmen or ushers or whatever."

I shake my head. "There is no one else. Just me. And Brooke's best friend, Jordan."

"But there must be hundreds of people out there," Sawyer says.

"That doesn't mean you have to have more attendants," I explain to him. "You don't know much about weddings, do you?"

"Don't care to," he says. "I've only been to two of them, and both times I was wasted. Weddings and funerals – *so* not my thing."

And in true Sawyer Mills style, he chips away another piece of my heart.

This man is truly incapable of love, despite the fact that I'm sure he loves me. I once read that insanity is doing something over and over again even though you get the same undesired results. That pretty much sums up my entire life right now. Sawyer won't change. I can't change him. I've tried. And I'm crazy to think I can.

Then again, he's here. At a wedding. Because I asked him to be. Even though he hates them.

I look at the clock. "It's almost time," I say, straightening Bass's tie.

"My cue to leave. I'll see you out there, man. Break a leg," Sawyer says to Bass. "And good luck to the hottest 'best man' I've ever seen."

When Sawyer walks out the door, Bass's parents come in to wish him luck. His dad shakes his hand and gives him some fatherly advice. His mom looks at me with such sad eyes, I want to scream at her. Then again, she may be the only sane person in this room. And part of me wishes she would have the guts to tell Bass to walk away. Because he should. He should walk away before someone gets hurt.

I laugh at myself when I realize if there were anyone ever in greater need of walking away from something, it's me. Because every day I stay hurts a little bit more.

The minister pokes his head in the door and tells us it's time for us to take our places in the front of the church, right before the family gets escorted to their seats.

"Ready?" I ask, hoping beyond all hope that he reads my eyes that are begging him to turn and walk out the door. The *back* door.

"Ready," he says, holding out his arm, motioning for me to go first.

I paste a smile on my face as I walk through the door at the very front of the church. I eye the hundreds of people in attendance as I take my place by the altar. I scan the crowd and find Sawyer, thinking of how much I want this with him but can never have it. And I swear he looks at me, knowing it. Knowing he can never be the one to give it to me.

Bass walks in behind me, taking his place front and center, next to the minister. He looks at me nervously and I give him an encouraging nod. Because it's too late to back out now. He's committed to this. I just hope he's not making a huge mistake. I hope that even if he isn't in love with Brooke now, he can learn to be.

People can learn to do a lot of things. And if Bass can learn to love Brooke, maybe I can learn *not* to love Sawyer.

Music begins to play and Bass's grandmother is escorted down the aisle, his grandfather following. Then his other grandmother, the widowed one, is escorted as well. Bass's parents are next, filling up the front right pew.

After that, Brooke's two sets of grandparents are escorted in. Her mother should come next. But she doesn't. The song ends and there is a brief silence. Then the song starts up again and we all look to see if Brooke's mom is being escorted down the aisle. She's not.

When the song comes to an end for the second time, the whispers among guests become louder. Bass turns to look at me and I shrug my shoulders. Has something happened to Brooke's mother? To Brooke?

The room is abuzz when the side door opens and Brooke's father comes through, motioning for Bass to follow him back into the room from where we came.

Bass grabs my arm, pulling me along with him. Brooke's father takes a long look at me and then shuts the door behind us, separating us from the sanctuary.

"Sit down, son," John says, motioning to the couch.

Bass gives me a curious look and then he takes a seat. I remain standing. I feel like an intruder. John is *looking* at me like I'm an intruder. But Bass's eyes implore me to stay, so intruder or not, I'm staying.

John puts a hand on Bass's shoulder. "I'm sorry. Brooke has changed her mind. There isn't going to be a wedding today."

"Changed her mind?" Bass asks. "What do you mean there won't be a wedding *today?*"

"There won't be a wedding at all," he clarifies.

"Sir?" Bass says, confused.

"I'm sorry, this is awkward," John says, looking at me again. "Brooke feels she isn't the woman for you. She's coming back to live with us for a while. You can stay in the apartment. We'll arrange for her things to be picked up in a day or two."

"So she's just … gone?" Bass asks.

John pulls an envelope out of his suit pocket, handing it to Bass. "She left this for you. It'll explain things better than I can." He heads for the door but then turns around. He nods to the envelope in Bass's hand. "Along with Brooke's letter, I've written down the information you'll need to go to Hawaii as you had planned. There's an extra ticket now. You can take whomever you want."

"John, I couldn't," Bass says.

"You can," John says. "Even if she isn't the one for you, Brooke is still at fault here. I'm truly sorry she didn't come to this decision earlier. Take the tickets. Enjoy Hawaii. Think about what you want out of life. Good luck, son."

He walks out the door, leaving us stunned and speechless.

Bass opens the envelope and pulls out the letter. I read it over his shoulder. She's not mad at him. She's mad at herself for not ending things earlier. She's not willing to be anyone's second choice. My name comes up more than once, making it clear that I'm the reason this wedding is not happening.

He folds the letter up and puts it away. "Want to go to Hawaii with me in six months?"

I want to go to Hawaii more than anything. The problem is, the man sitting on the couch is not the man I want to go with.

I point to the letter. "Based on what's written in that letter, I'm not sure that's a good idea."

He nods sadly. "Yeah, I guess not."

"I'm sorry," I tell him.

"Are you?" he asks. "You never wanted me to marry her."

"Only because I know you don't love her. Not *that* way. Not the way you should when you make a life-long commitment. But I'm still sorry. I know you care about her."

"I do," he says. "But part of me is relieved."

"So, what now?" I ask.

"Now I go out and get shit-faced. Isn't that what everyone who gets left at the altar does?"

"Where to?" I ask. "I'll take you anywhere you want to go."

He laughs, but it's not a happy laugh, it's a pained one. He runs a finger along the edge of the envelope. Then he throws my words back at me. "Based on what's written in this letter, I'm not sure that's a good idea."

We lock eyes and I see it. I see something change within him. He needs distance. Distance from me. Because the only way to truly get over someone is by getting away from them.

There's a knock on the door and then Sawyer sticks his head inside. "Is the coast clear?" he asks.

"Come in," I tell him. "There isn't going to be a wedding."

"I know. Brooke's dad just told everyone." Sawyer walks over to Bass. "You okay, Briggs? Your parents are waiting outside the door. They thought you might need a minute with Aspen."

Bass looks up at me with guilty eyes. "Actually, I think I need a minute *without* her."

I know that's my cue. My cue to walk away and give him the space he needs to figure out his life. I just hope once that happens, there is still room for me in it.

"Take him out," I say to Sawyer. "Get him drunk. Make sure he gets home safely."

Sawyer nods. "I'm on it. I'll crash on his couch and go to the game from there tomorrow morning."

"Thanks for taking care of him," I say.

"No problem. See you at the game?" he asks.

"Yeah, okay," I say insincerely, knowing that, just like Bass, I need to figure out *my* life. And I need distance. Lots and lots of distance.

~ ~ ~

I walk into the townhouse much earlier than I expected to tonight. I wonder what Sawyer and Bass are doing. I wish I were with them. But I'm glad I'm not.

I laugh at myself. Being confused as hell is the story of my life these days.

I walk over and sit down at the piano. Playing the piano is the only thing that makes sense to me anymore. I play a lot. He thinks I don't know that he watches me when I play. He doesn't know that he's the reason I play so much. When he watches me, he's not doing it because of the contract. Or to keep up appearances. Or to save his job. He watches me like a man watches the woman he loves.

Will he keep the piano when I'm gone? Will he sit on the bench and long for the times he watched me play? Or will he have it taken away, removing all traces of me from his life?

I stop playing when my phone rings. Maybe Bass changed his mind and he wants me with them.

But I don't recognize the number. However, I do recognize the area code. It's from Missouri.

"Hello?"

"I'm in trouble, Aspen."

"Denver?"

"I have to be quick. You're my one phone call."

My heart sinks. "You're in *jail?* What happened?"

"I screwed up, Pen. But I don't have much time. I'll explain later. I didn't know who else to call. I have no one."

"That's not true. You have me."

"You've done so much for me already."

"You're my brother, Den. I'll do whatever it takes to help you. What do you need?"

"Can you contact a decent lawyer? I'll end up in prison if I go with the public defender. I know it will cost money. Money I don't have, but—"

"Don't worry about it. I'll take care of everything."

"They won't let me out on bail this time," he says.

"Sit tight. I'll figure something out."

"They say I have to go."

"Hang in there, big brother."

"Thanks, Pen. I love you."

The phone goes dead.

I look around the townhouse. The townhouse that isn't mine. The one that belongs to the *man* who isn't mine. Everything in my life is fake. Manufactured. Just like the butterflies on the walls. The ones he uses to protect himself.

I walk over and pull my favorite one off the nail it's hanging on. The one I sit and stare at when he's down in the basement making more. When he's down there figuring out all the ways he can distance himself from me.

Then I walk upstairs and pull my suitcases out of the closet. Because I know what I need to do. I've known for a while now. Maybe it just took the failed wedding and the phone call from Denver to make me realize it.

Chapter Thirty-seven

Sawyer

My eyes are laser-focused on the pitcher. I watch for the tell-tale sign that he's about to start his pitching motion. It's different for everyone. Some of them shift their weight slightly. Some make a small head movement. Some have something as subtle as a finger twitch. But all of them do something that lets me know it's time to run.

This guy cocks his head to the left, right before the wind-up. I take my lead and play my favorite game – the one that has him trying to throw me out even before I try to steal. And I know he's going to step off the mound and go for me. I know because he hasn't cocked his head to the left yet. When he goes for me, I make it back to the base. I always do. Nobody ever throws me out going back. It's the going forward, the stealing, that's dangerous. But it's also exhilarating.

I've broken a finger more than once stealing bases. I've been stepped on, kicked in the face, and hit by balls. You name it, it's happened to me on the steal. But more often than not, I win the battle and steal the base. It's why my name will go down in history this year – the third consecutive year that I'll hold the league record for stolen bases in a season. In ten years, they'll be asking, '*Rickey who?*'

After the pitcher tries, unsuccessfully, to throw me out four times, he finally cocks his head and I take off for second base. I run so fast my helmet almost flies off my head. Thank God it doesn't, because I end up diving head-first and I touch the outer edge of the base just as I hear the ball hit the second baseman's glove.

I laugh. I had a good two seconds more before he would have tagged me.

I stand up and look down at my filthy clothes and smile. "Ninety-three," I say to myself. I don't dare say it to the second baseman – he's one huge mother fucker.

The Diamondbacks pull their pitcher, and as the new one throws a few warm-up pitches, I take time to look up into the stands, hoping to catch a glimpse of Aspen, but I can't always pick her out of the crowd when she wears the same hat and jersey as everyone else.

I know Bass won't be here today. He's sleeping off one hell of a hangover.

I feel sorry for the guy. The woman he loves doesn't love him back, and the woman he settled for left him at the altar. No wonder he drank himself to within an inch of his life.

That dude likes to talk when he drinks. And, holy crap, he's into Aspen. I knew he was, but I didn't realize just how much. The guy is seriously in love with her. Sometimes I wonder if he isn't the one she should be with. He's a nice guy. A firefighter, no less. He's a fucking hero every goddamned day.

But when I think about her with him, with *anyone*, all I see is red.

~ ~ ~

"Rick wants to see you in his office," one of the batting coaches tells me as I'm getting out of the shower.

I shake my head. What could he possibly want now? I've just had my three best games of the season. But nothing good ever happens when I'm called to his office.

I dry off and put my street clothes on, eager to get this over with and go out to share the win with Aspen.

"You wanted to see me?" I ask, sticking my head into Rick's office.

"Come in," he says. "Close the door."

I sit down, looking at his desk for a folder. Surely he's not going to threaten me some more after the weekend I've had.

"Notice anything different in here?" he asks.

I look at the furniture – all the same. I look at the television hanging in the corner – nothing's changed there. I look at the walls. That's when I see it.

My jaw goes slack when I see a picture of me right alongside those of Brady and Caden and some other players who have stood out on the team. I think the photo is from yesterday's game. I'm stealing third base. Man that was a good steal.

"Did Jason make you hang that here?" I joke.

He snorts through his nose. "No, he didn't." He gets up and touches the edge of the frame as if to straighten it, but it's already perfectly straight. Then he puts a fatherly hand on my shoulder. "I don't know what the hell changed you this year, but I have to say, maybe a bit begrudgingly, that you're an upstanding member of the Nighthawks." He laughs at himself. "I never thought I'd say those words, you know. But it's true. And I believe you just might lead us to the Series this year, son."

Son?

"Uh … thank you."

"Why do you look so surprised?" he asks.

"I guess because the only time you ever call me in here is to chew my ass."

He sits back down behind his desk. "If anyone had told me at the beginning of the season that you'd beat your record from the previous two, I'd have called them crazy. But you've done it. You've beat your previous records and the season isn't even over. You're on your way to the Hall of Fame if you play your cards right. So whatever you've been doing, keep it up."

Funny when he says that, the one thing that pops into my mind is Aspen's face. Not my teammates. Not my statistics. Not all the money I'll make and the fame I'll achieve. It's *her*. She's the reason I'm even sitting in this chair right now. She's the reason my picture is hanging on Rick's wall.

And all I want to do is go find her. I want to tell her about this moment. I want to recap every play of the game, because I know she'll sit and listen with a smile on her face. She always does.

I look back at the wall. I'm finally worthy of being up there. Or at least Rick thinks I am. What he doesn't know is that it's all fake.

And right now, right this second, I realize I don't want it to be. I don't want a fake girlfriend. I don't want a fake fiancée. I don't want a contract that dictates she has to be with me because I'm paying her.

I want it to be real. All of it. I want her.

And for the first time, I know I want more.

"Is that all?" I ask Rick. "There's someone I need to see."

"I assume you mean that girl of yours," he says. "Seems like a good one. You should hold on to her."

"That's exactly what I plan on doing."

"Go on. Get out of here," he grumbles in his usual fashion.

I'm almost the last one to leave the clubhouse. By the time I get out front, the fans have mostly dissipated. I sign a few autographs for the stragglers who remain as I scan the small crowd for Aspen. I don't see her. She must have gotten tired of waiting.

I grab a cab, excited to get home and tell her everything. She's the only one I've ever wanted to tell everything to.

The ride is quick and the townhouse is dark when I arrive home. And eerily quiet.

"Aspen?" I call out, walking through the living room.

Then I see something. Or rather, I *don't* see something. One of the butterflies from the living room wall is missing. I look around the room. The table where she puts her purse is empty. The extra pair of shoes she keeps by the front door is gone. I walk over to the piano to see it conspicuously absent of sheet music.

I dart up the stairs to her room. The sheets have been stripped off the bed. I open the drawers to find them barren. The closet's only contents are a few boxes that are packed and labeled and pushed to the side.

"Shit!" I shout to the ceiling.

I sit on the edge of the bed and that's when I see it – an envelope bearing my name perched on her pillow. I immediately have flashbacks to last night when Bass showed me the envelope he received from the girl who left him.

She left me.

I open the envelope and read the words I know will slay me.

Sawyer,

I've known for a while that leaving is the right thing to do. I just didn't have the guts to do it. But a lot of things have happened lately to push me in the right direction. So I'm going back home where I belong. Where my family is. Denver needs me. He needs me now more than ever.

You don't have to pay me the final payment. I didn't fulfill my part of the deal. And I hope you'll allow me to get out of the contract peacefully since there's so little time left in it anyway.

You did what you set out to accomplish. People look at you differently now. They see what I see. They see the guy I met that very first night. They see the man you've become these past months. I hope you got everything you wanted. I hope you have a long career with the Hawks.

I wish only the best for you. You're a good man, Sawyer. You have one of the biggest hearts of anyone I know – you proved that to me the day I met Danny. I hope you open that heart to someone someday. Because you deserve a life full of love.

Not a day will go by that I won't think of you.

Love,
Aspen

p.s. – I hope you don't mind, I took a butterfly.

I drop the letter on the bed. Then I scoot across the mattress and lie down on the pillow, hoping it still smells like her. It does. I close my eyes and think back to the one time we made love on this bed. That night was one of the best of my life. In fact, these past five months have been the best I've ever known.

She thinks I didn't open my heart to her. But I did. She fucking *owns* my heart. She owns *me*.

I bolt out of bed and run from her bedroom to my office across the hall. Then I tear it apart — I look through every drawer, every file folder, every notebook — until I find what I'm looking for.

Chapter Thirty-eight

Aspen

"I'm a fraud, Pen," my brother says into the phone, looking at me through the thick glass separating us.

"You are not a fraud," I tell him.

He shakes his head. "You're the only person on the planet who thinks so."

"What happened, Denver? Nobody would tell me anything."

"I was stupid. Again. And they're right. Everyone's right."

"Who's right?"

"The guys at the bar."

I furrow my brow. "I'm going to need more than that," I say. "I have a meeting with a lawyer as soon as I leave here."

"I went to Joe's Bar after work. You remember the place over on Twenty-third?"

I nod. "It was Dad's favorite place."

"Yeah. It's why I go there sometimes."

I wish I could reach out and touch him. It makes me incredibly sad knowing my brother lives in a city where he has no one. He's an outcast here. And the only friends he has are an old bartender named Joe and the ghost of our father.

"Anyway, the TV was on and there was a story on ESPN about you and Sawyer, something about your engagement. Some of the guys started ragging on me, asking why I couldn't be more like my sister. Saying I was the bad twin. Telling me what a fraud I am. And Joe heard it all. He put a couple of shots on the bar. 'Your dad's favorite,' he said, feeling sorry for me as I sat alone.

"I drank one of the shots and then left shortly after. But on the way home, I got a flat tire. I swerved out of my lane a bit when the tire popped, and then I pulled off the road." He shakes his head in frustration. "That's when I saw the red and blue lights behind me. And as luck would have it, Hank Marron's kid, Kenny, walks up to my window. You remember who Hank is?"

I nod. How could I forget? Hank was one of the veteran cops who ruined my brother's life. He was one of the assholes who took my money, his money, and the money of a dozen other people. The money Denver has to pay back in restitution.

"When Kenny saw it was me, he couldn't wipe the smirk off his face. I told him I had a flat tire. I even got out of the car to point it out to him, but he threw me against it and frisked me. Then he made me take a breathalyzer test. I failed."

"You were drunk?" I ask.

"Just," he says. "I tested right at the legal limit, so he cuffed me, put me in the back of his vehicle, and impounded my car."

"But the only reason you swerved was because of the flat tire."

"I told him that, but it doesn't matter," he says. "I failed the breathalyzer."

"Did he even have a right to test you?"

"If any other cop had been behind me, I'm sure I wouldn't have been tested. In fact, anyone else would have helped me fix the flat. I wasn't slurring my words. I was fine. The legal limit is so low now you'll practically fail the test if you're on cough medicine. But none of that mattered. Because Kenny's a cop and I'm a convicted criminal. They're going to put me in prison, Aspen." He closes his eyes. "Maybe that's where I belong. Maybe they're right. I am a fraud."

I shake my head. "If anyone is a fraud, it's me."

"What do you mean?"

"I'm not Sawyer's fiancée. I'm not even his girlfriend." I look around to make sure nobody can hear me. "He hired me to play the part, Den. He needed to legitimize his personal life to save his job. And I needed the money."

I watch my brother process the news. His jaw opens and closes. Then he sighs into the phone as his eyes become angry and then glassy. "You did it for me," he says. "I should have known something was up. The baseball star. The money. The way you've been acting these past months. It's all so unlike you."

"I'm sorry I lied. But I'd do anything for you," I say. "You'd have done the same for me and you know it."

"You slept with the guy for money?" he shouts quietly into the phone.

"No. Of course not. It's … it's more complicated than that. We became close over the past few months. Closer than he would like. But it's over now. I'm done. I can't do it anymore. When you called me on Saturday, I knew it was time to leave. I'm back for good now. I'm moving home."

"Let me get this straight," he says, anger consuming his handsome features. "He hired my sister to be his girlfriend, fucking her while he paid off her delinquent brother's debts, and you went and *fell* for the asshole?"

I blow out a deep breath, knowing everything he's said is true. "He fell in love with me, too," I say, a tear finally spilling from the corner of my eye.

He studies me through the glass wall. He's good at reading me. He always has been. I can tell he's conflicted. He wants to play the protective brother, but he also wants me to be happy. He gauges the sincerity of my words. He sees the truth in my eyes.

"Then what the hell are you doing *here?* Why did you leave him?"

"You're my brother, Den. My family. Something he can never be. He's incapable of having a real relationship."

"You mean unwilling," he says, angrily.

"Either way, it's over, and I'm back where I belong."

I spend the next few minutes telling Denver everything I've wanted to tell him for the past five months. Then a guard tells us our time is up.

"I'm going to get you out of here," I say before I hang up. "We'll get through this."

He puts the phone in the cradle on the wall and then holds his hand up to the glass window. I place my hand opposite his and mouth the words, *'Twin promise.'*

~ ~ ~

On the drive back to Denver's place, it dawns on me that it's been four days since I've heard from Sawyer. Four days since I've heard from *anyone.* It's like when I left New York, I fell off the face of the earth. I was sure Murphy or Rylee would try to contact me. But I guess when they said I was their friend, they meant only if Sawyer and I stayed together.

I'm still giving Bass some space. And apparently, he's letting me since I've not heard a word from him either.

And with Denver still in jail, waiting on his court date, I realize I've never felt more alone.

I need to look up some of my old friends from high school. See if they are still around. I just haven't had the chance. I spent my entire first day back contacting lawyers, and then I had to get Denver's car from the impound and start searching for a place to live. Not to mention visiting the university to see if they'd let me start my master's program in January.

I've been busy. But not so busy that I don't miss *him*.

Because I do. I miss him. I miss him every second of every day.

I think about him every waking minute and dream about him when I sleep.

I wonder what he's doing. Is he thinking about me? Regretting pushing me away? Moving on and sleeping with some groupie?

The thought of him moving on makes my stomach turn. And I realize I may have to avoid all television and social media so I don't hear about anything that will break my heart more than it's already been broken.

I pull up to Denver's apartment building, sure that I'm seeing things. Because even though my eyes think I see Sawyer sitting on the bench out front, my mind knows better. It knows that Sawyer wouldn't come after me. And that even if by some miracle he wanted to, he couldn't. Because today is Wednesday. He's supposed to be in Minnesota. I know his schedule as well as he does. Maybe even better. Because that is what obsessed, love-sick women do.

I park the car and blink my eyes over and over, but he doesn't disappear like I expect him to. And when I look more closely, I see two large suitcases on the sidewalk next to him.

I get out of Denver's car and walk over to him. He smiles as he stands up.

"Don't you have a game to play?" I ask.

"Yes. But I have to get my new uniforms first. That can take a few days."

"New uniforms?"

He pulls a baseball hat out of his back pocket and puts it on his head. Not a New York Nighthawks hat. A Kansas City one.

I cock my head to the side and study him. "I don't understand."

"I play for Kansas City now," he says, handing me a folder.

"You *what?*" I take a few steps back as if someone had pushed me. "Why? I thought your job was safe now." I cover my mouth and gasp as I open the folder and glance over the contract that has Sawyer being traded. I sit on the bench, guilt washing over me. "I did this, didn't I? When I left, something happened. Did they find out you hired me? Oh, my God, this is all my fault."

"It's not your fault," he says, sitting down next to me. "Actually, that's not true – this *is* your fault. It's your fault for making me see clearly. It's your fault for making me want to be a better person. And it's your fault for making me fall in love with you."

I look up at him, not quite believing what he's saying. "But you love New York. You love the Nighthawks. Everyone said you had a good shot at going to the World Series this year."

"We do. Uh, *they* do. But some things are more important."

"Some things?" I ask, hoping beyond hope that I'm one of those things.

"I want to be here because this is where *you* are. You don't like New York. You only tolerated it because of Juilliard. This is where you need to be. And *I* need to be with you."

"But—"

"I know about Denver," he says.

"You do?"

He nods. "Your letter. I figured something must have happened. I had a private investigator do some digging and he found out about the arrest." He fishes a card out of his pocket and hands it to me. "My attorney, Sarah, said this guy is the best lawyer in Missouri. He's expecting your call. We'll do whatever it takes to help your brother. And as soon as Denver is able, he can start his new job with the team in Kansas City."

My eyes go wide. "You got him a job?"

"It's nothing fancy. Grounds crew. But the pay is decent and the benefits are good."

"How did you manage that? You haven't even started playing for them yet."

He shrugs. "I made it part of the deal for getting me."

"You did that for him? For *me*? What changed, Sawyer? What changed since last week when you were so adamant about not being in a relationship? How do I know you can do this? How do *you* know you can do it?"

"This weekend was the best and worst weekend of my life. I played three incredible games. Games I wanted to share with you. Nothing is real anymore unless I tell you about it. Rick finally hung my picture on his wall. Can you believe it? He pulled me into his office on Sunday and showed it to me. He said he was proud of me. I've worked for the guy for four years and that's the first time he'd ever said those words. And all I wanted to do was go home and tell you about it. And when I got home and found that you had left, all I wanted to do was follow you. Because I realized that having my picture on his wall means nothing to me if I can't be with you. So the day after he hung it there, I brought him the contract he made me hold onto for the season – the one threatening to trade me. I brought it to him signed."

My throat is tight with unshed tears. Everything he just said is everything I've wanted to hear for so long. "What did he do?" I ask.

"He had a fit, of course. He said he wouldn't trade me. So I confessed to everything. Deceiving them. Hiring you. Can you believe that even then, he still wanted to keep me? But I'd already talked to my agent who negotiated a pretty sweet deal with Kansas City. And ultimately, the decision wasn't up to Rick, it was up to Jason, the team owner. He and I had a heart-to-heart on Monday. He recently lost his wife, so I think he gets how I couldn't risk losing you. The Hawks won't have me anymore, but they're getting two great players in return."

"Can you take it back?" I ask. "If you told them you changed your mind?"

"Why would I want to do that?"

"Because I can't have you giving up what you love to chase me, Sawyer. What happens in a month or a year when you realize this isn't what you want. You'll always hold it against me."

"I'm not giving up what I love. I still get to play ball," he says. "On Saturday, when Brooke's dad stood in front of the church and said there wasn't going to be a wedding, I realized how devastated I would be if you left me. And then the very next day, you *did* leave.

"When I came home to an empty house on Sunday, I didn't even have to think twice about it. I tore my townhouse apart to find the contract. There wasn't even a small piece of me that hesitated to walk into Rick's office and ask to complete the deal."

I look at him skeptically, wanting so badly to believe everything he's saying.

"More? You need more? Okay. Do you know where Kansas City holds spring training? In Arizona. I'll be less than thirty minutes away from Danny for almost two months every spring. If that isn't a sign, I don't know what is. Everything makes so much sense now, don't you see?"

I look over at his suitcases, still trying to absorb what this all means. "So, you're moving here? And you want to date me? Like for real, date me?"

He laughs. "I don't just want to date you," he says, pulling another folder from his suitcase. "I have a new contract for you to sign."

I huff in displeasure and then stand up and start to walk away. "I knew you would never change. It's why I left. Go back to New York, Sawyer."

He comes up behind me, placing a gentle hand on my shoulder. "At least look at it, Aspen."

He hands me the folder and I open it, angry at the thought of what he wants me to sign this time. But when I read the words at the top of the first page, I gasp. It reads: **Prenuptial Agreement**.

I spin around to see Sawyer down on one knee, holding up a ring. And this time it's not Murphy's ring. It's not a huge, flashy ring like the old Sawyer would have gotten. It's a modest platinum band with a just-big-enough diamond. Because he knows that's what I like. Because he knows *me*. It's the most beautiful ring I've ever seen.

"Are you kidding?" I ask, trying to focus on him through my tears.

"There's nothing fake about this ring. Or this proposal. Or how I love you. Because, I do love you, Aspen Andrews. I've loved you for a while now. And everyone except me seemed to know it. But right now it's just you and me. There aren't any cameras around this time. Everyone else can have the fake proposal on the internet. This one is just for us. And I promise you, everything from here on out will be real. No more hesitation. No more games. No more hiding behind the memory of my father."

"Do you trust yourself with me?" I ask.

He shakes his head. "I don't know. I want to. I want to more than anything. But I can't be sure. So I made sure you have a safety net." He points to the prenuptial agreement. "If I ever hurt you in any way, you get it all. Our house, our kids, our bank accounts, everything."

"Kids?" I say through my tears.

"Kids," he says. "And it's not just the prenup that will protect you. I told everyone everything about me. I told Brady and Caden and their wives. I told Bass. And as soon as I can, I'm going to tell Denver. If you ever feel threatened by me, you go to them. They know about my mom and dad now. They know about Danny. They will protect you if you ever need to be protected."

I put my hand on his cheek and rub my thumb along his jaw. "I won't need to be protected from you. But I don't understand. None of them said anything after I left. Nobody tried to contact me."

"I asked them not to," he says. "I didn't want anyone to spoil this. I needed you to be without me, without us, for a while. I needed you to be as miserable without me as I was without you. Please tell me you were miserable without me."

I laugh and nod my head. "Like you wouldn't believe."

"Good. But neither of us needs to be miserable any longer." He nods to the ring he's still holding. "Look at the inscription," he says.

I take it from him and squint my eyes to read the tiny words engraved inside. It reads: **Iron-clad contract**.

Tears spill over my lashes. "I always knew you were a romantic."

"That's because you know me better than anyone else." He shifts uncomfortably on the pavement. "Now my knee is fucking killing me, so what do you say, Aspen Andrews, will you marry this self-centered son-of-a-bitch and make me happier than I ever thought I could be?"

I grab his hands and pull him up to me. "Now, *that's* a proposal I'll never forget."

"Is that a yes?" he asks.

"If the ring fits," I joke.

"I'll *make* it fit," he says. "Because I'll do anything to have you, Penny, including bending platinum with my bare hands."

I raise my eyebrows at him. "Penny?"

"Yeah. All the men who love you call you that, so I thought I'd give it a try."

He slips the ring on my finger. It's a perfect fit.

"I've never loved my nickname more than I do right now," I tell him.

He cups my face in his hands, looking at me with so much love it literally hurts my heart. "I've never loved *anything* more than I do you right now," he says.

He leans down until our lips meet. And as he's kissing me, I try to recall what the date is. Because in my book, *this* is the date it all happened. Not the date our arrangement was made. Not the date he publicly declared his fake love for me. *This* date – today – is the date it became real. Our first real kiss. Our own private engagement. And if the heat in his eyes is any indication, the first time we make love. Real, honest-to-God love.

As we part, something tickles my ear. A butterfly is fluttering around us. We both stare at it, taking in the beauty of its multi-colored wings as it weaves a flight path around our heads.

I put my hand over his rib cage and rub my fingers across his tattoo.

And when the butterfly starts to fly away, I look up at Sawyer as he tries to control his emotions. "Bye, Mom," he says after it. Then his gorgeous icy-blue eyes find mine. "I think she approves."

I reach up and wipe his falling tears. "I think she does, Tom Sawyer. I think she does."

Epilogue

Sawyer

She finally got us to Hawaii. After more than a year of hearing Bass talk about how it was the best trip of his life, she was able to put it all together. So now, I sit here with my best friends and their wives, the six of us on a beautiful beach in Kauai, taking in the sunset on Christmas Eve.

Caden and Murphy are each holding one of their two-year-old twins. Brady is tossing a baseball to his seven-year-old son over in the grass. Rylee is rubbing her five-month belly.

I look over at my wife and watch her watch the sunset. I'm amazed at how she loves life. I'm amazed at the way she grows more beautiful every day. I'm amazed by how much I love her.

"I wish Denver were here," she says, looking back at me.

I can only smile. She has no idea that her brother and his girlfriend are flying in tomorrow to surprise her. It's one of my gifts to her. I'd do anything to make this woman happy.

I come up behind her and brush her hair aside, kissing the butterfly tattoo she got on the back of her neck after we were married. It's just one of the many places I enjoy kissing her.

"Mmmm," she mumbles, leaning her head back onto my shoulder. "I could get used to this."

"Too bad Hawaii doesn't have a team, huh?"

"And leave Kansas City? No way," she says turning around and lifting my right hand to admire the World Series ring I'm wearing. "Not after what you've done there."

"Not after what *we've* done there," I say. Then I hold up my left hand. "Besides, the only ring that matters to me is *this* one."

"Me too," she says, putting her left hand alongside mine as we admire the rings we've worn for just short of a year.

I take both of her hands into mine and then I kiss each of her fingers. "I love these," I say. "I love the music you play with them. Have you given any more thought to the job offer from the university?"

She shrugs and smiles at me. "Come on," she says, grabbing my hand and leading me out toward the water. "I know you love surprises. Are you ready for one of your Christmas presents?"

"Here?" I ask.

She leads me across the soft sand, out to where gentle waves have the water lapping at our feet. She stands in front of me, pulling my arms around her so my hands rest against her stomach. Then she stretches her neck around and gives me a brilliant smile.

My heart leaps in my chest. "Really?" I ask, rubbing my fingers across her flat belly.

She nods. "I found out last week. I hope you're not mad at me for not telling you. I thought it would be more romantic if I told you here. I'm nine weeks along. I think it happened the night you won the Series."

"Oh, my God. I'm gonna be a dad?"

"You're not just going to be a dad, you're going to be the *best* dad," she says. Then she pulls something out of her pocket. "And if I were you, I'd start getting some advice from Caden."

I look at the ultrasound photo and try to make sense of what is the very first picture of our child. Then I ask, "Caden? Why not Brady?"

Then she just smiles at me. She smiles at me until I get it.

Acknowledgements

Ending a series is always hard for me. I have to say goodbye to the characters who have become like family to me. I think it's why I like to revisit old characters from time to time. I know readers like it, but I also do it for myself. It's like keeping in touch with old friends. And someday, I promise to write stories about some of your favorite kids (keep the requests coming, it fuels my fire!)

Thank you to my extremely hard-working editors, Ann Peters and Jeannie Hinkle. It's difficult to read the same book over and over (and over) and still come back for more. But you do it wonderfully.

I don't have enough words to thank my incredible beta readers, Joelle Yates, Shauna Salley, and Laura Conley. Your keen eyes for detail put the finishing touches on this book. Sawyer thanks you!

Thanks one last time to baseball coach and former MLB player, Talmadge "T" Nunnari, who helped me with the many baseball details throughout this series.

I don't think I've acknowledged my awesome family in a while, so I'll take a second to gush about how supportive they are. Thank you, Bruce, for cooking dinner so I don't have to stop what I'm doing. Thanks to my younger kids for putting up with me yelling, "Quiet!" when I'm in the middle of a scene and can't lose my focus. Thanks to my older kids who had the decency not to tell me four years ago that they never thought my writing would amount to anything more than a hobby. That you are proud of me is one of my greatest accomplishments in life.

Finally, a huge shout out to my Facebook reader group, Samantha's Sweethearts. You all keep me motivated each and every day. I visit the group first thing in the morning and each night before bed. I'm touched and honored that so many people are as passionate about my books as I am.

About the author

Samantha Christy's passion for writing started long before her first novel was published. Graduating from the University of Nebraska with a degree in Criminal Justice, she held the title of Computer Systems Analyst for The Supreme Court of Wisconsin and several major universities around the United States. Raised mainly in Indianapolis, she holds the Midwest and its homegrown values dear to her heart and upon the birth of her third child devoted herself to raising her family full time. While it took time to get from there to here, writing has remained her utmost passion and being a stay-at-home mom facilitated her ability to follow that dream. When she is not writing, she keeps busy cruising to every Caribbean island where ships sail. Samantha Christy currently resides in St. Augustine, Florida with her husband and four children.

You can reach Samantha Christy at any of these wonderful places:

Website: www.samanthachristy.com

Facebook: https://www.facebook.com/SamanthaChristyAuthor

Twitter: @SamLoves2Write

E-mail: samanthachristy@comcast.net

Made in the USA
Middletown, DE
17 December 2020

28664010R00236